Where the

Water-Dogs

Laughed

The Story of the Great Bear

Also by Charles F. Price:

Hiwassee: A Novel of the Civil War

Freedom's Alter

The Cock's Spur

*W*here the
*W*ater-*D*ogs *L*aughed

The Story of the Great Bear

by

Charles F. Price

For Arletta, another admirer of Nathanael Greene. Best Wishes Charles F. Price 10/9/03

High Country Publishers, Ltd

Boone, NC 2003

High Country Publishers, Ltd
197 New Market Center, #135
Boone, North Carolina 28607
http://www.highcountrypublishers.com
e-mail: editor@highcountrypublishers.com

Cover design by Russell Kaufman-Pace
Text design by Schuyler Kaufman
Bear photo courtesy of Hugh McRae Morton

A portion of this book previously appeared in the
Raleigh News&Observer

Library of Congress Cataloging-in-Publication Data

Price, Charles F., 1938-
 Where the water-dogs laughed, or, The story of the great bear /
by
Charles F. Price.
     p. cm.
 ISBN 1-932158-50-2 (hardcover : alk. paper)
 1. African American families—Fiction. 2. Racially mixed people—
Fiction. 3. African Americans—Fiction. 4. North Carolina—Fiction.
5. Race relations—Fiction. 6. Mountain life—Fiction. 7. Black
bear—Fiction. I. Title: Where the water-dogs laughed. II. Title:
Story of the great bear. III. Title.

 PS3566.R445W47 2003
 813'.54—dc21

2003008443

First Printing November, 2003

This too is for Ruth

Tusquittee Bald is a prominent peak in the Tusquittee Mountain range, overlooking the valley of the Hiwassee River in south-western North Carolina. The Cherokee people who lived in that region for many generations called the peak Where the Water-Dogs Laughed. The name is based on an old story from Cherokee myth involving an amphibious salamander called a water-dog, which frequents muddy waters. A hunter once crossing over Tusquittee Bald in a very dry season heard voices, and creeping silently toward the place from which the sound proceeded, peeped over a rock and saw two water-dogs walking together on their hind legs along the trail and talking as they went. Their pond was dried up and they were on their way over to the Nantahala River. As he listened, one said to the other, "Where's the water? I'm so thirsty that my gills are hanging down," and then both water-dogs laughed.

– Adapted from

History, Myths, and Sacred Formulas of the Cherokees

– by James Mooney

Part One

The Forgotten Covenant

Chapter One

Two hundred-odd feet down in the wet and dark of the Axum mine, Hamby McFee was drilling a round of shot holes in a thick vein of mica-bearing quartz. It was an overhead vein and Hamby had to hold the big Ingersoll air drill up at an awkward slant while keeping enough forward pressure on it to make the bit cut firmly into the rock. Though the drill was braced on a jack's leg, still it bucked like a wild horse and it took all Hamby's strength to hold it steady.

Its hammering racket deafened him. Its exhaust blew the narrow chamber full of stinging grit. He wore a bandanna tied over his nose and mouth but even so, he couldn't help breathing in the grit and it scoured his throat and gave him continual spells of dry coughing. His only light was the pale glow of the carbide lamp fixed to the front of his hat and because of the dust and rock debris the drill showered down on him, he had to keep his eyes slitted almost shut and so was working nearly blind as well as deaf.

From time to time he would pause for a few seconds to rest his arms and the muscles of his back. Then, if he leaned close to the face of the drift, the dim blue light of his lamp would show him the gleaming edges of a big book of red mica running crosswise in the matrix of yellowish quartz. The sight made him grin.

He was setting the holes in such fashion that when he shot it, the round was going to pull the rock and break that big book loose all of a piece and in the morning when the damn muckers came in, they would find the whole of it laying there on top of the muck shining like one big slab of pure garnet and they would know it for Hamby's work and the sight of it would make them swear with rage to think the damn high yaller had shot another round neater and more perfect than any white on the gang could shoot, even Clyde Rainey. And they'd report it to Rainey and Rainey would know, goddamnit, know *again*, that Hamby McFee was a better driller and powder man than anybody, better especially than Rainey himself; would know that hell, even if the owners of the Axum were paying Hamby ten cent an hour and Rainey twenty-five, Hamby could still blow a privy sky-high and not even singe the hair of a man taking a shit inside it.

Finishing at last with the drill-holes, he untied his bandanna and wiped his face with it and afterward lugged the Ingersoll into the main shaft and stowed it and then dismantled the jack's leg and made ready to shoot the face. Aboveground that morning, he had made up several waxed-paper cartridges of black powder and now he loaded the holes with the cartridges and inserted a slow-match Bickford fuse into each. He tamped the charges with moist clay scooped from the floor at the edge of the iron turning-sheet leaving the Bickford rat-tails hanging out. Then using the flame of his lamp he lit the rat-tails one by one and came into the main shaft hollering, "Fire in the hole!" and rang the bell five times and clambered up the balsam-wood ladder to the first ledge and pulled the ladder up after him, hanging it by a rung from a hook sunk in the rock. Then he settled on his hams to wait.

All was quiet in the mine save the drip of the seepage and from time to time the ragged hack of his own coughing. Between coughs he took big open-mouthed gulps of air. The air was thin and damp and smelt of sulphur and very faintly now of the burning of the rat-tails below.

Pull, you son of a bitch, he said to himself, and then the charges began to go.

Wump-wump-wump-wump they went, and at each shot the rough wall of the shaft behind him gave a slight shiver and he hunkered there counting them in sequence as they pulled, *wump-wump-wump-wump*, cut-holes, relievers, edgers, lifters, every damn one of them was touching off and he heard the rumble of the plug of rock down there as it fell and then he visualized that lovely big book of red mica laying in the middle of the muck on the turning-sheet and he laughed out loud. In his head he said, *Take that, Old Rainey. Cram it up you ugly white ass.*

When the winch brought him up into sunshine and warmth Hamby climbed wearily out of the muck bucket and stood awhile in the headworks gazing off along the spine of the ridge toward the peak of Young's Knob in the distance. He kept on coughing. His old high-necked sweater and his jeans britches were sopping wet and even in the sun he shuddered with the chill that the mine-drip had put deep in his bones. He dragged off his rosin-stiffened hat and scrubbed his face again with the bandanna and this time the cloth came away smeared with blood from the cuts the rock debris had made falling on him as he drilled.

But he paid these small hurts little mind. He was forty-eight years old or thereabouts and used to hurts of every sort. He lit his pipe and presently ambled down the path a ways and sat in the bare dirt and unwrapped the lengths of fuse from around his pantlegs that kept the rock litter out of his brogans and then he stretched himself on the ground propping his head on one hand under the huge bright dome of afternoon sky. Contentedly he smoked, coughing between puffs, letting the sun dry him.

The spine of the ridge as it sloped away from him bristled with the dark pointed tops of the spruce trees and further down its side the ridge was black where their wedge shapes grew thick and crowded, and it was only when you saw the trees near at hand, just yonder beyond the slashing at the edge of the camp, that you could see the green in them as well as the black. The green was dense and shaggy and forbidding too but the shadows under the green and the straight rust-colored trunks of the trees and the bed of red needles they stood on were good to look at and made you want to go and lie there in the cool and dark and take a rest in spite of what the darkness of the woods wanted to say to your heart.

It was very different country from what he could not stop himself calling home. That was a place where the bottoms were broad and gently rolling and the mountains were round and plump as a woman's bosoms and stood far off and sometimes had a cast of delicate pale blue that might have been the color of the sky itself, if the sky were not bluer still. There was space around you. Light. Air. There was good rich dirt that would grow anything.

Here, the darkness was in everything and the land stood on end steep and brushy and sharp-topped and shoved together, the trees were soot-black, the valleys so cramped between sheer hills that the sun only lit them in the middle of the day, the creeks ran icy cold, the soil was stony and gave scant yield. High up, as here, it was pretty enough. But down below it was hard, damn hard.

He had not thought of the home country in a long time. It had been eight years since he left it and for much of that time he had not let it come into his mind at all because if he thought of it he would get mad about what had happened there at the end. But now the notion of it had stolen up on him unawares, and he found to his surprise that it had not made him mad after all, but only wistful. He let himself remember the slow-running Hiwassee and his place on Downings Creek and the Curtis farm and Carter's Cove. He remembered the woman who had been his sister in all but blood and hue, and he remembered what had befallen her and he was sorry for it but not so mad any more. He was marveling about this when Considine came down the path and knelt beside him and broke into his mood asking, "Any of them holes miss?"

Now that he had finally allowed into his head what he'd been staving off so long, Hamby hated to let it go; he was annoyed at Considine for making him do it. Besides, what Considine had asked was goddamn stupid, given Hamby's dead-perfect record. He sat up, blew a jet of smoke, snorted, "Hell, no. Ain't nobody drilling into no miss on a'ry round *I* shoot. You want to fret about misses, go and see old Rainey. He shooting tomorrow, ain't he?"

Considine frowned and furled his heavy lips. "You ought to lay off of Rainey, you know."

A gust of coughing shook Hamby. Bitterly he burst out, "Rainey a sorry-ass powder man. He gone kill somebody."

"You need to watch how you talk, McFee. I'm telling you that for your own good."

Hamby leaned and hawked up a bright blob of blood, jabbed the stem of his pipe back in his mouth and lustily puffed. "Rainey be shooting tomorrow. You watch and see. He leave a miss, next day some poor son of a bitch go to drilling, hit a lifter, you be washing guts up with a water hose."

Considine wagged his head. "You know what Rainey is?"

"Hell, yes, I know," Hamby laughed with a hollow note. He looked off down the ridge. To the west the sun was lowering toward the notch of the gap so the shadow of the gap was slowly climbing the flank of the ridge, leaving the narrow divide between them sunk deeper and deeper in gloom. But the top of the ridge shone like hammered brass. "I been knowing that kind all my damn life." He sighed. "Piss on Rainey. And piss on them. And on they goddamn nightgowns too. Rainey *still* a sorry-ass powder man. You the foreman. You ought to fire him. You don't, one day you be spreading quicklime on the mess he make."

Considine rose and stood. He still wore that scowl. He turned his head aside and spat and then remarked, "McFee, I can't figure how you've managed to live as long as you have."

Hamby shrugged. "Me neither."

At dusk he went down to the cookhouse and got his eats on a tin plate and came out again and sat on a stump by the compressor. When he had finished, he fetched his plate and cup and flatware back inside where the others were still at table and the whole time he was in the cookhouse he felt Rainey peering at him with his damn little beady pig's eyes but managed to act as if the son of a bitch wasn't there at all, not because he was scared of Rainey but because he was too give out to mess with him. The others watched warily between them and Considine stood motionless by the door ready to step in if things turned bad, though he plainly hoped he wouldn't need to. But nothing came off and afterward Hamby walked out to the little muddy fenced-in lot where Strickland kept the winch mule. He dumped a pail of corn in the manger of the lean-to stable and then folded his arms on the peeled top log and lounged there looking on while the mule drowsily munched.

That was one tired old mule. His ribs showed through his hide like the tines of a hay fork. There were nasty sores on his withers that had come of the constant rubbing of the hoist harness, and his flanks were raw from the whipping he got every time Strickland wanted to turn the drum of the winch. Strickland, the bastard, loved to ply that lash of his. There was a mess of maggots in the sores and hurts. So when the mule got done eating, Hamby climbed in and cleaned them and dabbed ointment on them and then stood petting the mule and pulling his ears and talking to him, at the same time cussing Strickland with the part of his brain that wasn't soothing the mule, and presently the dark settled in and the stars came out and the moon glowed and the whole ridgetop turned to silver around them, and Hamby stayed by the mule an hour or more, till it was time to turn in.

❦

His sleeping place was not in the bunkhouse but in a corner of the headworks where he kept a bedroll and a few belongings wrapped up in oilskin that he used for a pillow. That night he laid himself down extra easy, for he was sore as hell from the rock debris dropping on him and worn out from coughing and from breathing the bad air of the mine and from the aches in his bones from the damp and from the jolting of the heavy Ingersoll. It was true that he was accustomed to his torments and didn't mind them much; but not minding them didn't stop them hurting, and tonight he had to admit he felt nearly as used up as that poor damn winch mule of Strickland's.

Lying there on the hard concrete, racked on occasion with a rattling cough, he thought again of the home country and recalled how badly he had once longed to leave it, how much he had wanted to wander free in the great world. Well, he'd wandered all right. He'd worked a steel mill in Alabama and a salt works on the Kanawha. Made tar and turpentine down in the pine barrens by the Great Dismal. Mined coal in Kentucky and stoked an iron bloomery in Georgia and sharecropped tobacco in South Carolina. Fought game chickens in Chattanooga and mucked stables in Knoxville. Graded right of way on the Chester & Lenoir Railroad. Run a sash mill on the Cape Fear River. Dug corundum in Macon County and copper at Copper Hill and cobbed feldspar on the South Toe River. Mined mica at the Sink Hole near Bakersville and the Ray Mines above Burnsville and for Jake Burleson at Penland and on Cane Creek and Georges Fork and now for Reed Considine here at the goddamn Axum.

Wandered? Hell, yes, he'd wandered. But wandered free? He made a wry face and rolled over and spat past the edge of the slab. Freedom. Nobody had ever offered *that*. But he reckoned he'd got some anyway. Got it by taking it, by God. Yet he wasn't sure he would ever get more than he'd already lost. Maybe in leaving home he'd put aside as much freedom as he was going to get in life. Maybe freedom was just having a name folk knew and to which they gave a deal of credit. That little and that much. He wondered if there was anybody left in the Hiwassee country who remembered the name he used to have and gave it credit. He was wondering that when he fell asleep.

◆

Next morning he was sitting on his stump beside the compressor eating breakfast when Rainey came by on his way to the cookhouse. Rainey had a fashion of looking that he seemed to think showed how dangerous and full of rough dealing he was, though Hamby believed it just made him resemble more than ever a sow hog sated full with slop. Rainey stopped and looked down at Hamby that way now and commenced to nod as if to agree with himself that nothing as revolting as Hamby had ever come to sit on a stump anywhere near him. Hamby kept on eating in hopes Rainey's desire for breakfast would make him lose interest in baiting him. But it didn't. Just then Loomis came up the path from the bunkhouse and as Loomis approached, fat old Rainey turned and remarked to him, "You know what the trouble with this country is, Loomis?"

Loomis was more dumb even than Rainey and he stopped and scowled in a dull way and said no and Rainey laughed his guttural laugh and explained, "Why, they's too many goddamn niggers in it, that's what."

The pair stood guffawing while Hamby nibbled his pone. *Long as they been hating coloreds*, he mused, *seem like they could think up a slur you you ain't already heard a million times.*

Buffum had stepped out of the bunkhouse just as Rainey spoke and now he strolled up the path toward them with his hands stuck in the back pockets of his overalls and he was laughing too. He was smarter than Loomis and Rainey and unlike either of them he had a sense about Hamby that made him a little careful of him, so he didn't laugh very loud or very long after he got a glimpse of the spark of light in Hamby's blue-gray eye. Instead he stopped on the cinder path and watched close while Hamby sat sopping up the last of his bacon grease with the pone and then slowly ate the pone. Buffum kept that waitful air as Hamby put the tin plate by and tilted his cup aloft and drank down the last of his coffee and turned and set the empty cup on top of the plate and then stood and took a step in on Rainey, and Buffum moved back a yard or two.

"Hell," Hamby grinned, pushing his face so close to Rainey's that he could smell Rainey's rancid breath and dirty underwear, "I reckon a whole lot of niggers be just what this place need." He nodded. "Raise up the tone." He worked his nostrils elaborately and sniffed near Rainey's bevy of chins. "Improve the air." Then he turned and bent and picked up his plate and cup and started for the cookhouse.

Rainey and Loomis had quit their sniggering somewhere in the middle of Hamby's talk and for a second or two afterward the power of speech seemed to have left them. But by the time Hamby reached the cookhouse door Rainey got hold of his tongue. "Hit's you niggers that stink!" he hollered. "You coons and them others. They's Dagos and Arshmen too. Bohunks. Sheenies." In his rage he sputtered and blew beads of spit. "Ruining the country. Taking white men's work. Not a one of you knows how to act." Loomis and Buffum looked on ashen faced as Rainey waved a sausage-sized finger in the air. "You got to learn how to be. Us that knows, we got to teach you. I warn you, McFee, I've got friends . . . "

Hamby nodded. "Thass good," he said. "I 'spect you be needing 'em." Then he passed inside.

◀️

Later in the morning Rainey was sitting cross legged on a sheet of canvas fifty feet from the headworks loading his cartridges from the powder keg when Hamby happened by pushing the muck car along the rails toward the dump. Rainey would be shooting a round in another hour and Hamby had been down in the mine and seen the face and hadn't liked its looks. So he stopped and leaned on the rim of the muck car and told Rainey there was a big cracked rock hanging in the top of the drift that ought to be dug out before the round was shot. "Otherwise," he warned, "you go and shoot, that old rock come down. Block the face. Take us a whole goddamn shift just to break it up."

Rainey glared. All of a sudden it looked like his face was a balloon that somebody had started puffing up; but oddly, the more his face swelled, the smaller and closer together grew his little sow's eyes. He flung down his wooden powder spoon and little copper hammer. "By Christ," he burst out in a choked voice, "if you ain't smarting off, you're telling me my business like I don't know it."

Hamby watched him levelly. "If you knowed your business, I wouldn't have to tell it to you." He shrugged. "Go on ahead then. Shoot the damn thing. Maybe that rock drop on *you*."

Rainey looked up at him almost in appeal. Under stiff yellow lashes his pale eyes showed a glimmer of wet. He shook his big head. "You don't never stop, do you?" He sounded plaintive and sad and puzzled, maybe even hurt. "You don't leave a man a inch of space." He paused. Then he said, "You're a *nigger*, McFee. Don't you know it? Don't you know it yet? Ain't nobody ever taught you?"

Hamby was an old dog and knew the signs. He took a long breath and stepped away from the muck car with his arms hanging loose. Rainey uncrossed his legs and put both hamlike hands flat on the tarp and pushed himself to his feet and Hamby knew from the heavy way he moved and from the bloat and congestion of his face that Rainey had got past his fear at last and there would be no more bluster and the time had come as it always must come, sooner or later, everywhere, to all like Hamby who had the same feature of blood.

Yes, it was fear that men like Rainey felt. Hamby knew that, had finally learned it. And once you learned it, you could even feel pity. He felt the pity now as he retreated another step and held his hands away from his body. His razor hung inside his shirt from a lanyard around his neck but he wasn't about to go for it no matter what Rainey did. Not even he could afford that. Not here. Not with this one.

Out of the tail of his eye he saw Considine coming at a half run. Considine said Rainey's name but Rainey seemed not to hear. His eyes had emptied out. He pulled a folding knife from his pants pocket and put it sideways in his mouth and opened the blade with his teeth and bent down in a clumsy crouch weaving the knife before him and Considine called his name again but he came at Hamby anyway flicking the knife first down and then up as if to gut him. Hamby whirled away from him and got behind the muck car and snatched a big hunk of quartz out of the muck car and when Rainey made his next pass he walloped him over the ear with it and it made the hard hollow *thwock* of a buckeye dropping on a fence rail and Rainey gave a grunt of surprise and sagged sideways and fell.

◄

Though it was but Wednesday, Considine paid Hamby six dollars for a full week's work of ten-hour shifts. He said he'd got three dollars' worth of fun just watching Rainey's eyeballs roll back in his head before he pitched over. Still, Hamby was fired. And he'd better get down the mountain pretty damn quick before Rainey came to. "That old boy'll send for his Kluxers," Considine warned, "and they won't dilly dally." Ruefully he drooped his head and sighed. "I hate to lose you, McFee. You're about the best blaster I ever had. But you're a troublous sort of a darkey, ain't you?"

Hamby shrugged. They shook hands then and Hamby stood and left the little office walled off with beadboard from the cookhouse, and came down the wooden stoop and picked up his hickory staff with his budget of goods tied on the end and laid the staff over his shoulder and then waited awhile looking around him. He looked at the mouth of the mine with its wooden trap door in the middle of the headworks and at the hoist with the mule hitched to it and at Strickland standing by the winch drum and at the muck cars and the rails they ran on and at the muck dump and at the whole ugly sore of the Axum there on the side of ridge and then at the ridge itself rising beyond it in its long run toward Young's Knob and finally at the black-green forest that clothed it and at the sky.

When he'd looked his fill, he walked over to the hoist and petted the winch mule for a spell and stroked one of its ears while Strickland glowered and cussed at him. He said to Strickland, "I told this mule. You whup him, he be kicking you deader'n hell." Strickland gave a scraping laugh. Hamby turned off and left the headworks and crossed to the waiting mica car. Buffum walked down after him. Climbing in, he sat on the shiny heaped-up books of mica holding his staff and poke of goods straight before him like the flag of a just cause. Standing by the car Buffum gave him a solemn bob of the head and Hamby nodded back and then Buffum threw the levers and the chains clanked and the car jerked and started down the mountain. At the foot of the slope where the sled road commenced, the empty mica car began to climb up toward him on the parallel set of rails. He watched it come.

Then as it passed him, he leaned and spat a gout of blood into it.

Chapter Two

There was a new sound in the forest and it came to Yan-e'gwa as he slept in a laurel brake at the head of a cove and after a time it awakened him. He raised his head and listened. The sound was harsh and grating and it repeated itself in a quick rhythm that reminded Yan-e'gwa of the panting of some great beast that has made a long run and is now catching its breath. Although it was new and strange, the sound also had in it part of another noise that Yan-e'gwa had heard before. The noise he remembered was small and thin inside the new and louder one and was a hollow knocking. But in both, Yan-e'gwa recognized the voice of the metal that the Ancestors used as they kept on changing the world.

He heaved himself to his feet and shook the twigs and litter from his shaggy pelt. He pushed his way through the tangled boughs and slick tapered leaves and emerged from the brake and paused between the trunks of two huge red spruces that were as big around as several of Yan-e'gwa himself would be if gathered together in a bunch. The trees rose so high overhead that Yan-e'gwa could not see halfway to their tops, or even to where their first branches began to sprout.

Above, the crowns of the spruces grew out and joined and wove together to make a dark canopy that broke the sun into pieces of light so small they fell on Yan-e'gwa in motes like a soft rain of shining. All around him rose the trunks of more spruces *waiting in royal stillness for the next breeze to stir their mighty tops. The needles they had shed and the thick cushions of moss the needles had fallen on made a softness under the pads of his paws. This was the mountain called Where the Water-Dogs Laughed and was a sacred place. Yan-e'gwa was grieved to think that the Ancestors had disregarded that, as they had disregarded so much else.*

He cleared his nostrils with a blast of snot and rose with a grunt to his full height, standing on his hind legs in the fashion that showed how his kind and the Ancestors had once been the same. His front paws curled at his chest, he lifted his nose and sniffed delicately at the air and many odors came to him, the bitter spruce, the tart laurel, the nearness of the frost to come, bobcat, ground squirrel, the rot in blown-down trees here and there on the floor of the woods and the grubs and wood roaches and worms that lived in the rot, juncos and chickadees and small birds of every sort and the hawk and the sleeping owl, voles, mice and ants going about their business in the earth everywhere around him, the dry mast of acorns and chestnuts that covered the slope lower down, and then finally the smell of the metal of the Ancestors burning in the air and the smell of the Ancestors too, which in some ways was like the smell of Yan-e'gwa himself but was very different also, more oily and as bland as fat meat and without the good coarse smell of the robe of hair that Yan-e'gwa and his kind had grown to cover them when they were transformed. Yan-e'gwa dropped again to all fours and set off down the cove with his swinging gait.

The cove was grown thick with hemlock. Although with his short sight he could not see it, a vast hardwood forest soared on either side of the narrow wedge of evergreen. It mounted toward the peak of the mountain in broad folds and pleats. There was yellow poplar and beech and chestnut and sugar maple and basswood and already some of the leaves were beginning to turn and Yan-e'gwa could see the colors only dimly but he could smell every tree and could distinguish each kind from the other and could divine the state each was in, so he knew that the sap was draining from their leaves and changing their nature. He knew without seeing them clearly that every one was a giant and towered aloft even higher than the hemlock. But he also knew that the size of the hardwoods was a deception. Since their clothing of leaves fell off when winter came, it was plain that the ordeal of the seasons was too severe for them and that they were weaker than the spruce and hemlock which never surrendered their garb no matter how hard the weather.

So Yan-e'gwa who was brave himself descended through the bravest of the trees disdaining the timid ones, and the further down the cove he went, the louder and more annoying became the new sound that was like panting and the older noise of knocking and the stronger grew the smells of the Ancestors and of their metal. Presently some of the steepness began to go out of the ground and soon the brave hemlock gave way to more and more of the poplar and also to other cowardly growth like white and red oak and black cherry and linden and black walnut, some of which were enormous and stood to great height no matter the weakness of their spirits. The crowns of these were less thick than the tops of the evergreens and more sunlight now fell on Yan-e'gwa. But under his coat of fur he did not feel its heat any more than he would feel the cold when the snows came later. His nose and his ears told him this was the place to be careful – even here, higher on the flank of Where the Water-Dogs Laughed than the Ancestors had ever come before.

It troubled and saddened him to hear the note of their metal in this new and old way, so far up. They had not come so far before with their changing. That they did so now made him fear for the world and for all in it. He and his kind had never changed and had always kept the bargain of sacrifice they had made with the Ancestors at the start of things. But the Ancestors had changed and changed and had forgotten the bargain and were changing the world more and more all the time. They did not even sing the old songs entreating the sacrifice or ask the pardon of Yan-e'gwa's kind before killing them.

They were very near. As he heard and smelled them, he felt a vestige of fondness even in the grip of his foreboding. He revered them for the kinship he shared with them. But he was sorry for them too and he wished they were better than they had be-

come. Yet still he wanted to love them if he could. Going quietly now he passed through clusters of fern and a thicket of sassafras and then entered the open forest floor where he smelled the odors of the beasts that the Ancestors kept and that grazed free in the woods and had eaten away all the mast and underbrush.

He came at last to a twisted old dogwood that bore the claw marks he had made long ago to signify the border of his range. He noticed a stand of cedar nearby and because the cedar was very holy he prayed to these and asked them to sharpen his eyesight so he could rightly judge the seriousness of the changes the Ancestors were making in the world. Then his prayer was answered and he could see everything.

One was killing a tree with the tool that made the knocking noise. Two more were dismembering a tree they had just killed. They mutilated it by standing at either end of a long tool that ran from side to side and was narrow and shiny, and it was this tool that made the sound of hoarse panting that Yan-e'gwa had never before heard. Several other trees lay dead too. These had already been severed into parts. Below, horned beasts stood motionless in a paired line along a path. Yan-e'gwa smelled the dying of the trees and even though they were only timid hardwoods, he mourned them. The place of the killing and severing was a great hole in the world. The sight made Yan-e'gwa sadder than he had ever been.

Rufus Middleton had been chopping an undercut out of a big leaning ash for the past two hours and wasn't even a quarter of the way to the heartwood yet. Standing before the cut he stopped and leaned on the haft of his axe to catch his breath and commenced cussing himself for choosing to bring down a leaner that you couldn't saw, rather than a good straight-standing one that would take a crosscut. But ash was what Weatherby wanted and ash was what Rufe was going to give them. That and walnut and poplar, the kinds of timber that were already logged out of the woods up North. And for all its leaning, this one was fit – more than a hundred foot high and least fifty foot to the first branch, big enough through the butt that you could set a supper table on the stump for the whole family to eat a meal off of – if you could ever get through it and *make* a stump. She had three good six-teen-foot logs in her at least.

Shedding a cascade of wood chips, Rufe dragged a soiled rag from the pocket of his britches and mopped his streaming face. The muscles of his arms ached and the constant rubbing of the haft of the axe on the palms of his hands as he chopped had aggravated the calluses there so badly that some of them had started to seep blood at the edges. He wouldn't have thought that was possible, as hard as his hands had got from thirty years of every kind of horny-fisted work, and he felt a little ashamed to be bleeding like some damn Willy-boy. He dabbed at the blood with the bandanna and stood back critically eyeing the cut. He guessed he had an hour's chopping yet to go before he could do the back cut and bring her down. If he didn't cut deep enough before laying the faller to the back of it, the damn tree was going to shatter bottom to top and ruin itself. Hell, he might have to forget the saw altogether and chop her all the way down with the axe alone.

His left hand was worse off than his right so he wrapped the rag around it and tied it with a knot that he drew tight with his teeth while turning about to look downslope to where Absalom, his oldest, and one of the hired hands were cutting up a big yellow poplar they'd just felled. They plied the six-foot crosscut with a swaying, regular motion that looked tireless though it surely wasn't. Luther, the middle boy, was standing on top of another section of poplar just beyond them, nosing the end of it with a poleaxe so it wouldn't dig itself into the ground on the skidroad down.

The youngest boy, Seth, waited just below on the skidroad itself with five more of the hired men. They would use peaveys and canthooks to roll the log down and hook it to the oxen with a dull chain whenever Luther got done nosing it. It would be the last one to go down that day. Four other logs were laying near the road where Seth and his team had wrestled them. They and Absalom's poplar and Rufe's leant ash, if he ever felled her, would go down tomorrow.

The six yoke of Red Devons that would pull Luther's log stood on the skid between the fender logs patiently chewing their cuds. Watching them, Rufe fetched a plug of Winesap from his pocket and bit off a hunk relishing the first squirt of bitter taste on his parched tongue and began to grind his own jaws in slow unconscious mimicry. He wondered as he always did how they could stand so content, given what was about to befall them. It wasn't that they didn't know – your ox was smart, smarter by a damnsite than any horse and nearly as smart as a mule, though unlike the mule, the ox didn't figure it deserved an opinion about whether or not it wanted to work. No, those old steers remembered from one day to the next. They knew what they were in for. Just as Rufe knew, with that hour's chopping ahead of him. Sourly he pondered the parallel. He reckoned he and an ox must be about even when it came to brains.

While he rested, an impulse of vanity took him and presently he grasped up a hatchet and went about cutting and peeling saplings till he'd made a half-dozen stobs, each about two foot long. Then he went and stuck those stobs in the slope of the ground every few yards along the line he knew that ash would take when it fell. He could tell the line from the way the cut was set in the tree and he often took a boastful pride in dropping a tree so true that it would drive a row of such stobs into the earth not missing a one. Doing that today with this troublesome damn leaner would give him a needful lift. He hummed under his breath. Now and then as he worked he bent to the side and unleashed a bountiful stream of Winesap juice. His old redbone bitch followed him. She sniffed at each stob as he tapped it in place with a blow of the flat of the hatchet head and at each spot where he'd spat too. But when he turned back to the cut she lost interest and trotted off up the mountain with her dugs aswing and soon he heard her somewhere in the woods yonder, barking at something. Likely a possum or a groundhog, he thought. Soon she quit.

Bracing himself in his calked boots he resumed his familiar rhythm. *Whock, whock, whock* went the axe. Each stroke sent its echo racketing off through the space where the woods used to be. Chips flew. He smelt the sharp sweet fragrance that breathed out on him as he cut deeper and deeper into the pulp. The smell was cool and moist and something about it was special but Rufe didn't know what that was and didn't care either. The smell might have made him conscious that he was cutting into a thing that lived. And not only lived, but had lived a long time, lived longer than Rufe himself had been alive. Longer than North Carolina had been a state or America had been America. But it didn't. This old ash was just one more out of millions. There wasn't any end to them and they all smelt pretty much the same when you cut into them. The whole flank of Tusquittee Bald that bulked high above him was covered with masses of them and others like them, and the Weatherby Hardwood Company had bought forty acres of them on the stump and it had been a bad year for the corn and tobacco that Rufe raised on his farm down by the mouth of Big Tuni and he needed the extra money to help feed his woman and twelve younguns through the coming winter and if a goddamn tree happened to split while you were sawing it or a log jumped out of the skidroad when the tow started to run or if a log lost its ride and rolled over on you someway, it could kill you or cripple you quicker than hell or break the legs of your oxen and you had to kill *them*, and it was Rufe's job to clear that forty acres of everything bigger than eighteen inches across the stump and then snake the logs out of the woods and load them on the big-wheel wagon and tote them over the range to the bandmill on the Nantahala River without any of those bad things happening to him or to his boys or to his hired men or to his teams, and that was all there was to it, no matter that he was going to leave the whole top half of this big old ash laying on the floor of the woods to rot because the knots it would have in it where the boughs sprung out were no good for lumber, no matter how sweet and tart the fragrance of its long living in his nose, no matter how his calluses might bleed, no matter what.

❧

Captain Moore heard them coming down. He drew rein and sat his saddle for a moment in the middle of the skidroad. The black mare Dixie shifted under him, chopping her hooves in the soft earth that had been gouged and plowed by the passing logs till it lay in loose dark mounds that were fetlock deep. She had heard them before he had. She loathed cattle and was mortified to find that some were near. Snorting, she kept laying her ears back in disgust and then pricking them nervously upslope toward the bend in the road. Up there, still out of sight beyond a laurel hell and a heap of lichen-spotted rocks, whips were popping and heavy chain was rattling and Dixie heard the sounds and smelled the oxen that were coming down and shivered with outrage and misgiving.

Irish Bill laid a hand on the side of her neck and spoke to her in a confiding voice and stroked her mane in reassurance. She steadied a little then. When she was calmer, he clucked to her and turned her off the road. She stepped daintily over the fender log into what had recently been woods but now was a wilderness of stumps and lonely bent-over saplings and chopped-off limbs and wilted tree crowns and a litter of wood chips and sawdust. He checked her there and waited.

Presently the first yoke of oxen came around the bend and started down. They were the color of red wine and had white stars on their foreheads and the tips of their horns were capped with bits of brass that now and then caught the sun in winks and glimmers. They came very slowly and with enormous effort, heads low, eyes bulging. By turns they staggered for purchase in the soft footing and then, finding it, hardened with unimaginable force, their muscles and veins starting like cables from the strain of the load unseen at the end of the chain around the bend of the skidroad behind them. Ropes of slobber dropped from their muzzles. Seth Middleton walked beside them wielding his whip of plaited hickory bark. At every lick of the whip's cracker a hank of hair would jump off the back of one ox or the other. The two bled in a dozen places but the blood was the same red color as their hide and was hard to see unless the light fell on it a certain way and made it glisten and then you could see the bright runnels of it all down their flanks.

Dixie tossed her head with a clash of bit chains and neighed her contempt for kine of any sort and young Seth glanced up at the sound and saw Irish Bill and nodded and said, "Hidy."

Captain Moore gave him a tip of the head. The second yoke had rounded the heap of rocks and came down now and began to pass. These were larger and longer legged but moved with the same agony of effort and were the same deep red and had the same white blazes on their foreheads but lacked any of the brass sparklers on their horn tips which Irish Bill recognized, now that the first yoke was going by, as forty-five-caliber pistol shells neatly hammered on for ornaments.

Seth passed on down cussing and whipping. Above him at the bend, a third yoke – these were hornless muleys – and then a fourth appeared, herded by some of Middleton's hired hands flailing more whips that snatched out bits of hair and made the blood fly. The chain between them hummed and chirped from the stress on it. The legs of some were raw where they had scraped against the chain and the fender logs. Their eyes stood out like doorknobs. Their tongues writhed and dangled. Under the yokes of all of them a froth of sweat showed like clabber and creamy spills of it ran out from under the yokes and down over their withers to drop white splashes in the dirt of the road.

Down below, Seth's swearing fluted higher and Moore looked that way and saw that the bull-poles meant to act as a bridge to carry the log over a depression in the skidroad were out of place. Something or someone had knocked them sideways. If they weren't repositioned, the log the oxen were pulling would come down the skid and dig its head straight in the dip in the ground and there would be hell to pay ever getting it out again. Seth glared at the poles in hate, then hollered up to the others and told them to stop the tow and they did. The oxen stood gasping and shuddering. Seth threw down his whip and went to work putting the poles back the way they were supposed to be.

As he bent to the task, a great impact shook the whole hillside – Irish Bill felt its jolt in the ends of his bones and remembered how it had felt when a roundshot killed his horse at Chickamauga and for an instant he thought Dixie had somehow, impossibly, been similarly struck. Then he realized the shock came from above, beyond the bend. Immediately it was followed by a shriek of tortured chain, a chorus of men's yells, steers bawl-ing piteously, the crackle of underbrush and the trunks of small trees snapping, and finally another crash as vast and reverberant as the first. "God *damn*," Seth swore, looking up white-faced. Some of the hired men dashed uphill and around the bend to see what had happened. In a moment one returned. "Damn log jumped the road," he called down between cupped hands.

"Anybody hurt?" Seth wanted to know.

"The damn wheelers broke their back legs. One's got a hoof tore off. Log rolled till it fetched up on a rock. Twisted them critters like a goddamn corkscrew."

Seth swore a second time. Irish Bill spoke to Dixie and started her up the slope beside the road through underbrush and past broken saplings and hundreds of round yellow stumps that shone in the sun like huge coins dropped everywhere. Around the bend he passed another yoke of steers kicking with their hind legs at the chain that no longer trailed behind them but instead angled off into the bend of the skidroad, taut against their heels and fouled with gouts of laurel and ivy; and just beyond, on the naked slope cluttered with the ruins of the woods, he saw an immense poplar log lying crosswise against a boulder with one end jutting high.

The log was probably five feet across the butt, looking nearly as fat as it was long. In many places its bark had been chipped and flaked off from banging against the fender logs and hitting rocks in the skid. Each of its wounds showed a pale center like a piece of exposed bone encircled by the red pith of the bark. The head of it wore a thick beard of black earth that it had dug out of the ground as it came down. The wheel steers, hopelessly entangled in the dull chain that had slipped off the log to snare them, hung suspended with hindquarters in the air and heads turned sideways on the ground at an angle no heads were meant to bend. They flailed weakly with their mangled back legs but made no sound except for the *whuff-whuff-whuff* of their breathing against the earth. Men were fussing with the chain and the oldest Middleton boy was swearing and kicking at the big slabs of bark laying about that had been sheared off the log when it rolled. Luther Middleton was checking the loads in a pistol. Irish Bill rode on.

At the top of the skid he found Rufe Middleton. Rufe had just cut down a big ash tree and was standing with his hands on his hips regarding the fallen monster in a satisfied way. It had been the last tree left on this part of the slope and now that it was down, the mountainside it used to stand on looked so bald there was something alarming about it. The emptiness made the Captain think of the head of a man he had once seen who had been scalped by some bushwhackers up in East Tennessee during the war. He dismounted leaving Dixie reins-down and shook hands with Rufe and joined him to stand gazing out across the slant of ground that was covered with every kind of woody scrap and scrub and with the several logs yet to be skidded down and with that mighty felled ash, all of it laid bare to the sun and dominated by a shocking view of the mountain above them that no man had ever seen before because the trees had always obscured it. After a time he asked, "You cutting for Weatherby, Rufe?"

Middleton nodded in a conclusive way that showed he didn't aim to let Irish Bill take on any airs with him. "I am," he replied stoutly. Then he began to call for his bitch hound that he said had wandered off. "LuLu," he bellowed in the direction of the line of woods above them. "LuLuuuu!" His shout echoed eerily across the strange new vacancy they stood in.

Moore shrugged and inclined his head to signal that he understood even if he didn't approve. "I know. I've had these mineral and timber men after me too, wanting to buy ridgeland, stumpage, surface rights."

He paused and Middleton sung out again for his dog, "LuLuuuu, come up!" Rufe's left hand was wrapped in a bloody rag. There were chips and splinters lying all around the brim of his hat like some kind of ill-considered decoration. Around the back of his neck the thick coils of his graying hair had turned a greasy black with sweat. "LuLuuuu," he boomed, "here to me, you gal!"

"Weatherby's people came to me," Irish Bill went on, "just like they did you. Wanted to give me fifty cents a foot across the stump for all the poplar I had. A whole mountain of it."

"*Did* you?" Even though he'd asked, Rufe had to already know the answer. He knew Irish Bill just as everybody up Tusquittee knew him. But Moore guessed Middleton would still rather not hear confirmed the thing he already knew to be true. Not waiting for an answer, Rufe started up the slope toward the woods. "LuLu! Come up, gal! LuLu! LuLuuuu!" He moved with a rangy absence of grace that emphasized his long bony legs and pointy elbows.

Irish Bill took a breath and followed after him, a step or two behind. "No, I didn't," he answered at last. Rufe called the dog again and that same weird echo came back to them. Pushing himself up the slope, Moore noticed from behind how Rufe's sweat-soppy shirt clung to his back and moulded the shapes of his two sharp shoulderblades and the cleft of his slumped spine. There were deep creases in the skin at the back of his neck and the creases were shiny and black with sweat and grime. The knuckles of his hands were raw and scabbed. He cocked his head and spat tobacco juice off to the right. They climbed higher among the stumps and scattered remnants of trees. There was a stand of cedar at the edge of the timberline a hundred rods or so above them and Rufe headed for that.

"LuLu!" he called, then all of a sudden stopped and turned back and gave Moore a look that the Captain felt all the way to his sock heels. "Hit's good, I reckon, to have a choice," was all he said. But it was enough. There was all the steely condemnation in it that a poor man could pack into what he wanted to tell a rich one.

Moore blinked but held the look with his own. He felt the force of Middleton's remark and could even admit some of the rightness of it. But he'd been poor himself once and had never let himself forget it. "Yes," he said at last, "I'm fortunate that way. I confess it. Because I've got means, the choosing's easy for me." Only then did he glance aside from Rufe's accusing eye. They waited a few seconds unspeaking, then he turned back and added, "I'll not judge them that lack the luxury I enjoy. I think you know that, Rufe."

Middleton said nothing in response. He just scowled as if puzzled. "How come you not to sell?" He leaned and spat. "You talk like there was principle to hit."

"Maybe there is," answered Irish Bill. "*I* think there is. Some of these mineral and timber fellows are our neighbors and are looking to do business right here on our own ground. Or have settled in to live, like that fellow Cover that owns the new tannery in Andrews. I don't begrudge them. Why, I've cut lots of oak and chestnut and hemlock and sold the tanbark to Cover. And I've cut other timber and sold to mills hereabouts that some of the boys in Clay and Macon run. And made ties for the railroad."

He took off his hat and dried his brow with his sleeve and replaced it. "But most of the big lumber people – like Weatherby – why, they're from off," he continued. "Think about it. Where's Weatherby at himself? Pennsylvania, isn't he? Sure, he's got him a summer place over the ridge yonder, but his home's away in Yankeedom. Some's from Maine, I know. Illinois, Michigan, New York. Hell, I heard of one in Glasgow, Scotland. Seems to me if we sell to these foreigners, why, we're giving over our birthright. In time we'll be the slaves of strangers. Be doing the bidding of them that scorns our interests while holding their own close."

Middleton spat and wiped his mouth with the back of his bandaged hand. "They're a-paying," he pointed out in his dogged fashion. "And the stuff's here. The iron in the ground. The trees in the woods." He stopped and his face shaped itself into hardness and his slate-gray eyes went cold with judgment. "Some of us would rather sell than starve," he said.

He whirled then and resumed his awkward climb toward the cedars. Watching him go, Irish Bill made his peace with his old hard-luck neighbor and spoke to his back in warmer guise. "I hope Weatherby's men gave you a good price then."

Middleton vented a dry laugh and rounded smartly on him and once more shot a stream of bright amber to the side. "Well," he said with a crackle of fury in his voice, "I'll tell you one thing – they never give me no fifty cent a foot. I reckon that's the price they give a high-station man." Wheeling back, he went on with his tramping. "LuLu!" he roared. "LuLu, goddamnit! Come up!"

Moore stood where he was. He wanted to say something more to Rufe but couldn't think what it would be. A long time ago he and Rufe had been just about even in life. But fortune had smiled on him since then and had frowned on Rufe. That had changed all there was between them or could ever be. Nothing could mend it now, nor ease its pinch. It irked him. He looked on as Rufe mounted the last of the steep. Rufe had to crouch over to keep from sliding back. He steadied himself by putting one hand on the pitch of ground and used the other to push at the top of his knee and drive himself on up. Finally he reached the clump of cedars and pawed in among them and then Moore saw him come to a halt with a kind of jerk and stand stock still afterwards and he knew at once that Rufe had discovered something uncommon. "What is it?" he yelled up.

But Rufe sent back no answer and Irish Bill gave in to his curiosity and dug his heels sideways into the slope and went clambering. He covered the last few feet by scrabbling at the mountainside with his clawed hands and pulling at the sparse undergrowth. He had forgotten, as he often did, that he was sixty-seven years old and by the time he dragged himself into the little bower of cedars his heart was throbbing and he was fighting for wind and feeling more than a little giddy.

He sank down wheezing next to Rufe, who was on hands and knees now, peering intently at something on the ground. There was no bitch dog to be seen, but pressed into the soft loam covered with cedar needles was a fresh bear track. It was the biggest one Irish Bill had ever seen. He placed the flat of his hand inside the track to get a measure but he was a small skimpy fellow and the size of his hand didn't much signify. Rufe was six feet two or three, and even if slight, had a damn big foot. He moved up a ways and bent and stuck his calked boot inside the track. His was only half as large.

Chapter Three

If young Will Price had been inclined to show the world a pursed and peckish face and a worse disposition than a galled mule's, few who knew his case would have wondered. Bereft of his mama through sickness when but a lad, cast off by a vagabond daddy that preferred to flee West rather than stay and raise his get as he ought, Will came up ten years in the home of a man most called a saint out of Heaven but those closest knew wore a different face behind his own door. What Jimmy Cartman's real nature was, only Will could have told. Him, and Jimmy's wife Laura. Now Laura, she *was* a saint. All could agree on that. And Will knew she had to be, to stay wed to Jimmy.

Yes, young Will and sweet Aunt Laura knew the truth. But if the truth was that Jimmy was a worse Pharisee than Caiaphas, they weren't telling it. Outwardly they cast their lot with those that thought Jimmy embodied some fine figure from Holy Writ. Yet even they had to concede he'd sprung from the Old Testament and not the New. His Godly love was as hard as some people's hate. Not even his best admirers would go so far as to liken him to the Savior. Fact was, Jesus looked a little weak next to Jimmy.

But Will would never say a syllable against the man who'd taken him in when his daddy spurned him. Instead, he spoke of owing Jimmy all. He beamed and laughed and sang his songs – he had a fine bright voice that he loved to tune to the old Methodist hymns. If he was in fact no better than Jimmy's nigger, he acted like it was a privilege. The boy looked to be not just content but even gay. Of course none of this had ever stopped Will's grandpap, old Oliver Price, from trying to pry out the blacker tale he was convinced Will kept hidden behind his smile.

So on this particular rainy autumn afternoon when Will stepped into Oliver's shoemaking establishment on the Hayesville square and told him hello, old Oliver laid down his hammer and a handful of shoe pegs and started right in on him. This was also Oliver's way of answering the question that Will never had to ask whenever he stopped by, the question about Ves, Will's daddy. "The little old bald-headed slavemaster gave you a road pass, did he?" Oliver inquired far louder than was necessary. "Finally let you off the old plantation for a spell? How many lickings did you have to stand this week, to earn the trip?"

Will hardly felt the disappointment any more, so the grin he gave back wasn't as much of a mask for his feelings as it used to be. Only once had the unspoken question ever been answered as he wished, and that had been so long ago that Will no longer expected another one as good. Colorado had been the answer then. The conversation he and Oliver were going to have now, or one like it, had been going on between them for a long time and was a substitute for the new answer that Will wanted but never got. Still, he would've liked to know if it was still Colorado. "Dad's never laid a hand to me," he reminded Oliver mildly, "and you know it." Yes, he even named Jimmy Dad, though of course Jimmy wasn't that at all. But in all the ways that mattered, Will thought he was.

"Don't know nothing of the kind," Oliver insisted, waving a dismissing hand. "I've been acquainted with Jimmy Cartman since he was no bigger'n a riding boot. Him and that brother of his." He gave a snort of distaste. "Jimmy and Andy. They're quare, the both of 'em. Always was. And Jimmy's the quarest of the two."

"He's got his ways," Will admitted, shaking the rainwater out of his rubberized coat. "Uncle Andy too. But I'm treated good. Me and Sister both. You just don't want to believe it." He shrugged out of the coat and hung it on the hatrack and sat down opposite Oliver running a hand through his soggy yellow-brown hair. He had looked up Colorado in an atlas that Dad owned. He had even found the town, Littleton. Even though he no longer expected a new answer, he sometimes wished he could at least find out if it were still Littleton, and on one or two occasions he had even tried to imagine what Littleton might be like.

"No, sir, I don't," Oliver agreed. "You're right. I've never cared for that pair, nor them for me."

"That's not so, either," Will declared with his usual show of stubborn patience, that came of knowing how deep was Oliver's shame that Ves had skipped out leaving Will and Minnie no better than foundlings. Oliver gulped and bit a corner of his mustache and gazed through the window at the gold leaves of the maples in the square that looked so bright against the drizzly gloom. He'd wanted to take Will and Minnie in himself but couldn't afford to because of being a widower and poor and crippled up, and Will knew how he'd hated it that Will had had to go to Jimmy and Minnie to Uncle Andy, who weren't even kin. "Why," Will pointed out now, "you even helped Dad and Uncle Andy build their houses a long time back."

"Yes, and that's how come I know just how confounded quare they are," Oliver blurted. "The two of 'em, pretending to be twins when they ain't, when Andy's younger. Doing everything the same. Marrying sisters. Both childless. Dressing the same. Driving the same kind of buggy, even the same color of horse. One taking you and the other taking Minnie. Building houses just alike and side by side. You should've seen 'em, measuring and comparing and doing their sums to be certain one house was just like the other. Counting bricks to make sure they both had the same number in the fireplace. The only difference between 'em is Jimmy's a Democrat and Andy's a Republican, and the Lord only knows how *that* come about. Otherwise, the way they behave ain't noway natural. Never was. I can remember when they was younguns, they used to run around wearing the same kind of sailor suit. By gum, they'd even talk to a-body both at the same time, like a confounded duet. They're quare, I tell you."

"You cut your name on a brick when you built Uncle Andy's chimney," Will pointed out. "I've seen it."

Oliver made another motion of impatience. "I done that so when the part of the house that Andy built fell down and that chimbley stayed up, folks would know it was *me* that done the chimbley."

Will laughed. "You did it because you liked Uncle Andy and were proud to help him."

Oliver frowned and squirmed in his chair and fiddled without purpose at the shoe last before him. "Well, Andy ain't the case we're addressing anyway, is he? It's Jimmy we're talking about."

But today Will had something else on his mind besides the unasked question and the good-humored bickering that was an excuse for an answer. He waited before bringing it up so as to organize his thoughts, and in the stillness that fell between them they could both hear the drumming of the rain on the roof and the rattle of it in the downspouts. The sound was restful and together with the familiar aromas of Oliver's shop – the fresh hides in their bins and the fish oil and beef tallow that made them pliable, the beeswax he used for waterproofing, the smoky odors of all the old pieces of leather lying about – helped ease Will's nerves. "There's something I want to do, Grandad," he said when he was ready. "I want to ask your opinion about it."

Oliver turned serious as he always did whenever Will came to him with a worry or to seek counsel. He wanted to be as much of a daddy as a grandpap could be, to make up for what Ves had done. He put his elbows on his knees and folded his small hands that were getting knuckly with age; expectantly he leaned at Will. "What's that, son?"

Will blushed a fiery red and glanced away from him and sat looking at the assortment of tools that lay on Oliver's work table, at the peg rasps, gauges, heel shavers, nippers, awls – looking but not really seeing them. "Well," he stammered, "well, there's a girl . . . "

"Oh, Lordy!" Oliver exclaimed, raising both hands before him as if to ward off calamity. "Is it time for that already? How old are you, boy?"

Due to embarrassment there was a second or two when Will couldn't recall, but then his own age presently came to him. "Why, I'll be sixteen in two months' time."

"Sixteen? Is that so?" Oliver bit at his mustache some more while he considered. "Well, you're older'n I thought." Then he held up a warning hand. "But not old enough to be thinking about a gal with such ceremony that you need to be bringing it up to your old grandpap."

Will pulled a painful face and crossed and uncrossed his legs and then crossed them again. "Well, I can't hardly bring it up to Dad."

With thumb and forefinger Oliver tweaked his stubbly chin in thought. "No," he agreed with a somber look, "you're right about that. He'd say you were bound for the lake of eternal fire just for making mention of a gal atall."

Will let his head droop and his blush got redder. "Well, maybe I am."

Oliver stared aghast. "What in the world d'you mean by that?"

Now Will peered miserably aside at the box of shoe patterns near where he sat. When he answered, it was in a bashful whisper. "I get some awful naughty notions sometimes," he confessed.

Oliver bounded up out of his chair as if the seat of it had unexpectedly turned red-hot. The motion was so violent it made Will flinch. "You're *alive*, ain't you?" Oliver bellowed down at him, then commenced to pace excitedly back and forth across the narrow room, every step of his crippled leg making him pitch so sharply to the right that he looked in danger of falling over, though he never did. "Got breath in your lungs and blood in your veins? What you're thinking's only rightful for a young sprout at your time of life."

He stopped and turned and steadied himself by grasping one end of the shelf that held his pots of waterproofing. He glowered hard at

Will. "I'll bet Jimmy Cartman's put it in your head that it's wrong to ponder the raptures of the flesh that God put in us." He stopped and sighed and passed a hand over his face in what Will could see was an attempt to get the better of his temper. But he succeeded only in part – when he spoke again his voice was quieter but no less charged with feeling. "Now I'm a religious man, son," he said. "You know it. I yield to nobody in professing the faith. But there's a sort of a Christian that hates life, God forgive 'em, and Jimmy Cartman's one. He names a sin the very parts of life that make it worth the living. No wonder he's childless. Why, he's probably never had no congress atall with that poor Laura, lest he put their souls in jeopardy of damnation."

Will blinked and shrank from that, wishing he hadn't heard it. But Oliver limped back over to him and sat down and rested his hand on his shoulder and fixed him with a steady gaze and kept on. "You can't listen to him, son. Not about that. There's nothing bad about dwelling on the sweetness of our natures. Lord knows, living's hard enough without denying ourselves the few delights that come free and natural."

"I hope you're right."

"I *am* right," Oliver proclaimed, and pounded his fist on his good knee to drive the point home. "Depend on it. I had the same notions myself at your age. Had the same things happen to me in the night when I dreamt. There's no shame to it. It's the way the Good Lord made us." He paused and contemplated Will with narrowed eyes as blue as the blue you sometimes see in mother-of-pearl. "Now. Who's this gal, anyway?"

"Mr. and Mrs. Tom Carter's eldest, Lillie Dell."

A light of approval kindled in Oliver's countenance. "Lillie Carter?" He leaned back in his chair and gazed on Will with what seemed a new respect. "Well, I'll be." Then mischief came to tug lightly at the ends of his mouth. "What d'you want with her?" he teased.

"Well," answered Will, trying to sit as straight as he could in the cane-bottomed chair to demonstrate how formal he thought the matter was, "I'd like to court her. And when we're old enough, I'm thinking of marrying her."

Oliver smiled. "You are, are you? You've ridden that mule pretty far down the pike, haven't you? Planning to marry when you ain't even gone a-courting yet."

Will shrugged. "Well, I've known her all my life. I fancy her. And I have reason to believe she favors me back."

Oliver squinted doubtfully at him. "I thought you was going to be a railroad man."

"I want to be," Will confirmed, "once I'm free." He gave Oliver a dogged look. "Railroad men can have wives."

"They can," Oliver agreed with a smirk. "But then if they're married, they ain't free. Are they?" Next he furrowed his brow and sadly shook his head as if some dismal truth that he had allowed himself to forget had just reclaimed his notice. "Oh, I don't know, son. Why, I don't believe you can marry Lillie Carter."

The outsides of Will's ears caught fire with alarm. Urgently he bent closer. "How come?"

Oliver was the picture of dejection. "Well," he murmured with a sigh, "there's an awful tangle of relations there, you know. She must be some kind of cousin of yours. I wouldn't be surprised if she wasn't too close to you in blood. Why," he mused, cocking a mournful eye at Will, "if you was to marry Lillie Carter, you might get younguns you wouldn't want folks to see."

Will glimpsed the little twitches that had started again at the ends of Oliver's mouth and saw what was up. The fire around the edges of his ears went out and he relaxed in his chair to let Oliver have his little merriment. "What d'you mean, Grandad?" he asked, pretending to be worried.

"Well," Oliver went on in over-solemn vein, "let's figure it." He counted on his fingers. "Her mama was a sister of Jimmy's mama, so Lillie's Jimmy's cousin. And an aunt of hers is married to Tom Carter's brother. And Tom's her pappy. And you're Jimmy's boy, so . . . "

"You're funning me now," Will finally laughed out loud. "Me and Lillie are no kin atall."

Oliver grinned and slapped his thighs with the flats of his hands. "Yes, I'm joshing. Fact is, I love Lillie Carter like she was my own. She's Rebecca Curtis's littlest, granddaughter to Judge Madison Curtis, my old friend from the long-ago days. You know how dear to my heart I hold the Judge and poor Becky's memory."

"I thought you'd approve," Will nodded. "And I don't mean to rush into things. I won't be free till I'm twenty-one. But if I can, I'd like to get Lillie bespoken anyway."

"You sound mighty sure of yourself. Have you took this up with Lillie yet?"

"Not yet. I'll need Dad's blessing first."

"Yes, you surely will."

"Like you say, him and Lillie are cousins. And if I've any chance of land and goods atall, it's through him. He's got a right to have a say."

"Won't Lillie bring a dowry of land from her mama's portion?"

"I don't want to count on that, Grandad. I want to stand on my own."

Oliver turned and looked out the window and through the blur of rain to the courthouse of patterned red and rose-colored brick in the middle of the square. "Nobody'll lay hands on anything of Jimmy's till he's dead," he said grimly, then added with another flare of ire, "and if I know him, he'll outlive us all from pure meanness." Then his gaze came back to Will and it was hard with resentment. "What is he, forty? Forty-two? In spite of his bald head and the miseries in his joints and his cranky ways, he's a young man yet. And he's the rankest skinflint I know. He may have took you in, but you're no better'n a servant to him. Not even as free as a sharecropper. He's only adopted you till you come of age. After that, he don't have to give you as much as a stick of furniture. And when he passes – if he ever does – why, it's Laura who'll inherit."

Confidently Will shook his head. "You're too harsh, Grandad. He'll do right by me." He could see that Oliver would never agree to what he felt so certain of. He even knew the evidence appeared to be against him. But he had faith in the love he thought Dad bore him. He saw, though, that it would be futile to fuss at Oliver in hopes of changing his mind. Instead he ceased and sucked in a quick breath because they had come to the nub of it now. A nervous flicker went through him. Then he said it: "But I'll need help getting him to agree about Lillie."

"Whose help?" Oliver inquired. Then he saw. His jaw dropped and his shaggy eyebrows shot upward. "Mine?"

Will gave him an imploring look. "Yes."

"*Mine?*"

"Yes, Grandad."

For an instant Oliver sat speechless, staring at Will in a mixture of horror and disbelief. Then he cried, "What in the world makes you think Jimmy Cartman's going to credit a thing *I* say to him?"

"Because he respects you, Grandad," Will told him stoutly, since he knew it was true. Then he smiled. "Just like you do him."

Oliver tried to muster an explosion of outrage but couldn't quite manage it and ended by looking as sheepish as a youngun caught stealing pies off a windowsill. Now it was his turn to redden with embarrassment. He wouldn't meet Will's look and instead sat glaring at the floorboards and gnawing his mustache in chagrin. "If I was a cussing man," he grumped at last, "I'd cuss."

Indulgently Will nodded. "I know, Grandad. But you aren't. And you won't."

❧

Six-year-old Will and his daddy stood at the edge of the wagon road. His daddy held him by the hand and his daddy's hand was cold and wet where it held his. Minnie was asleep in the crook of his daddy's other arm. With his free hand Will clutched the end of a pillowcase that was slung over his shoulder. Inside the pillowcase were an extra shirt, a pair of drawers, some stockings and his only toy, a bull-roarer that his daddy had made for him on his last birthday. Before them a new lane turned out of the road and went down the slope between a hill on the right grown over with scrub oak and spindly pine and a rolling pasture on the left in which a number of cattle grazed. Ahead lay a broad bottom and beyond it some blue mountains that Will's daddy told him were in Georgia.

The brush and saplings that must have been cut when the lane was made lay to either side in a bristly clutter. The lane was laid with smooth stones which Will's daddy said the Cartmans had toted up from the river in wagon and wheelbarrow loads, a quarter mile each way. His daddy sneered when he said this and Will understood why, for he knew his daddy well. What he did not know was why his daddy wanted to give him over to folk he held in scorn.

On the flat below, the lane met a carriage road. A house fronted the road on the left and – some distance along – another fronted it on the right. Will saw that the two houses were exactly alike as to size and shape and color and that even their barns and outbuildings were set out in the same way and painted in the same hues. Minnie awoke and sleepily inquired after her mama and Will's daddy impatiently told her for the hundredth time that Mama had gone to be with the Lord Jesus. But Minnie was such a babe she couldn't remember a lot of the time who the Lord Jesus was and the answer only puzzled her more and made her ask when Mama would return from her visit. She wanted Mama to sing her the sour-apple song. Will's daddy told her she was the most bothersome and tiring creature anywhere around. Yanking Will by the hand, he started off down the pebbled lane. Will commenced to sing the sour-apple song as they went. But Minnie told him to hush, as Mama was the only one so entitled.

They went to the left-hand house that his daddy said was going to be where Will would live. It was a white frame house of two storeys with steep gables. They mounted a rock stoop to a small porch and Will's daddy knocked on the doorjamb and the door opened and a handsome smiling woman appeared and then stepped aside to let them in. The house swallowed them. Within, it smelt of a poplar fire and the walls gave off a pleasant fragrance of new-cut wood and Will could see from the freshness of the siding of the hallway that the house was new, each yellow unfinished board as wide as a man's opened hand and every one expertly fitted to its neighbor.

They turned left and entered a room that was more full of furniture and knicknacks and doodads than any room Will had ever been in before and made him think how bare had been the house where he'd grown up, whose only decoration was a strip of newspaper strung across the mantelpiece that his mama had cut up fancy to resemble a piece of lace. In a corner stood a big spruce Christmas tree trimmed with tinsel and strings of popcorn and little candles set on wafers of tin. It had a five-pointed pewter star at its peak. The star almost touched the ceiling. Till now Will had seen but two Christmas trees up close and they were more the size of bushes and had no more decoration than a few thimbles his mama had put on the ends of branches. He marveled. The window curtains of this room had been drawn and lines of bright light from outside showed around the edges of the curtains. A fire burned in the fireplace and due to the fire and the shut windows the room was stifling.

A man dressed in Sunday black rocked by the hearth. He was wreathed in friendly smiles and nodded a greeting to Will's daddy and to Will himself and apologized for not getting up – he was suffering a bad siege of rheumatism, he said. Will's daddy stooped and placed Minnie on the rag rug. Then with Will in tow he crossed to the man and shook his hand and prodded Will forward so the man could take him by the shoulders and draw him close and place a cold wet kiss on his brow. The man smelled of camphor and breath sweetener and the lye in his freshly-washed shirt. "God bless you, son," he murmured, hugging Will tight against the rough cloth of his coat.

Then he held Will out again at arms'-length. His eye was a light gray that put Will in mind of faded denim. "My name's Jimmy," he said, though Will already knew that. "Folks mostly call me Uncle Jimmy. But in time I hope you'll be calling me Dad. My wife here, her name's Laura." He chuckled warmly. "I say Lar, for a pet name. She'll be your mother, when you're ready."

The woman smiled too and settled into a ladder-back chair on the other side of the hearth and bade Will's daddy take a seat and Will's daddy did. Will laid down his pillowcase of goods but was too nervous to sit even after Uncle Jimmy urged him to. He kept standing by the fire glancing from his daddy to Uncle Jimmy and back to his daddy. The hot room began to make him feel a little swimmy-headed.

Uncle Jimmy was bald and had a thick mustache that reminded Will of a push broom. Will knew him from a distance but had seldom before seen him up close. He gave Will an amiable study and his eyes sparkled in the firelight. Then he began to tell how he himself and his brother had been orphaned much like Will and Minnie, how they had gone first to his grandparents old Madison and Sarah Curtis and then, after they passed, to Aunt Rebecca Curtis and finally to other Cartman kin.

"It was a blessing in the end," he declared. "Grandma Cartman took us into her heart and treated us as her own, though she had six children of the blood and her husband was sickly from wounds taken in the war and went to his Heavenly Home shortly after." Fondly he nodded. He gestured with his big, coarse hands – Will had heard he was a fine blacksmith and the sight of those powerful hands made him believe it. "Bravely and trustfully she took up the burden," he said, employing a rounder and more fruity tone, "and she faced an uncertain future without flinching." It was the same tone Will remembered him using for holy communion at church, when as lay leader it was his duty to shepherd the congregation to the altar, solemnly intoning, "As these retire, let others come forward." Communion at Quarterly Meeting was the only time Will's mama could take him to church since his daddy forbade it otherwise.

Uncle Jimmy raised his eyes in reverence to what Will took to be Grandma Cartman's likeness, one of several hung about the room in heavy dark frames. Indeed, Will thought, she had a good face – much in contrast to the others portrayed, who wore looks that seemed reproachful and whose dour regard, he sensed, might follow darkly after him no matter where in the room he might retreat. "Sabbath morning always found her taking us children to Sunday School," Uncle Jimmy resumed. "We spent many hours gathered at her knee where she taught us the great Bible truths and principles of right living." He sighed in pious fashion. "She was one of our pioneer mothers, you know, Brother Price. She loved her Bible, sermons, religious books and her church paper. She read them daily. She lived a beautiful, unassuming Christian life. She shed an influence of. . . . of . . . what-you-may-say . . . of *wonderful serenity* both in the home and throughout the community."

Will's daddy had an uneasy air, for he had purposely lived his whole life as far away from religion as he could get. It was another reason Will couldn't see why he wanted to give over his son to folk that were as lifted up and saved as these. Now again Uncle Jimmy set a mild and loving look on Will. "In taking your boy into my home, Brother Price," he said, "I am hopeful – umbly hopeful – of emulating the example that blessed woman set for me. I mean to pass on the kindness my brother and I were shown." Sweating, Will stared doubtfully back.

Uncle Jimmy remarked that a paper that Lawyer Kope Elias had drawn up must be taken to the courthouse to be signed and recorded. He drew it from the bosom of his coat and laid it on the marble-topped table that stood between him and Will's daddy. There was a big leatherbound Bible with gilt pages on the table too. Will's daddy leaned and looked at the paper, then nodded and pushed it back toward Uncle Jimmy with the end of a finger. Uncle Jimmy fetched it up, folded it and returned it to his inside pocket. He suggested they meet next day at the courthouse to conclude the transaction. Brother Andy would come too, he said, to do the papers on Minnie. Will's daddy agreed.

They talked awhile longer. Then it was time for Will's daddy to go. They all stood save Will, who abruptly chose that moment to seat himself on a footstool by the hearth and huddle there to gaze stonily into the low red flames and bright embers. Will's daddy reached down and touched the top of his head. "Get up, son," he said, "and say goodbye to your pap." But Will would not rise. Nor did he even want to make any show of having heard. At this sign of dudgeon Uncle Jimmy only made a sympathetic cooing sound and his woman plucked up a corner of her apron and held it to her eye and dabbed away a tear. Will saw this out of the edge of his vision and felt it touch him and he bit his lip. He wanted to think of his mama then but couldn't afford to and so did not.

Will's daddy kept his hand on Will's head a spell longer. While he did, they all listened to the clock ticking in the outer hallway. The wood in the fire whined and popped. Then Will's daddy took his hand away and bent to one side and with a grunt hefted Minnie up off the floor where she had been crawling and blowing big bubbles of spit. Despite his rheumatism Uncle Jimmy struggled to his feet and walked Will's daddy to the door using the cane Will had seen him ply whenever his pains were plaguing him. Will could tell from the halt of their footsteps that his daddy had paused at the door to peer back at him in farewell. But he would not turn on the stool to meet the look. Instead he sat and glared hard into the fire trying not to remember his mama.

❧

When Uncle Jimmy came back from sending Will's daddy on his way, Will was amazed to see that his welcoming smiles were gone and the eyes that had been so kind and twinkly before had turned hard and the light in them was now a glitter as dangerous as broken glass. Giving his jaw a sideways jut Uncle Jimmy pivoted on the point of his cane and rounded on Will and leaned down at him pushing forth a red and scowling face. "Well, young mister," he scolded, "I see you have a rebellious spirit, continuing to stand when your elders have told you to sit. You are willful, young mister, willful. We'll have to break you of that."

Will froze in confusion. Uncle Jimmy seemed to have taken his decision not to sit when he first came in as a sign of defiance. For an instant he wondered what had become of the genial man who had wanted to be called Dad. But then he realized that the alarming change in Uncle Jimmy was his fault – by not sitting when invited, he had hurt Uncle Jimmy's feelings and angered him. Now he wanted very much to say he was sorry and explain the misunderstanding. But he was ashamed of himself and frightened by how different Uncle Jimmy was and couldn't speak a word. A drop of sweat slowly crept from his fringe of hair down behind an ear into the collar of his shirt while Uncle Jimmy bent lower and went on berating him, "I expect you've come by your surly nature through that no-account father of yours."

Crossing his hands on the head of the cane Uncle Jimmy straightened and stood shaking his head in disparagement. "I've known Ves Price all my life, I'm sad to say. He's a sorry low scoundrel. Always has been. And he'll *be* a scoundrel till the day he dies." The head wags turned to nods. "I reckon that's *your* bent too. Got that . . . what-you-may-say . . . that bad Price blood in you. Well, you won't get by with it in this house. No, sir. I'll not raise any boy of bad character under *my* roof."

The woman's soft voice stopped him. "The child's had a terrible shock, Jimmy. Don't you think?" She spoke quietly and with a becoming respect but Will noticed that at the sound of her voice Uncle Jimmy turned his head and put a glare on her that was like a gleam of steel. She pressed on, though. "He's lost his mama and his papa and his home. And you and I are nothing but strangers to him. Don't you think he's in need of love and not correction?"

Uncle Jimmy watched her for a second or two. Then he brought his attention back to Will and talked at him but he was speaking to her and not to Will at all. "You're a kind and forgiving soul, Lar," he remarked, though in saying so he made it sound like a failing. Will in spite of his shame and fear did not like how Uncle Jimmy was treating the woman. Although he was at fault he tried to look sternly at Uncle Jimmy, for he wanted to protect the nice woman. Uncle Jimmy looked sternly back.

It was a test; but it was the kind of test that grownups always had to win, and in a moment Will looked away. *Dad*, he thought. *This is my new daddy.*

"God loves the compliant," Uncle Jimmy was telling him, "and He will love you too."

"God loves you already, son," Aunt Laura insisted in her gentle way. She smiled at him and Will wanted to smile back but decided he had best not.

This time Uncle Jimmy didn't turn toward Aunt Laura even by the slightest fraction of an inch as he replied staring down at Will. "Yes, Lar," he conceded, "of course God loves the boy. He loves us all." In the gray eyes Will could see the cold fierce flare of his temper. He could almost feel its chilly breath, as when you hold a piece of ice close to your face. "But the more umble and obedient we are," continued Uncle Jimmy, "the more He loves us."

Aunt Laura colored and folded her hands in her lap and said no more.

Uncle Jimmy nodded to Will a final time and turned then and crossed to the marble-topped table sharply rapping the floor with the end of his cane at every step. He took no further notice of Will. He had something else on his mind now. From her ladder-back chair Aunt Laura quietly watched him as he grasped up the Bible and sat and put by his cane and opened the Bible and began to turn its flimsy pages with a kind of ferocious energy. Soon he found what he was searching for and marked it with a finger and then resumed paging till he had located the next place and similarly marked it. All this while Aunt Laura sat looking on in that same quiet way. Will realized that she was waiting.

"Proverbs eleven," Uncle Jimmy all of a sudden proclaimed in a triumphant voice, "verse twenty-two: 'As a jewel of gold in a swine's snout," he read, "so is a woman without discretion.'"

Looking up from the book he glowered at Aunt Laura till sweetly and compliantly she nodded and answered, "Yes, Jimmy."

Vindicated, Uncle Jimmy bobbed his head and made a little pleat of his lips and quickly turned to the other place he had marked. The tissue pages of the Bible rustled in the stillness. He offered the big book upward with buoyant lifts of his hands as he read. "First letter of the Apostle Paul to Timothy, second chapter, verses eleven and twelve: 'Let the woman learn in silence with all subjection. Suffer not a woman to teach, nor to usurp authority over the man, but to be in silence.'"

Aunt Laura looked more contrite. She had lustrous auburn hair that was beginning to turn white and she had wound it about her head in long braids that were held in place with ivory combs. "Yes, Jimmy," she said. Will felt it was because of him that Uncle Jimmy was chastising her. She was suffering for having given him a few sentiments of solace. He wanted to ask Uncle Jimmy to stop. But he was too frightened.

Now Uncle Jimmy closed the Bible with a thump and slid it back on the table. But he wasn't finished. He lashed a bony finger at Aunt Laura. "And Paul says in another place that women are commanded to be in obedience, and if they will learn anything, let them learn it from their husbands, for it is a shame for them to speak."

Aunt Laura kept her look meekly downcast. Again she nodded. "Yes, Jimmy."

"Now let us go to the Lord in prayer," he commanded. She obliged him by sinking to her knees on the rag rug. Because of his aching bones Uncle Jimmy couldn't kneel, but he scooted forward and perched himself on the front edge of his chair in a half-crouch and propped himself there with his cane. While Aunt Laura bowed her head, Uncle Jimmy raised his high – the better to address Heaven, Will guessed – and closed his eyes tight and once more unleashed that plummy Quarterly-Meeting communion voice. "Our Heavenly Father, we beseech Thee, look down with pity on this Thy erring servant Laura, who cometh now on bended knee entreating Thy forgiveness. She hast given way to turbulence and willfulness of spirit. Her tongue hath ruled her when it should have kept silent. She has fogotten the submission which is the duty of the woman before the man. She repenteth now of these transgressions, Lord. She rueth them. Henceforth she will endeavor to bear herself in all modesty and seemliness. Give her the strength to remember her duty of obedience and keep to it. Shew her Thy grace, we pray. We ask this in the Name of Thy Son Jesus Christ Our Lord. Amen."

"Amen," Aunt Laura echoed. Rising to her feet, she managed to catch Will's eye and somehow seemed to smile without smiling at all, though it was a sad smile, and this time Will did smile back, though Uncle Jimmy failed to see.

Supper was consumed in total silence after Uncle Jimmy offered a blessing that Will thought was closer to giving a sermon than saying grace. Neither Uncle Jimmy nor Aunt Laura seemed bothered by the absence of conversation, though Will found it unsettling. He guessed maybe they preferred keeping quiet and he reflected that if he were in Aunt Laura's place he would certainly rather listen to nothing than to Uncle Jimmy. But it did seem a wonder, after all the talking he'd done earlier, that Uncle Jimmy could keep still so long over his rations.

Afterward Uncle Jimmy – Dad, it was going to be Dad now – ushered Will into a side room of the house and sat him on a daybed upholstered in black horsehair and took a wicker chair beside him. From the way Uncle Jimmy grinned and winked and offered a stick of peppermint candy it seemed he was trying to be friendly again, and this was so different from the way he had acted earlier that Will was once more startled and puzzled and wary. Uncle Jimmy even reminded Will that Christmas was coming in a few more days and told him that Christmas, in addition to being the natal day of Our Savior, was a time when boys who had been obedient often received treats and play pretties. "Son," Uncle Jimmy added in kindly vein, "I'd like to tell you a story. Is that all right?"

"Yes," Will replied, sucking on the peppermint stick. What else was he to say? It was Uncle Jimmy's house and Uncle Jimmy was surely the king of it. Will shifted his weight on the mattress of the daybed and set to scratching his elbows.

Uncle Jimmy gave a nod. "It happened long time ago," he commenced, "when I was about the same age you are now. This was a year or two after the war, and the times were still unsettled. One hot summer day my brother Andy and I were playing down by the river when I noticed a whole lot of butterflies swarming on the ground in the shade of a big willow. There must have been a hundred of them, all fluttering and beating their wings. They were blue and black butterflies – you've seen ones like them; they're right common – and to me the whole mess of them looked like . . . what-you-may-say . . . like a thick bed of flowers that had come alive. I thought they were the prettiest things I'd ever seen. I thought the whole mess of them looked so flightsome they might be able to take wing altogether and it would be like seeing a whole flowerbed soar aloft. Andy and I went closer to admire them, and that was when we got the smell. It was a smell something like the spray of a skunk, only not as strong and a little more sweetish. And I knew it for rot, for the stink of death. That was a dead man those butterflies were swarming over."

The image was a compelling one and made the peppermint stick lose its sweetness and Will felt a thrill of horror as Uncle Jimmy conjured it up. "It turned out some bad fellows had murdered this man and left him there and the butterflies had come across him and they were feasting on him," Uncle Jimmy continued. "Under all that beauty that I had praised he was laying there bloated up with corruption fit to burst, with maggots crawling on him and his skin burnt waxy black by the sun. But covered over with all those lovely butterflies."

Will took the stick of peppermint out of his mouth and sat holding it. Uncle Jimmy paused and rested one of his big gnarled hands on Will's leg. His voice assumed a confiding note. "Now this world has its beauties, son. Beauties that can . . . what-you-may-say . . . can ravish your senses to witness. But just as those pretty butterflies cloaked that rotting corpse, why, the beauties of this world are but a cover for its evil."

He nodded to confirm it. "The Devil is in the world and means to snare us and drag our souls down to Hell. He's sly and knows how to use the world's beauties – the beauties that God made. That's how bad Satan is, twisting what God's made for his own ends, so as to lull and tempt us and draw us to Perdition. We've got to be strong to resist that. Now I've made myself strong against the powers of Lucifer. Those around me, I make them strong too, for I love them and want to keep their souls from the Devil's grasp. Maybe I'll seem harsh to you in that strength of mine. But it's meant to save you. Bring you to redemption. Yes, I'll be harsh. But if you get past me, you'll be a match for Satan, you can lick him. I promise it." Dad, Will thought. *Dad.*

*

Will didn't cry that night. He had already cried for his mama and his daddy and for Minnie and for himself. He was all cried out now. Besides, the time for crying was over. Starting tomorrow, everything was going to be different. It was going to take all he had to get through it. He knew that the biggest thing he had to get through was to learn how to love Uncle Jimmy. His mama had taught him that he must always learn how to do that – to find a way to love – and he had always tried his hardest to do it.

He had learned how to love his daddy although that had been terrible rough. He thought he was already starting to love Aunt Laura. But loving Uncle Jimmy was going to be a job of work. Lying on his pallet under one of the gables, Will put his mind to the problem. He thought about the story Uncle Jimmy had told. It seemed to him that Uncle Jimmy had drawn the wrong lesson from the story, had got it turned wrongways-around. Uncle Jimmy thought beauty was just a face that evil showed to fool you. But Will wondered if evil wasn't the face and beauty the reality. Beyond doubt the world was cruel. It had surely proved that to Will. But maybe beauty was the thing life gave you that made you strong enough to stand the bad. He believed that was so. His daddy hadn't. Will had felt sorry for his daddy, that he couldn't see the good for the bad. But that had been the beginning of finding out how to love his daddy. Maybe, he thought, that was the way to learn to love Uncle Jimmy too. By remembering how afraid Uncle Jimmy was of the world.

Chapter Four

Doubtless the reporter for the *Asheville Chronicle* would nourish certain smug preconceptions about what a Pennsylvania timber baron would be like. George Gordon Meade Weatherby was determined to dash them.

He would not arrive in regal fashion, borne in a carriage with liveried driver and footmen, but simply, alone, on horseback. He would not come garbed in deerstalker, chinchilla overcoat and tweed shooting jacket, but instead in a much-used mackinaw, workmanlike corduroy and his plainest boots, topped off by an old slouch hat. And if the normal expectation was that every logging mogul must be superannuated and as plump as a Christmas turkey, Weatherby – just thirty-four years of age, vigorous, muscular, whipcord-lean and tipping the scales at a spare one hundred fifty pounds – knew how nicely he refuted it.

Not that he actually lived the unassuming life he wished to imitate on this dazzling October morning. Like any nabob he was deeply fond of the trappings of his wealth and station. But he knew when it was wise to trim his sails; this occasion was one such. It would not do to ape Vanderbilt or Pack and come off so pompous that news of him would arouse resentment among the rustic mountain folk whose trust he so needed to inspire. He had even chosen his worst mount to carry him to the interview – an old white-faced bay hunter whom many years of jumping at Monongahela and Laurel Hills had given a weak back, bad knees and a hacking gait that Weatherby thought looked suitably plebeian.

So as he rode down the ridge between Wolf Creek and Big Choga to meet the reporter who awaited him at his sawmill on the Nantahala, Weatherby for all his millions looked no more grand than some mildly prosperous local husbandman. Yet it was his ridge – all five square miles of it, from the peak behind him, thirty-five hundred feet high and crowned by Wildwood, the turreted mansion he whimsically called a hunting lodge, to the joining of the two watercourses just ahead.

And a mile further on, where Wolf Creek emptied into the Nantahala, he owned another fifteen acres of riverbank and of course the mill itself, forty thousand dollars' worth of mill, with a big Clark bandsaw and a bank of circular saws in it, and thirty-five men working – a mill capable of an average cut of fifty thousand feet of straight stuff per day, with a narrow-gauge track running out of it that shipped the finished lumber downriver all the way to Beechertown on the Southern Railway and thence south and west up the Valley River to Andrews and then to Murphy and finally on to a junction with the Atlanta, Knoxville & Northern and so outward to the great world beyond, where all men of means knew very well who and what G.G.M. Weatherby really was.

He stopped on the last of the high ground that would offer him a broad view of the valley and the mountains that rimmed it and of the river that wound through the valley and the covered bridge that crossed the river and of the mill. He sat his horse and took in the prospect. Although the mill was large – a vast two-story central structure with four tall stacks, several outbuildings, lumber docks, a log-pond – still it was the smallest thing in view. Across the river the ragged head of a mountain the country people called Beech Cove Knob towered over it and beyond that, the high serrated wall of the Nantahalas. On the left bulked a round-topped range whose name Weatherby had not yet had an opportunity to learn. Back of him, had he turned to see them, the Tusquittees loomed. But he was pleased to remark that the mill – small though it seemed in relation to what surrounded it – had a power that the landscape, for all its immensity, lacked.

A hanging veil of its smoke obscured all but the profiles of the summits; he knew that the parts of the heights whose woods had not yet been cut were brilliant with autumn color, but behind the blue-white shroud the gay tints paled, were lost. And much had been cut bare and had no color to lose and through the film of smoke these tracts showed only a surface of coarse matte gray stippled with even grayer spots which were the stumps of thousands of felled trees. In the dulled sky the sun had faded and become a bloody disc. The long river meandering by twinkled in the light but the haze dimmed the twinkles to wan glints and upstream from the boom that had been spread from bank to bank to catch them, big drives of logs stripped of their bark choked the river and gave its surface the look of a floating boneyard.

While Weatherby watched, the little twenty-ton short-barreled Climax locomotive chugged slowly away from the docks drawing behind it a string of flatcars piled high with yellow lumber. He admired the red lettering on the gable of the mill that said WEATHERBY HARD-WOOD COMPANY. He saw with satisfaction that a row of water barrels had been set along the peak of the roof to protect against fire, as he had directed on his last trip down. All was well. He pondered the effect which he, one man, had had. It was large. He had diminished what had been colossal, what he supposed some were wont to call sublime. But to Weatherby it was the mill that was sublime – the mill and its power, which after all was no less than the wholesome power of commerce and improvement, which must always bear mankind upward, ever upward, to higher and higher realms; sublimity was the mill, and it was himself.

◀

The reporter's name was something-or-other Hotchkiss. He had a pocked face, round shoulders and a stoop, and proffered Weatherby a hand disagreeably limp and moist. He proclaimed himself a native New Yorker, though transplanted South when a babe and now a confirmed Carolinian. Weatherby had small use for journalists as a class – thought them purveyors of smut and sensation catering to the lowest of popular tastes. To encounter one sprung improbably from the original settler breed was disheartening; but to ponder his raddled countenance and slouchy deportment speaking of bloodlines now gone bad was worse – it confirmed a long-held and recently-intensifying belief of Weatherby's that the old American stock had entered upon a steep decline, tending toward degeneracy.

But it was important that the scribbler be cultivated even in the face of evidence suggesting a tainted lineage. Weatherby knew from long practice how to swallow his distaste when duty required. Affecting a congenial air, he responded with enthusiasm to every question, beginning with the inevitable one about the origin of his name.

"I was born," he explained, as had been necessary so many times before, "on the third of July, eighteen hundred and sixty-three. You may recognize the date. It was the last day of the great battle at Gettysburg during the Rebellion – or the War for Southern Independence, as I believe you here in Dixie prefer to call it. General Meade, you will remember, was the commander of the National army on that occasion. Meade was a Pennsylvanian, you know, as were we. My father was a great patriot and an admirer of Meade, and named me for the general on account of his victory."

"Was your father in the war?"

"Not as a soldier, no. At the outbreak he was too old to serve." In fact he had been but twenty-two; when the draft called him he had purchased a substitute, a poor Irishman from Pittsburgh who soon perished in battle, erasing Father's obligation to the Republic without the inconvenient necessity of Father having to die himself. "He had become well established in lumber" – that was true, up to a point; when the war commenced he was operating a single small sawmill in the Alleghenies. But it was the war itself that had made him. "He supplied the National army, you see. He became a contractor furnishing ambulance and wagon bodies and other needed wood products. As I say, he was a patriot." Or a profiteer, depending on the point of view.

While they talked, Weatherby conducted Hotchkiss through the mill. He demonstrated how the cleated chain of the jackslip fetched logs up the gangway from the pond and how the flippers then boxed each log into the log deck and how the deck tilted the log toward the carriage, where the stays captured it and afterward rolled it into the carriage to be held in place by the steam nigger. As they moved about, Hotchkiss displayed a dragging, shuffling walk – more evidence of the spoilage of the ancient strain that saddened Weatherby to see. They watched as the carriage shoved the log smoothly to and fro into the wicked teeth of steam-driven bandsaw traveling at blinding speed over its two rotating wheels.

"How did you begin in the business?" Hotchkiss shouted a few moments later over the screaming of the circular saws and the cutting of the lines.

"Cutting white pine for my father in the Tuscaroras and the Blues," he replied. "Later," he continued, "as our commerce grew, I worked at our operations in Maine, Vermont, New Hampshire, New York. When I had learned my way sufficiently, I began to manage our enterprises west of the Lakes, in Michigan, Wisconsin and Minnesota. As a consequence, at one time or another I've performed every task there is in lumbering – chopper, fitter, foreman, saw filer, road monkey, knot bumper, grab driver, even cook. My father insisted on a most complete apprenticeship. So when he passed on and I assumed the management of affairs, I knew the trade in the most intimate and practical manner, from the bottom upwards."

One by one the sawed boards were turned down to travel on live rollers to the edger. "And what decided you to come South?"

Why, thought Weatherby with bitter impatience, *this is where the timber is, you idiot. This, and the Far West. Everywhere else, it's all been cut.* Outwardly he was more earnest. "I am in hopes of giving employment to the men of this region. And of helping engender wealth among them so as to raise the region up. And of course I plan to engage in certain philanthropic activities which will benefit the people." He withheld his other, secret purpose; it was not for the ears of a prying wretch who was himself an example of what Weatherby had resolved to root out.

"I suppose," remarked Hotchkiss with a cynical curl of lip, "you are not averse to turning a profit too, whilst you are so busy improving all about you?"

Weatherby chuckled to hide the rage that the impertinence called up. He uttered but a mild reproof. "Ah, that was cruel, Mr. Hotchkiss."

The reporter reddened and grew stern. Weatherby could see he that was an anticapitalist zealot as well as the fruit of impure blood – all the more reason to detest him. "We here in this country have seen a few capitalists of late," Hotchkiss declared through flattened lips. "Some have made themselves quite conspicuous with unseemly displays. We have known them to distract us with philantrophies whilst they set about plundering our natural treasures."

"No doubt," said Weatherby, still maintaining his mask of jovial composure. "But I hope when you come to know me better, you will draw me somewhat mild in contrast to those you speak of. But you may be assured, I do love a profit as much as any man of affairs. I will not conceal it. But I ask you, is it not the guiding spirit and supreme purpose of all commercial enterprise that the accumulation of capital shall benefit not the capitalist alone but all those who prosper from his initiative?"

Hotchkiss made a sour little trap of his mouth and chose not to answer. "At any rate," Weatherby went on, "I have other reasons for having come to Western Carolina. Reasons relating to a purely personal predeliction. You see, I fancy myself something of a sportsman. I especially enjoy hunting the black bear, having done so from my youth, both in the highlands of Pennsylvania and later on the Upper Peninsula of Michigan. Here in these hills I am told the bear abounds. I look forward to stalking him."

As he spoke he ushered Hotchkiss outside to show him the bullpen and the kilns and docks. They stood for a while in silence gazing at the stacks of lumber air drying on the docks and at the steaming kilns. Presently Hotchkiss roused himself from his disapproving sulk sufficiently to inquire, "You will make your home here, then?"

"Not at all, sir. My permanent residence is in Philadelphia. Oh, I do maintain some minor holdings in Western Pennsylvania." Prudence forbade any mention of the particulars of the farms at Monongahela and Laurel Hills, which had incited envy on the Main Line for years. "My place here is but a humble holiday retreat, I assure you. A refuge from the confusions of the city. I am a man of simple tastes." He leaned toward Hotchkiss as if to share an ironic confidence. "*I* need no Biltmore," he laughed. Then he stood apart and with his arms pantomimed the aiming of a rifle. "From my rude cottage, I shall sally forth in quest of great black bruin, your *Ursus americanus.*" He dropped his arms and laughed again. "And do a little business too, of course."

"I should like to see your . . . cottage," Hotchkiss said with a narrow smile. "Our readers would no doubt be reassured to know how modest it is."

Weatherby nodded equably. "No doubt. But I am afraid that will be quite impossible. I readily confess, sir, that I am something of a fiend when it comes to my privacy."

"Ah," sighed Hotchkiss. "Too bad."

"Yes, too bad. But you may surely rely on my account of it."

The reporter smirked in an infuriating way. "I am sure that I can." He gestured toward the mass of naked logs floating in the river. "Tell me, sir, how do you come by your supply? Do you cut it all yourself?"

"We do have cutting crews. I own some acreage outright and of course we cut that, as you can see on the mountainside opposite us. On other tracts, held by individuals, I have bought timber rights and can cut there. But much of the supply comes from farmers who cut timber we have previously purchased, on their own lands, after their crops are in. They ship the logs here, by wagon mostly. Some float them down, as you see, by river."

"How do you keep track of who supplies you?"

"Each brands his logs with his own mark."

"Ingenious."

They ended where they had begun, at the edge of the log pond. Again Weatherby took the sodden hand. Immediately he was seized with a longing to wash his own. "I shall look forward to your account of our talk," he blustered in cheery vein. In fact he felt drained hollow from the effort it had cost him to treat the odious person decently. Yet he had to bear it a little longer, pleasantly smiling and waving in farewell, as Hotchkiss climbed aboard his buggy and took his solemn departure.

❦

As they parted, Weatherby became aware of a train of three mule-drawn log wagons approaching the ramp that sloped down to the millpond near where he stood. The logs were poplar and ash, big ones, held in place by heavy chain. It looked to be pretty good stuff. Weatherby moved a little distance off to be out of the way of the unloading and was thinking of going to see the mill manager before heading home – Poindexter had said there was a problem that needed seeing to – but something about the way the driver of the lead wagon carried himself made him pause and take notice.

Like many another country fellow this one was rangy, wry-necked and gaunt of face and had the wintry look in the eye that came of a lifetime of hard going. But he was young yet – no more than twenty-five, Weatherby surmised – and still moved with the catlike grace that always seemed to mark the best of them till age and toil bent and slowed them. He set his brake with a stroke of one foot, expertly wound his reins, dropped off the box and set about loosening the log chains all in one fluid sequence of motion. He worked swiftly and expertly – the word graceful came to Weatherby's mind – and had freed his load before the others had even managed to dismount from their wagons.

Grasping up a peavey, he caught the outermost bottom log with it, gave the tool a single upward twist, and his whole load, thus neatly dislodged, rolled off the wagon with a noise of muted thunder. He stepped away from it so nimbly that the move would have reminded Weatherby of a dancer's had it not been so natural and unconscious. One by one the logs tumbled down the ramp and splashed into the pond. Before they had ceased bobbing in the water he was rounding impatiently on the others and Weatherby smiled to see how comically their own unloading speeded up under his silent rebuke. Clearly he had the gift of command.

In another moment the two remaining loads had been dumped. Then to Weatherby's surprise the man turned and came purposefully along the top of the ramp toward him. Approaching, he did not remove his hat or glance bashfully aside as many country men did to show deference. Instead he looked Weatherby square in the face. His manner announced, I *may be poor but I'm every bit as good as you.* "You're Weatherby," he declared.

Not *Mr.* Weatherby. Just Weatherby. Not a question, a statement. His only concession to rank was that he did not presume to offer his hand – a distinction between station and merit that Weatherby thought quite elegant. "Yes," he said with growing interest, "I'm Weatherby."

The man briskly nodded. "Reckon I work for you, then. In a manner of speaking. Name's Absalom Middleton. My pap's Rufus Middleton."

"Middleton. Yes, I know the account. You're in the next valley south. Big Tuni Creek. We have forty acres stumpage rights of you, I believe."

"That's so."

Middleton had a frank and open countenance and a good clear blue eye and a full head of silky blond hair – the perfect Anglo-Saxon, Weatherby noted with approval. "What can I do for you, Mr. Middleton?"

"I've had a notion lately. It might be worthwhile to us and you both."

"What's that?"

"Wouldn't it be an advantage if we brought you finished lumber in place of logs you've got to saw? What if we were to get one of these little donkey mills – the kind you can move about from place to place? Take her right into the woods with us. Set her back in the mountains middleways of what we mean to log, pull logs into her from all around, saw 'em up, and move the lumber down to you. Then shift her to the next place. Just keep on moving her back in the woods as we go, pulling our logs in to the mill on the ground. And haul the lumber out to you on wagons."

Weatherby grew more and more impressed as Middleton explained himself. Here, he thought, was a business mind at work, crude perhaps, untutored, but clear as polished glass – almost as clear as Weatherby's own. Middleton used the idiom of his class and the twang of the mountains lived in his tone but there was such uncommon clarity and precision in his speech that Weatherby began to think he might have gained some modicum of learning, perhaps from one of the mission schools Northern churches were now founding in the highlands. "You'd have to know how to grade the lumber," he pointed out.

"You can teach us that," was the instant and confident reply.

Weatherby smiled at the fellow's self assurance, so robust that it bordered on impudence. He found it amusing and somewhat touching and, yes, even inspiring. And it was agreeable to find that one could still be inspired, even in the smallest of ways. "Have you got the where-withal to buy a portable mill?"

Middleton was ready with his answer and it was as plucky as the rest. "You can loan us the money. We'd pay you back in lumber."

Weatherby could not help laughing. The fellow was a delight. "I have to go and see Poindexter," he said. "Come in with me and we'll talk your notion over. I think we may be able to work something out." Middleton gave another perfunctory nod and called back to his partners to wait for him. Then the two of them started along the lip of the ramp toward the mill office. Yes, Weatherby thought, the fellow was a delight. But perhaps he was more. Perhaps he was also a discovery, a strike as promising as ore in float or a gem embedded in common rock, its value waiting to be assayed and smelted or chipped out by the jeweler and polished for display – something fit to be set into the bright coronet that was Weatherby's plan for the saving of the race.

✦

That evening Weatherby sat before the rock fireplace in a lower chamber of Wildwood that was paneled with California redwood and trimmed with honey-colored primavera imported from South America. He was busy cleaning and oiling his octagon-barreled Model 1886 Winchester hunting rifle. Admittedly it was a lot of gun for the job. It was bulky and front heavy, tiring to carry, and chambered for .50-300-110 Express, enough of a load to knock down a buffalo. But according to Poindexter, the boys had said the bear was an uncommon one, the largest they had ever seen – and they were all natives and claimed to know the bears of these parts.

The bear had come into one of the logging camps high on this side of Tusquittee Bald night before last and had broken up the cook shack and killed two dogs that tried to fight it. But then it had gone into the stock pen and killed an ox. Killed it wantonly, Poindexter said. Poindexter had never known a bear to do such a thing before. It was strange. It spelled trouble, he thought.

But what had looked like trouble to Pentland Poindexter was only a welcome challenge to G.G.M. Weatherby, above whose arched fireplace of fitted river stones hung the mounted heads of four black bears and, in the center, that of a great silver-backed grizzly he had shot two years ago in the Powder River country of Montana. Besides, he took all tales of bear size with a grain of salt, having inflated his share of them to excite the wonder of his peers. Still, whatever this one turned out to be, big or small, it would be bully good fun going after him.

Squinting in the firelight and the mellow glow of the kerosene lamp beside him, Weatherby finished by polishing the burled walnut of the rifle's stock and forestock with linseed oil. He missed the brilliance of the electric lights in his Philadelphia townhouse – no need to peer and peek to see one's work in the library there. But he had to concede there was a nice quality to the warmer radiance in this dim, snug room smelling of woodsmoke. How finely the soft light picked out the checkering of the pistol-wristed stock of the rifle and the rich red and gold tones of the paneling in the room.

He sat with the rifle across his lap gazing contentedly into the fire. Soon Cassandra, his daughter, would arrive from Swarthmore. They would dine on bear meat. She would hate it. He would extol its nutritional virtues. He smiled in happy anticipation. Duncan, his butler, brought him a brandy.

Chapter Five

On the twenty-ninth day Hamby got across the Nantahalas and started down the head of Shooting Creek into the valley of the Hiwassee. Those last few miles were the hardest. He was footsore and lame from walking the whole distance from Caney River. The trip had taken him over the high range of the Blacks to the North Fork of the Swannanoa and then down past Asheville and along the Hominy to the Big Pigeon. Next he'd gone through Balsam Gap and across the Cowees into the Nantahalas. Altogether it was better than a hundred and sixty mile of some of the steepest country God ever stood on end.

Not that he had tramped it all in a single stretch. He was tough but not *that* tough. From time to time he would stop and take a rest of a day or so. His old bones ached and his wind was short – it had been short ever since the year before, when he'd taken the first of his coughing fits at the Sink Hole. And besides, Reed Considine's six-dollar payoff from the Axum mine had only got him as far as Waynesville. After that, he'd had to stop every few days and find a piece of work to earn the money to keep on.

Even so, the damn hike had very nearly used him up. And now that it was almost done he couldn't even say why he'd made it. Coming out of the mountains there was a place on the shoulder of Chunky Gal where he could see down the Shooting Creek drainage and he paused there leaning on his walking stick to gaze and shake his head and ask himself, *Why in hell you drag your sorry ass back here?*

There wasn't any answer that he could think of – save the vague notion he'd had back at the Axum, that this was the one spot on earth where folk had given his name a bit of notice and as much freedom as came of that. So he just stood looking. The air was clear and he could see all the way into Georgia as far as Brasstown Bald. The valley yonder lay bright in the sun but where he stood was still under cloud and the November wind blew in his face and it was piercing cold and smelt of winter. He turned up the collar of his coat. Presently he went on.

Likely it would have been nearer to go down from the headwaters of Perry Creek, by way of Tusquittee. But he hadn't done it. And he didn't know the reason for that any more than he could tell why he had come back at all. Tusquittee lay no closer to Carter's Cove than Shooting Creek. But somehow it had *felt* closer, and that was enough to make him take the other road. He didn't know if he was ready for any of what he was going to find but he knew for sure that he wasn't ready yet for Carter's Cove. Now and then the memories from there would come flying at him. But he would stave them off with cussing so not a one could take hold. Although they no longer made him angry as they once had, still he did not want them around him, not yet anyway.

Seeing the land again, he did remember why it had fetched him back. It didn't appear quite as fine as he had recalled it – but then, nothing ever did. The open-pit mines at Corundum Hill and on Buck Creek were bigger and deeper and their flume lines ran every which way on the mountains. There were lumbermen in nearly every patch of woods cutting the slopes clear and hauling logs out. Farmsteads had sprouted in coves that had been wilderness when Hamby left. The air stank of tanneries and coal smoke. It all looked leaner and poorer and more shabby than he had expected, especially now that the leaves were mostly off. The rich greens of his memory had given way to the bleak browns and tans and grays of the season. Still, the hills were as soft and hummocky as ever and the ring of mountains roundabout just as china blue. The sky soared just as high. Even ravished by mines and mills and dulled by late autumn, it sure as hell beat the dark and spiky-topped mica country.

By early evening he had made his way down as far as Pitts Cove. He turned north then and went up the cove and through Smackass Gap. And he was there. The Downings Creek bottom lay before him sheltered by its familiar rim of low wooded hills. He could see the wagon road that led up through the hills and out by what had been the Curtis plantation, where he had been born in shame and in bondage. And closer by he could see the turnout to the cabin and the forty acres it sat on where he had later grown from child to man, no longer in bondage but still in shame and in the rage that sprung from the shame.

He did not think of the cabin and the farm as his – to him it was still, always, his stepdaddy's. It was old Daniel's. He did not really think of it as home either, because he figured home was a place you felt you belonged in and even though it had been better for him on Downings Creek than anywhere he had ever lived, he had never felt he belonged on it. But he had stayed there longer than in any other place. And if he had not been content, at least he had got closer to contentment there than ever before, or since. But it wasn't his. It was old Daniel's.

And Daniel McFee was a mystery that Hamby had never been able to puzzle out. Standing there gazing at the cutoff that led to old Daniel's he had a sudden surprising thought. Maybe not being able to solve the mystery of old Daniel had *kept* the farm and Downings Creek and the valley of the Hiwassee from becoming a place that he could belong in. Or a place where he could lose the shame and the rage that ate at him. Shame and rage had eaten at Daniel too but before the end Daniel had got past them. Got past them in ways Hamby couldn't understand and even condemned and despised. Now in a flash it occurred to him why he might have come back. Maybe, without knowing, he had come back to try to solve old Daniel's mystery – which after all was his own mystery too. Then he brayed a scoffing laugh. *Shit*, he told himself, *you a damn fool now for sure.*

◀︎

Limping up the lane he saw that the spirit tree was gone from the dooryard. The place where it had stood was covered by a patch of carrots and turnips and other such cool-weather kitchen truck. He remembered that the tree had had some rot in it when he left and he reckoned it had decayed and got taken down in the time since. He was surprised to find how badly he missed it now. Old Daniel had started it, dressing the ends of the limbs with pretty bottles of every hue. After Daniel, Hamby had kept it up, never with any affection for the tree itself and certainly not out of any belief in the powers some superstitious niggers would have given it, but just because keeping it up had seemed a way to do right by old Daniel. He propped himself on his staff and bent left and right massaging his aching shins. He saw that the garden had also taken up the space where he used to pen his gamecocks. More memories tried to come then but he pushed those away too.

There were other changes. The woodlot nearest the wagon road had been cleared and was sown in what looked like winter oats. The meadow behind the cabin where Daniel used to pasture his horses and where Hamby had kept his jenny was a cornfield now and although the corn had been harvested Hamby could see that the leaves of the cornstalks left standing had been cut off for fodder and that the stalks in the part of the field nearest the cabin had already been plowed under. At least whoever had the place now knew how to farm better than most.

Also there was grass in the dooryard instead of swept dirt and the grass was neatly mowed. The shack had a new tin roof. Hanging on either side of the front door were some fancy doodads made of feathers and beads that looked to Hamby like Indian charms. The frames of the doors and windows had been painted blue and the rest of the house had been freshly whitewashed. Hamby guessed it was neater than it had ever been in his time, though to his taste it appeared much too fussy and womanish.

As he stood critically taking in the sight of it the door of the cabin swung open and a coppery-brown old man with a red cloth tied around his head came out, and with him a dog the likes of which Hamby had never seen in all his life. The critter ran at Hamby not frontwards but scuttling along broadside and sideways. It was crookbacked and as lumpy in the body as a stocking stuffed with yarn balls, save in the middle where it had a sunken place that looked as if somebody had sat on it and mashed some of the yarn balls flat. It was so kinked it had to peer over its own shoulder to see where it was going. It stopped a few feet from Hamby and glared at him with its cranked head and gave a couple of coughing barks. Hamby gaped and couldn't help asking, "What the matter with that dog?"

The old man smiled and let himself down in the rickety fashion of old men and sat on the doorstone. He had a shock of white hair that the red cloth could not contain and that hung in a shaggy mass down his back except for two thin braids dangling in front. "Bear walloped him," he answered. "Knocked him up agin a rock. Kindly rearranged his insides."

Hamby shook his head in wonder. "He goddamn funny looking."

The old man gave a cackle. "You ort to see him try and shit. Has to fix hisself just so. Twists around like he's trying to look up his own asshole. Can't do his job nohow if he don't. Groans like forty."

The dog ceased to bark and all of a sudden made a distorted hump of itself and then lurched violently backward. Hamby was alarmed – maybe the damn thing was mad – till he realized these were only the preliminaries to its sitting down. It had to sit hindwise to Hamby so as to watch him over one shoulder. Panting, it studied him with limpid brown eyes that were as pretty as it was ugly. "Whyn't you put the damn thing out of its misery?" Hamby wanted to know.

"Oh, he don't suffer much," the old man said with a languid wave of a hand. "And he's still a right good old bear dog."

Hamby was more amazed than ever. "You fooling me now. Why, he can't even walk a straight line."

"Well, he does have to take hisself a right good bearing on where he means to go, afore he starts," the old man admitted. "And then he kindly has to go on the bias to get there. But he purely *hates* a bear. I expect he wants to pay 'em all back for what that one done to him." He eyed the dog fondly. "He's mostly Plott hound – got a good cold nose, can pick up a cold trail at a far distance – but there's a right smart of cur dog to him too. Tracks like a Plott but fights severe, like a cur will. Won't tangle with other dogs, though, the way your Plott hound wants to. I've kilt six bears with that dog. You a bear hunter?"

"I hunted some. Never with no Plotts, though. Redbones and bluticks. Mostly I hunts by myself." He examined the dog and it examined him back with its liver-colored tongue hanging out. Its fur was thick and brindled but it had pale spots above its eyes like a black-and-tan. There were deep scars on its muzzle and one ear was torn swallowtailed. Hamby could see that it was an honest dog even if it was deformed. "What you call him?"

"I call him Cattywampus Dog," the old man said with a crinkly grin.

Hamby nodded. "I can see why."

The old man reached in the front pocket of his greasy canvas coat and fished out a corncob pipe and stuck it in his mouth and sucked on it cold. Cocking his head to one side he closely studied Hamby with little yellowish eyes. His face was deeply wrinkled and looked as tough and pliable as an old leather purse. He might have been sixty or ninety, there wasn't any telling. He had a redkskin's coloring but his features were sharp and narrow like a white's. "You'd be McFee," he declared at last.

Again Hamby was surprised. "How you know that?"

The old man shrugged. "Folk hereabouts, they always say, 'Old McFee, he be back one day.'"

"Humph," snorted Hamby, "they knowed more'n *I* did." He frowned in confusion. He had never imagined that anybody in the valley would think about him at all, much less go to the trouble of predicting his return. He couldn't tell if he liked that or resented it, and his divided mood turned his temper gruff. "What you doing here?" he blurted out, still annoyed about the spirit tree and the rooster pens.

The reply was mild. "I crop shares for Mr. Sanders Carter."

That was the Carter who lived at the old Curtis place. Tom Carter's brother. Tom Carter of Carter's Cove. The name stung. Hamby pressed the old man, meaning now to be rude. "You a Injun?"

The old man took the stem of his pipe out his mouth and sweetly smiled. "I'm a Injun the same way you're a nigger," he said with a sparkle in his eye.

Hamby waited a moment still holding onto his scowl. He thought about being offended. But then he decided he liked the remark pretty well. "Then you a Injun," he declared, and they both laughed at the same bitter truth. He walked up to the stoop and put out his hand and the old man gave him a callused paw and they shook. "What they call you?" Hamby asked.

"Mordecai Corntassel." He put the pipe back in his mouth and fished a tobacco pouch from a side pocket of his coat and opened it and tamped the bowl full. Hamby put down his stick and settled on the grass next to the doorstone where the old man roosted and untied his brogans and took them off and set to rubbing his bare feet while the old man lit the pipe. The dog sat backwards to them watching them over its shoulder panting. The old man puffed awhile on his pipe. When Hamby finished with his feet he got his own pipe out of his budget of goods and lit up too and the both of them sat smoking as the dusk started to come down. Now and then Hamby would cough and spit a little ruby spot of blood on the grass. Each time he did it the freak dog would come and lap up what he spat with a greedy relish.

After awhile the old man spoke up. "I reckon you'll be wanting your place back."

Hamby wagged his head. "'Tain't no property of mine. Not no more. I give up my right to it. Never kept up no payments. You got a contract with Sanders Carter, I 'spect the law say this place be his, he can do what he like – rent it to you, whatever. I ain't in the picture nohow." He paused. He had decided the old man was all right and had started to accept the varmint too. He coughed and leaned and spat again and watched as the dog licked it up and then he said, "But I be obliged if you let me stay the night – just till I find me a hole of my own."

"You can stay," said Mordecai Corntassel, "but you got to sleep in the loft. Cattywampus Dog, he gets the spot by the fireplace."

◄

They ate a supper of fatback and pone washed down with cider from a demijohn that the old man brought up from the spring house. The cider was too fresh to be much good but it was spicy and tart and it spread a tingly warmth from the belly outwards that commenced to heal the hurts that the long walk had put in Hamby's joints. After supper they sat by the fire and had another smoke and finished off the cider. Hamby shoved his naked feet to the blaze to ease their soreness. The dog lay curled on the hearth in such contorted fashion it was hard to see how it could get any rest at all. By and by it slept.

The old man stayed silent a long time and Hamby savored the quiet and the rest. Firelight flickered on the walls in a way that made him pleasantly drowsy. But the chimney didn't draw any better now than it ever had and in time they were both blinking and weeping from the sting of the smoke that backed into the room, and that waked Hamby up again. The place smelt strong of smoke and had another odor too that was smart and rank like what fills your nose when you come near the den of something wild. There were bear pelts and the skins of coons pegged on the walls and bearskins thrown on the dirt floor for rugs. Racked over the fireplace was an old trapdoor Springfield needle gun and standing in a corner was a Model 1866 Winchester whose brass receiver had gone brown with tarnish.

Hamby had been looking for something in the room that might be familiar – something that he or even old Daniel might have left, some trace to show they'd lived there. But all he could see was the firedogs on the hearth that he remembered forging at the Curtis smithy. Nothing else. He reckoned that in living here so long after Daniel passed, he'd wiped out every sign of Daniel's living. Now the old man was wiping out every sign of his.

After a spell he raised the matter of where he might find work. The old man said he doubted if Sanders Carter had any. "*I* handle any-thing Mr. Sanders has got – or is going to get," he boasted. Still, he didn't mind if Hamby asked. What about old Captain Moore, up Tusquittee? Corntassel agreed that Irish Bill might have something. "Or the Middletons on Big Tuni," he went on. "You recollect them? Sure you do. Mr. Rufus and them three boys of his? They got 'em one of them portable sawmills. It's up on Tuni there somewheres. They been sawing away like hell up yonder, a month or more now. Had 'em a splashdam too, flooded logs down to the mill. They sell the lumber to Weatherby over on the Nantahaly."

Hamby nodded. He'd worked many a sawmill in his time. And Big Tuni was away up. Far from Carter's Cove. Maybe he'd try that. Cattywampus Dog whimpered in his sleep. Hamby pointed at him with the bowl of his pipe. "He in pain?"

"Might be. But I always reckoned it was him a-dreaming."

"Dreaming how, you think?"

"I bet he dreams of the bear."

"The one that hurt him?"

"Not just that 'un. More'n that. I expect he dreams of what a bear *is*."

Hamby frowned. "What that be?"

"Oh, a mighty figger. I dream of it myself."

"What you dream?"

"Lots of things. One thing that I seen for real, when I was just a youngun. I was a-hunting in the woods one day up near the head of the Lufty when I heard what I thought was a woman a-singing to her babe. It was the sweetest song I ever heard. Why, it just beguiled me. So I followed it up a branch till I come on a cave under the bushes. And the singing was coming out of this cave. Well, I parted them bushes and peered in. And you know, a big mother bear was a-setting in there. And by God, she was rocking her cub in her paws and a-singing to it. Singing this sweet babysong."

In disbelief Hamby blew out a gust of wind. "It never."

"No, it did. She was a-rocking this cub just like a human mother would do. And what she sung was:

Let me carry you on my back
Let me carry you on my back
Let me carry you on my back,
Let me carry you on my back,
On the sunny side, go to sleep,
On the sunny side, go to sleep.

It was a lullabye, you see. 'Course, she sung it in Cherokee."

"You telling a lie now," Hamby scorned him.

"No, I ain't. I seen that with my own eyes. Others seen it too. Told it. It's a tale of my mama's people. But what was just a story to me till then, why, I *seen*. And I dream of it still. I tell you, the bear's a mighty figger. But not the way you might reason. Now there's a big one lives up on Tusquitte Bald. Them as got a look at him says he'll go eight, nine hundred pound. More brown than black, they say. Rared up, he's seven foot tall. A strange bold bear. Like none afore him. Been troubling that sawmill camp of the Middletons'. Killed a mule, some dogs. Yonside of the ridge, went after some steers of Weatherby's. He's a mighty figger – in his way. But his ain't the proper nature, you see. Not for a regular bear."

"What is?"

"Why, the bear's *us*. Don't you know that? He's us afore we soured. He's us when we lived right. Ain't no power greater'n *that*."

Hamby shook his head. "I never heard a man tell so much shit all at once."

"Well," the old man hotly declared, "you're just about plumb-ass ignorant, ain't you? Most niggers I know're smart. But I reckon you was absent when they passed out the brains to the darkies. Now I got to educate you. I'll tell you a tale."

"You just got done doing that."

"Well, I aim to tell you another'n. And you'll profit from it if you'll listen."

"I reckon this the price I got to pay for a goddamn place to sleep. Go ahead on."

"A long time ago there was a clan of folk called Ani-Tsaguhi. One family of this clan had a boy that liked to leave home and go and spend all day up in the mountains. He'd go oftener and stay longer till finally he stopped eating his rations in the house altogether but would go off afore daybreak and stay back in the hills and not come home again till after dark. His folks'd scold him but it done no good, for the boy still went off to the mountains ever day afore dawn and wouldn't never come back till way in the night. Then they noticed he was a-growing hair all over him. Long dark hair. And they wondered and asked him why he was a-growing all this hair and why he wouldn't eat his rations and why he spent all his time in the woods.

"And this boy told 'em, 'I find plenty to eat in the mountains and it's better than the corn and beans we got here in the settlements, and pretty soon I'm going to go and live in the woods all the time.' Well, you can bet this vexed his folks. They commenced to begging him not to leave. But he said, 'It's better in the hills than here, and you can see I'm starting to be different already, so I can't live here no more. But if you come with me, there's plenty for all of us and you won't never have to work for it like you do now. But if you want to come, you've got to fast for seven days.'" He leaned confidentially at Hamby. "Fasting – that means not eating."

Hamby pulled a wry face. "I know what fasting is, goddamnit."

"Well, I'm just a-saying," the old man nodded. "Now this boy, his folks talked it over and then went and told the headman about the fix they was in. And the headman called a council. And the whole clan met in council and pondered the matter over. And they said, 'Here in town we got to work hard and still we don't always have enough. And this here boy says there's always plenty in the woods without work. We'll go with him.' So they all fasted seven days – the whole clan of 'em. And on the seventh morning all the Ani-Tsaguhi left the settlement and followed the boy up into the mountains.

"When the people in the other settlements heard about it, they was worried and confused. They sent their headmen to try and convince the Ani-Tsaguhi to come down out of the woods and live at home again. But when the messengers found 'em, they was already a-growing long dark hair all over their bodies. You see, they hadn't took no human food for seven days and already their nature was a-changing. And they refused to come back.

"And this is what they said to the messengers: 'We're a-going up in the woods where there's already plenty to eat. After this we'll be called *yanu* – that's Cherokee for what a bear is – and when you your-selves get hungry, you can come into the woods and call us and we'll come down and give you our own flesh to eat. You don't need to be afraid to kill us, for we'll live always.' Then they taught the messengers some songs. They said the people would have to sing these songs to call them down out of the woods for the sacrifice they'd make of theirselves. But the people must always kill them with thanksgiving and reverence. The people must ask their pardon every time. For it was a great sacrifice they was willing to make. And the messengers agreed to this.

"And when they'd finished a-teaching the songs, the Ani-Tsaguhi started on again and the messengers turned back to the settlements. But after going a little ways they looked back. And all they seen was a big drove of bears going into the woods.

"So that's the true nature of your bear. That he come of us. Us when we was good and not yet spoilt. *He's* the best we ever was. And he gives his life over to us. Lays down that sacrifice. Does it of his own notion. So's we can eat. But we're supposed to honor him for it. And that's the sorry part. For we don't do him no honor. Not no more. Now even my mama's people don't ask his pardon afore they kill him. Nor sing the sacred songs. We've broke the agreement them old messengers made. Lately I been a-wondering about that'un up on the Bald – the one that ain't acting right. I been a-wondering . . . Maybe he's an answer to that wrong. Maybe he's a kind of a . . . visitation."

Hamby snorted. "First he Jesus. Then he the Devil. Which way you want it?"

"'T'ain't how *I* want it," the old man said. "It's how '*tis*."

◀

Next morning Hamby set out to see Sanders Carter about getting work. It was but a short distance – less than a mile by the carriage road that followed the low ground instead of the old wagon road that was higher. Yet it felt like the longest mile he'd ever walked. Remembrances bounded up out of every foot of it. There wasn't a tree or a shrub or a piece of ground that didn't want to retell its story. About old Daniel, about the Curtises. About her. He warded them all off. He had taken special pains to armor himself against whatever the place wanted to say or do – he'd known that today would be the roughest yet. But the weight of the armor he had put on was heavy and toilsome to carry.

He took the turnout to the old place, saw it yonder on its hill. The sight of it punched him in the belly like a fist. God *damn*, he swore. The two-tiered gallery in front, the hipped roof sheathed in tin and the rock chimneys at either end, the big magnolias and oaks and maples in the yard, the double row of boxwoods leading up from the turnaround – it was all the same. Eight years' time had not altered an atom of it. It was as if he had never gone away, as if all the ones long dead were still alive and would step out on the gallery any minute and hail him.

He clamped his lips tight and went on. *No,* he said to himself, *all I be doing is get me some work.* But it was like wading in mud up to the knees. The gravel of the drive crunched under his feet and he remembered that sound from before and then had to make himself not remember it. The morning was crisp but he was sweating into the collar of his shirt anyway, till it made a cold wet ring around his neck. His wind came shorter and shorter. Finally a spell of coughing took him and he had to stop and bend over and give way to it till it ran its course. Then he wiped the blood off his mouth with his sleeve and went on.

He was still some shy of the house when he spied the old phaeton parked in the turnaround. *Shit.* He stopped, spat angrily sideways into the weeds beside the lane. That was Tom Carter's goddamn rig. Tom Carter, piss on him, come to visit his brother. What a sorry piece of luck this was. Hamby glared in contempt at the phaeton's rusty hood. *All this time, the cheap son of a bitch still got that same damn old raggedy-ass buggy.* The dun horse hitched to the phaeton pricked its ears and looked curiously at him. *At least the damn horse is new.* Hamby took a step back. He couldn't go on now, not with Tom in there. *Shit*, he said again. He was trying to decide what to do when the front door opened and some people came onto the porch. Before they could glimpse him he dodged out of the road and got behind a laurel bush to hide himself. He was going to watch. For he wanted to watch. He wanted to see who it was. Even though he feared to see.

He recognized Sanders – he still had that scraggly beard. And there was Tom, a little heavier. And a slim brown-haired girl of fourteen or fifteen. He looked close. His mind told him who the girl was. She was Tom's daughter. *Her* daughter. She was Lillie Dell. That was what his mind said. But his eyes said she was not herself at all. They said she was her mother. He turned away quick then and started back the way he had come. *By God*, he scolded himself, *older I get, the more I be going soft.* He was toting a flask in the hip pocket of his jeans that still had some lightning in it. He was going to find himself a spot away off in the woods somewhere and he was going to lay himself down in that spot and he was going to drink that lightning up.

❦

"After I got done a-telling tales last night," Corntassel remarked that evening as they lounged by the fire after supper smoking their pipes, "it come to me, you're a tale yourself."

Hamby wasn't much in the mood for talk. There had been less whiskey in that flask than he thought – not even enough to dull the edge of what ailed him, now that he'd seen what he'd seen. He sat staring into the fire, seeing it – seeing her – still. The dog slept at his feet, a mis-shapen lump that now and then whined. Dully he roused himself. "What you mean by that?"

"*You're* a tale. Folk tell it."

Hamby barely heard him. "What tale is that?"

"'Bout a mixed-blood living 'twixt the two ways," the old man said. "Whites name him nigger, coloreds call him white. Born to slaves, a slave hisself. Then free. But not free of hate. Hating what he be. And hating them that made him so. But bound too. Free, but bound. Bound to the ones that held him property afore. Them Curtises of old. Bound as if by blood, yet they ain't no tie of blood. What bound him? Them as tells the tale don't know. Can't nobody say."

Hamby had begun to listen now. The cadence of Corntassel's voice was different. It had a kind of singsong to it. And the language was different too, though Hamby couldn't have said exactly how. "He had him a stepdaddy," the old man was saying, "a full nigger, Daniel McFee by name. Curtises used to keep this Daniel in bondage too. One day roughriders come. The stepdaddy got kilt in place of them that used to own him. Tried to save 'em, it looked like. That was back in Reconstruction time. But *he* never had the grace his stepdaddy had. On account of the hate in him. Yet he's bound closer'n Daniel ever was. And he's bound to no Curtis nearer'n he is to that youngest gal-child, Becky by name. None can explain it. 'Twasn't kin. 'Twasn't the longing of the flesh. But they's bound. Mortally bound. Long as she lived, he was by her."

Hamby had turned still as stone. He had the feeling that if he moved, something would break – something inexpressibly delicate – and that if it did break, even delicate as it was, why, the world might crack open under him. He hardly dared breathe. Cattywampus Dog whim-pered again and commenced to twitching as if he dreamt of running and Hamby wanted to stop him making a commotion that could cause the thing to break but then chose not to stir lest his own motion break it. In the stillness he heard the thumping of his heart.

"Time come," Corntassel went on, "he offered hisself up to save a white. Much as his stepdaddy had. But not with his stepdaddy's grace.

With hate. With that hate still a-rankling in him. Hate and all, he done it. Why? God knows. 'Tis a riddle. Quare thing is, 'twasn't Miss Becky he done it for – her that he favored, and that favored him. 'Twas a worthless piece of nigger-hating white trash that he went and saved. Not even a Curtis. Not even one of the ones he felt bound to. Bad 'uns had snared this one. Blockaders. Ves Price was his name. Held prisoner up Tusquittee. They was fixing to do murder on him. *He* went up. He bred gamecocks then. Took some roosters, wagered with the bad 'uns for the life of this dirt-eater. It come to killin' in the end. But they come out of it, him and the scamp both. So he done more than even his stepdaddy had. But he done it still with hate."

Hamby wanted to tell him to stop but didn't, couldn't. He just sat looking into the fire while the dog trembled and cried on the hearth and the old man's voice droned on like a chant. "Miss Becky was sickly then. Consumption, I heard. She wed Mr. Tom Carter. Him that lives over to Carter's Cove. Brother to Mr. Sanders Carter that hires me. She lived six years. He stayed by her. Honored that bond, whatever it was. But the bile never went out of him. Finally she passed. Same day she died, he up and left. No word ever come of him in the years since. Been gone a long time. Yet the folk all say, 'One day, Old McFee, he be back.'"

The old man fell quiet then and Hamby was relieved. He let a long time pass. Then he said, "That quite a tale."

Corntassel nodded with enthusiasm. "Gets bigger ever time they tell it. Why, it's got sacrifice in it too, just like the bear story I told you before. Did you take note of that? Yep, I like it. I like it 'cause the case seems right close to mine. They say my mama was kin to Nimrod Smith, old Tsaladihi, that used to be the Principal Chief of the Cherokee. But my daddy was a trader up from Charleston, white as sweet corn. So I'm mixed too. Neither the one nor t'other. I took my mama's name, 'cause my daddy forswore me. The case is near, like I say." Slyly he smiled. "'Cept *I* ain't never tried to give myself over for sacrifice, to save folk not my own. Nor ever had such hate in me. Nor has anybody ever told a tale of me, like they done you."

"I ain't him," Hamby growled. "I ain't that."

Chapter Six

Will Price was cutting crossties in the oak woods on the brow of Spoon Hill. From there he had a clear view across the river bottom to Jimmy Cartman's house and on occasion as he worked he would pause and gaze that way and wonder if his fortunes were prospering or not. And then he would drag off his hat and clasp it to his breast and offer up a prayer entreating the favor of Heaven on the proposition his grandad was advancing to Dad just then. Then he would replace his hat and go back to cutting ties. But pretty soon he would get to fretting again and have to stop and peer across and resume his wondering and then take off his hat and yield up another prayer.

For his cause was by no means assured. By nature Dad would oppose the notion of his paying court to Lillie Carter – Dad tended to count a sin anything he thought might gratify someone other than himself. So it was up to Grandad to argue him around to the place where he'd forget that it was Will he was obliging and see a side of the matter that might profit him alone.

There was nobody better to do it. Oliver Price might be but a poor cobbler with scant learning, yet he was sly and powerfully gifted with ready talk. And few cleaved to the Methodist doctrine any nearer, not even Dad – and Dad knew that and had to honor it. But Dad was tough as a hickory nut and no matter how fluent and guileful Oliver managed to be, nothing short of the help of the Lord was going to crack that shell Dad wore over him.

Will completed his latest prayer and put his hat back on and reminded himself with a sigh that he must set his distractions aside – he knew of a boy on Greasy Creek who'd daydreamed while cutting ties and sliced all the toes off his left foot and ended up a hobbling cripple. He bent once more to the work, plying the broadaxe with care. He had already felled a chestnut oak and cut off the crown and branches and used iron wedges hammered in with a wood mallet to split the trunk. He had chopped the splits to the right lengths. Now he was hewing out the ties.

Ties only needed to be flat on two sides and a lot of fellows were satisfied to smooth the tops and bottoms and leave the sides rough, sometimes even with the bark still on – the railroad didn't care. But Will did. He liked to finish his ties on all four sides. And he always finished them clean. It was a matter of pride with him. If you looked at one when he was done with it, you'd have thought it had been planed by hand instead of hewed out with a broadaxe. His mama whom he could no longer call to mind had left him with a maxim that he had never forgotten, that no matter how mean the task, it should be finely done; a person's work was a measure of his character. He always shaped himself to every saying of his mama's that had stayed in his head.

Whenever he cut ties Will would think of the rails that would lie on them one day and how the trains ran on those rails and how the trains went everywhere in the whole country. A-body could pay a quarter and get on one of the six main-line trains that stopped at Murphy or Culberson and be in Atlanta or Knoxville or Asheville that same day and if he had some more money he could connect there with other trains that would carry him off to all the different corners of America. He could even travel as far as Littleton, Colorado if he wanted to. Will knew that because Dad's atlas that he had consulted showed a little crosshatched line that denoted a railroad – the Denver & Rio Grande, it said – running right through Littleton. A-body could catch a train in Atlanta or Knoxville and then take other trains in other places till finally he got on the Union Pacific and he could ride the Union Pacific all the way out to Denver and in Denver he could change trains and then go south on the D&RG and in no time at all he would be in Littleton.

That was something he often thought about. It was a part of the reason he had always wanted the life of a railroad man. As long as he could remember he had longed to be a brakeman or a conductor or a fireman or even an engine driver, to be free to ride those long distances to far places. Places like Littleton. Where his actual daddy was. He didn't know if he really *wanted* to go and seek out his daddy. He never imagined actually doing it. He never thought about what he would say to his daddy if he ever saw him. He tried not to ponder his daddy at all. But somehow it was a comfort to know he could see him if he wanted to and if he took the right trains. So he would think about it but never plan on doing it.

Mostly he just fancied the railroad for its own sake. When he first came to Dad's ten years ago, the whole Hiwassee country was afire with excitement about the coming of the tracks. The Richmond & Danville was at Topton then, building west toward Murphy through an open cut, and the Marietta & North Georgia was already at Murphy and had a depot across the river on the bench of land behind the ice plant. Will could remember riding the ferry across the Hiwassee with Dad, carrying wagon loads of pulpwood – five-foot sticks of skinned poplar and maple – over to the depot. He would stand on the platform of the depot filled with wonder as the locomotive of the up-train came rumbling in wrapped in clouds of steam like a storybook dragon.

Later the Richmond & Danville got to Murphy too and built its depot. The names were different now – the Georgia line was the Atlanta, Knoxville & Northern and the R&D was the Southern. Whatever they were called, nothing stirred him nearly as much. There was a livestock corral next to the Southern depot and a big wooden water tank and a coal yard. When the trains came, men would load cows into the cattle cars and copper ore and quartz and marble into the hopper cars and crossties and lumber on the flatcars and Will would think how the copper had come from up the Little Tennessee and the quartz from Big Snowbird and the marble from Hyatt's Creek and the wood and ties from everywhere in Clay and Cherokee Counties and how it was all going out on the trains to cities and towns from one end of the country to the other and he wanted to go too, go and never come back.

But like with his real daddy, he thought on it without ever believing it would happen. He thought about marrying Lillie and being a railroad man but as he thought about it he understood that even if he and Grandad did overcome Dad's objections and he took Lillie to wife, he would no more become a railroad man than he would ever in all his days look again on his real daddy's face. Somehow he knew that what he had was pretty much all he was going to get. He could dream as much as he wanted, but his dreams weren't going to come true. They were just a way of amusing himself with an imagined life while his real life went on happening.

◀⁞

After his voice changed Will had developed a fine tenor voice and while he enjoyed singing any time at all, he especially liked to sing whenever he was vexed – the fullness of music in his throat had a way of easing him like nothing else. And he was truly vexed now from waiting to hear from his grandad. So when he finished cutting the ties and began to stack them he resolved to render up some of his cherished hymns as he worked. There was a practical reason for singing too: He had uttered so many prayers during the course of the afternoon he was afraid God might be getting worn out listening to them. He figured a hymn was nearly as good as a prayer. So if he switched from prayers to hymns, he might get the same effect and also have the benefit of variety by not taxing the Lord's patience. He started with his most favorite:

"What a friend we have in Jesus,
all our sins and griefs to bear!
What a privilege to carry
everything to God in prayer!

O, what peace we often forfeit,
O, what needless pain we bear,
all because we do not carry
everything to God in prayer."

He sang all three verses. He enjoyed the sound of his bright tones soaring over the distances in the crisp still air. It was a cloudy day but the clouds were high and thin enough to let some sun seep through and the air was clear and he could see the mountains off in the distance and even the texture of the trees on the mountains that had mostly lost their leaves by now, making the peaks look like they were covered with scatters of iron filings. He paused long enough to finish neatly stacking the ties – he didn't need to stack them, of course; he could have left them scattered helter-skelter, for in two days' time he would be bringing the steer cart back to load them and take them into Murphy and in the meantime it hardly mattered how they lay; but that wouldn't have squared him with his mama. When he was done, he leaned against the stack and wiped his brow with his handkerchief and sang his second favorite:

"Sweet hour of prayer! Sweet hour of prayer!
That calls me from a world of care,
and bids me at my Father's throne
make all my wants and wishes known.

In seasons of distress and grief,
my soul has often found relief,
and oft escaped the tempter's snare
by thy return, sweet hour of prayer!"

He sang all three verses of that too. Between Spoon Hill and Dad's place stood the house where Will's sister Minnie lived with Uncle Andy and Aunt Samantha Cartman. Whenever Minnie heard Will singing she always sought him out if he was close enough by and her chores permitted. By ordinary they didn't get to see a great deal of each other – they were too hard-worked for that. But Minnie knew today was an anxious time for Will and wanted to be with him for a spell while he waited to know his fate. Yet she was enough of a sister that she wasn't going to betray that. Instead, she took on an air of spite. "How come you want to marry Lillie Carter anyway?" she blurted as she came flouncing up the slope through the grass at the edge of the woods that the November frost had turned sere. "Why, she ain't even pretty."

"*Isn't* pretty," Will corrected her, "not ain't."

Minnie climbed up on the stack and sat there kicking her heels against the ends of the ties. "That's what I just said."

"No. I mean, you said 'ain't' when you should've said 'isn't'. You ought to talk right if you're going to grow up and be a lady." Minnie was thirteen now and Will thought it was high time she commenced behaving in proper fashion. He was disappointed that Uncle Andy and Aunt Samantha weren't doing a better job on her than they were. "And Lillie *is* pretty too," he added.

"No, she ain't. She's got little squinty eyes."

"*Isn't.*"

"Ain't."

"*Isn't,*" Will insisted. "And her eyes are beautiful and not squinty atall. She's the prettiest girl I know."

Minnie frowned and quit kicking her heels against the ties. "What about me?"

Will laughed. "You? Why, *you're* the ugly one. Talk about squinty eyes. And look at that little nubbin of a nose. And all those freckles. If I were you, I wouldn't go around talking about somebody *else's* looks."

Minnie made a face and twisted a ringlet of ginger-colored hair around a finger and resumed her kicking. "You don't mean that."

He grasped the toe of one of her brogans and playfully tugged it. "No, I don't." Then he hunkered down next to the stack of ties and picked up a wood chip and put it in his mouth to chew on. "But I'll try and tell you why I want to marry Lillie." He mused awhile trying to think how to explain it. "It's like . . . well, it's like she was me and I was her."

"Shoot," said Minnie. "That don't make no sense atall."

"*Doesn't.* Doesn't make *any* sense."

"That's what I just said."

This time Will let it pass. He was too intent on telling what he wanted to tell. "I mean, I don't have to say a thing to know she understands what's in my mind. And not just in my mind but in my heart too. Because sometimes your heart knows things your mind doesn't. And I can do the same with her. So it's like we're the same person but there's two of us. And it's always been like that."

"Well," Minnie declared, "it still don't make no sense."

"*Doesn't.* Doesn't make *any* sense."

"See?" she burst out with a peal of laughter. "You agree with me!" She had trapped him so nimbly that Will couldn't help but laugh too.

They were still laughing when Will happened to cast his eye across the way to Dad's and spied his grandad limping down the front steps and saw at once from the stoop of Oliver's shoulders and the halting way he moved that the Almighty had a plan for Will that was different from the one that Will had been praying and singing for. His spirits wilted but before he could get downcast he told himself sternly *Blessed be the name of the Lord* and reaching out he stilled Minnie with a touch on her ankle and said, "Here he comes, Sister. Let's go and see him."

With a squeal of delight Minnie dropped off the stack of ties and set off through the yellowed grass. Will followed slower, watching in the distance as Oliver unhitched his mule from the iron jockey in front of Dad's house and awkwardly climbed onto its bare back and shook its one rein of plowline and started down the carriage road with his bad leg sticking out to the side. Oliver's head sagged and bobbed with every stride of the mule as if the ordeal of negotiating with Dad had somehow worked it limber on his neckbone. The road came past Uncle Andy's and turned up a swale that ran alongside the foot of Spoon Hill and that was where Will and Minnie met him.

Minnie dashed up giggling and Oliver favored her with a wan smile and then she saw his distress and stopped short of him and stood on the shoulder of the road hopping from one foot to the other not knowing what to do with herself. "Hello, children," Oliver said, pulling up the mule. His voice was husky from talking, maybe from shouting. He gave Will a sad study. "Well, son, I'm afraid he's dead set against you. I used all my wiles. I'm plumb give out from haranguing. But I couldn't budge him."

Gravely Will nodded. There was another plan, that was all. He just didn't know yet what it was. "What's his reasons, Grandad?"

"That you're too young. You and Lillie both."

A small geyser of annoyance spouted up inside of Will despite his best efforts to quell it. "You've been in there with him three hours or more," he burst out. "Did it take that long for him to say that little?" But as soon as he spoke he was ashamed of himself and looked down at his feet and felt his ears start to scald with embarrassment and regret.

"I was a-saying *my* piece too, part of the time," Oliver explained. "I done everything I could." A hard glint kindled in his eye. "Short of killing the stubborn little billy goat like I wanted." He hesitated as if to summon up a more seemly manner and cleared his throat, then it was his turn to shift his eyes away. Finally he conceded, "I reckon he did say . . . more'n that. Somewhat." Oliver seemed about to speak further, then didn't.

"Well, what else *did* he say?" Will prompted him.

Vigorously Oliver shook his head. "Nothing. Nothing that mattered. Nothing you ought to pay any heed to." He worried at the end of his mustache with his side teeth.

Will didn't need Oliver to repeat what else Dad had said. He knew Dad had said the same thing to Oliver that he had already said to Will a hundred times or more – the thing about Will's blood being bad from his real daddy. About Will going rotten in time, just like the rascally Ves. Will nodded again. He put out his hand and laid the flat of it on the coarse hide of the mule by Oliver's good knee. "I know you did your best, Grandad. And I know it wasn't easy. I'm much obliged – you taking time off from your work and all."

Oliver still wouldn't look at him. He examined the crest of the rise before them and said, "I'm sorry I couldn't do more for you, son." A second time he cleared his throat. Then he murmured, "Well, I got to get on. There's shoes yet to make afore dark. I'll see you two tomorrow at church."

"Goodbye, Grandad," Will and Minnie said together. He shook his rope and the mule plodded on. They stood by the road and watched him ride slowly up the hill with his game leg poked out. Will thought how much he loved this old man who wanted to be the daddy he had lost, though he couldn't be that no matter how hard he wished it. "Well," Minnie remarked, "now you can't get bespoken after all. I guess you'll just have to stay a bachelor." She looked sharply at Will. "You won't get mad and stop singing, will you? Even if I have to hear you tell me I'm ugly, I still like to hear you sing."

Will smiled. "I'm not mad. And no, I'll not stop singing – I won't ever do that. But I *am* disappointed." He took a breath and flattened his lips into a firm line and added, "But meaning no disrespect to Dad, I still aim to marry Lillie Carter." He had decided that the difference in divine plans was but a matter of timing – that God still meant for it to happen, but later rather than sooner. And if he had learned anything so far in his life, he had learned patience.

"How can you?" Minnie wanted to know. "Uncle Jimmy forbids it."

"The day I come of age, Dad can't say me yea nor nay any more. And that's when I'll ask her."

"Supposing she won't wait that long. What'll you do then?"

"She'll wait. Remember what I said, about us knowing what's in each other's minds and hearts? Well, I know she'll wait. You just watch and see."

·

After Minnie went back to Uncle Andy's, Will returned to the crown of Spoon Hill to collect his broadaxe and wood mallet and poke of wedges. Once he had gathered everything up, he sank to his hams at the tree line and watched the dusk darken over the valley while he set in to thinking. He knew that when he got home Dad was going to fuss at him for sending Oliver to be his advocate. He could even predict the words Dad would use to reproach him. *If you think you're man enough to get married, why, you ought to be man enough to come to me yourself, instead of sending your old grandpa.*

That would smart because it would be true. Will had meant to approach him. As soon as Oliver agreed to speak for him he had resolved to raise the matter, fully expecting to meet with an abrupt refusal that would have opened the way for Oliver's intervention. But Will had lost courage at the last moment. Just as he was drawing a big breath to speak, Dad had launched into a tirade about the degrading of the Curtis line. Tom Carter had managed to offend him in some business transaction and he disparaged all Carters and lamented the sad fate that had seen his Aunt Becky Curtis, Lillie's mama, marry one. "It's a constant sorrow to me," he declared, "that Aunt Becky's daughter's half a Carter. I sure hope she marries well. If she weds beneath her like her mother did, why, the blood's spoilt for sure."

Was it happenstance that he would say such a thing at just that instant? Or had he somehow divined what Will wanted to ask and decided to preempt him by bringing to mind the purity of the Curtis line and the poison he said ran in Will's veins that would sully it? Whatever Dad meant, Will took the meaning that made him unfit – the meaning he thought Dad intended. He let it stop his tongue in his mouth. So it was true that he had let his granddad fend for him. Shamefully true. He hadn't been the man he ought to be.

He sighed and wished he were better than he was. He wanted to keep on believing what he had believed when he first came to the Cartmans – that while the world was without pity, every day it held up a face of beauty for a person to see if he wanted to. And that beauty was greater than the world's evil. And if you let it inside you, it was stronger than the bad and could defeat it. He wanted to keep on believing it and he still did.

But he feared the belief was getting thin. He felt like he was standing on a sheet of ice that was melting under him and was apt to crack at any time. Underneath the ice flowed a dark cold river. If the ice broke, he would sink in the river and be lost.

It was hard to keep his faith in the grace of the Lord and listen to Dad too. Will loved God and thought God loved him back. He hoped he would live a virtuous life and go to Heaven when he died. Even if he couldn't see all his dreams come true, he hoped for a life that might be small but still rightful. But Dad would read out to him the passages of Scripture that told how the blood taint had come to him through his real daddy. Employing that fruity tone he reserved for pious utterances, he would offer the big leatherbound Bible with its gilt-edged pages heavenward with small lifts of his hands intoning, "And the Lord will by no means clear the guilty; visiting the iniquities of the fathers upon the children, unto the third and to the fourth generation"; or, "Our fathers sinned, and are no more; and we bear their iniquities"; or, "The fathers have eaten sour grapes, and the children's teeth are set on edge."

If it was in the Bible, it had to be so. But Will knew there were other things in Holy Writ that promised a person could be redeemed of sin if he repented. The parts that Dad read seemed to say the sin that got passed down from fathers to sons couldn't be washed away by the Blood of the Lamb, but had to be borne. How to reconcile the two? It was worrisome to puzzle over what looked like contradictions in sacred text. But one thing was sure, it was all the Word of God. Somehow or other, it was all so, even the parts that didn't look like they matched up.

How was it just that Will could be condemned for what his real daddy had done before he was even born? Maybe the Almighty wasn't bound by justice. Maybe He held larger considerations in mind. Still, Will didn't want to think that he was already marked like Cain. If that were true, it would cut him off from every good choice in life and then from the promise of salvation after death.

Why, if it were true, it was pointless for him even to pray and sing hymns and worship the Most High and try to do right. If it were true, he was wrong to want to marry Lillie Carter – because by wedding her, he would infect her with his blight of sin and infect their children too, when children came. Infect them unto the third and fourth generation. If it were true, he was already damned; he was bent toward Hell before he ever had a chance to fairly set foot on the path of life.

But it *was* true. In some manner that he couldn't fathom, it was true. That was the knowledge that ached in the middle of him all the time. It was the ache that he sang and prayed and laughed and was gay and loved Dad all the time to try to soothe.

Chapter Seven

Perched on an outcrop of rock above a fire-scald on a saddle of ground between two mountain peaks that he could no longer see because of the thickening mist, Weatherby shivered in the damp and hugged his Winchester close as if it had the power to warm him. The day had started out sunny and clear but by midmorning clouds had formed and a cold wind had commenced to blow and the first of several rain showers had swept over him and then the fog had come. It drifted up the divide in wisps and then in skeins and then in long trailing streamers and at last it drew its shroud over everything and he was embowered in cloud as thoroughly as any angel.

The improbable image evoked a dry smile. Perhaps this was as close to Heaven as he was going to get. If so, it was a relief to find that Paradise was as boring a place as he had always imagined. There wasn't even a view. At least before the mist came he had been able to see down the divide into the valley of the Nantahala and that had given him something to look at while he waited – slopes of woods partly bare and partly clothed in brown leaves not yet fallen, giving way to yet more slopes and then more that dwindled yonder into a maze of far-off folds and wrinkles, all of it spread out under a bright and limitless sky. Now, anything farther than twenty feet from him was lost in whiteness. Even if the bear came, likely it would pass him by unseen.

He swore. Using the tail of his woollen muffler he began wiping beads of moisture off the barrel and receiver of the Winchester. The life of a stander on a bear hunt was an ordeal of tedium under the best of circumstances. In his younger days he had always loathed it. One of the felicities of the rank he had now attained was that as master of every hunt he could assign someone else to the thankless task. But this was the fourth day of the hunt and while they had found plenty of sign and had even struck the trail of two that eluded them, they had not seen the bear they wanted; and everyone else in the party had done a turn at standing and in a gesture toward democracy Weatherby had felt he should volunteer too.

It was the last day – had to be, because tomorrow he must go down to the railroad to meet Cassandra – and he had realized that if he agreed to be a stander at least once during the hunt Absalom Middleton and the others would think the better of him for it; and it was important to him that they – that Middleton especially – should think that.

Of course if you were a stander and the bear decided to come through you to get away from the dogs and the drivers, monotony was no longer your problem. Then in a twinkling you had to find your nerve and aim true and shoot straight – something Weatherby had never failed coolly and efficiently to do. If it should happen, he would be ready. He would relish a test of skill as he always did. Most often, though, the dogs got to the bear first and then the drivers followed the dogs in and it was the drivers who did the killing while the poor stander loitered on some remote gap or knob listening wistfully to their gunshots in the distance.

Still, there was that one small chance. The bear might come his way. He hoped it would, though if it did come the mist would prove a considerable disadvantage. Left to his own devices he was the equal – no, the superior – of any beast of the wild. Admittedly this one seemed a shade out of the ordinary. By all accounts its behavior had been erratic. Most blacks were shy and timid yet it roamed boldly about and came into the settlements and seemed to have no fear of man. It had killed livestock. Destroyed property. And from the sign Weatherby himself had seen it was quite large, more the bulk of a small grizzly than a black. But he had hunted and taken bigger game – not just grizzlies but Kodiaks too. He felt no dread of the brute regardless of its size or disposition. Even so, he wouldn't fancy having any kind of bear at all coming at him out of this confounded murk.

He shivered again and cradled the rifle nearer. He hated exposing its fine finish to the elements. When this was over, he would break it down and give it a meticulous cleaning. That was the trouble with a beautiful gun – you hated to foul it with use even as you longed to employ its precision. He sighed. Then from somewhere far down the divide he heard the faint baying of a dog.

He felt a stab of excitement and got quickly to his feet and stood with sharpened senses and the cry came again, muffled a little by the fog, and this time he recognized the plangent note. It was Middleton's bitch, that old bluetick-walker crossbreed. The strike dog, Poindexter's black-and-tan, wouldn't be sounding; that meant they had come upon a fresh trail and had unleashed the pack. Sure enough, in another instant the rest of the dogs tuned up – the redbone, the Plotts, his own two Airedales. He smiled. To a bear hunter it was a music sweeter than Mozart's.

But the noise soon faded and he realized with a sink of disappointment that they were trailing across the divide and not up it. They were heading away from him. He resumed his seat on the rock and sulked as the belling of the dogs receded to the west. Democracy, he glumly reflected, had its price. But after a time he began to console himself with thoughts of Cassandra and her impending visit.

What great sport it was going to be to joust again with his willful daughter! At Swarthmore they were stuffing her head with notions even more radical than the ones she had hatched on her own by reading Saint-Simon, Fourier, Marx and Proudhon in Father's rather too extensive library. She had been the next thing to a syndicalist when she left home; God knew what heresies she might be preaching now. That was half the reason he had taken her out of school for a term – female education was all well and good so long as parents had a chance now and then to intervene and correct it.

Still, he delighted in Cassandra's spirit nearly as much as he ridiculed her beliefs. Had she been a male like that wretch Hotchkiss the politics might have been a concern. But politics in a woman were irrelevant apart from the amusement they afforded. And Cassandra was smart for a female and really quite articulate and joyously full of irate passion and Weatherby loved to match wits with her, playing the grasping plutocrat to her fiery idealist in shouted arguments that could go on for hours but always dissolved into good-natured laughter at the end – perversely, the two were as devoted as father and daughter as they were opposed in their convictions.

Again he dried the Winchester with one end of his muffler. Sometimes he did worry that by so fervently championing the rights of the working class and denouncing the evils of capitalism Cassandra might discourage the attentions of men of means – one of whom she must inevitably wed in time. After all her husband, whoever he turned out to be, would have to manage the Weatherby enterprises which she would inherit. Naturally the man must come from the very highest realms of finance or business. And of course none but the purest blood would serve. But just now that worry was a small one; the pleasure he took in Cassandra dwarfed it. He tried not to think about how she was going to react when the time came for him to pick the fellow or about what kind of marriage she was going to have afterward.

For now it was enough that he doted on her. And that she in no way resembled her mother. Another shower of rain briefly spattered him and he hunched his shoulders against its pelting and against the chill of the mist. All unwanted, the doleful image of Isabella rose in his memory. Poor creature. Bearing Cassandra had ruined her insides. A fallen womb. Holes in her uterus. Beautiful as a Sargent portrait but stinking all the time of the shit that oozed from her privates. It had been a blessing when she died of pneumonia at only nineteen, when Cassandra was but a year old.

What a paradox, that he with his commitment to the improvement of the race had taken to wife one so unsuitably delicate. She had come of good stock – one of the best families of Rhode Island. It showed how pernicious was the debility that now beset even the noblest of the original strain. Who knew how it had insinuated itself into the lineage of the lofty Arrowoods?

Thankfully Cassandra seemed to have escaped the incubus. He regarded it almost as a miracle, knowing as he did how obstinately the blot usually clung once it found lodgement. But she was robust as a thoroughbred mare, thank God. Eminently suited to breed up the line. She had the broad pelvis and the rounded breast recommended by Abbot Kinney in *The Conquest of Death*, his fine volume on the religion of reproduction, and in all ways that Weatherby knew about was anatomically perfect. Furthermore, in looks she struck the golden mean – she was neither so beautiful as to pass on traits of vanity and shallowness nor so ugly as to transmit ill favor. She wholly possessed Kinney's first requisite in a woman to be selected for a wife – the physical capacity to bear children who would be an improvement on the parents.

A loud crackling of brush near at hand interrupted his musings. Hardly believing his ears, he bounded up with the Winchester at the ready just as the trunk of a sapling snapped with a noise like a pistol shot somewhere to his right and very close to him. He heard the fluttery rattle of its dry leaves as it fell. He turned in that direction remembering that a patch of woods – rhododendron and young mountain ash – jutted there, ending no more than thirty feet away; but the mist was denser now and he could see nothing save the rock he stood on and maybe ten square yards of the fire-scald tilting toward the invisible treeline below. His heart thundered in his chest. It was a bear – he could smell it now, the smutty, rank, musklike, deep-woods odor he knew so well. But was it the one they sought? Or had another come his way by happenstance, frightened by the racket of the dogs?

In the stillness he heard it breathe. A hoarse chuffing like a locomotive laboring up a steep grade. He dared not move. There was a round in the chamber of the Winchester but he would have to cock the hammer before he could shoot and as close as the bear was, it might well hear the snick of the hammer and bolt back into the forest. Weatherby sure as hell didn't want that. But neither did he want a scared bear blundering over him by accident in a blind fog.

He considered his options. His heart might be throbbing from the thrill of his plight but he was as calm as he had ever been and as he debated what to do he could not help noting with pride how serene and confident he felt, how certain of his own mastery. Above the chuffing of the bear he heard its great weight shift in the rhododendron, heard the stalks pop and the leaves shiver. Another wave of its bitter smell passed over him. The moist air hung heavy; he could feel no breeze; if the bear were so close and had not yet caught his scent, he must be in its lee. Like all its kind the beast was nearsighted; the fog was thick as fleece; maybe it didn't even know he was there. If that was right, then he had the advantage.

He rested the tip of his thumb on the knurled spur of the hammer. That was when the bear came. Nothing had ever moved so fast. All he saw was a blur of cinnamon as huge as the side of a boxcar. That, and the sweep of a mighty paw. He only had time to feel the opening up of a round and empty hole in the middle of him that he had never felt before but that he nevertheless knew was the fear he had always denied, and then there was a shock; the Winchester sailed end-over-end; a blast of hot breath scorched him; and he was down. Stunned, he rolled off the rock and lay on his back in the wet bracken. Somewhere a bird sang.

◄

He had summoned them by blowing the ram's horn Poindexter had loaned him. He sat on the rock examining the Winchester which was bent into a dogleg and whose lovely burled stock was scored with deep claw marks. They watched him from the fire-scald but only with the edges of their eyes. Whatever they were thinking they did not reveal it and he was grateful. The weary dogs lay about them panting. He was sore from the glancing blow the bear had dealt him but he was not otherwise hurt save in a way that he was trying to keep secret even from himself. "Mr. Middleton," he asked, "can you remain another half-day? Stay in the woods tonight and try again in the morning?"

"I expect it's for you to say." Absalom Middleton had done so

well with the portable sawmill on Big Tuni that Weatherby, more impressed than ever with his initiative, had hired him and brought him
over to the big mill at Nantahala to be trained as he himself had been
trained – doing in rotation every job there was. Just now he was saw
filer. His father and brothers were running the little mill Weatherby had
financed – which, thanks to Absalom, had already come near paying for
itself. In every way the young man was measuring up to the high expec-
tations Weatherby had had of him. He very badly wanted Absalom with
him now. "Dockery can keep the saws sharp," Middleton drawled. "But
there's that train you want to meet."

"We'll have time," Weatherby assured him. "The train's not due
till tomorrow evening." He turned to the mill manager. "Poindexter?"

The manager shook his head. "We've got that big lot of logs from
Indian Camp to cut."

"Can you leave the dogs?"

"The strike dog, yes. But them Plotts is one-man critters. You
can't do a thing with 'em. The black-and-tan'll mind Middleton, though."

"All right. What about Bascom and Ledford?" He had picked his
men off their jobs for their bear hunting skills but now he had to think of
business. Ledford was a scaler and Bascom handled the set works.

"The dogger can do my setting," Bascom spoke up eagerly. "Half
a day of it, leastways." If it was a choice between setting the carriage
and chasing bear, and if he was being paid either way, Bascom didn't
see a choice at all.

"I can scale the logs myself," Poindexter put in. "We can manage." So it was settled. They would try again. And if they did not take
the bear tomorrow they would come back another day. They would keep
coming back. They would come back again and again till they got him.
Him. It was a Him now. He had a smell and a color and a way of moving
that was his own and he and Weatherby knew something very important
about each other and they were intimate now as only mortal enemies
were intimate. What The Bear knew about Weatherby The Bear could
not be allowed to keep on knowing. And by killing what The Bear knew
Weatherby would also be killing what he had learned about himself. At
least that is what he hoped.

◄⋮

The next day's hunt was in vain as Weatherby came quickly to
know it would be. At noon they started down. The route, according to
Middleton, would take them from Signal Bald along the tops of the
Valley River Mountains to Wolf Creek Gap. And indeed, when they

came to the gap, Weatherby found he could look down the drainage and see the familiar turrets of Wildwood rising above the bare treetops. Why not go straight down Wolf Creek? he ventured to ask. But Middleton insisted with convincing authority that it would be longer to the railroad that way. Instead he led them along the ridgetops north and east through what he said was Junaluska Gap and then down a watercourse – Dick's Creek, Middleton called it – and from thence to the river, coming out some miles downstream of the mill on the narrow-gauge track that connected the mill to the railroad.

Presently the little Climax came puffing down from Beechertown pulling a string of empty flatcars. They hailed it and soon it was backing its way up the track with the hunting party crouched on the cars clutching the leashes of the alternately cowering and snarling dogs. They made it to the Beechertown flag stop with half an hour to spare. When the Southern down train arrived, Cassandra and her chaperone, Weatherby's elder sister Margaret, stepped off and stood on the ballast gaping in astonishment at the men in their muddy and briar-torn clothing and at their abundant weaponry and at the gaggle of hallooing dogs. "Is there a war, George?" Margaret sniffed in her best disapproving schoolmarm style.

"If there is," laughed Cassandra, "surely these are losers."

"No, my dears," Weatherby bluffly assured them. "I must disappoint you in the matter of the war. But we have been on a hunt, and I am sorry to admit that we have lost *that*." He came to kiss them both.

◆

"Oh, Father," Cassandra burst out as the Climax carried them between the clear-cut hills, "look how you've devastated the mountains! I'm appalled." Reclining amid her baggage on the sawdust-covered bed of the open flatcar she appeared perfectly at ease as the soot of the little geared locomotive settled liberally over her. She had even removed her bonnet and shaken out her long coppery locks as if to revel in the grit and grime and icy winds.

Weatherby gazed worshipfully at her. But she had challenged him, so he must wrangle with her. "Would you rather everyone in America lived in earthen huts?" he scoffed. "Do you know what the annual requirement is for housing in this country? Twelve and a half million cubic feet of lumber. Would you like to dispense with the railroad which just delivered you to me so efficiently and in such comfort? That's a million four hundred thousand cubic feet. How about fuel to heat homes? A mere seventeen and a half million cubic feet. Somebody must cut the wood, dear."

Cassandra tossed her head in scorn and her green eyes brightened as she warmed to the argument. "Well, I can quote some figures too, Father. Do you know how much timber is lost each year to forest fires? Over ten million acres. Add to that your horrid, wasteful destruction. Why, I've read that in California the tie cutters waste timber to the value of a dollar and eighty-seven cents to make a railroad tie worth only thirty-five cents."

"Whatever happened to Latin and Greek?" he inquired with a grin. "The Romantic poets? Shakespeare? Algebra? Plane geometry? What sort of curriculum do they offer up there?"

"She does her own reading, George," Margaret interjected, very much offended by the rude circumstances of their travel. She clasped her feathered bonnet to her head with one hand while pressing a lace handkerchief over nose and mouth with the other. Now and then she used the handkerchief to dab in futility at the growing number of spots on her gray serge traveling dress. Her face was blue with cold.

"I know," Weatherby replied, secretly enjoying her discomfort. "To my cost."

"The point is," Cassandra went blithely on, "at the present rate of our consumption of timber, combined with the annual loss due to natural causes, we shall soon denude our forests."

"Even as we cut the forests, others grow," said Weatherby. "And there is a vast supply. We shall never exhaust it."

Cassandra vented a croak of contempt. "Tell that to those in Michigan who now gaze out upon great expanses of emptiness where once the white pine grew."

"Tell me, dear. What are you now? Bi-metalist? Utopian? Communist? Readjuster? Anarchist?"

She laughed brightly. "An anarchist, by all means. It's much the most fun." Her gaze drifted rearward. It settled on the men of the hunting party crouched on the bed of the car behind them. He saw her face sharpen with interest. "Father," she asked, "who is that fine-looking fellow with the golden hair?"

"His name is Absalom Middleton. I'm training him in the trade. A most remarkable man. Provincial, unschooled, even backward by our lights. But quite shrewd in his own way. And unspoiled. Absolutely unspoiled. The pure Anglo-Saxon . . . "

"Ah, eugenics again." She cocked an amused eye at him. "Are you still obsessed with purifying the racial stock? Father, is Mr. Middleton by any chance one of your . . . experiments?"

He chuckled. "Quite possibly, my dear. Quite possibly."

⁕

At her first sight of Wildwood – its sixty-eight-foot central tower surrounded by sets of peaked and latticed gables, its Romanesque turrets each with its conical cap shaped like a witch's hat and not one carved like its neighbor, its balustraded porch, all of it fashioned from native woods – Cassandra was aghast. "It's a monstrosity!" she shrieked. "An oppressor's castle! This is worse than Versailles! More excessive than Chambord! How conspicuous! How utterly pretentious, extreme and vainglorious! How many rooms has it?"

"Twelve," he beamed.

"You had this built just since I went to school? You cannot safely be left alone, Father. Where on earth did you get the plans?"

"A fellow lumberman, Carson by name, on Humboldt Bay in California."

She shuddered. "It's entirely hideous."

⁕

In the dining room dozens of candles awakened mellow splendors in the paneling of oak and heartwood pine and a fire burned lustily in the double-flued marble fireplace with its inset of stained glass and framing of Philippine mahogany. In lieu of the bear meat Weatherby had counted on but failed to provide, they made do with venison and pheasant. Afterward Margaret complained of a headache and retired. Weatherby and Cassandra withdrew to the music room. Duncan served them brandy – Weatherby had conceded Cassandra the privilege the previous fall when at sixteen she had become the youngest woman ever to be admitted to Swarthmore.

She sank into the leatherbound cushions of the sofa and quizzically examined the organ, the harp, the piano, the guitar in the corner, the ornately-carved oak music stand. "Father, since neither you nor I can play a note of music, don't you think this rather an unseemly display?"

"Not at all, my dear. One day when I have the leisure I hope to take up music. And Margaret plays the piano."

"Ah, but you have leisure now," she pointed out. "Nothing but leisure. You are the idle rich. You wallow in indolence surrounding yourself with luxuries paid for by the sweat of the workers."

"Nonsense. I work harder than the meanest laborer. But you know me, Cassandra. I am unapologetic. I will not paint myself as more benevolent than I am. I admit I came to these mountains because I believed they afforded a magnificent opportunity for investment and speculation. I mean for them to make me one of the richest and most influential men in the country. And I am but the first of many. When the extent of the resources of this region is fully understood, it will be a revelation to other capitalists of the North and West."

Cassandra made a contemptuous face. "And they will flock here and sack it as the Vandals sacked Rome."

"You are incorrigible, dear," he smiled indulgently. "But hear me. The store of wealth that lies buried in the hillsides of the South and the timber that stands thick upon its mountains can do more than increase the personal wealth of men like myself – it can furnish employment for a population twice as great as that of the United States today. It can give the South what it has always needed – a capable middle class and workers who are vigorous, sturdy, wholesome . . . and white."

She nodded with a sarcastic laugh. "I thought you'd get to that."

"Think of the North, Cassandra. Immigrants from strange European and Asian countries have overrun it. The laboring classes there are now almost entirely composed of foreigners – Russians, Poles, Italians, Hungarians, Irish. Alien cultures. The sweepings of old and decaying civilizations."

"Charmingly put."

"But true. You must admit the truth of it."

"I will admit there has been an influx of immigration. But I will never characterize it in the vulgar way you have. Why not construe it as a stimulating admixture? Perhaps it is the American stock that is exhausted and decaying."

"Precisely my point. The old settler strain *is* in decline. But it will not be improved by mixing its blood with that of mongrel nations. No, we must seek elsewhere for the wherewithal to restore the purity of our race. We must look here, to the mountain South."

"Here?"

"Yes, here. What do we find? We find a people of immaculate, undiluted Anglo-Saxon heritage. Native born. Homogeneous, unadulterated, respectable, free, independent, patriotic, distinctly American. Devoted to religion. Noble of spirit. Sturdy of character. Republican in politics. During the Rebellion they clung to the Union while others in the South allowed themselves to be seduced by the heresy of Secession."

"And they're white," she reminded him archly.

"Yes, white. For too long the philanthropists have wasted their energies on the undeserving Negro whose apathy and ignorance have doomed him to political and moral degradation. It's the whites of the South who possess the potential for uplift and improvement. And the mountain white especially, for in his isolation he has not been contaminated by prolonged contact with the Negro. He is more energetic, more able, far more potent for good."

"He is also, is he not, a degraded primitive? Famously poor, backward, violent and lawless? A remorseless feudist? A maker of illicit whiskey? Is this your savior of the white race?"

"You've seen Mr. Middleton. Is he what you describe?"

Her color reddened. She looked away and for a moment did not speak. Then she murmured, "It would seem not."

"Indeed. And he is, I'm convinced, a representative type. It is through him that I will prove my theory that it is the white of the highland South who, if given the chance to rise, can do so."

She smiled bitterly. "Will you let him rise as high as you?"

"Don't be absurd, dear. My goal is to reverse the present calamitous trend toward elimination of the old stock. I leave it to you to erase the lines of class."

"I shall do my best, Father," she promised, raising her snifter in salute.

"I know you shall. Now pass the brandy, my dear, if you please."

◀

Later that night he sat alone by the fire in his study turning the scarred and twisted Winchester this way and that before him. The blow had been but a grazing one and the gun had taken the brunt of it but his arms and shoulders still ached from its impact and that impact spoke of an immense power. Immense, he reflected, but not dealt full force. Had The Bear swatted him and not his rifle, he would be lying dead or gravely injured this very moment. Was that happenstance? Had all that power been simply wasted in a near miss? Or had it perhaps been . . . withheld? Withheld . . . by calculation?

His sense would not let him give the preposterous answer that his gut knew. But he remembered something now. Something besides the fear he had discovered that he had not known was in him. He remembered that in coming for him The Bear had looked at him. Slinging its head from side to side it had looked. And he remembered what he had seen in The Bear's darkly burning eye. He had seen volition. He had seen reason.

Chapter Eight

Now that the trees with the weakest medicine had shed their clothing of leaves and the air had begun to smell of winter, Yan-e'gwa had to stop trying to keep the world from being killed long enough to feed and start to grow the robe of fat he would need to keep him warm during the time of cold. So he left the top of Where the Water-Dogs Laughed and ranged over the mountains to another place where he remembered that the feeding was good and where the Ancestors had not yet intruded.

Yellow birch and red maple and hemlock sheltered it. There were also many oaks and hickories whose nut-bearing limbs could be torn off and their bounty consumed. Under the dry leaves that covered the ground there were acorns and walnuts and buckeyes and many plump insects. He only had to rake back the leaves to expose them. There were deadfalls full of sweet grubs. Small streams wended through it where fat trout swam. In the low places there were sedge marshes rimmed with fern where bog turtles lived that could be toyed with in idle moments although they were not practical for eating. Rhododendron and laurel grew in dense tangles and Yan-e'gwa could break down the thickets to make himself a nest for sleep during the times when he was not feeding.

While feeding Yan-e'gwa thought only of that. But sometimes as he rested he remembered his war. The war that he was waging against the Ancestors was the first ever mounted by his *kind. But he knew from the tales of his mother that once before, long ago, the bears had come close to making the same fight.*

While rocking him in her arms in their cave-den singing songs and telling stories, Yan-e'gwa's mother had told him how the Ancestors had forgotten that they and the bears were related. The Ancestors began to ignore the covenant they had made after the Ani-Tsaguhi were changed into bears. They were no longer grateful for the sacrifice that the bears were willing to make to give them their pelts and meat in return for reverence. They forgot that they were to show respect to the bears and to all the animals. They neglected the prayers of pardon they had promised to say before killing. And heedlessly they began to slaughter the large animals and the birds and the fish for their flesh or their pelts, while the smaller creatures such as the frogs and worms were crushed and trodden upon without thought, out of pure carelessness and contempt. So all the animals decided to consult about what steps they might take to protect themselves from the thoughtless Ancestors. The bears were the first to meet.

Yan-e'gwa's mother told how they gathered at their council house under the Mulberry Mountain. The old White Bear Chief presided. Each bear complained about how badly the Ancestors were behaving. Finally it was decided to begin war against them. One bear asked what weapons the Ancestors used. "Bows and arrows," cried all the bears. "Bows made of wood with strings made from our entrails." Someone suggested that the bears make bows and arrows and use them against the Ancestors. So one bear got a nice piece of locust wood and another sacrificed himself for the good of the rest in order to furnish his entrails for the string.

But, said Yan-e'gwa's mother, when everything was ready and the first bear stepped up to shoot an arrow, his long claws caught the string and spoiled the shot. It was proposed that his claws be trimmed and this was done and at the next shot the arrow went straight to its mark. But the old White Bear Chief pointed out that the bears needed their long claws to climb trees. "One of us has already died to make the bowstring," he said, "and if we now cut off our claws we must all starve together. It is best to trust to the teeth and claws that we were given when we were transformed, for it is plain that the Ancestors' weapons were not intended for bears to use."

So the council was disbanded. The bears could not find the means to correct the behavior of the Ancestors without changing their own ways. Yan-e'gwa's mother said they had seen that it was more important to be true to their ways than to go against them, even in order to defeat the Ancestors who were killing them. So ever afterward the bears had been compelled to tolerate the disrespect of the Ancestors.

That was why in waging his war against the Ancestors who were behaving worse than ever now and who he feared were killing the world, Yan-e'gwa was doing a serious thing. He was changing the way all the bears had agreed to act. The common decision of all the bears was supposed to be binding and none of his kind had ever gone against it before. None would join him now. He was alone in what he did. He hoped that by changing in himself what a bear was, he could stop the Ancestors from killing the world. But he would be the only one to change. The other bears would go on abiding by the decision they had made.

But if by changing, Yan-e'gwa succeeded in stopping the world from being killed, the others would be grateful. And if because of what he did the world were not killed after all, maybe even the Ancestors would finally come to remember the covenant they had made. Maybe they would begin to sing the sacred songs again and beg the pardon of the bear before killing him and give him the reverence he deserved.

But although Yan-e'gwa was making war he had no wish to kill any of the Ancestors or even to injure them. He only wanted to drive them off the sides of Where the Water-Dogs Laughed and keep them from going on to kill the whole world. So in order to discourage them he was slaying their beasts and ravaging their possessions. But he was still enough like all other bears that he had no desire to taste the Ancestors' blood. He only wanted to remind them of their obligation. He wanted to love them. For they were his kin. They had only forgotten it.

So he had slapped the stick from the hands of the one Ancestor in the fog rather than hurt him. He had been excited that time. It was the closest he had ever been to one of them. Yan-e'gwa had not seen the Ancestor at first because of the mist, nor had he smelled him because the wind was wrong. Also Yan-e'gwa was very tired from running away from the barking and baying of the Split-Noses and he was ashamed to admit that he had not been paying proper attention.

But he had heard the Ancestor stir on his rock. And when Yan-e'gwa came close enough to see the Ancestor and smell him, he had seen and smelled his fear too. He had looked into his eye and although he and Yan-e'gwa were kin, the eye was white and not dark like a bear's and Yan-e'gwa was intrigued to see its whiteness but also sad to see so much fear in it. The Ancestor was so small and frail and almost ridiculous that Yan-e'gwa became sorry for his frightened brother and knocked away his stick and ran on.

Perhaps he had discouraged that one. Perhaps that one would now go down from Where the Water-Dogs Laughed and not come back. Perhaps he would be the first to stop trying to kill the world.

Only once in his life had Hamby ever removed his hat to show respect and that had been for Miss Becky on her deathbed. But she had chided him fondly for doing it and told him he ought to keep his ugly shaven head covered up and almost with her last breath had laughed with him about it. So now as he stood over her grave permitting himself to re- member that he kept his hat on. But he wanted to take it off. He read the words chiseled on the headstone:

REBECCA CURTIS CARTER
AUGUST 26 1855 – APRIL 12 1889

He wasn't any good with ciphering and couldn't quite figure how many years that was without putting pencil to paper, but knew it wasn't many. Yet she had been awful broke down at the end, and not just from the consumption either. No, it was life that had killed her.

Around his neck on a separate cord from the one that held his razor he wore the little carved wooden angel she had given him that last day. His fingers went to it now and softly handled it. All its edges had been so worn from handling and it was so soiled from his touch that it no longer resembled an angel at all but was as round and smooth as a river pebble and as black as a piece of coal. He had carved it himself. It had been his gift to her when she first fell sick and seven years later she had passed it back to him and with it they had exchanged the same wish for each other, though he had known that while his wish for her would certainly come true, hers for him never would.

He hadn't meant to visit the grave, not yet anyhow. He had left Corntassel's that morning to go over to Sanders Carter's to look for work and somehow had ended up here. He had taken the Carter lane down to the turnaround in front of the house and this time there hadn't been any Lillie gal to balk him. He had followed his usual habit and climbed up on the top rail of the worm fence and lit his pipe to sit there smoking till somebody took note of him. He wasn't about to creep around to the back like some woebegone nigger. But he wasn't going to knock at the front door either, as if he considered himself white. He wasn't white. He was one damnsite better than *that*. He would perch his ass on the fence and when one of them happened to glance out and spy him, why, then they could come out to *him*, by God.

It was Miz Martha Carter who finally did. She was Miss Becky's older sister and the sight of her was what changed Hamby and made him let himself remember Miss Becky full-on for the first time since he came back and think how she lay buried in the little graveyard back of the Methodist church on the hill behind Hayesville. Miz Martha had never done harm to a living soul that Hamby knew of and save for Miss Becky he thought she was as good a white woman as it was possible to be. It surprised him that she looked like an old lady but she did. Being wed to Sanders Carter must have been as bad a job as getting stuck with his fool of a brother like Miss Becky had. "We heard you were home," said Miz Martha.

Home. Again he was taken aback to think folk were paying him so much mind. And that in her talk Miz Martha was giving him the same home she had. "Yes'm," he said.

"You staying at Mordecai's?"

"Yes'm, I be looking for work."

"My husband's over to Sweetwater today," she said, "but he's got no work, not beyond Mordecai's. I'm sorry." He could see that she really was. "Can I give you a bite to eat?"

"Nome, but I be obliged."

From there he'd gone on to the cemetery. Cattywampus Dog was with him. When he left out of Corntassel's that morning the dog had uncoupled itself off the hearth and come scuttling crabwise after him and Corntassel had laughed and remarked, "You're the first man other'n me that critter's ever took to," and Hamby had looked down in pity at the poor malformed thing and then had taken thought of himself and how solitary he was in the world and said, "I reckon this dog and me, we got something in common."

They had set out then and the dog had not only kept up in spite of its awkward gait but sometimes had even run scrambling up the road in its sideways fashion so as to get ahead of Hamby and take a peek at him over its back – probably because with its cranked head it couldn't see him from the rear but only had a view of its own tail. For all its handicaps it wasn't even winded when they reached the graveyard and by then Hamby had begun to wonder if it wasn't able to chase bear after all, just as old Corntassel claimed. Now while Hamby stood at the foot of the grave Cattywampus Dog sat with its back to him watching him over its shoulder with its pretty eyes.

Seemingly in addition to its other virtues it was a tolerant dog. It ignored a bird that Hamby noticed hopping in the grass nearby. This was a type of bird Hamby didn't know at first. It had a creamy white head and a straight yellow beak and a breast of rust red and a gray back and black wings trimmed with the same white that was on its head. From time to time while he stood thinking, Hamby would look up from the grave and there the bird would be. It seemed not to have any fear of him or of the dog. It hopped close about them and now and then it fluffed up its feathers as if it had an itch and sometimes it sang a little song that went *tweep tut-tut-tut*. It wasn't hunting for worms. It was just hopping to and fro among the gravestones. Finally Hamby focused his attention on it and after a moment of bewilderment he decided from its song and from the way it stood that it was a kind of freakish robin.

He thought if it truly was a freak white-headed robin, then all the ordinary robins would probably be shunning it. Maybe no female would mate with it. Maybe it was an outcast and that was why it kept so close to a man and even to a dog, without any fear. Maybe it wanted companionship. He smiled. Freak bird, freak dog, freak Hamby – hell, that made sense. *We all three the same*, he told it without words. He watched it some more.

Then a notion no bigger than a gnat flew into his head and as quickly flew out again as he denied it with a curse. *Goddamn hocus-pocus*, he swore to himself. He reckoned enough of Africa ran in his veins that now and then some of its voodoo had to get into his head much as he hoped against it. But if the notion was gone, its tiny shadow lingered. Maybe that bird meant something. Maybe it *was* something.

Quickly Hamby wrestled free of that. He coughed and spat a blob of red to the side of the grave far enough away not to defile it; Cattywampus Dog waddled over and licked up what he'd voided. He felt himself getting mad. Being at the grave had made him mad for the first time since that day at the Axum mine when he found he could think of the Hiwassee country not with anger any more but only with some sadness. But today he stood over her grave and felt of the wooden angel that hung around his neck and he was as mad as hell. Mad at the disease that took her and mad at Tom Carter for the dry husk he'd made of her and mad at all her people – her folks that she'd tended all through their dotage and her brother who'd lost his wits and finally had to be put in the asylum and her sister who'd come home to die in her arms of a childbirth gone wrong and her nephews she'd had to raise till others could take them in.

Mad at himself for not being a better friend. Mad too at other things. At Clyde Rainey for his meanness and at Loomis and Buffum and at Strickland who liked to beat his winch mule and even at Reed Considine for condoning it all. Mad at Ves Price. Mad at Sanders Carter. Mad at all whites and mad at every nigger. Mad at living for being what it was. If he'd have thought there was a God that had set things up as they were, he'd have been mad at Him too. But there wasn't any damn God. There wasn't anything. Nothing but humankind acting as low as it could.

Thinking about how mad he was made him think about the tale Corntassel had told of him. About how he'd done all he'd done with so much hate in him. About how old Daniel had lost his hate but Hamby never had for long, though he'd risked almost as much for others' sake. Corntassel's tale had vexed him on account of how queerly it had dovetailed with his own reasoning. When he heard it he'd only just guessed himself that maybe his purpose in coming back was to learn how Daniel had lost his hate and how he could lose his too.

But he wasn't losing his hate. Not any more. He was getting more and more of it back. And now he didn't *want* to lose it. He wanted it to grow. He wanted as much of it as he could get. It was a grudge he wished to keep.

That night at Corntassel's he and the old man drank up the last of the cider and as he drank he kept thinking how all of Creation was smothering in mortal shit and how much he had loved a few parts of Creation in his life but how, as time had passed, the parts he hated had overtaken the parts he had loved and now his main wish was that he had the power to fetch the whole goddamn mess to a close. In a fit of temper he told Corntassel that.

"You do," the old man answered.

"Do what?"

"Have the power. Every man does."

Hamby scowled. "Howso?"

"Where's it all at, anyhow?" asked the old man. He tapped the side of his head with the end of one finger. "In here, ain't it? And if it ain't in here, where is it?" He nodded with conviction. "Gone, that's where." He leaned back in his chair puffing on his pipe with Cattywampus Dog asleep on the hearth before him. "So you can get shet of it any time you want to," he said. "Anybody can."

❧

Riding up from Tusquittee Creek to the road where it passed by his house, Captain Irish Bill Moore found Hamby McFee hunkered in the weeds of the roadside patiently smoking his corncob. Moore remembered from years ago how that was Hamby's way of getting a parley without lowering himself to ask. He smiled in his beard. It was good to see Hamby squatting there defiantly waiting to be noticed and it was good too to remember that. He turned Dixie through the gate and into the road and walked her along the fence to where Hamby waited and checked her and said hidy and Hamby said hidy back. Hamby did not rise and did not remove his hat. Nor did the Captain expect him to. Hamby looked Dixie up and down although he never put his eyes on Moore himself. "What become of that big brown stud you used to ride?"

The Captain reached and patted Dixie's neck. "Crockett? Oh, Crockett died, I'm sad to say."

Hamby nodded and turned his head aside and spat the other way. What he spat was bright red. "He a good old horse," Hamby remarked. He knocked the ashes out of his pipe against the heel of one hand and put the pipe in the pocket of his coat and stood now with a grunt, straightened, pressed the flats of his hands into the small of his back and shook out first one leg and then the other to rid himself of his kinks and cramps. For the first time Moore found himself thinking that age was starting to catch up to Hamby McFee who had always been hard as new wire. Hamby moved close and took Dixie under the chin with a cupped hand and examined her more critically and considered awhile and then declared, "This a right fair animal too." He paused, then in the interests of precision added, "For a mare."

Irish Bill tried to catch his glance but Hamby still wouldn't look up, so he told him what he wanted to anyway. "I was pleased to hear you'd come back."

Hamby's color darkened and he frowned as if offended. He let go of Dixie's chin and moved back several steps and leaned against the fence and sternly crossed his arms. His gaze went to the stones of the road and fixed there unmoving. "I looking for work," he mumbled. "You got any?"

Moore well remembered the calculated rudeness and seeing it again after such a long time amused and even touched him. He shook his head. "Afraid not. I'm all hired up." Even if he wasn't, he didn't think he would have wanted to hire Hamby, given the mulatto's tetchy ways and his own hot temper. Sparks and gunpowder, that would be. He plucked at his bottom lip in thought. "But I know somebody further up Tusquittee that needs a hand."

Hamby again spat red. "Them Middletons?"

"That's right."

"Heard about them." Still not looking at Moore he gave a short bob of his head. "I try them."

Irish Bill mused a spell longer. "Tell you what," he said. "I've got to ride up that way this afternoon. I'll take you up and vouch for you."

Hamby turned even darker. Uncomfortably he stirred against the rails of the fence. The planes of his face hardened and his look jerked sharply left and right over the ground. A long moment passed while he appeared to struggle inwardly. Then he nodded and spat again and muttered, "I be obliged." From his manner he might have been agreeing to let himself be crucified.

"Good," the Captain said. He was beginning to enjoy persecuting Hamby with kindnesses. He took note of Hamby's worn-out brogans and the the way his ragged coat hung on him soppy with sweat despite the cold. "You walking? You can't get around afoot. I've got a good old mule I'll let you have."

Hamby's patience was wearing thin under the relentless shower of boon after unwanted boon. He hunched his shoulders in surly guise. "Got no money," he growled.

"Oh, that's all right," Moore breezily replied. "Pay me what you can when you can, after you're hired. He's old but he's a good mule."

Hamby uncrossed his arms and stood away from the fence and stuffed his hands in the side pockets of his old coat. He had the depleted air of a soldier who after a long and losing fight has at last seen the necessity of retreat. He shrugged. "I be obliged."

"All right." Moore gathered Dixie's reins. But he couldn't resist inflicting a final indignity. "You come on to the house now," he insisted, "and I'll get Miss Hattie to fix you a lunch. You're looking right gaunt. After we eat, we'll go up the Jack Holler and get your mule."

But Hamby had conceded retreat, not surrender. He drew himself straight and finally raised his look but only as far as Irish Bill's knee. He regarded the knee steadfastly. "No," he said with a dogged firmness, "thass all right, I wait here." He blinked, frowned, blew out a sigh. Then he gave one more dip of his head. "But I be obliged."

◄

"Who's that darkey?" Miss Hattie inquired when Moore stepped inside and shrugged out of his coat and hung it by the door. She was Miss Hattie to him today just as she'd been Miss Hattie forty years ago when he commenced courting her and she was a blushy girl living in a fine house in Franklin and he was a poor mudsill of an Irishman with naught to recommend him. She was quality then and she was quality now and he thought quality ought to be saluted – in this case with a special name that recalled her maidenly sweetness – even if she *had* lowered herself to marry a wretched case like himself. Whatever he'd achieved since then, he'd got for her.

She was in the dining room setting the table. "He's been dawdling out there half the morning, off and on," she said of Hamby. "I went out a time or two to see what he wanted but he said he was waiting for you. Mighty sulled up, he was." She came to the entry of the dining room pushing stray strands of hair back into place with the ends of her fingers. Her hair was white as rime ice on a ridge top but still lustrous and silky smooth and it still made him want to take it down and run his hands through it. He stopped in the hallway to admire her as she went on. "He reminds me of that terrible Hamby McFee that used to live over on Downings Creek."

"Well, guess what," he grinned. "That's just who it is." He came on down the hall and leaned to peck her on the cheek and breathed in and savored her fragrance of soap and cornmeal and her own natural essence which was something like the cool brisk air that comes off a clear-running stream. She kissed him back and stood aside to admit him. "But I don't know about Hamby being terrible."

"Why, he killed that blockader up on the mountain that time," exclaimed Miss Hattie.

Moore drew back in mild alarm. "No, he didn't. He was there all right, but it was somebody else handled the shooting. Why, Hamby was doing good that day. The 'shiners had kidnapped Oliver Price's boy Ves – you remember him, you patched him up once when he was hurt. They were fixing to murder Ves for informing to the Revenue and Hamby went up to save him." Moore paused and pondered, then mischievously thought he should make himself absolutely clear. "So

Hamby didn't kill that 'shiner. Of course I don't know who *else* he might've killed. Or not killed."

"I remember him perfectly," Miss Hattie declared, paying no attention to his mischief. "He's a terrible man." Ten-year-old Nannie, their youngest, came downstairs as Miss Hattie spoke and took her place at the table and wanted to know who was so terrible and Miss Hattie told her to never mind. Irish Bill sat down at the head of the table and winked at Nannie and said he and Mama were discussing a reprobate.

Nannie knit her brows. "What's a reprobate?"

"Somebody Mama don't approve of."

He and Nannie giggled but Miss Hattie ignored them with her usual serenity which made the traits of all others seem silly and trivial. She commenced dishing out helpings of pork and beans. "What on earth does Hamby McFee of all people want with you?" she demanded. He told her.

While he was talking Jim and Charlie came in and shed their wraps and took their chairs and Moore broke off explaining long enough to return thanks. He was not an especially religious man but he was grateful for the many blessings he enjoyed and most of all he was grateful that he hadn't worn out Miss Hattie's patience after all these years and that Nannie and Jim and Charlie were still at home to comfort him in his old age. Without them – the last of his ten younguns still unmarried – this big old house would be just too still and empty to bear. He told the Lord all that and then said amen and they fell to eating.

Jim and Charlie had been putting new siding on the barn and they reported on the progress of the work. Miss Hattie set a platter of cornbread on the table and then finally settled at her place next to the Captain and as was her habit watched the rest of them dine while she rested. "Well," she said after a pause for thought, "I reckon I'll make up a poke of eats. When you're done with your dinner, you can take it out to Hamby. He's so lean he don't half cast a shadow."

Moore knew better than to smile but he did send another wink Nannie's way and Nannie winked in reply. "Why d'you want to take him to Rufe Middleton anyway?" Miss Hattie continued. "All you do anymore is complain about the Middletons ruining the forest. Hamby'll just help 'em do it faster."

He shrugged and wiped his mouth with his napkin. "Rufe's going to cut whether I like it or not. And Hamby needs the work. And I want to see that he gets employment; I enjoy having him around. I've missed his cussedness. I find that he . . . ." Moore hesitated till he had sought and found just the right word. "Entertains me."

"Humph," Miss Hattie snorted, "you've always been far too fond of entertainment."

"I know," he smiled. "It's my besetting sin."

◄

The mule the Captain picked out for Hamby was surely up in years – about thirty-five by its teeth – but it still had good eyes and good wind and it wasn't lame nor a kicker. It was a horse mule and was shod because Moore had used it pulling wagons on the roads as well as drawing a plow. Moore guaranteed it sound and after looking it over Hamby didn't gainsay him, though he turned down the old Confederate saddle the Captain offered. He did deign to accept a bridle and reins. And he did consume the poke of ham biscuits Miss Hattie had fixed him. It was about one o'clock in the afternoon when they struck out up the creek.

The day was a blustery one and the wind cut sharp at them but the sky was mostly clear and betweentimes when the wind lulled they could feel a little of the warmth of the winter sun on their faces. Scraps of cloud were scudding overhead and sometimes the clouds briefly hid the sun and then when the gusts blew, the cold would go bone deep. They rode higher and the country got rougher and the peaks above them got sharper and more rugged. As the light came and went on the high tops the mountains changed from pewter-gray to russet and back to gray again.

Hamby was no talker but the lack of a respondent had never yet stopped Irish Bill from having a conversation, even if it had to be only with himself. He talked and talked. He told how in the old days the Tusquittee road used to be a turnpike and how when it was court week down in Hayesville all the judges and lawyers and solicitors of the Circuit Court would come over Chunky Gal from Franklin and stay the night at his house on the way. He told how they used to inscribe their names on the front wall of his parlor and how the autographs of all the famous men of the Western North Carolina bar could still be seen there – David Schenck's and Augustus Merrimon's and David Coleman's and Kope Elias's and those of many another eminent pleader.

He told how in eighteen-and-sixty-one he had a contract to build a road across the Tusquittees to Buck Creek and how he was working on that road with a gang of men when the war came and he had to quit work and go to fighting. He told how before they went into the army he and his gang had buried all their tools in a big hole around the crook of the mountain, expecting to come back when the fighting got done and finish that road. And he told how those tools were still buried up there in that same hole thirty-seven years later.

He was telling how his boy John was a lawyer in Florida and was saying how proud he was to have a son that was a man of the law just like all those famous men who'd signed his wall when they came to the first of the Middleton boundary and that was when he stopped talking altogether. The Middletons were taking the acid wood for tanbark now as well as the poplar and ash and walnut for lumber and the hills round-about were cut bare of all but the spindliest growth and were littered with piles of slashing and were studded with thousands of raw stumps and the sight of them dropped something as heavy as a lead shot into the bottom of Irish Bill's stomach.

He drew rein and stared while Hamby sat the old mule beside him without comment and without any reaction at all that the Captain could see. Part of the sorrow Moore felt came from knowing that Hamby wasn't seeing what he saw. He saw destruction; Hamby saw a paying wage. Hamby saw what the Middletons saw. What more and more men of the mountains who had toiled and scraped to eke a living from this hard land were seeing now. He couldn't bring himself to blame such fellows for what they saw. But he grieved. He grieved.

When they finally started on, he retailed no more stories. Grimness had him by the throat. He liked to think of himself as a progressive man. Politically he had been a Whig before the war and had been in favor of internal improvements and development of the western part of the state. He had known slavery was evil and had loathed the men who led the South to war and ruin to try to save it. After the Surrender he had anxiously awaited the coming of the railroad which he confidently expected would give highlanders like himself easier access to the markets of the wider world. Nowadays he was in favor of universal schooling and of women's suffrage and even of equal rights for the blacks and he deplored the unholy practice of lynching and he thought it would be good if everybody in the mountains had electric lights and the telephone and indoor toilets that flushed and he wanted to see the region prosper in every way it could.

But he was a husbandman. He always had been. He had husbanded the land too long not to revere it. And many of the changes that he saw coming so fast around him were consuming or degrading that very land that he held nearly sacred. Timber titans like Weatherby and poor men like the Middletons who longed for ready money for the first time in their hardscrabble lives were wrecking the woods and then the soil of the waste places they left behind washed away in the rains and the rivers ran red with silt that had once been the good rich earth. The locomotives that traveled on the railroad that Moore had once eagerly awaited now belched sparks that set fire to the crops and forests and killed the livestock that had wandered free for generations and now strayed innocently onto the tracks to be struck and crushed by the great hurtling machines. The timber cutters left acres and acres of dry slashings that mischief makers or even dry strikes of lightning could ignite starting conflagrations that raged over the country consuming even more of the forest. And the railroads controlled the courts so no ordinary man could get justice if he were injured by the losses.

There were subtler changes. Yes, the railroads had opened markets. But they had also driven down the price of livestock and feed and brought in cheap goods that undersold the products men like Moore had made their way selling. Improved breeds of cattle were introduced that could fetch a dearer price on the hoof than the local stock. This together with the clearing of the forests spelled the end of the old open range; more and more the raising of cattle was becoming a business of fenced pastures and controlled feeding that big corporations could afford more easily than any single mountain farmer.

Captain Moore had favored progress because he wanted to see the end of the woes that had beset the highlands since the war. But now that the isolation of the country had been breached he rued its loss. Now the mountains were awash in boomers, boosters, trimmers, rowdies, vagabonds, strangers with strange ways. The rush of modern industry was sweeping away the seclusion that had nourished the people since the old pioneer times. And its excitement bewitched the young who were bored with the solitudes of the hills.

Moore's own boy Charlie at twenty-three had heard the siren song and had gone down to work one season on the railroad but thank God had not traded his birthright for a mess of pottage after all – he was a husbandman at heart too, Irish Bill reckoned – and Charlie had returned home pretty quick, disillusioned but wiser. Wiser than many, wiser than most.

※

On the broad bottom by the mouth of Big Tuni the Middletons' donkey sawmill roosted in a nest of culls and splinters and slabs of bark-covered edgings and pieces of punk timber. It resembled some unsightly featherless goose incubating eggs from which fowls even worse looking than itself would one day hatch. For a neck it had a thin smoke pipe and for a body a rusty boiler through whose several holes squirts of live steam blew. A pulley attached to the boiler's engine ran a single whirling circular sawblade that screamed like a tortured woman as Seth Middleton worked the levers that ran the carriage back and forth slicing logs into boards. Seth's brother Luther and a number of hired men were hooking logs off a big pile and across a littered rollaway to the carriage. There was a slapdash roof of sorts – some planks laid over a rude frame. But mostly the outfit lay open to the elements. Around it stood the stripped hills already seamed with deep new gulleys like the lines on an old crone's face. Nearby, a stagnant pond scummed with wood-trash gave up a clammy stench even in the chill of the weather.

The pond was the child of the Middletons' splash dam. Last winter, before they got the donkey, they'd dammed Big Tuni higher up. Till then Moore would never have thought the creeks in these parts were big enough to make the flow needed to flood logs. Now he knew it wasn't the natural fall of the creek that made the force, it was the rush of water from behind the dam when blown with dynamite. Down it came, water and cut timber and all, and the torrent took everything on both creekbanks with it – trees torn out by the roots, boulders as big as bowling balls, tons of mud and earth dredged up from the bed and washed from the sides. It wouldn't have been pretty.

But Rufe Middleton had figured it was the answer to his poor luck, just as the donkey was his answer now. In the bottom the flood had scoured out a deep ragged-edged hole that the rains and the seepage of groundwater had then filled to make the pond. In the time since, silt draining out of the widened watercourse had closed off the pond and landlocked it; now it lay hard by the donkey giving off its woeful stink.

The road carried them below the mill and the pond and they crossed the creek on a small wooden bridge and headed for the Middleton farmhouse where it sat in its cove sheltered by the only two full-grown poplar trees left anywhere in sight. It was a plain log saddlebag house with a stick chimney and a roof of oak shakes held down with rocks. There was a dogtrot between the two wings and but one window in the right-hand wing and it was covered with oilcloth. Several of Rufe's littler younguns ran bare bottomed in the yard of beaten dirt oblivious to the cold.

Irish Bill checked Dixie and sat his saddle looking up the slope to the house while Hamby rode a few yards on and then stopped and circled the mule back and waited for him. *This is Rufe's*, Moore thought as he watched. *This is what Rufe has to cure.* Just then two riders – a man and a young woman – came around a bend in the road ahead of them and turned up Rufe's lane and approached the house. Moore recognized the man. It was Absalom, Rufe's eldest. He didn't know the girl. But he noticed her coppery hair.

Chapter Nine

Chestnut Grove Methodist was Jimmy Cartman's church. Not just the one he attended. It was *his*. It belonged to him.

It was true that five other men and their families had helped Dad set up the church seven years before. They had given money the same as he had. J.A. Rutland had donated the acre of wooded hilltop the church stood on. And because Dad was so hindered by his rheumatism, Mr. Rutland and Uncle Andy Cartman and Sanders Carter and George Blood and Lander Blodgett had cleared the land and cut the timbers and hewed the shingles and actually built the church out of the logs of the chestnut grove it stood in. But Dad had supervised.

It was also true that Mr. Rutland got to be the first Sunday School superintendent and Reverend D.H. Lowman got to be the first preacher. But Dad was lay leader and tycoon of the whole outfit and it never occurred to anyone – Reverend Lowman least of all – to doubt his authority moral, temporal or otherwise.

It wasn't that he abused it. He didn't. His rule was enlightened and benevolent. Each Sunday morning Will found himself amazed anew at the change that would come over Dad as the buggy clattered up the hill from Downings Creek and approached the church, Uncle Andy and Aunt Samantha following along behind in their identical rig drawn by an identical white mare. Sweet tolerance would settle over him. He glowed with benevolent smiles. No one could have been gentler or more affable.

Yet all the way up from home, past Cemetery Hill and Sanders Carter's and the grist mill on the creek and even as far as the fork that turned off to the church, he had been a fount of sarcasm and reproof, berating poor Maw – Aunt Laura – for her choice of hats or for having burnt the bacon at breakfast or for speaking out of turn somehow; or rebuking Will for having sowed the seed corn two feet four inches apart yesterday in the lower field instead of two and a half, or for neglecting to lubricate the crosscut saw with kerosene and getting the blade stuck in the pine they had been felling last week on the hill above the wagon road.

Yet as soon as he guided the mare into the churchyard all his ill humor melted away and Dad became the soul of Christian charity. Descending, he handed out peppermint sticks to all the children. Lovingly he patted every tow head. He sought out boys named Jimmy so he could tell them in fond complicity that all Jimmies must stick together. Despite his aches he bent to kiss the little girls. He shook hands cordially with men Will had heard him disparage by his own fireside for their idle ways or want of religious zeal or even for their outright sins.

There had been a time when Will wondered which Jimmy was real, the one he saw at Chestnut Grove or the one he saw at home. But he no longer wondered about that. He had decided that both could not seem so real – *feel* so real – if they were not. Just as his cruelty at home cut to the quick those nearest him, at church Dad's goodness warmed and healed the hearts of others. You could see their faces shine with grateful affection when he spoke to them. Yes, both were real. The mystery was how they could be.

And that too was something Will had quit trying to penetrate though he did on occasion envy the ones he saw Dad favor as he seldom favored Maw and Will himself. Dad was what he was. It was Will's task to revere him however he chose to be. For the debt that Will owed Dad was far greater than he could ever repay. Dad had taken him in when his own flesh and blood had cast him off like a used-up soup bone. If not for Dad he might've gone wandering alone in a pitiless world. So like Maw, Will was content to bask in Dad's good humor when it was on display for the benefit of strangers and didn't complain when he chose to vent nothing but spleen under his own roof.

Will relished church not just because it was the place where it was easiest to appreciate Dad but also for the sense it gave him of coming close to sanctity. Because of what Dad kept saying about his having bad seed, Will guessed he couldn't get as close to God as he wanted to. But sitting on the hard bench pew listening to Reverend Lowman pray and extol the Word and looking at the pretty brass cross on the altar table and standing to sing the old hymns, all these made Will think that maybe the Spirit of the Lord did dwell in that little wood-paneled sanctuary and was in fact near by, and if due to his taint he couldn't get as close to the Almighty as he longed to, maybe God at least knew he was there and held a merciful thought of him.

Of course another reason Will liked Chestnut Grove was that sometimes Tom Carter and his family came over from Carter's Cove for services. When that happened they would sit with Sanders Carter and his family, and then Will could see his sweetheart Lillie even if Dad disapproved of his speaking to her, forcing him to adore her in silence and only from across the aisle. There they would be, all in a row like crows on a fence – Mr. Tom Carter and then his second wife Maggie who had been a Greenwood and then Lillie and next to Lillie her brother Homer and then her sister Ethel and after them the younguns Mr. Carter had got with Miz Maggie, three of them stairstepped down in size save the littlest that Miz Maggie was holding on her lap swaddled in a blanket.

But Lillie was the only one he watched. Afterwards he would always get on his knees and beg the Lord's forgiveness for how his eye kept wandering to her when he ought to be attending to the holy offices. But she was so bright and fetching. She made it hard to pay the hymns and prayers and sermons proper mind. With Dad and Maw on one side of him and Uncle Andy and Aunt Samantha and his sister Minnie on the other, it was hard to do more than steal a sideways peek at Lillie now and again and not betray his addled state of mind and earn a scolding. But more often than not he managed it.

She was little and delicate in her motions. But all the same she had a withy look that made you think of tree creeper, tough and flexible – she'd bend every which way but never snap. Her manner was crisp and saucy and sometimes could cut. She had a temper. But underneath she was as sweet as clover honey. Her look was straight and honest and her blue-gray eyes were deep sunk and had a bit of a slant – that was why Minnie criticized her for being squinty-eyed – and when she set that look on Will something sharp would stab him behind his heart so bad that he would want to faint dead away. There was something poutish about her mouth but it didn't seem like a sign she was surly but maybe showed she was just determined. He knew she was. Her hair was chestnut color and parted in the middle and pulled back to a bun. Grandad had once told Will it was the same brown gold as her mother Rebecca's.

Naturally Will couldn't take in all of this on the sly while in church. But he snuck looks at what parts of her he could glimpse quick and then later he would put the parts together in his mind. The times when he got the leisure to see her all at once and cherish the sight of the whole of her were rare indeed. That was why it came as such a miracle when one

Sunday in December after church he unexpectedly got to spend the whole of an afternoon in her company.

It was Grandad's doing. Oliver attended Chestnut Grove too and when the service let out he pulled up beside Dad's buggy in his battered old Studebaker wagon just as Dad was handing Maw in and he announced to Dad, "I'm taking the boy for the day. It's high time he saw his grandpap." Dad could hardly argue that Will ought not visit with his own blood kin. Reluctantly he gave his assent and Will mounted to the box of Oliver's wagon and Oliver spoke to his brace of mules and drove away but instead of heading to his own place he went on through town and out to the road that followed Qually Creek and went along the winding, hilly track in and out of the piney woods till he came to the mouth of Carter's Cove and he turned up the cove and Will knew then that he was taking him to see Lillie. He was doing it to make up for not being able to convince Dad to let Will go courting. "Thank you, Grandad," Will murmured.

"I don't know why you're a-thanking me," Oliver mumbled, pretending Will had mistaken his intention. "I'm just going by Tom's to drop off a pair of shoes I made up for him."

"Well," said Will, trying to swallow the lump in his throat, "I'm obliged anyway."

Oliver had brought along a hamper of boiled eggs and dried apples and bread and a jug of buttermilk and they had consumed a lunch on the way knowing that by the time they arrived at the head of the cove the Carters would have already eaten. The day was mild for the start of winter, though clouds clogged the sky and the sun was but a pale smudge hanging low over Wiggens Top. There was a wind with a mild chill to it. It was two o'clock or so when they took the Carter turnout and went rumbling up the lane toward the little frame boxed house sided with vertical boards. When they stopped, Lillie came out the front door and just then the sun broke through and lit her hair and made it blaze.

❧

Oliver and Tom Carter and Miz Maggie took coffee in the front room that was papered with old newsprint and the younguns all scattered to play and Will and Lillie sat on the high back porch looking out over the round hills that cupped the head of the cove. They discussed topics appropriate to the Sabbath. They speculated on why the Baptists went in for foot washing when the Methodists did not. They wondered when the Southern Methodists and the Northern Methodists were ever going to get together and debated whether they should. In the case of baptism they argued over the merits of sprinkling compared with those of full immersion.

Their talk ran back and forth between them with the almost magical fluency that Will thought was born of the way their hearts and minds so perfectly matched. It resembled a dance done in words or a weaving not of threads but of notions, or maybe some other kind of craft that came naturally to people inspired by a thing greater and better than they could be by themselves. Lillie was his partner in the dance and the threads of her words and his joined on the loom and the two of them were both apart and one, all at the same time.

Rarely had he been as happy in all his life as he was to be sitting there on the porch talking with Lillie even if they were disagreeing. But presently Lillie changed the subject and went off of religion and what she brought up stopped the dance and the weaving both. "Did you hear?" she inquired. "Hamby McFee's come back."

Will frowned. He knew who Hamby was but preferred not to entertain his name too much because it was linked to the other name that he sometimes wished to remember but at other times didn't. Just now he didn't. It annoyed him that Lillie had made mention of Hamby – and through him the other. So he bowed up his shoulders and with unaccustomed bad grace grunted, "Who's that?"

"You know who that is," Lillie chided him. "He's that yellow man that saved your real daddy when the blockaders had him."

Now Will got to frowning for sure. Glumly he muttered, "What did he do that for?"

"How would I know why he did it?"

"I don't mean that." He pondered what a rogue Ves Price had been and how it had afflicted his own life. Ves by being what he was had given Dad a reason to view Will always through a dark glass of misgiving. And Will himself could never entirely make up his mind whether he loved and missed his real daddy and wanted to take the railroad west to Littleton, Colorado to see him or whether he hated him and hoped never to gaze on his features again. "I mean," he finally said, "what good did it do anybody to save him?"

Lillie gave a sigh of exasperation. "Well, I don't know what good it did." Then she took thought and presently spoke again but this time in reverent vein. "Maybe the Lord worked a purpose through it."

"What in the world purpose would that be?" scoffed Will.

"Maybe your real daddy went off somewhere afterwards and did a lot of good in the world. Maybe he helped others."

Now it was Will's turn to be exasperated. The notion was so silly it almost made him mad – would've, had anyone but she given it utterance. And he missed the dance and the weaving of their normal talk together and he blamed her for breaking it off. "Lillie," he burst out, "if he was a good man, don't you think he'd have come back for me and Minnie by now?"

She looked at his reddened face and went pale when she saw how she'd put him out. But at first she didn't want to concede that he was right to resent the idea that Ves Price could ever be any good. So she got mad herself and snapped back, "Well, I surely can't say about that." Then as soon as she'd spoken she regretted her harshness and bent close and laid a hand on his and told him softer, if still a little grudging, "But I'm sorry to mention it. I never meant to hurt you." Then she took her hand away and sat back and resumed her former subject. "Did you ever see Hamby?"

Will was never one to sulk. He began to brighten a bit. "No," he answered, "not that I can recall."

"I remember he was there the day Mama died," Lillie mused. "I remember he didn't smell bad that day. He must've washed. Most of the time he didn't care to wash and that's what I remember about him most – that smell. Papa says he liked to offend folks by not washing. But I expect he washed that day. Mama loved him like a brother. I don't know why. I wish he'd come for a visit, now he's back. I'd like to see him. Maybe I could tell why she loved him so. I wonder if he washes yet or not."

While she spoke Will began to fiddle with the knees of his britches, plucking them up between thumb and forefinger, letting them go and then plucking them up again. All of a sudden the topic of Hamby wasn't an irritant any more; not only that, it had lost any interest it had ever had. He was thinking of another matter now. A larger, more immediate matter. Oddly, the breaking up of the dance and of the weaving of their talk had momentarily put Lillie at such a distance from him that it had made him think how near they were, or ought to be. He badly needed to bridge that gap. Then it came to him what he would do. He hadn't figured to do it just yet but now he saw that he wanted to, had to. So he sat plucking at the knees of his pants. He was getting his nerve. When he'd got it, he blurted, "Lillie, I want to say something to you."

She was still talking about Hamby when he broke in, but she stopped at once and gave him a questioning look and saw that he hadn't meant to be rude but only had got something important on his mind. "Well," she shrugged, "why don't you?"

He wouldn't look at her now. Still plucking at his britches he said almost in a whisper, "I'm not sure I'm right to want to do it."

"Why?" she smirked. "Is it indecent?"

He blushed and then chuckled. "No, of course it's not indecent." Then he turned serious again. "But I'm afraid it might not be . . . I don't know. Fit. It might not be fit."

"Fit how?"

He squirmed. "Well, Dad says . . . "

"Says what?"

"Says *I'm* not fit."

"Not fit how?"

"On account of my real daddy," Will muttered, still plucking at his pants legs. "How he was. That I've got his blood and maybe his nature too and on account of him, maybe I'm . . . like he was. Like Ves Price was."

"Why, I never heard of such a thing," cried Lillie. "You've got your share of failings but I never yet saw any sign you were fixing to turn out a rowdy. Nobody that knows you would even think it. Not even Jimmy can think it – not really. He just told you that to keep you under his thumb."

She turned to him and grasped him by the shoulder and because she was riled used her sharpest voice. "You know what your biggest failing is? It's not that you're apt to be a scamp like Ves Price. It's that Jimmy holds you down and you let him. He's my cousin and I know him. You're the best hand he ever had and he don't even have to pay you a cent. You're the finest bargain he ever struck. If he loses you, why, he'll have to get back to work himself."

Will shook his head. "Dad works harder'n I do."

She snorted. "He just complains more."

It was true that Dad moaned an awful lot about the rheumatism. But he did work hard in spite of it, Will thought.

But Lillie hadn't quit. "You forget about being fit or not fit," she instructed him smartly. Then she surprised him by giggling. She sat back in her chair and commenced to rock. "You were going to say something to me," she reminded him. She looked away from him and smiled in mischief at the faraway hilltops. "I'd tell you to go ahead and say it, except I already know what it is." Then she stopped rocking and gave him a sassy look. "You want me to tell you?"

He quit fiddling with his britches and made a face. But he was pleased because the dance and the weaving had started up again. "You're going to anyway, aren't you?"

Lillie gave a confident nod. "You're aiming to bespeak me."

"Bespeak you?"

"Bespeak me. Ask me to marry. Aren't you?"

Will was flabbergasted. "Well . . . well," he stammered. "Well, yes. I was. Am. I am. Asking you to marry. When I'm of age."

"When'll that be?" she wanted to know.

"Nineteen-hundred-and-three."

"That sounds like a long time off. How long off is it?"

"Five years," he replied. "I just turned sixteen. On the seventh of December in nineteen-hundred-and-three I'll be twenty-one. I'll be free then. And I want to get married before the next New Year."

"Well, *I'm* but fifteen yet," she told him briskly. She lifted her chin and took on a haughty air. "A lot can happen in five years. A girl has to be careful and not drive her ducks to a bad market. What if I was to agree to marry you and then I met somebody better?" She looked sly then. "Somebody that wasn't under somebody else's thumb? Somebody that didn't think low of himself?"

Will laughed his big brassy laugh. "Whoever he was, I'll bet he wouldn't be able to sing like I can. Or tell funny stories as good as me. Or laugh as hard. Or work as hard. Or like you as much."

"Now you're boasting," she mocked him. "Pride's as bad as self-pity, you know."

"Anyway, you'll be sixteen in another month," he told her. "You'll soon be an old maid. You'd better promise me." He felt splendid now. He bounded out of his chair and paced up and down on the porch and declared, "I'm going to sing now, to remind you how good I am at it." And he did, sending out over the cove what he knew was his brightest and most glorious tenor:

> *"The World, the Devil and Tom Paine*
> *Have tried their best, but all in vain.*
> *They can't prevail, the reason is,*
> *The Lord defends the Methodist.*
> *They pray, they preach, they sing the best*
> *and do the Devil most molest.*
> *If Satan had his vicious way*
> *He'd kill and damn them all today.*
> *They are despised by Satan's train*
> *Because they shout and preach so plain.*
> *I'm bound to march in endless bliss*
> *and die a shouting Methodist."*

"Who's Tom Paine?"

"I don't know. But he must be a terrible sinner to get mentioned in a hymn along with the Devil. But I still have to tell you a story. Let's see. I'll tell the one about the old preacher that said he could face down the Devil."

"All right, but it better be a good 'un," she warned him.

She rose from the rocker and went to the railing of the porch and yelled to the younguns telling them that Will was going to conjure up a tale and they all came running, Homer and Ethel from the barn and Fred and Carrie from the yard and one from the road whose name Will could never call, and they climbed up and settled around on the stoop and on the railing and in the doorway making a ring of expectant faces all turned up at Will, and Will took a deep breath and commenced: "Old Preacher Fanshaw, they called him. He claimed he could face down the Devil himself. Old Fanshaw was one of these shouters that you used to see at protracted meetings in the brush arbors. A shouter and a jumper. A flyer. He was *animated*! Why, he would prance, he would spin, he would leap, he would stomp and paw the air. Thrash his arms like he was fighting bees and shake that old Bible at you. And holler. Law, could he holler! Blow the bricks out of chimneys and the shakes off roofs. Set weathervanes to whirling."

The younguns listened spellbound. By now Oliver and Tom Carter and Miz Maggie had come to the back door – Will was famous for his stories and nobody ever wanted to miss a one of them. But what mattered most to Will was that Lillie was looking up smiling at him and there was nothing in her face but admiration and that made his heart soar high.

"Old Fanshaw came to this one church to preach a revival," he went on. "And the sad truth of the matter is, Old Fanshaw, well, he was vain. Vain about the power of his preaching. Lillie just now told me I was showing pride, and that made me think of Old Fanshaw. You were right, Lillie. Pride goeth before a fall, like the Good Book says. And Old Fanshaw, he was all swoll up with an unbecoming pride.

"So before the revival commenced, in his pride and his vanity he got to bragging and he told the congregation, 'Brothers and sisters, my preaching's so hard, why, if I was to be a-preaching and Satan was to come right up out of the ground, why, Preacher Fanshaw would stand right here and face him! I'd preach him right back into Hell.'

"Now of course that arbor where they held the revival, it had a dirt floor. And during a revival, straw would be spread on the floor to keep down the dust. Any extra straw would be set over in a corner to use later. The revival went on all week. Every night Old Fanshaw would preach a hot and heavy sermon and always end it saying, 'If the Devil was to come right up out of the ground, Preacher Fanshaw would stand right here and face him.'

"Well, there was some rowdy boys in that community, going to that same church every night for the revival and dehorning cattle during the daytime. They heard this boast of Preacher Fanshaw's and decided to play a prank on him and see if he was up to facing down the Devil as much as he boasted. They got a pair of bull horns and strapped them on the head of one of the boys and before the service commenced, they hid this boy with the horns on him under that pile of extra straw off to the side of the pulpit. So that evening when Old Fanshaw got to preaching at his hottest, why, this boy with the horns, he started to raise up from under that straw. Raised up slow. And he poked those bull horns through that straw and it looked for sure like the Devil was coming up out of the ground.

"Old Fanshaw was at full holler just then. He was caught up in a sacramental frenzy. He sprung. He bounded. He revolved. He gyrated. He spouted forth the thunders of Jehovah. And just when he was reaching the peak and pinnacle of his argument he commenced to pounding on the pulpit hollering, 'And if the old Devil was to come up out of the ground, Preacher Fanshaw would stand right here and face him!'

"And right then he turned around and spied that straw rising up and those two horns poking out and his eyes got as big as biscuits and he lit out of there so fast his coattails stood out straight behind him. And as he ran on down the road out of sight the congregation heard his old voice fading kind of pitiful in the distance and he said, 'Would one of you faster boys fetch Old Preacher Fanshaw his hat?'"

Amid shouts of laughter Will sat down blushing and bathed in the sweat of his labors. "I believe I heard that old fellow preach a sermon after that," Oliver joked when they had quieted. "He was *still* nervous." There was another round of merriment. Then the group broke up and scattered and presently Will and Lillie were alone on the porch as before. For a time they kept silent to savor the pleasures of the tale. From the moody expression in Lillie's eyes Will guessed she might be proud of him. And maybe inclined to him too. So, flushed and perspiring as he was, he took his leap. Earnestly he bent toward her. "Now, are you going to promise me?"

But when she answered him she sounded sad and not happy as he'd expected. "It's true you sing like a warbler and that you recount a fine tale. You've a grand laugh. You aren't all that handsome." She gave him a teasing smile. "But then beauty don't make the pot boil." But after the smile the sadness came back and it struck him odd that she was saddened to list his virtues. And then he began to be sad as well.

"You're a hard worker," she kept on. "You're honest and a good Methodist. As far as I know you've got no vile habits." There was a place there for some more humor but she passed it right by. She sighed and looked away from him and after a short pause went grimly ahead. "But you've not got the backbone God gave a snake. If you did, you'd not be wishing Jimmy Cartman would let loose of you, you'd go and tell him to his face, and you'd make him like it too."

Embarrassment scorched him. Shame, too. He knew she was right but he didn't want her to be. He didn't want to face the truth she was saying. He hung his head. "I'm bound, Lillie. I'm bound to him till I'm twenty-one."

"What are you afraid of?" she shot back. "That he'll cut you off? Cut you off of what? Do you think he's put you in his will? Why, he'll not give you the snot of his nose if he can help it."

Miserably Will wrung his hands. "You don't understand. He's . . . he's my dad. He gave me a home when nobody else would. Without him, I'm . . . I'm not anything."

Lillie stood up then. She stepped in front of him blocking his view of the hills and he was strangely moved to see that she was the same height standing up as he was sitting down. She bent toward him and placed both hands flat on the arms of his chair and pushed her face close to his and looked him square in the eye. "You listen to me, Will Price. What you are, you got to be on your own. And you did it in *spite* of Jimmy Cartman, not on account of him. Look at you. You're warm and gentle and funny and strong and tender of heart and full of grace and fair dealing and everybody that knows you loves you and gives you high respect. And look at Jimmy. Sure, he's got a lot of people fooled into thinking he's a saint. And maybe he is, in his own way. Many bow down to him, I grant you. But you're not him. And he's not you. You're *better 'n* him because you're truer. He can't *be* a saint all the time and with everybody. He can only do it now and then. A good deal of the time he falls short. But you. You're always just who you are. Who you *made* of yourself. Just that. *All* that."

She straightened and moved back against the railing and folded her arms across her bosom. There were tears standing in her eyes now and the sight of them brought tears to his own. They stung him and blurred his vision till he could scarcely see her. She became a cloudy vision. But he could still hear her. "Only you don't know that," she said. "Or believe in it."

He wiped his eyes with the backs of his hands and her image came clear again and he saw that her tears had spilled over and were streaming down her face and he knew that she was as angry at him as she was hurt and sad for the two of them. When she spoke next her voice was as low and loving as it had ever been but there was a hardness in it too, like a thin braid of steel. "And if you want me for a wife, then by gum, you've got to know that and believe it. And then after you've come to know it and believe it, why, you've got to grow yourself some backbone and go and tell Jimmy Cartman what's what. Tell him you want to get bespoken and you'll marry who *you* want, and when *you* say, not when he says, or who he picks."

She nodded then and through her tears gave him one more wistful smile. "When I see you do that, then I'll know you honor yourself as much as I do. And *then* is when I'll give you my promise."

Chapter Ten

Not till the second week of January did the Asheville *Chronicle* finally publish its sketch of Weatherby based on his interview with the journalist Hotchkiss of more than three months before. When Weatherby read the piece he understood at once why it had been so long delayed. Somehow, in defiance of his explicit prohibition, Hotchkiss had managed to creep secretly onto the grounds of Wildwood and spy about. Then he had snooped in even more distant parts.

Taken as a whole, Weatherby had to admit, the account was surprisingly evenhanded. Hotchkiss offered at face value Weatherby's own account of himself, his background and his motives. Only the mildest hint of what Weatherby knew to be the reporter's anticapitalist leanings could be detected. Yet the clandestine tour of Wildwood had clearly engaged the man's proletarian sympathies and he had resolved to paint Weatherby as a callous oppressor.

But he went slyly about the work. He arraigned Weatherby not on the most obvious ground of having built a conspicuously lavish country estate in the midst of the poor folk his enterprises were exploiting, but instead for having modeled his villa after someone else's, and for doing it in bad taste – an accusation far more shrewdly damaging.

Of course the account sent Cassandra into transports of hilarity. That evening in the sitting room she insisted on performing the relevant passages aloud in the manner of a dramatic reading, with Weatherby and Margaret as an unwilling audience. "'The edifice lacks even the virtue of originality," she declaimed, "being as it is nothing but a shameless copy of an even more extravagant pile built some years ago above Humboldt Bay by William Carson, a logging titan of Eureka, California, whose plundering of the Northwestern redwood forests we must hope Mr. Weatherby does not plan to imitate here in the virgin woods of Macon and Clay.'"

However did the whoreson learn that? Weatherby wondered to himself. *Did he go to California? Did he write to Carson? Did Carson give him the plans? No, Carson would never dare.* Whatever his sources, he had committed the worst possible offense: He had held G.G.M. Weatherby up to ridicule. Calumny, Weatherby could ignore. Loathing, he could abide. But ridicule – that was something else. His head swam with hate. He longed for an exquisite vengeance. Already as he sat listening to Cassandra's recital he was busy imagining ways to crush the creature – though naturally he let slip no outward sign. He had always taken pride in an iron self control which had stood him in good stead in so many business transactions. He would no sooner gladden Cassandra by showing any least flare of ire than he would have tipped his hand to a client or competitor in some affair of commerce. He listened impassively as she gloated on:

"'Imported French tapestries; fireplaces of Mexican onyx; stained glass windows; sideboards inset with beveled mirrors; chandeliers of alabaster and cut crystal; medieval statuary; English clocks; a grand spiral staircase; a dining room of finest oak modeled after a hall in the great castle of Chapultepec in the City of Mexico; and eleven more commodious rooms paneled with mahogany and redwood and priceless primavera, as well as with the local heart pine cut from our own heretofore untouched hills – this is the stuff of which Mr. Weatherby has knit what he so modestly terms his 'rude cottage' and 'humble holiday retreat.'"

Weatherby decided to yield up a clever remark to demonstrate the coolness of his composure. "At least," he quipped, "I didn't paint the roof red, white and blue, like Carson."

"George, how can you make jokes?" Margaret burst out. "This base person has actually been in the house – you must find out how! Or at the very least he has obtained an inventory of the contents! Or looked in through our windows. A low sneak, violating our privacy! A peeping tom. You must sue him, George. Sue him for slander and have him indicted for trespass. And sue that miserable sheet he works for as well. You should ruin them both."

Ordinarily Weatherby dismissed his sister's opinions – the childless woman *was* a zero, as Abbott Kinney had so rightly written – but tonight he found himself in hearty if silent agreement with her. Naturally enough Cassandra demurred. "Pshaw, Aunt Margaret," she burbled. "The account has the considerable merit of being truthful.

And since the views of the writer and my own so nicely coincide, I'm thinking of traveling over to Asheville to make his acquaintance. I sense there might be a great amount of fellow feeling between us. If he should prove as appealing in the flesh as he seems in print, why, I believe I shall ask him to marry me."

The comment gave Weatherby a jolt, accustomed though he was to Cassandra's impertinence; and his facade of calm dropped away. The girl was just adventurous enough to act on such whims. Yet it could never be. "Do not say so, dear," he warned her sharply. "Not even in mockery." For Cassandra even to meet such a specimen was unthinkable. "Remember, I know the man. He is, as Margaret says, quite base. And remarkably ill-favored too, I might add. You would find him repulsive. To say nothing of the difference in backgrounds."

Coltishly Cassandra tossed her bright curls. "I believe it's for me to determine whether I find him desirable. As for our backgrounds, they are irrelevant."

"Not to me," Weatherby answered hotly. He had indulged her enough. Now she must listen to reason. He rose from his chair and approached her with such unaccustomed energy that she inadvertently drew back – though she recovered at once and stubbornly held her ground. "Nor," he went on, bending close, "if you are true to your heritage, to yourself either. Nor to anyone of our descent. Background, as you very well know, is all. *All.*"

"I know you believe it to be," Cassandra snapped back. For an instant they stood glaring. Between them the old chasm suddenly yawned – that rift far too deep and wide ever in their lifetimes to be permanently bridged. It did not often gape but when it did it showed them how far apart they really were for all their closeness in other ways. The sight of it always frightened and then sobered them. It did now. Saddened, Cassandra stepped back from the brink. "I was only teasing, after all."

Now he could step back too. He caught her gently by the elbows. "I know, my dear. And normally I love your whimsy. I love it so much that I sometimes egg it on. But – "

She touched the tips of her fingers to his mouth. "Don't say any more, Father. Please." He nodded and fell silent. That was how they kept their friendship. It was still something they could keep, though each of them knew that one day it would have to end and when it did, it would end badly. But the end was not yet; they still had a little more time. He kissed her on both cheeks and she kissed him lightly on the lips and then they parted and she whirled away from him and snatched up the newspaper and resumed her recitation.

❧

As furious as he was with Hotchkiss and as maliciously as he savored his fantasies of destroying the cretin, Weatherby knew better than to strike back. For form's sake he would write a letter of protest to the editors of the newspaper. Certainly he would call together the Wildwood staff and ferret out and discharge whomever Hotchkiss had bribed to gain access to the grounds. But beyond that he would choke down his mortification and seek no revenge. He was shrewd enough to understand that if he sought redress he would play straight into the hands of those in the region who, like Hotchkiss, wanted to see him only as a reckless power monger and might rally to oppose him should he bestir himself.

Besides, other than to question his taste the article had presented him more fairly than he had any right to expect. It had granted him the standing he thought he deserved. And by scorning his taste in architecture it had even managed to make him seem somewhat vulnerable and . . . well, passably human.

At the conclusion of her reading Cassandra bade them goodnight and retired upstairs. Duncan brought brandy and Weatherby and Margaret sat before the fire sampling their drinks and trying to soothe their tempers. Of course, Weatherby reflected to himself, the hullabaloo over the article was nothing but a farce, absurdly trivial next to the matter that had been preoccuping him ever since his encounter on the mountain.

As angry as he was at Hotchkiss, he hated even worse the memory of what had transpired there. Tomorrow he must see Poindexter and Middleton and arrange another hunt. Boar bears didn't go to den in winter as sows did; somewhere up there on Tusquittee Bald the beast would have made a bed of rhododendron and laurel broken down and raked together, and would be sleeping there during spells of bad weather. But when he got hungry he would venture out to feed.

Margaret's scolding voice broke his reverie. "You are not consistent in your judgments, George," she lectured in her adenoidal whine. "That young country man – what's his name? Middleton, isn't it? He is hardly of a background commensurate with ours, yet you encourage Cassandra's friendship with him. You can't blame her if she fails to make the proper social distinctions. In fact, it's your fault that she can't." Margaret despaired of Weatherby as a father. But then Margaret despaired of everything and everyone except herself.

Wearily he sighed. "Nonsense. The cases of Absalom and that execrable reporter are not at all alike."

"And why not, may I ask? The Middleton boy, as you so often remind me, is the best of the old Aryan-American stock. And I distinctly recall your telling me that Mr. Hotchkiss descends from the original settlers of Old New York. Surely there is little to choose between the two of them, breeding wise."

It was hard to be patient with her. How could she speak of considerations of breeding? In breeding terms she herself was a dead end. A mule. He could never look at her without a faint sensation of disgust. She had failed in woman's chief duty. What good was she now? She wasted the very space she occupied. In her barrenness she was as much a part of the calamity that was befalling the race as were those of the old blood who were either taking steps through abortion or contraception not to breed at all or had given themselves over to a sterile debauchery. The melancholy result must be the yielding up of the future to the hordes of immigrants now flooding the land – ignorant masses steeped in darkest superstition but prolific, woefully and fatally prolific. This was the burden of Kinney's book – the book that had inspired Weatherby to take up his grand cause.

"There is every difference," he replied with a show of strained patience. "Men like Hotchkiss are but the lees of a once-fine vintage. Absalom, on the other hand, is unadulterated."

Margaret frowned. "But surely – in point of civilized attainments, if nothing else – he is the inferior of the journalist?"

She had the pretensions of high breeding without its sense of responsibility. Childbearing was her job and she was childless. Like Kinney, Weatherby – were he a tyrant with absolute power – would have made it a legal obligation on every woman – every qualified woman, that is – to breed. Yet Margaret was his sister. Perhaps it was not her fault that she was plain and no man had ever desired her and the one man who had been willing to wed her to lay hands on her fortune had died in a carriage accident before she could conceive.

Now she was shopworn goods as well as plain and no man wanted her fortune desperately enough to marry her to get it. Again Weatherby sighed and mustered another sum of patience. "You must understand me, Margaret. I regard Absalom as an extraordinary type. But he is also a primitive; he is in an absolute state of nature. Like all his kind he is raw, unfinished. I have taken it as my task to . . . to shape him, smooth him, make him into what he can be. But he can never be what you and I and Cassandra are. His strain may be pure but it is still common."

Duncan entered the sitting room to refresh their brandy. When he had left, Weatherby went on. "You know that I encourage Cassandra to see Absalom because he has qualities that few men of her normal acquaintance will ever posses – the old virtues, all in the pure state and all as rare as rubies. He offers much that persons of our class have lost – I think we can admit that much – and it will benefit her to see them displayed, so that she may emulate them to the extent that the circumstances of her future life will permit.

"Yet Absalom lacks – and always will lack – the one ingredient that makes us and our kind what we are. He can never *be* us, no matter how much I may refine him. He must not even aspire to it. He is forever barred."

"I am much relieved to learn that you understand that," Margaret fluted in her primmest tone.

"Of course I understand it." Then he gave her a cynical smile. "It's all a matter of timing, isn't it? Remember Father? He became rich as Croesus and was an intimate of the powerful and had a library worthy of Jefferson and a mind the equal of Voltaire's yet no one ever thought of him as a man of quality because he had commenced as a poor ignorant sawmill hand and the odor of pine rosin always clung to him and he never shed the rude ways of his youth no matter how much he had improved himself otherwise. He was regarded to the end as a jumped-up mechanic."

She nodded but without his ironic humor. She had never approved of Father, nor he of her. Weatherby sipped his brandy and laughed. "I, on the other hand, am counted a member of the elect. Why? Because enough time has passed for our unfortunate tincture of rosin to dissipate. And because I went to Yale and obtained Yale manners. A generation or two are required before one's lowly origins may be, if not erased, then . . . at least conveniently redrawn. So, if Absalom Middleton may not ever be a gentleman, perhaps his sons may. And his grandsons surely will, assuming the process of improvement be continued. And of course it *is* within reach of Absalom to become as much as Father was."

Perhaps because of the brandy he felt the warm surge of his purpose and turned to her now for the first time with enthusiasm. "I've told you before, Margaret, that I have a policy for this place. I mean to use my wealth and influence to uplift these mountain types, to purify in all ways what is already pure in but one, and that one the most precious of all – the original bloodline which everywhere else is dying out. Because his taproot is in Scotland and England the highland white can restore what we are wasting. His is the sturdy old Elizabethan breed. His vigor can revive our expiring race. Absalom will be my proof of it."

"But there could never be any . . . connection – "

"With Cassandra? God in Heaven, no. We've been over this before, you know. And it makes no more sense now than it did when you first brought it up. How you can even imagine such a thing?"

Gravely she shook her head. "I fear Cassandra imagines it."

Weatherby made a negligent gesture. "Don't be ridiculous. Cassandra plays at rebellion but she understands more than she is willing to admit. She certainly understands *that*."

Margaret's head rose imperially. "I hope you are right, George. But I fear that you may be very wrong."

Yan-e'gwa slept under a blowdown. A drizzle of cold sleet was falling but he did not know it. He was covered with pellets of sleet that had filtered through the limbs of the dead pine above him but his thick coat of fur and fat kept out the chill and he slept in comfort. He dreamt. He dreamt of the stories his mother used to tell him while she rocked him in her arms in their cave above the river. He also dreamt of the songs she would sing to him in between the telling of the tales.

He dreamt of the great leech that lived in a deep hole in a river at a place called Tlanusi'yi. His mother had told him this creature could cause the water of the river to boil and burst out of its banks so as to drag its victims down to be eaten. Then he dreamt of the giant snake that his mother said dwelt on the cliff at Nun'day'li and moved in jerks like a measuring worm. Then he was dreaming more agreeably of the song the rabbit sang to escape from the wolves, which his mother had taught him and which he could still sing perfectly. He was dreaming that song when he heard the baying of the Split-Noses and awakened and remembered his war.

He crawled out from beneath the deadfall and shrugged off the sleet and bark litter and pine needles that clung to his robe and then he threw himself up on his hind legs and cleared his nose with a snort and smelled the air. He could not smell them. The wind was wrong for smelling. But despite the sighing of the sleet it was good for hearing and he heard them clearly in the still air. Each had its own note. He knew them. But while he remembered the voices he could not remember a style of fighting to go with each voice. He *had not fought with these or he would be able to remember that. They had chased him before but had not turned him.*

He dropped to all fours and started up the slope. He went through a tangle of rhododendron and over a scree of rock that was now slick with a thin coat of ice. He followed a steep and stony ravine that went higher and higher under scrub pines leaning this way and that. The sleet changed to a light snow and he climbed out of the ravine and loped heavily across a glade where drooping ferns were turning white with snowflakes. He was pleased that the Split-Noses were coming. If the Split-Noses were coming, so were the Ancestors.

The Ancestors were bringing the war to him now. This was good. Maybe if the Ancestors spent more time chasing Yan-e'gwa they would have less time to kill the world. He would lead them far up. He would take them to the highest and worst place. Then if they kept on coming, he would turn and make a fight. He would make a strong fight. Maybe if the fight he made was strong enough it would remind them of the covenant.

Up and up he went. The belling of the Split-Noses kept coming on from behind and below. He worked his way through a dense growth of laurel and creeper and through patches of briars and he splashed over a partly frozen brook scattering the little shards of ice to all sides. He passed through open places that were whitening with snow and then through places under stands of evergreen that were still dark and wet where snow could not fall because the heavy boughs of the evergreens kept it out. He clambered over many fallen logs.

The ground grew steeper and steeper but he climbed nimbly among the slippery rocks and moss and wet bracken, blowing clouds of vapor before him, his forepaws pulling him up, his powerful hindquarters thrusting him forward. Still the Split-Noses followed. From their barking and crying he could tell that they were gaining. It was all right if they were gaining. It was even all right if they turned him – as long as they turned him at the place of his choosing. The highest and worst place. Up and up he went.

He was not going toward the gap. The gap was where he had encountered the Ancestor with the stick whose fear he had smelled. There were often Ancestors with sticks waiting in the gaps. He did not go there. Instead he went to another place. He broke out of the spruce woods and lumbered in the blowing snow across open ground where a lot of trees had died and fallen long ago and were lying in rotten tangles and as he ran through this place the decayed trunks and branches snapped under him and flew up in pieces around him. Clumps of snow that had covered the pieces jumped up with them. The sky was huge and empty above him. He came to the boulder field that bordered the place where he was going. He made his way over the boulders swiftly but carefully because of the caps of snow they wore and he got over them without any trouble. He had been running for a long time but he was not winded. He felt fine. He was in good shape. He was strong. The Split-Noses were very near and it was all right that they were near, for he was almost at the place he wanted to be.

Where the boulders ended a flat wedge of rock slanted up and out over nothing. Yan-e'gwa came to it and trotted out to the very tip. With his bad eyesight he did not know from seeing it how long the drop was from the tip of this rock down to the bottom. But he thought it was pretty far – the pebbles he had knocked loose when he had come here before had always taken quite a while to fall. He was satisfied that it was far enough. He turned and put his back to the vast empty space. Now the Split-Noses and the Ancestors could only come at him from the front. He waited. He did not wait long.

The first of the Split-Noses came alone and was not baying. Because of his short sight Yan-e'gwa heard it before he saw it. What he heard was the sniffing of its nose and then its panting. Next came its smell. It had a bitter odor. Finally he saw it as it came scrambling over the boulders with its nose down smelling out his trail. It was a dark one. When it spied him it stopped and looked at him and then began to run from side to side along the base of the wedge of rock glancing at him edgewise as if it did not want to see him any too clearly and Yan-e'gwa understood that this one was not a fighter but was only for tracking.

Yan-e'gwa heard the others coming. The yammer of their

voices was loud and irritating. He heard the crackle of the rotted limbs and trunks of the downed trees as the Split-Noses ran through them and then he could hear the scrabble of their toenails on the rocks of the boulder field as they got over those and then he heard their voices change and go higher and sharper and that was when he began to see them, some dark like the one that still ran back and forth in front of him peeping at him edgewise and some light colored with short wiry hair, and then all the Split-Noses save the peeping one rushed at him through the swirl of snow showing their fangs and swarmed him growling and snarling and he felt their small teeth biting at the thick hair around his flanks and hams and belly and as they worried at him their smells washed over him, a different smell for each, and one of the light colored ones bounded up to make a try for his throat and almost casually Yan-e'gwa reached out a paw and scooped that one up and drew it to his chest and it snapped at him and he closed his mouth over its muzzle and with a wrench of his head tore off its lower jaw and dropped the jawless Split-Nose on the backs of the others and two of the dark Split-Noses turned on it then and the three of those started to fight. Yan-e'gwa spat out the piece of jaw. He popped his teeth and bent his back and looked down left and right and another light colored one leaped at him and he swung at this one and clubbed it solidly in mid-air and it flew end-over-end out and down past the edge of the rock and Yan-e'gwa heard its fading squeal as it fell.

By now the jawless Split-Nose had run off and the two dark ones that had attacked it now came at Yan-e'gwa again and he plucked one of them up and threw it as far as he could and his claws tore open its stomach as he threw it and its guts uncoiled in the air as it went. One by one Yan-e'gwa kicked with his back legs at the others that were still chewing at him.

He kicked one free. It was a dark one. It landed on its side but quickly scrambled to its feet and then to Yan-e'gwa's surprise it ran right up his belly and chest as if it were climbing a steep bank and it fastened its teeth in his throat and Yan-e'gwa felt the teeth go deep and he roared his fury and hugged the Split-Nose close till he heard its ribs pop as twigs do when stepped on and then the jaws that were biting his throat relaxed and he let that

*one go and the others drew back making a great noise of barking
and baying and that was when Yan-e'gwa saw the Ancestors coming through the boulder field.*

*It was never easy to distinguish an Ancestor because if one
was far enough off he looked as much like a deer as an Ancestor
and even when he drew nearer he often resembled a bear that
was standing up. And at first these that Yan-e'gwa saw stepping
gingerly among the white-covered boulders were so sprinkled with
snow that they made him think of snowy hemlocks that had learned
to walk.*

*But when their smell came to his nose he knew them for
what they were and he began to shift his head from side to side
looking for a way around them but there was no way. He dropped
to all fours and growled and dashed a short distance down his
rock toward them in hopes of frightening them but they did not
run away or even stop, and one of them made a hissing noise with
his mouth and as if in response to this the Split-Noses swarmed
Yan-e'gwa again biting and chewing and worrying and he batted
at them with his forepaws and kicked at them with his back legs
and shook his great shoulders where one had attached itself by
its jaws, and then he had to stand up to fight them better.*

*The Ancestors had advanced to the base of Yan-e'gwa's rock.
They paused there, a scattered line of them. They spoke warily
together. They carried sticks. Till today the Ancestor whose fear
he had smelled that foggy day in the gap was the only Ancestor
Yan-e'gwa had ever been close to. He suspected that the sticks
the Ancestors always carried were weapons but he did not know
what kind. He had often fought the Ancestors' Split-Noses but he
had always defeated them and made an escape before the Ancestors themselves could arrive and corner him.*

*So Yan-e'gwa did not know what use the Ancestors made of
the sticks. Now he saw one of them point a stick at him and har-
ried by the clamoring Split-Noses he waited to see what would
happen. He was curious. The Ancestor was too far away to hit
him with the stick and did not hold his stick as a bow and arrow
are held. The Ancestor looked odd pointing his stick as he did.
Then a noise came that was like thunder but much harder and*

more shaped and a violent impact struck Yan-e'gwa and almost knocked him down.

He was stunned and offended. He had been taken advantage of. He staggered but did not fall. The unexpected blow enraged him and even before the pain of it came he reacted to the rage and dropped again and charged down his shaft of rock toward the line of Ancestors with one Split-Nose still clinging by its teeth to his back and another with its fangs sunk in his side and he ran over some others in his rush and sent one more tumbling and then the pain came, a pain that split his skull, and he was among the Ancestors then, smelling them, and the hard shaped noise sounded again but this time there was no jolt, and he drove his body into one of them and the Ancestor gave a strangled cry and fell and Yan-e'gwa took the odor of that one in his nostrils and knew it was the same one he had met at the gap and this surprised him.

But another Ancestor was pointing his stick and Yan-e'gwa whirled on that one and took part of him in his mouth and lifted him off the ground thinking how light he was, how delicate, how fine his blood tasted, and the Ancestor screamed and Yan-e'gwa gave his head a mighty shake and the Ancestor made a turn in the air and struck the edge of the rock. And Yan-e'gwa ran for the boulder field carrying the foreleg of the Ancestor in his teeth with the two Split-Noses still dragging at him and the others chasing after him and then more of the hard shaped noises came from behind but nothing struck him except the pain in his head, which got worse and worse and worse with every jump he took.

Part Two

The Scourge

Chapter Eleven

Hamby started out tending the boiler on the Middletons' donkey mill. It was his job to keep enough fire and water in the boiler to run the saw. Every morning he would fill the tank from the creek and get the fire going and run the pressure high enough to pop the valve, and that would set the drive wheel to turning at the right rate. Then while the least Middleton boy cranked the logs back and forth in the carriage Hamby would hold enough steam in the boiler to keep that valve popped up so they could saw logs all day long.

The saw was set right over the creek and the sawdust from it went into the creek. Now and then Hamby would have to get down in the creek with a shovel and scoop the sawdust out from underneath the saw where it was apt to clog the flow. He'd shovel it further downstream so the current would wash it on into the Tusquittee.

That was toilsome because the water was ankle-deep and sometimes knee-deep and it was always freezing cold. Worse, a shovel full of that soggy sawdust was as heavy as so much rock and Hamby's wind had gone bad owing to his lung ailment and had left him puny and peaked. He could handle the boiler work fine but that business in the creek with the shovel bested him. He got cramps in the calves of his legs and lost the feeling in his feet from the chill of the water. His hands and the muscles in his arms would go to trembling so bad he could barely keep a grip on the handle of the shovel. He couldn't get his breath and pains would shoot through his chest like he was being stabbed with darning needles. He'd cough and spit up big gobs of blood and the blood was getting darker and darker all the time.

It shamed him that his body was failing him. He had always been one to work. They were paying him seventy-five cent a day for a job that would have been worth a dollar had he been white, but seventy-five cent was close to fair for colored pay and anyway he was drawing a wage for a day's work and a day's work was what he owed and he meant to give it. Besides, he had always stood up to whatever came. That was who he was. If he wasn't that, who in hell was he?

But those rough days shoveling wet sawdust in the creek not only left him achy and tired out but sometimes kindled fevers that racked him of a night so he lay wakeful on his pallet bathed in sweat and shallowly panting. When that happened he would start to count his breaths. He counted them as if they were coins. He was spending breaths out of a dwindling treasury just the way a man might spend down a hoard of money. *Goddamn*, he reproached himself, *What you be – a sick old man?*

Well, maybe he was. Maybe he was giving out. It amazed and fretted him to suspect it but maybe it was true, and against his will he began to entertain a thought that before now he would never have let into his head at all. Maybe he ought to go to Old Man Middleton. Maybe he ought to beg to be let off the shoveling and just do the boiler work. He was damn good with the boiler and any fool could shovel that shit down the creek. It would mean a cut in pay. Not to mention the shame it would cost him to ask. But he was actually thinking that. Cussing himself but thinking it. But then they moved the mill and changed his job and he was spared the belittlement he'd been nearly ready to set on himself.

The Middletons' plan had always been to log out one area and then move the donkey higher to another part of the woods and then take the donkey higher yet when they logged that out. They meant to go the whole way to the top of Tuni Gap before they got done, cutting their own logs and sawing them. Then when they got on top of the gap they were going to build a slide and run logs down the other side straight to the Nantahala and sell those to Weatherby to be sawed in his big bandmill. They had worked for better than three months logging out the trees around the mouth of Big Tuni. It was cut clean now. Nothing was left that would make more than a hickory switch. So the last week in January they looked higher up and found themselves a good spot in a stand of hardwood above where the splash dam used to be and they set about dismantling the donkey and moving it in pieces. By the middle of February they were set up in the new place and cutting.

Instead of taking Hamby up to the new site to man the boiler, Old Man Middleton gave him a bark spud and put him to stripping tanbark off the acid wood that some of the hired hands were cutting lower down the ridge in a hemlock cove and in a nearby stand of chestnut and chestnut oak. It was a good deal less of a job than the boiler tending but Middleton only reduced the pay by a nickel. Maybe that was by way of notice for the good work Hamby had turned in before now – Middleton was no worse a boss than many, even if Hamby was nothing but a coon to him. Being put to the simpler task was surely a comedown, no two ways about it. But he could still strip more damn tanbark than any two white men half his age.

So piss on it. He peeled that bark and scattered it out in long loose mounds so it would cure fast and when it was all good and dry he loaded it on a steer wagon and hauled it up Big Tuni on the logging road and took it over the gap and down Little Tuni on the other side of the mountain and on to the railroad at Topton and stacked it there by a side track. And when he'd stacked enough of it to make up a boxcar load, he'd spend a day loading a car to be shipped on down the line to the Cover tannery in Andrews. He reckoned that was a right smart of work for a bunged-up old man to do, if that was what he was. But he could do it at his own pace and between times he could rest on the trips coming and going and that way he could feel better about himself than when he was straining his balls trying to shovel all that damn soppy sawdust down the creek.

◄

After the donkey went into operation at the new site Old Man Middleton decided to drain the pond in the bottom near where his house set – the stink of it had got too much even for him. Hamby and Seth Middleton handled the job. Seth was some slow in the head but he was a fair hand at work and Hamby could stand him better than he could stand the others save Old Man Middleton himself. They had got used to one another when Hamby was tending boiler and Seth was running the carriage of the donkey.

The day they drained the pond was dim and rainy and a cold fog hid the tops of the mountains so that no more than the cut-over footslopes were visible roundabout mottled with black tree stumps. In the rain the gullies on the hills bled a red like blood. Hamby and the boy dug a ditch with pickaxes and spades and the pond commenced to drain and they withdrew to the shelter of a nearby lean-to to sit and watch it run. Seth tore off a chaw and Hamby fired his pipe and they sat for a time not talking, listening instead to the soft hiss of the rain and the suck of the pond water sluicing into the creek. It was a peaceful time and there hadn't been many such for Hamby of late and he puffed on his corncob in contentment savoring it.

They waited like that an hour or more, till the boy commenced to fidget. Hamby knew from working with him at the donkey that whenever he undertook to shape a notion that was bigger than his head could hold, Seth would go to fidgeting. Next he would get a vacant look on his face that was the look of somebody who has been hit in the back of the head with a big stick of kindling. Gradually now that look started to come over him. When it had fully come and set, he turned and inquired of Hamby, "What's a darkey think about, anyways?"

Hamby could see that the boy was in deep earnest, so rather than get wrathy he was amused and only grunted, "Niggers think about dumb white boys that spends they time wondering what be on a nigger's mind."

Seth considered this. Evidently it made perfect sense to him. He gave a somber nod. "My daddy, he says all a darkey thinks about is warm shoes, tight pussy and a good shit."

Hamby seemed to ponder, then answered in serious guise, "Well, that might be. Can't say on my own account. See, I be only *half* a nigger. My nigger half, it do think about shoes and pussy and shit, sure enough. But t'other half don't."

Seth squinted. "What's the other half think about?"

Hamby coughed, spat blood outside the lean-to. "Why," he declared, trying to keep from grinning, "it white. It worry what be in a nigger's head."

For a long time Seth examined him. The rain pelted on the roof of the lean-to and some of it dripped through and fell on them. From the dooryard of the Middleton house a rooster crowed. Seth's face worked itself into a frown and slowly began to redden. Finally he bent his look away and murmured, "I didn't mean no offense."

Hamby shrugged. "Didn't take none." He laughed. "You just dumb."

"Always was," Seth mused. He stated it as a settled fact and without rancor or embarrassment. Long minutes passed while he appeared to meditate on the condition with an air of melancholy. When he had given it ample consideration he spat and bobbed his head conclusively and remarked, "Brother Ab, now. He's the sly one. My daddy says he was always bad to read. Ended up, he went to that Piss-capalian school. Got more learning than was good for him, you ask me. Me, I can't read noways. Only use I've got for a book is to tear out a page and wipe my bottom."

That was all he had to say for some considerable while. They lounged under the leaky roof of the lean-to listening to the rain. Hamby rolled his sweater up into a damp ball and put it under his head for a pillow and resolved to take a nap. He was just drifting off when Seth, having managed at last to construct another thought, spat and cleared his throat and announced, "But Ab, hell, he knows ever'thing. 'Twas him got us in the sawmilling business to start with. Figured that out all by hisself. Now he's a-running that bandmill of Weatherby's." He paused and sighed and swept a mellow gaze over the bare hillsides. "My daddy says we're getting rich as hell logging these woods out."

Hamby yawned. "I expect you be."

Seth lapsed again into silence and sat morosely chewing. Hamby watched him with a half-open eye, trying to decide if he was fixing to say more, not wanting to get waked up again right on the verge of sleep. The boy sat slump backed and head hung, staring into the rain with hooded eyes. He looked sleepy himself. Hamby relaxed, dozed, gave way once more to slumber. "We been poor as rat shit all my life," Seth declared. Hamby cussed under his breath and roused. "If we're rich now," the boy went on, "I can't tell it. We dress the same, live in the same damn old house, eat the same food."

Sleep wasn't in the program, it looked like. Hamby rolled up on one elbow and hawked and spat aside another dollop of bloody mucous. He yawned a second time. "Your daddy, he be keeping it. Storing it up. It come too dear to spend free."

"Guess so," Seth agreed after a lengthy wait. "I'd like me a new shirt, though." He chewed on awhile, then shook his head in a wistful way. "Hit's making us rich but I do hate to see how skimpy them hills look when we get done cutting."

Hamby snorted. "'Tween getting rich and looking at a bunch of damn trees, I take getting rich. Cut all this down, it grow back someday; you die, you *dead*."

"I know. But I've hunted and played in them woods."

Hamby drew on his pipe and exhaled a drift of smoke. "Well, they gone now."

Seth's mind jumped that track and took another. It seemed to be moving quicker now. The boy had become a fount of words like never before. Maybe the more he talked the smarter he got. If this kept on, Hamby thought, he'd get to be a goddamn genius before suppertime. "How d'you reckon Ab knows what to do to run that big bandmill?" Seth demanded. "I wonder if he read that in a book? Or maybe old Poindexter told him how to do hit."

"Poindexter, he in no shape to tell nobody nothing. He lucky he still be living."

"Ab says Weatherby's been out twice more since then, a-trying for that damn old bear. Busted arm or not. Ab says all Weatherby wants to do any more is hunt that big old bear. Says he's as bad as Captain Ayhab." He stopped and scowled. "Who's that? Was he in the Army of Tennessee?"

"How would I know? But that Weatherby, he best watch out or that old bear be hunting *him*."

"Bullshit," scoffed Seth. "Ain't no bears ever go to hunting people. You know that."

Hamby was remembering what Corntassel had said about this one. That maybe it was a visitation. He didn't want to believe that. He was afraid if he believed that, it would mean he was one of those voodoo niggers. But he couldn't deny how different the bear was from the normal. And sometimes he even thought he knew how the critter felt and why it did what it did. Maybe that was voodoo too, but it was what he thought anyway. Men who'd seen the bear since it ripped up Poindexter and broke Weatherby's arm on the bald claimed it had a bad head wound now, a wound swoll up and festering and full of pus from Poindexter shooting it. Hamby knew what that was like, except his own wounds were mostly on the inside. The bear was mad and slobbering from the hurt done it. So was Hamby, in his way. Or had been, till now.

"Come to *this* bear," he told Seth, "you don't know a damn thing. Nor Weatherby nor your brother nor God Almighty neither one."

But by now the boy's thinking had run on ahead and circled around bears and returned to the subject of his brother. "Ab, he's right sly," he repeated. He spat and wiped his mouth with his sleeve and his jaws resumed their slow work on his chaw. "Risen above his raisin', though – hit's what my daddy says. Got a damn better portion than me, that's sure." His pale eyes hardened, the narrow chin jutted, his words came out clipped and sharp now with ill temper. "You can bet *he* ain't a-setting on his ass in the mud watching some dead-water pond drain. He's rose high and left me low, he reckons. Acts like he thinks he's better'n me – better'n all of us, I expect." Then as fast as it had come, the outbreak waned and he softened. "You seen that gal of Weatherby's he goes with?"

That was a subject Hamby dared not go near. All he said was, "I seen her," and set to emptying his pipe with a tap of the bowl against the heel of his hand.

"Now *she's* high-up. I've spoke to her once. She said a whole lot. I couldn't catch the biggest part of hit." He mused for a spell and then a look of wonder came over him. "I never in my life seen hair that color.

Nor eyes neither. How come you reckon she goes around with Ab? My daddy says hit'll come to no good. Says she's just a-dallying. Passing time with Ab till hit's time to go back North and be with them rich folk she comes of. But Ab, he fancies her. I can tell. He fancies her a right smart. I reckon he knows what to say to her on account of he's read all them books. But I'd sure hate to try hit. That one time, why, I couldn't say a lick to her."

Hamby sighed. An hour ago the fool could barely frame a word and now he couldn't stop blabbering. Anyway, Hamby had small interest in the trials that might beset a clan of rednecks on the path to fortune. While Seth maundered he again grew drowsy. Soon he slept.

◄

The boy and Old Man Middleton held to custom and kept Hamby apart in all the ways coloreds were usually kept but otherwise they acted mostly decent to him. Luther, the middle one, hated darkies but stayed as clear of Hamby as he could and as long as he did that, Hamby figured he had a right to feel however he wanted to. Absalom, the oldest, was never around and Hamby couldn't guess his mind. What Corntassel had called Hamby's tale was known to the Middletons – he'd overheard them speaking of it – and he surmised on that account they were willing to cede him a bit more space to move in than if he was just some commonplace kind of a nigger.

There were eight other hands on the place and they had not heard the tale. Even so, most of the time all but one of them were willing to let him be, even if they had no use for him. The one was called Boatwright and he was worse than Clyde Rainey at the Axum save that he had never been a White Capper.

Old Man Middleton had hired Boatwright at the same time as Hamby but had set Boatwright to cutting in the woods, maybe because he had smelt out the trouble Boatwright had in him and didn't want Hamby and him to mix. So Boatwright and Hamby had not worked in the same gang. And since Hamby slept by himself in a shed back of the Middletons', he never had cause to enter the bunkhouse the Middletons had converted out of their old chicken coop for Boatwright and the others. So the only time he and Boatwright ever came together was mornings and evenings when it was time to eat. And even then Hamby tried to stay clear of the bastard – another sign, he sourly reckoned, that he was getting old and breaking down. But giving Boatwright ground didn't help. He'd still start in on Hamby every time.

The others took their meals on a trestle table in the barn. Miz

Middleton and two of her hank-haired gals fixed the victuals and served them. Hamby would come up to the barn to fetch his plate and cup and then tote them back to his shed to eat. It didn't appease Boatright. He would want to know why he had to abide such as Hamby so close around him at mealtimes. He'd say the stink turned his stomach and spoilt his appetite. He'd complain it was degrading to have to dine with the sight of a nig revolting him.

None of the others ever backed him up or encouraged him. But none ever took Hamby's part either – no white could do that and keep his station, not unless he was a rarer man than any Middleton. So Old Man Middleton would just bend his head to his food and Seth would look sorrowful but hold silent and never meet Hamby's eye, and Boatwright would go on baiting.

Hamby wasn't the only thing stuck crosswise in Boatright's throat like a shad bone. Boatright wanted the bear. That was what they called it now, as if no other roamed the woods. And none did. Not now. Not since Poindexter and Weatherby on the bald. And not since all the ruction after that. Whatever else had once passed for bear had lost all standing now. There was just the one. Men mentioned it as ha'nts are mentioned, as demons are. Save Boatright.

Boatwright would stand at the edge of the woods and holler. Taunt that bear. Dare it to come out and let him kill it. He'd cuss it and swear till he sounded like a man raging against his worst enemy. He'd not only brag about shooting the bear, he'd pledge to befoul it, do it dog fashion like he took his women, and then skin it alive as he'd once skint a nigger. He'd howl things that made Hamby cringe, for he was saying them about a brute beast of nature and not about a human that knew what it did or what he said.

He had a thirty-eight Colt double-acting revolver that he wore all the time in a cartridge belt buckled around his waist, even when he worked. He bragged that a thirty-eight was all he'd need to get the bear. Weatherby and them that went out with big-bore guns and express loads were yellow as piss and all such heavy weaponry was bullshit. The only thing a man needed – a man that *was* a man – was to put the slug in the right spot; if he had grit enough, he could kill any goddamn bear living with as little as a twenty-two.

Hamby stood that just like he stood the abuse Boatwright heaped on him. Weeks and weeks he stood it. He remembered Clyde Rainey and told himself Boatwright was scared of Hamby and scared of the bear just as Rainey had been scared and he ought to let the fool *be* scared and go on with his ranting. He would let Boatwright be. He would ignore him. There was a job to hold, a wage to be earned, peace to be kept. He was old, he was jaded, his joints ached, he had no wind. He had been battling a long time. Up to now it had been his custom to pay back every slight; that was his tale. The hate – the hate Corntassel had told of – had fueled it. And the same hate burned in him now just as hot as it ever had. But he was weary of stoking that blaze. He was weary of the hate, weary of himself, weary of the whole sorry world.

Weary of letting every slight eat its hole in his vitals, of biding his time while the holes the slights ate got bigger and deeper and more raw, of waiting, of making the fine calculations that must be made in order to know when it was wise to let the resentment out and when not to, when it was safe to act and when unsafe; of waiting and waiting that way and then telling himself he must wait longer and then longer still, while the holes kept opening up in him, more and more holes each of which seared like a live ember, till finally the rage roiled up in him and came gushing out through every one of those holes and he hit back, striking sometimes when the time was right according to the fine calculations he had made and sometimes when the time was dead wrong as it had been with Clyde Rainey, wrong but no longer to be resisted, the offense was too bitter, and he hit back and broke bone and drew blood, he whipped ass, whipped it damn good, he reveled in the fierce joy of breaking bone and drawing blood, he was happy in that moment to do it and happy too to pay the cost of it, to lose that job and have to skip the country one jump ahead of the Ku Klux or some ravening band of crackers and go to walking the roads seeking work, and then the virtuous wrath waning at last, dwindling, dying out, giving way first to emptiness and then to a gnawing dread of starving or taking bad sick; and weary also of the next job when it finally did come, always some piss-poor miserable shit-licking job, another piddly job with another gloating son of a bitch like Rainey or Boatwright on hand to start spewing out the same slights, the same old slights, and the slights would start eating more holes in him, and he'd counsel himself to wait, wait, wait longer.

Trouble with you, he complained, *you ain't no more what you used to be.*

◄⦂

Early in March they made a road to the top of the gap and set to work in the bone-numbing cold building a log slide down the other side of the range to the river. They were logging both ways along the spine of the ridge now and the country was too rough and steep for the donkey so they were going to start running the timber down the slide to a landing on the river where the logs could be made up into rafts and drives and floated on to Weatherby's. While they worked they all kept watch for the bear.

It felt and looked queer to be on the high tops with the trees mostly gone off them. There wasn't any end to the sky and it was higher and more blue than Hamby had ever seen it and it looked like it still wanted to go on and be something even higher and bluer. The air was that clear it might have been polished. He had not suspected there was so much distance in the world. The valley was a quilt of gray and tan and yellow and every other faded winter hue and it trailed off into a smoky haze and away yonder beneath the film of haze he could just make out the sinuous curve of the river dimly gleaming, then the crags of the Nantahalas standing along the edge of everything in rows of snowy white. It was white where he stood too. Rime ice covered everything. It made curtain lace out of the piles of slashing and the cut-off tree crowns and it turned all the stumps to cakes with icing on them and all the felled logs along the ridgetops to bundles of sugar sticks.

To make the slide they took logs of maple and beech and birch and split them longways and set the halves angled against one another making a V-shaped trough that ran in a crooked and curvy line all the way down the mountain. They drove sharp-pointed iron goosenecks here and there through the sides of the trough that would stick up out of the surface and bite into the timber and slow its run as it slid down; and at the bottom of the slope they built a whipporwill switch that would shunt the running timber off at the landing. To smooth the run they smeared the slide with skid grease and in the evenings they poured water down it so it would freeze of a night and next morning that slide would be slick as snot.

Boatwright handled the towhorse that dragged the logs from the cutting ground to the slide and Hamby was in the gang that rolled the logs into the trough and linked them together with L-hooks to make a string of ten or twelve. In putting him in the gang Old Man Middleton had given Hamby back his nickel a day. His lungs had cleared up some and if he worked smooth and steady and doled out his strength he could keep pace.

It was the first time he and Boatwright had been ganged together. Seth Middleton was in the gang with them. Old Man Middleton managed the mule team and it was his duty to latch a J-grab onto the back log in every string they made up and then ease the string down the slide till it wanted to run. Then he'd jay off and let the string run loose and that string of logs would start down the slide riding on the coat of ice and grease and it would pick up speed making a roar and a rumble that shook the ground and down it would go lickety-split, sometimes so fast that the last log in the string would be flying a foot high in the air.

Boatwright was wearing that Colt on his hip. Every time he towed another log to the slide he would pass some remark. "Show me that old goddamn bear – I'll take my pistol and pop him under the chin and flat bust his brains out. One shot and he'll roll. Hit's a pity how lazy a nigger is and how slow the work goes on account of hit. Let that bear come on me, why, by God, I'll reach right down hits damn throat and grab hit by the root of hits tail and turn hit inside out. If a darkey wasn't closer kin to a ape than to a man, why, he might get further ahead in life." Even if he washed, Boatwright said, a coon smelt worse than the asshole of the towhorse Boatwright was leading.

Hamby kept his eyes low and his mouth bit flat. *Let the son of a bitch talk, he just scared, it don't make no never-mind.* With skidding tongs he and Seth caught the logs Boatwright towed up and rolled them one by one into the slide for the others to hook together and then stood by waiting for the next log, not speaking, not looking, trying to pay no heed, Seth darting quick nervous glances from side to side, up and down, anywhere but at Hamby, and Luther and Old Man Middleton keeping watch as they worked with naught showing in their faces save a keen but empty vigilance.

They made up one string and sent it down. Then Boatwright came up leading the towhorse by its bridle towing the next log. He was supposed to drop the log short enough of the slide so Hamby and Seth would have the space to knock the dogs out and catch it with their tongs and roll it in. But this time he dropped the log right next to the slide so it rocked over and wedged itself against the slide's outer rim where Seth and Hamby couldn't get at it without going to a good deal of trouble. Seth fussed at him for being careless but Hamby kept quiet and they bent to free the log.

That was when Boatwright jerked on the bridle of the towhorse and turned it so the big heavy dapple gray drove its shoulder into Hamby and forced him back against the lip of the slide. The horse snorted and tried to shy off. But Boatwright gave the bridle another yank and the horse lunged for purchase and pushed into Hamby again and its weight drove him sideways and over and he felt himself teetering and starting to fall and then he lost his balance and did fall, head over heels he toppled into the trough, then he was moving, slipping, sickeningly he felt himself start to slide on the greasy surface and he would have gone on down just like a string of logs, down and down skidding and tumbling, had he not caught the lip of the trough with his tongs and saved himself.

It was maybe five hundred feet down to where a couple of slide tenders were at work mending and keeping the trough greased and adjusting the goosenecks. Then it was another three or four hundred feet farther on to the first dead stretch where whatever came along would no longer slide; a team was waiting there to drag the logs to the next running stretch. So Hamby could have slid nearly a thousand feet before anybody could stop him. There was no way to grab hold because the canted faces of the trough were slippery with grease and ice. And all that way down the sharp noses of the goosenecks were jutting out at intervals ready to tear into him. If he hadn't snagged the lip of the slide with his tongs he'd have ended up at the bottom as nothing but a bundle of bloody rags.

Seth reached in and took him by an elbow and hauled him out of the trough and Hamby all covered with grease and grit and bits of bark got his legs steady under him and stood and commenced to shiver. He was cold but that wasn't why he was shivering.

By then Boatwright had led the towhorse away and up the path toward where the cutting crew was working and they could hear him up there laughing as he went, a coarse grunting of a laugh. "Where's that damn old bear?" he yelled. "Where's hit at? I want hit."

Old Man Middleton left his team then and crossed to Hamby walking slow and bent-kneed as if what he thought as he walked was so heavy that it bore him down with its weight. He rounded the head of the slide and waited till Hamby could lift his eyes and set a look on him and the two of them stood there blowing the white vapor of their breathing one on another, an exchange strangely and newly intimate, and then Old Man Middleton gave Hamby a solemn nod and said, "If you want to do something about this, you go on ahead." Then he turned and went back to his team in that same slow and heavy way. It looked like Old Man Middleton believed in Hamby's tale even if Hamby himself didn't.

That was a funny notion and as Hamby stood there shivering it gave him the warp of a grin.

❧

Before Hamby could take steps to get square with Boatwright or even begin to plot how to go about it, the fates did his work for him. The fates or luck or Providence or God – was God the same thing as Providence? – or maybe even some of that heathenish bear medicine Corntassel had spoken of. It did it right quick too. Next morning when the gang started up the mountain to the slide, Old Man Middleton left Hamby in camp to sharpen the saws and axes and keep out of Boatwright's way; and that same evening they brought Boatwright back down again in a makeshift drag pulled by his own towhorse with his guts lying next to him in a crokersack along with his double-acting pistol and his face bitten off and his belly laid open like a butchered hog's. The son of a bitch was dead as a hammer and Hamby hadn't had to bestir himself at all.

Seth said the gang was cutting in a grove of spruce on the south face of the ridge when they smelt something rank like meat gone bad and then the bear busted out of a big thicket of laurel and came in on them walking on its hind legs like a man and bringing that smell with it. The varmint was as big as a house, Seth claimed. More brown than black, with silver around the muzzle where you normally see a tannish color. It had an ugly place on the crown of its head that was mortified and looked like the bulb of a half-rotted mushroom. That was what was smelling. Its eyes burnt red as fire coals and it twisted its head from side to side like one will do when it means harm. It slung a yellow drool from its jaws. And it made straight for Boatwright like Boatwright was the reason it had come. Strings of ivy trailed after it and it was sprinkled white with the flecks of rime ice it had broken off in the brush coming through and it was blowing its breath like locomotive smoke.

Boatwright was carrying that thirty-eight of his but never made a move for it. He just stood there like he'd took root and watched that bear coming at him and his mouth was moving but not a word was coming out of it and he pissed himself, you could see the front of his britches turning shiny black and the black going down one leg in a long streak. Seth said the bear grabbed Boatwright in both paws and raised him up as easy as a babe, and him weighing near three hundred pounds and struggling and fighting, and it hugged him close and bent its big head over and went for his face with its teeth, Boatwright trying to scream but only making a bubbly sound from the blood pouring in his throat. Seth and the others belabored it with axes and cant hooks and such but it gave them no more heed than if they had been so many gnats. Finally it dropped Boatwright on the ground and rolled him over and took one swipe at him with its claws and opened him like a watermelon. After that it came down on all four feet with a thump that made the woods rattle and off it went, sashaying out the other side of the clearing like it hadn't done anything more than feed on a mess of blackberries.

While Seth talked, Hamby stood gazing down on what was left of Boatwright. The rind of Boatwright's gaping belly showed a line of fat the color of new butter but because of his being hollowed out he looked oddly flat and the claw-torn flaps and ribbons of belly skin sunk down and lay slack inside the hole that used to be his insides. The face was just a maw of red and a ragged leer of teeth. One half-winking eye. Hamby reflected. Corntassel had told him the tale of all the bears. Then he had told him the tale of this one bear, how it was different from the other bears and why. Suppose Corntassel was right and there was also a tale of Hamby McFee that folks told. If that was so, then it looked to Hamby like his tale and the tale of all the bears and the tale of the bear that had killed Boatwright were all twining together into one.

Chapter Twelve

The first of the fine weather awoke the little band of sprites and pixies that had slumbered all winter in Captain Moore's heart. Tramping the woods he reveled in the sight of the wildflowers springing up everywhere out of the dry litter of last year's leaves – the stately blue irises, the pointed white trefoils of the trilliums, the violets and bluets and bloodroot, all the small bright faces nearly forgotten over the long months of cold and gloom opening up again, offering themselves afresh, new but familiar, fondly remembered now, welcomed.

And on the hills above him he could see the flush of spring – the russet and burgundy brown and flat red of the budding hardwoods that flared like a foreshadowing of autumn and gave way here and there to patches of pale jade where the fresh leaves grew; the delicate fringe of new green around every dark pine; and the tulip poplars in the hollows tasseling out in plumes the color of unripe limes. The air felt moist and dense and had a rare flavor and smell of new life. Pollens swarmed in it so thick it made a veil over the mountains and the crags loomed behind it as strange and indistinct as ghosts.

All this put him in mind of stories he'd read in books of how ancient folk who lived in icy climes so longed for the end of cruel winter that they practiced incantations and charms and magic to bring it on, even sometimes sacrificed beasts and even humans to fetch it nearer, and when at last it came in all its glory and promise of abundance they celebrated its arrival with wild frolics and festivals and rites of fertility.

He guessed that was what happened inside of him every springtime: The sprites and pixies started from their sleep and broke at once

into carnivals of joy. Then the mischief they made would animate him and
he'd sally forth and earn anew the name he'd had from boyhood as an elf
and leprechaun remade. That self hid in winter and without it he tended to
turn morose, to brood as he'd brooded over the works of the Middletons
and of Weatherby and of the railroad, but now – with Charley and the hired
help handling the plowing and planting and Jim in charge of all the cares of
the farm – he gave himself up to whim and fancy as of old.

One sunny morning at the prompting of his imps he plucked up
his old infantry drum from its hallway corner and with it bounded into
the kitchen where Miss Hattie and Nannie were cleaning up from breakfast and announced the three of them were going into Hayesville that
same day to pick up a pair of boots Oliver Price was making for him.
"And I mean to take my Yankee drum," he cried, brandishing it, "and sit
on the porch of the post office and beat on it." He'd picked up the drum
on the battlefield at Chickamauga and kept it ever since as a memento
and whenever the gnomes took him it was his habit to play it in the Old-
Dan-Tuckerish style he fondly remembered from the war.

Nannie gave a shriek of delight at the news but Miss Hattie regarded him severely as he took his bear rifle from its rack over the door
and sat at the table to load it – what with all the trouble up on the bald of
late, it made sense to carry it along.

"I hope you're not going to try and ride that Dixie mare in one end
of the courthouse and out the other," Miss Hattie chided, "like you used
to do with Crockett."

"No, I won't," he agreed. "Dixie's got an unreasonable aversion
to doors and hallways." Regrettably some moderation had been forced
on him by the death of Crockett. He laid the loaded rifle on the table and
picked up the drum and his drumsticks and wove the sticks through the
cording of the drum to secure them for the trip. Then he flashed a grin.
"But I do pledge to ride around the square at full gallop and display my
dexterity by bending out of the saddle and snatching up all the roosters
I can. I'll do that after I've drummed awhile."

He even did a semblance of it on the way to town. Miss Hattie
drove the buggy as was her unfailing wont. Nannie rode beside her.
The loaded Winchester and the old Yankee drum were wedged between them. Riding in front, Moore swept off his hat and sailed it
ahead of him just as a lad might sail a pie tin, and when it had landed
crown-up fifty feet or so on in the middle of the road, he touched Dixie
with his heels and came at that hat on a dead hammering run and
spindly as he was, no more than a hundred pounds, sixty-eight years
old, white beard flying, he let go the reins and took hold of the pommel

horn with his left hand and rotated himself sideways out of the big
stock saddle, right foot set firm in the stirrup, the heel of his left foot
hooked under the cantle, the surface of the road rushing past inches
away from his outstretched fingers, and the hat came to him fast and
he grabbed it up with a whoop and a holler and, once he'd righted
himself in the leather, gave a full-throat Rebel yell that echoed eerily
across the narrow valley and off the faces of the hills to their left
around Sawyer Cove.

Trotting to the buggy, he was unable to stop himself boasting. He
crowed he'd done the trick nimbler than ever, nimbler even than when
he was a wiry young cavalryman aching to lick every coercing Yankee
he came across. Still, he knew he'd earned a rebuke from Miss Hattie
and sure enough, when he drew near he got it. She shook her reins in a
peremptory way that made him wonder if she'd even watched. "You
look silly," she grumbled, "cutting didoes and monkeyshines like some
addleheaded boy."

But Nannie, bless her heart, could be counted on to bathe him in
the praise he coveted. "You did not," she burst out more fervently even
than he'd dared hope, "you looked like a circus rider, Daddy." By way
of thanks he doffed the dusty hat.

Then Miss Hattie surprised him by hinting just the shade of a
smile and adding, though she didn't favor him with a look, "Of course
the reason is, you *are* just an addleheaded boy."

"Why, that's my charm and you do love me for it," Irish Bill
teased her, reining Dixie near the rig. Bending down, he fetched her a
buss on the cheek and when Nannie demanded one as well, circled behind and came up on the offside and leaned and obliged her too. "I'm a
fortunate man," he declared to the bright and ample morning, "for my
sweet ladies love me."

"*All* the ladies love you," Nannie giggled.

By now Miss Hattie had recovered her usual diffident air. "They
wouldn't," she pointed out, "if they knew you better."

Under a warm sun whose light came to them softly filtered by the
haze, they made their unhurried way down between the greening hills.
The woods around them were full of birds and Irish Bill listened happily
to their songs, especially the robust caroling of the wrens, his favorites,
so tiny were they yet so impudently and improbably loud. Swallows and
red-winged blackbirds and goldfinches darted overhead or perched on
the roadside fences watching them pass with curious twists of the head
till it was time to fly away. Up and down along Tusquittee Creek where
it ran beside the road kingfishers veered and wheeled twittering in their

anxious fashion.

Moore felt so buoyed up by birdsong that he couldn't help raising a melody himself, and once he'd got it started, Nannie had to join in and then Miss Hattie too, and that was how they crossed the bridge at Sanderson Ford and entered Hayesville, singing:

> *"For the beauty of the earth,*
> *For the glory of the skies,*
> *For the love which from our birth*
> *Over and around us lies;*
> *Lord of all, to thee we raise*
> *This our hymn of grateful praise!"*

On the boardwalk before Oliver Price's shop they found Oliver and his grandson Will sitting on a bench in the sun engaged in earnest talk. All save Moore made their manners, Will and Nannie fiercely blushing as was right given their genders and time of life. Then the gremlins got to working on Irish Bill and he bent on Oliver a darksome glower and addressed him in scolding vein. "Brother Price, I sure never thought to find you loafing before your own shop. And the day scarce begun. I fear for your character. It appears to be in decline. Those boots of mine had better be ready."

Negligently Oliver shrugged. "I figured the bears had et everybody that lived up Tusquittee. How'd you escape?"

Miss Hattie and Nannie watched sharp from the buggy. The encounter was shaping up to offer a deal of entertainment. Slowly Moore dismounted and tethered Dixie to a hitch rail. "There's not but one bear," he explained. "Nor but one man et – one man and one arm. And that Weatherby knocked over and hurt. The rest is all steers and mules, and a lot of gear wrecked. As you see, I'm whole. Whole," he added pointedly, "and in dire need of my boots."

"Well," Oliver said, "I reckoned you'd got et. So I sold them boots."

Irish Bill meted out a lingering and unblinking study. "You better not have."

Oliver ignored that and rested a hand on Will's arm. "Say hello to my grandson." He turned to the boy and tilted his head Moore's way. "Will, that's the richest old man in the county."

Will smiled, embarrassed again. "I know who it is, Grandad." Politely he nodded to Irish Bill. "Morning, Captain Moore."

"Morning, Will."

"Everybody lives in fear of Moore," Oliver declared to Will in robust tones, "on account of he's rich. Ain't nobody to say him nay."

The Captain grunted. "Nobody but you. Did you sell my boots?"

"I did. Sold 'em to a tinker that was passing by. He was riding a flea-bit old nag and he looked to me like he needed some boots. So I sold 'em to him. Told him I'd made 'em for a rich man but that rich man already had three pair of fine boots that I knowed of and anyway had been et by bears and I thought a tinker was in worse need, a-riding on a sorry nag like he was. So I sold 'em to him. Sold 'em cheap too."

The Captain leaned his elbows on the hitch rail and frowned, trying hard to hold his laughter in. "You didn't either. For if you had, I'd have wreaked a terrible vengeance."

Oliver was serene. "Well, I did. Anyway, I've got better things to do right now than cater to the whims of them that's laid up treasures on earth but not in heaven." Again he touched Will's arm. "This boy's got to go and beg permission to be engaged to marry, and his nerve's a-failing him and I've been encouraging him."

"Well," Irish Bill rejoined, "he'd better just up and ask her." He relished few things better than the giving of advice and turned now to Will and told him passionately, "Nerve's what's required. Putting it off'll do no good atall."

Oliver made a noise of disgust. "'T'ain't the *gal*. The gal's willing. It's Jimmy Cartman he's got to ask. Since he's Jimmy's adopted and not yet of age."

Moore spread his hands. "Why, that ought to be easy enough. Jimmy's the soul of kindness and understanding."

Oliver gave forth a bitter laugh. "He is, is he? Oh, I forgot, you're in the camp that worships the water Jimmy walks on." He wagged his head to show the contempt he felt for Moore's opinion. "Well, you're wrong but I know there's no arguing you out of it, so I ain't fixing to try. Important thing is, this boy needs bolstering."

The Captain took the matter under grave consideration. "Son," he said to Will, "it seems to me a fellow in your place has got two things to be afraid of. One may be Uncle Jimmy. But the other's the gal. Even if I grant what your grandaddy says about Uncle Jimmy being harsher than I think – even if he's mean as sin, which I doubt – why, his worst rage won't amount to a row of beans next to the aroused wrath of a gal that thinks her man's not willing to put up a fight for her. And when her wrath's spent, that'll be the end of you. She'll not look your way again. Not for a second." He rounded on the buggy with a hopeful smile. "I'm right, Miss Hattie, aren't I?"

She regarded him stonily. "You're telling it. This is men talking.

I've naught to say."

Undaunted, Moore squared back to Will. "Who is this young lady you want to wed, son?"

"It's Lillie Dell Carter, sir," murmured the boy. "Mr. and Mrs. Tom Carter's oldest."

"A fine lass," cried Moore. "Mighty fine. And spirited, I know that about her. She's got fire. If you don't do right by her, you'll rue it ever after and there'll be no one to blame but yourself. On the other hand, should you stand up for her and persevere to get her like a man ought, why, you'll win her whole heart, I promise you. I can illustrate what I mean. When I was courting Miss Hattie – "

"I hope you're not going to tell all that again," Miss Hattie complained. "Everybody's heard it a hundred times and in another hour it'll be time for dinner."

"Yes, I'm going to tell it," insisted the Captain with a spurt of impatience. "It's edifying. And it won't take any hour either. Fact is, I'm up in years now and my age has lent me wisdom – "

"And made you rich," Oliver put in.

"And it's the duty of elders," Moore went on, determined not to be put off, "to pass on their wisdom to the young – "

"It's wisdom, is it?" Oliver inquired.

Moore fixed a gimlet eye on Oliver and vigorously nodded. "It is. It surely is. What's the use of long life anyway, if not for the old to instruct the young?" With that he turned again to Will and resumed. "Now, son, I want you to listen to me. You'll hear me called Irish Bill. Why d'you reckon that is? Was I born in Ireland? No, sir. Not atall. I was born down in Rutherford County and raised right here in Clay – only 't'wasn't called Clay then, or Cherokee either. It was all wilderness, the Indians hadn't been run out yet, so I don't know what it was called, if it was called anything.

"Thing is, I was reared up yonder on Tusquittee and there'd been two generations of Moores ahead of me born on this side of the water, both of 'em right down flatside of The Ridge in old Rutherford, as it happens. It's not till you go back to my great-grandaddy, Aaron Moore, his name was, that you'll find a real Irishman – one that was baptized in the Roman Church on the Auld Sod itself. But that Irish blood runs true. True like all that wild high blood the English wanted to tame but never could. It runs in me as true as it ever ran in old Aaron." He paused and took thought, then inquired of Oliver, "What's a Price, anyway? Isn't a Price a Welshman?"

Oliver inclined his head. "He is."

"Well then." Moore raised a finger before Will's face. "Mind what I say. The Welsh are all singers. And what Irishman isn't a bard and a dreamer? Name me a Scotsman that don't love the lay and the keening of the pipes. All those old tribes were like that. Seekers of visions. Warriors. Conjurers. Dwelling amid the mountain mists. Harps, lyres. Music of a night. Poems chanted by the light of a peat fire. A fine ballad was better to them than a big castle. They'd rather roam free on the heaths and moors than live in a town and count money. Pride was better'n coronets of gold, freedom was better'n fine clothes, honor was better'n station.

"I'm satisfied the Welsh were that way, just like the Irish. And the Scots. We all had that romance in us, y'see. We were stormy and turbulent but sun-bright too, ready to laugh or raise a song. All of us lovers of love. Gaels, Celts, Scots, every man as good as the next. None of us lords – 't'was the cold-as-clay English had to be the lords. No, we were all common folk. Common but hot of blood."

"And rich," Oliver reminded him. "All you Moores got rich."

"After while, maybe. But not in my day. In my day I was poor. Which brings me to Miss Hattie – "

"I'm hungry, Mama," Nannie declared, her devotion to her daddy undermined by the state of her innards. "Isn't it pretty near dinnertime?"

"It's drawing nigh, sweetheart, sure enough," Miss Hattie assured her.

His daughter's defection was a disappointment but Moore hid his bruised feelings behind a mask of fatherly authority and told her to hush. "And Miss Hattie, you be patient too; I've not been talking five minutes yet." He set his attention again on Will. "Now Miss Hattie here, she comes of prominent people, the Gashes, out of Henderson County. And her folks died when she was just a wee thing and after that she was raised by her mama's folks, Germans by the name of the Sauer over across Chunky Gal in Macon.

"Now the Sauers were even grander than the Gashes. They lived in a big fine mansion and kept a great gang of slaves. And they had money on top of land and property; not many did in those days. Why, one of her cousins was in the State Legislature and a friend of Zeb Vance's. So these folks, you could say they were wallowing in splendor and luxury and you'd have the right of it. And me so poor I couldn't keep my wristbones from sticking out of the raggedy sleeves of my one old coat."

Miss Hattie interrupted him in a note of sarcasm. "Don't forget about the poor old horse you rode, first time you came calling, that fell down dead in the driveway of bots because you were too poor to buy the pint of syrup that would cure it."

"Well," Moore answered, facing her, "that happened."

"It never did. You made it up. If you insist on telling lies, you ought to keep to lies that others can't refute. It's a safer course."

"That horse died."

"It never did. And if it did, it died of old age. Anybody would've *lent* you a pint of syrup, for heaven's sake."

The Captain heaved a sigh. "We've strayed from the point and I won't be tempted further."

Once more he addressed the boy. "Listen to me now, Will. The Sauers looked down on me for I was poor and lived back in the mountains and I guess they thought I was some kind of a barbarian compared to them, swaddled as they were in lofty estate. And Miss Hattie herself, well, I don't know to this day what she thought of me back then. Maybe she figured I was a savage out of the woods too – whatever opinion she held, she's never told it to me. What she did say was, she's too young to think of marrying.

"And you know what that was, Will? That was a test. A test of my fortitude. Of my determination. She was testing me to see did I have the gumption to go to scrapping for her hand. And not just make some short little mild tussle of it either. No, I'd have to put up a good long hard fight – a whole campaign, even a war. Like old Ulysses S. Grant going at Vicksburg time and time again, this way and that, upriver and downriver, digging canals, ferrying troops, fighting, laying siege, till finally those poor old Rebel boys had to give up because he plumb wore 'em out. Only with me 't'would take years and years before Miss Hattie surrendered, where it only took Grant a matter of months to lay hold of Vicksburg. So I had to prove I was a harder man than even Ulysses Grant." A second time he swung about and appealed to his wife for confirmation. "I'm right, Miss Hattie, am I not?"

"Like I said, this is men talking. And it *is* near time to eat."

Chagrined, he came back to the boy. "Six long years I was at it. Went off to resist the Yankees and the whole time I was fighting for Miss Hattie too. A two-front war, it was. And in the end I lost to the Yankees but I triumphed with Miss Hattie. I did. Now it's true that in the same six years Miss Hattie grew up from a girl to a lovely young woman and so her original argument of tender age no longer applied. But whatever doubts else she might've secretly held to, about my spirit or my faith or my character or my resolution, I had overcome 'em. I had beat 'em down by persisting and enduring and striving on and on.

"And you know what kept the heart in me that whole time? What kept me on the attack to win Miss Hattie's hand? Why, it was the wild high blood of those old clans. Their passion was mine. No, I hadn't been born in Ireland. But I *was* Irish – Irish in my soul. I still am. I'm the Irish hurling themselves on old Oliver Cromwell's Roundheads; and more'n that, I'm the Highlanders coming down on the redcoats at Culloden and the Welsh that followed Hotspur and Glendower against those English kings too. On account of that blood. Same kind of blood you've got running in you, young man. Tribal blood. You've got to answer its call. You don't, sweet little Miss Lillie Carter'll turn aside from you. Leave you flat. And maybe even worse, in time you'll discover to your woe that you didn't just lose Miss Lillie, you lost the best part of yourself as well."

Later, after Irish Bill had played his drum till he wearied of it and then to the cheers of the townsfolk dashed around the square several times on Dixie snatching up hats and chickens and handkerchiefs and once even a piglet and satisfied himself that he was in fact as spry as he needed to be, the three of them were heading home in the soft slanted light of evening when Miss Hattie laughed and remarked, "All the times I've heard you brag about your Irish blood, I've wondered how come you never talk about the German and the Dutch and even the English and I don't know what-all else you've got in you, that your daddy told me you Moores had."

The Captain rode a few dozen yards alongside the buggy with the bear rifle balanced across the pommel of his saddle mulling the matter over before he yielded up his answer, then when he felt ready he gigged Dixie closer and leaned and said, "Well, the truth is, it's not *just* a matter of the blood. I reckon we're all of us mongrels, more or less. But then, a man's got free will, doesn't he? He has choice." Settling back he gave a brisk nod as if to affirm his notion. "So," he said, "*I* chose to be an Irishman."

Will walked home along the paths of beaten dirt that went in doglegs and angles around the edges of the various fields in the bottom between town and the river. He was sunk so deep in thought that he hardly noticed the activity around him. It was planting time and the signs were in the arms and the phase of the moon was right and those who took stock in such as that were putting in the Indian corn because they thought it would come up lower and the ears would shank and hang down better.

Some hailed him as he passed but he didn't hear them. He went trudging on with his head bowed and his poke slung over his shoulder containing the medicine powders and Ramon's Relief he'd bought for Dad's rheumatism and the gallon of bleaching and the yard of gingham and the several spools of thread he'd got for Maw, and the neighbors stood between the rows watching after him in wonder as he went, for Will Price was always one to speak and wave and smile a greeting and if he didn't, then something must be bad amiss.

Captain Moore's talk was whirling round and round in Will's mind. He'd witnessed many a speech of the Captain's – Irish Bill was famous for his orations – but never a one the like of which he'd heard today. Every time Moore got on the stump he said a whole lot and it was always hard to recall the bulk of it afterward. But one thing above all else he'd said today had stuck in Will's head like a burr on a pants leg – the notion of blood as a blessing. A blessing and not a curse.

It had not occurred to Will before that blood might be a good thing as well as a bad. That there could be power in it instead of shame. That one could take pride in it. That it could fill you up and not drain you. Continually Dad spoke of the Price blood as if it were the brand of Satan and held up the scapegrace Ves, Will's real daddy, as the example that proved him right; and if Will had ever resisted this, he couldn't remember when. No, he'd believed it. Had no choice but to believe it – or so he'd thought. Believed his own daddy was dirt. And believed he was too. And believing it had held him back from seeking Lillie's hand, from going to Dad to ask consent.

Yet there had always been a different sign before his face, had he been disposed to see it. That sign was his own grandad. Oliver had the same blood as Ves, didn't he? Both were sprung from the same line. Yet the one was a scoundrel and the other good. Why must it be that Will was blemished for having come of Ves? Ves had come of Oliver but Oliver's good hadn't been passed to Ves. Grant that Ves was bad. But if he was bad, what – or who – had made him so? Surely not blood. Not blood alone.

Another revelation smote him. Men spoke of blood as if it came of the male line only. But it didn't. It came of women too. Half of it was mothers' blood. Ves wasn't all of Granddad, he was half of him. The other half came of Ves's mama, Will's grandma, Oliver's first wife. What was her name? Nancy? Yes, Nancy. Who was she? She who'd died of consumption down in Georgia in the long ago. What was she like? What blood did she carry? Whatever she was, Ves was half of it. And Will was half of that. Half of Ves and half of Maggie Thompson, his own mama who'd died when he was six.

And who was Maggie Thompson? He scarce remembered her now. A cloud of brunette hair, a tart and spicy fragrance he couldn't name, a sound of singing, the click of a spinning wheel. Some teachings about how the finishing up of work no matter how lowly was a measure of virtue. About how one must always love others. Beyond this, he could recover nothing but the hole she had left in him by dying before he could know her. But half of his blood was hers. How was her blood? Did she come of heroes or scoundrels or ordinary folk? And if Ves was a pariah, why had she wed him?

Will thought then of all the mothers all through time who'd given their blood to their sons only to see the sons disavow the gift and look only to the fathers to learn who they were. He saw that every son had robbed his mother of all she'd done and felt and given. And not the son only. The father too. Men had wiped out the legacies of their wives. It was a plot all men had entered into. He saw the ugly pride in it. The evil. Will who'd had no mama he could bring to mind and no grandma either, and who'd grown up aching from the lack, could feel the wrong of what men had done like an echo of his own pain. They had spurned a thing Will had never had a chance to know. They had put aside a treasure too dear to count – Dad did it every day to poor Maw, not in the reckoning of issue but in the dismissal of what she was, which came to the same end. And in putting aside their own, they'd put aside Will's too. For they'd made it seem his mama and his grandma hadn't lived at all. They'd stolen part of who he was. Fate had taken his mama and his grandma and that was bad enough. But men had taken away the knowledge of whatever good those women might have put into him. And if it kept on and Will married Lillie Carter and the two of them made children together, would not the spite of men conspire in time to erase all trace of Lillie too?

At the foot of the swinging bridge over the Hiwassee, Will stopped. Beneath the bridge the river ran thick and full, the color of butterscotch. Somewhere upstream there had been a heavy rain. The river passed by with a murmurous rumble that spoke of the massive force that was in it, a force yet kept within bounds but always able to change at any moment, to swell and surge and burst out of its banks and do deadly damage. He watched the river. Smelt it. Beyond it lay Dad's fields. Beyond those stood Dad's house. He looked to the house. He remembered what was in it. Who was in it. What he owed.

Blood was a made-up thing. It was pretend. It was as much of a play-like as a children's game. You could make of it what you wanted. Dad had made it up to suit him. Captain Moore had made it up his way. So could Will. Will could come of Oliver as easily as he could of Ves. He could be the offspring of warriors and singers, those old Welsh the

Captain had extolled – he was a fine singer, after all. Or he could be part of what Maggie Thompson was, and Nancy, and their mothers, and all the other women away back in time whose gifts of love men had schemed to wipe out. Whatever that had been. He could be that.

Chapter Thirteen

She watched them as they came single file up the graveled drive between the rows of Lombardy poplars, Father in front on his sorrel gelding and then the dog handler riding a bony dun trailed by his pack of nondescript hounds and finally Absalom on his white-faced mule leading a small donkey packed with guns and gear. Her eye touched on Father long enough to learn from the defiant carriage of his head that he was unhurt save in his pride and that he'd had no more luck this time than he'd had the four times before, then it slid on past Father and over the man on the dun and came to rest where it had wanted to be all along, on Absalom.

There it feasted. From where she stood on the second-story deck of Wildwood she couldn't see his face – the slanted round of his hatbrim concealed it – but there was plenty else to admire, the coil of white-gold hair at the back of his neck, the narrow yet powerful set of his shoulders, the wiry torso, those strong and nimble freckle-backed hands on the reins that had been on her too, the whole strong hard length of him that had been pressed against her and whose memory her body kept now like an imprint that she never ceased to feel. Before her on the railing was a medallion of wrought iron that held Father's initials elaborately intertwined; she closed her hands on the rim of this and gripped hard, leaning into the figured metal as she remembered leaning into Absalom, into his firmness, tasting the hot flavor of his mouth as it opened on hers.

She sensed motion at the tail of her eye and glanced back that way in time to see Father's hand drop down; he'd waved. The memory of Absalom that her flesh was holding didn't want to leave but must and finally did; and a tremor of want shook her whole mood. Disconcerted, she returned Father's hail.

"How did you fare?" she called, knowing the answer but trying to sound cheery and hopeful and interested all the same, making the attempt but failing from halfheartedness. At the sound of her voice Absalom's face lifted at last. But duty kept her from drinking it in, forced her instead to smile approvingly down on Father as if his worsening madness of The Bear were not madness at all but wisdom or logic or at least some semblance of reason.

"The brute eluded us again," Father confessed, grim-faced. His rage beat out from him in hard pulses that Cassandra could feel. He checked the sorrel awkwardly with his ill-mended arm – he'd never been awkward in all his life till now and every time the awkwardness showed, it surprised and disappointed her and made her want to blame him; and then she was ashamed of wanting that and hated herself. He was going to sue the incompetent doctor in Murphy who'd made a mess of his arm and he was going to have it re-broken and reset when he returned to Philadelphia in the fall, and all of what he felt about that was in the rage that she could sense beating out of him.

He stepped down from his horse and handed up the reins to the dog handler and stood for a moment on the flagstones looking stiffly back at the yellowing poplars along the drive. He had bought them in Richmond for ornamentals thinking they'd look grand lining the drive. He had shipped them here on the railroad but something had gone wrong with the root-balls on the way and now they were dying. Dying in spite of him. Dying *to* spite him, he seemed to think.

Watching him in his rage Cassandra wondered if she knew him at all any more, this angry man she had always seen as the soul of composure, that she had always thought she understood. But then she had never seen him at what he conceived to be the bottom turn of fortune's wheel. Always before, the luck had run his way. Whatever he had willed, he had gotten. Now for the first time he had come against a thing big enough to stop him and bend him off his chosen path. It was not just a beast. It was a power. A malign power, volitional. A power to beat or be beaten by.

The dog handler led the sorrel along the path past the shoulder of the house toward the stables, the hounds trotting after him glancing alertly about, pink tongues hanging. Absalom walked his mule behind bringing the donkey at the end of its lead, slowly swiveling in the saddle to keep his gaze fixed on her. Just at the corner of the house he reined back, shifted sideways in the leather and held her with that deep look. Even at this distance the blue of his eyes shone like bits of pure October sky. She longed to speak or wave or give some sign. But she dared not.

She held tight to the curve of iron under her hands and imagined that she could send a part of what she felt for him through the air unseen, a telegram of herself transmitted without any need of wires, a message not made of words but of sheer passion only, that he could read and understand because of what they had known and shared of one another. She sent it. Then he clucked to the mule and rode on and seeing him go was like a tearing of vital tissue.

But Father was speaking now, saying something about Duncan and the drawing of a bath. She smiled down at him from between the fat balustrades but she was blind and deaf with feeling and she gripped the rim of the medallion and leaned hard against it and all she could think of was Absalom.

◆

To Father, Absalom was a sort of savior in the egg; hatch him right and he would go forth to cleanse the blood. You had to know that to understand the project Father had devised for him and Cassandra; for it *was* a project; it was the test of a theory, calculated and finely reasoned and quite remote from the messy randomness of the actual world. It was an exercise in logic conceived in such isolation that while it made a measure of sense within its own vacuum, when framed against everything that was real, it looked absurd, even mad.

Father was convinced that the same traits that made Absalom so very different from Cassandra might also serve to improve her. And he believed the transfer of those qualities from Absalom to his daughter could occur innocently, without danger. But he reckoned not how love might spark into flame even between opposites and then wax so hot that the lines of caste would melt in its heat.

Cassandra and Aunt Margaret had been at Wildwood but a week last fall when, over a dinner of steak and duck, Father had made his announcement. "Cassandra, I've asked young Middleton to take you under his wing awhile. You'll remember him from the other day, I believe."

She was astounded. Remember him? How could she not? Father had taught her how to judge horses and the first time she saw Absalom among his dogs and guns and knapsacks on the flatcar behind them as they all rode up to Nantahala on Father's little logging train, she had been vain and thoughtless enough and false enough to her true convictions to appraise him as if he were a racer or a hunter or a jumper – his looks were that fine and that alien and she had admired them in the same way and from the same distance, which was the distance not to be traveled that separated one species from another.

He had looked magnificent – magnificent as a bold stallion is magnificent. But what had stirred her was primal. She had looked across that mystery between kinds and seen a beauty not of her kind and had felt something of its strange power and answered to it from the place deep inside her where there was still a vestige of the original kind from which all other kinds had sprung long ages ago. But it had seemed only a flicker of low instinct, some deep memory in the blood that rose unbidden and spoke of more ancient, baser origins. She had dismissed it almost at once – or so she'd thought.

Now as Father spoke she felt the same answer to the same power. Yet she was also a child of privilege no matter how much she sometimes wished to deny it and the notion of being squired about by an ignorant country oaf – even one as striking as Absalom – came as an insult at the same time that it intrigued her and set her heart to pounding with excitement. The two urges collided head-on, left her vexed and bewildered. Nonetheless she thought it best to feign a serene indifference. "Under his wing?" she replied, laughing as lightly as she could. "He's an unlikely brood hen."

Blithely Father nodded and took a sip of claret. Seated in his high-backed Renaissance chair upholstered with Belgian tapestry, lit by a nimbus of gold light from the onyx fireplace behind him, he looked like a monarch on his throne – a monarch whose least whim all must obey. "Indeed," he purred with an indulgent smile. "But I think you'll find him a pleasant surprise – as I did. He's agreed to give you a few hours every week or so, take you riding, show you the country and its ways, get you accustomed to matters as they are here. I'm too busy, I can't do it, and you need to know these things. He's a bit roughcast, I admit. But he has religion and he's been schooled a little. You'll find him quite congenial."

Aunt Margaret's disapproval broke over them like bad weather. She laid her fork down with an emphatic motion, as if eschewing by force of will the temptation to use it to stab Father, perhaps fatally. "Is that wise, George?" she inquired in the steely tone she reserved for the topics she found most repellent. "After all, the man's a rustic." She made an effort to smile but failed. "I'm sure you're right that he's a cut above the run of his kind. But even so, I imagine he's subject to . . . well, to certain vulgar urges . . ." She almost shivered where she sat, so hideous was the prospect of the lout in a state of carnal arousal. ". . . which he can hardly be expected to understand, much less control."

"You *would* imagine that, wouldn't you, Margaret?" Father

chortled in easy contempt. "What a haughty old snob you are. You'd do better to remember our own humble origins. Besides, Absalom is no degraded immigrant from the slums of Pittsburgh; he's – what's the old term? – he's the Noble Savage. Common clay but pure. Ready to be molded, bettered. And while I work to shape him, why not let his simple soul and native goodness be a beacon to a spoiled, willful girl too long incubated in the hothouse of Main Line society? It will benefit her. I assure you, there's no risk. The fellow knows his place. Besides, he owes me far too much ever to think of taking advantage. Nor would Cassandra permit any such liberty."

"You speak of me as if I were not present," Cassandra blurted, a spout of anger jetting up from the turmoil within. "Am I to be consulted in this at all? Or am I simply to be auctioned off without my consent? I was under the impression that slavery had been abolished. I know nothing of this man. And what about *his* concerns? How do you know *he* wants to spend his free time playing nursemaid and tour guide to the daughter of his employer?"

"Absalom will do as I ask," Father declared; there was an absolute certainty in the remark that chilled her. She felt the old chasm open between them and saw again how different they were and knew once more that they would never be the same no matter how alike they might seem in small ways.

He sent her a look in which both reproach and amusement were mingled. "My dear, you should beware. You tread upon the brittle edges of hypocrisy. You're constantly haranguing me about the virtuous poor and the exploitation of labor, about the universal fellowship of men of every sort and condition." Coals of sarcasm gleamed in his eyes. "Do I understand now that you disdain the company of the very same humble toiler you've always insisted was your brother-in-arms at the barricades?"

Horrified, she glimpsed the kernel of truth in what he had said. A flush scorched her cheeks and throat. "No," she stammered. "No, not at all. Of course not." She discovered to her astonishment that she was trembling. Under the tablecloth she knotted her hands, found them moist with embarrassment. "How can you think it?" she finished lamely, then sat speechless, aghast.

Father made a negligent gesture with his napkin. "Spend some time with the fellow, then. Get to know a *man* at last – a real man, one with calluses on his hands and the odor of sweat about him from honest labor. Learn that all men aren't idle fortune hunters or ne'er-do-wells living on their trusts. Of course you will remember that the proper distinctions are to be maintained. That you are his superior in every way save perhaps in the things that are simple and direct and without guile or subterfuge. For now, learn from him. It will stand you in good stead later on."

So there might never have been more, if not for Father and his need to put his hypothesis to proof. She might have gone on, content to steal occasional glimpses across that mystery between kinds, admiringly but absently too, distantly, as she might glance at a great horse running free in its pasture and be stirred in the ancient way and savor for an instant its grace and force and beauty. But that was not how it would be.

The first time he called he was plainly under compulsion. That would have been clear from the misery written on every inch of him had Father not already told her he was coming that afternoon. He filled the doorway with his solid height yet what he radiated was not the unaffected manliness Father had spoken of but the agony of a timid boy forced forward in alien company. He blushed the color of a new brick and hung his head like a captured cutpurse. So closely did he examine the toes of his boots that she'd glanced down too, to learn what had riveted his attention there. He held his hat against his breast with a grip that turned his knuckles white. And with his free hand he held out to her a wreath of galax leaves. He had woven it himself.

They rode that day. Cassandra took Omar Khayyam, the Arabian she'd had transported from Laurel Hills. Aunt Margaret overcame her loathing of horses and insisted on doing duty as chaperone; she chose Patience, the gentlest mare in Father's stable. Both were blooded animals and beside them Absalom's white-faced mule looked laughably coarse. But the mule – for some reason he called it Pequod – soon proved itself far nimbler and better suited to rough country than the pretty thoroughbreds and Cassandra could not help thinking perhaps this was an example of the plain sense Father kept praising in him.

Aunt Margaret held such a vigilant eye on him that Cassandra half-suspected her of hiding a pistol in a pocket of her riding skirt, to be used in defense of their collective virtue when he fell victim to his primitive urges. But on that score he proved a disappointment. Far from giving way to uncontrollable bouts of lust, he looked as if he feared for his own chastity, hedged about as he was by possibly predatory females. He apologized. He was sorry to take up her time with foolishness. He knew she must have many things better and far more agreeable to do. But it had seemed to please her father for him to come calling. He wouldn't do it again if he could help it. And if he couldn't help it, then he pledged to keep his visits short. She loathed him beyond all reason. She told him to hush, that she hated it when people kept apologizing for themselves. She behaved horribly.

But the day kept wanting to open her up to it and to him. It was late in the season and there were still rags and shreds of coral and madder-red and a lesser red like burnt copperas on the oaks and tiny coins of old bronze dangling on a few of the locusts and some maples were yet part scarlet and part yellow though some were mostly bare and the horses waded to their knees sometimes in the mounds of fallen leaves, tan leaves and brown and amber and wine-hued ones, some as purple as bedewood, every tint and every fine-edged shape, dry and whispery under the hooves. Others were blowing about them and it was as if bits of the world were swirling confetti-like, all the tones and colors of the world broken up small and scattering over them just for her to wonder at. The sky was a rare cool blue – yes, the same blue that his eyes had – and the air felt so clear and icy-crisp that you wanted to take a bite of it to see if it would crackle and start to melt between your teeth the way you thought it might. The nostrils of the horses blew white jets of vapor and their own noses blew smaller ones.

When she got home she threw his galax wreath into the fire and watched in malicious glee as it shriveled and burned. She was indignant. She repented of having listened even for an instant to the glory of the day as it sang to her. It was ludicrous for a young woman of her rank to be seen with such a bumpkin, even if he were as handsome as a god and much cleaner and better mannered and more well-spoken than she'd expected. No rubes, please. And certainly no gentle rubes. She did not long for gentleness. She could overawe gentleness, she always had. Ferocity was what she craved. A ferocity to match her own.

But after the galax had burned to ash she felt badly. She took thought of her principles. Had Father not been right? Was she not on the side of such as Absalom in the struggle against the tyranny of capital? Whose cause did she espouse if not his? She had scorned Father for professing to admire the same poor mountain whites he would never invite to dinner, much less treat as equals. How was she any different? She wasn't. She was a hypocrite. She preached the welfare of the common man but pride bore her too high to tolerate being seen with one. She . . . She . . . With a roar of exasperation she threw herself on her bed, then burst into peals of ironic laughter, burying her face in a lace-covered sham to stifle the noise.

What a fool you are! she raged. *What a smug little shrew! Can you only think in slogans? Is there nothing in your head but polemics? Or rebellion against Father telling you what to do? Or snobbery even worse than Aunt Margaret's – worse for being hidden, even from yourself?*

Anything to shut out the truth. It wasn't politics. It had nothing to do with politics. Or with rebellion or snobbery either. It was him, Absalom. It was her. It was his power calling to her and it was her blood answering.

◀️

On the third of their outings Patience shied at a squirrel that darted across her path; and poor Aunt Margaret, never a horsewoman, was quite unceremoniously dislodged. Not thrown; dislodged. Emitting a series of whimpers that grew ever more shrill she rotated side-ways, gradually at first, then at an increasing rate, till finally she lost her reins, pitched headfirst and tumbled into a nest of rocks, painfully fracturing a collarbone. The injury forced her into an unwill-ing convalescence. By then she had already come to the reluctant con-clusion that Absalom meant Cassandra no harm – his bashful deference had succeeded in quieting her worst misgivings. But if Absalom no longer seemed dangerous in himself, she continued to believe that the situation surely was.

She argued the point constantly to Father, begging him to assign another chaperone; but all in vain. Cassandra, he asserted, was in hon-est hands. "This is not Spain," he told her with a snide curl of the lip. "We require no *deuñas* here." After that she could do no more than plead with Cassandra herself to guard against overfamiliarity. But Cassandra only patted her hand and crooned, "Aunt Margaret, you've spent the last sixteen years instructing me how to behave. Now the time has come when you must trust me to put your teachings into practice." She could tell that Aunt Margaret was not reassured.

◀️

The first time they rode out unescorted, Cassandra was amused to find Absalom far more nervous than he'd been under Aunt Margaret's gimlet-eyed surveillance. If he felt any relief, his terror at finding him-self alone with her seemed to cancel it out. But at least he was able to shed some of his reticence – fear, she guessed, had loosened his tongue. Perhaps as a way of filling up the time and also of keeping Cassandra at a safe distance, he began to tell stories – wonderful, fantastic tales drawn from the mountain life he and his people lived, fables that could not be more foreign to her had they been recounted by a Mongol shaman in a yurt on the steppes of Asia.

He told her about snakes that took their tails in their mouths and rolled along like hoops. He told her about a coachwhip snake whose tail was plaited and could lash its victim to death. He told her about a snake whose head had been cut off and hours later bit a dog. He told her about a milk snake that would come to the barn every night and milk a cow. He told her about snake dogs – the dogs most every farmer kept that roamed around the country looking for copperheads and timber rattlers. Snakes abounded in these parts and the highland folk despised them. The dogs attacked the creatures wherever found and killed them. Often the dogs were bitten. When this happened, said Absalom, "why, they crawl up under the house and they either get well under there and come out after while and go to snake hunting again, or they die and start to smell. And then you've got the choice of going under there yourself and dragging 'em out or just leaving 'em to lay and smell till the smell quits."

He told her about a rattlesnake that was found frozen stiff one winter and was carried indoors where it thawed out and forthwith began to sing. He told about a kind of snake that broke into pieces when struck only to mend itself whole again by morning – he told that one with a straight face. There must have been a hundred snake stories. The snake seemed to him a terrible and mystic being. How odd, she thought, that these people living so close to nature had never taken the serpent for simply what it was – a lowly reptile squirming on its belly. To them it was a figure possessed of recondite powers.

The bear also – she remembered he and Father had been hunting a bear that first day when they came down to the railroad to meet her. Bears must be almost as common in these hills as snakes. Yet they too were seen in mythic guise. There was the bear called Honest John that was so wily no man had ever been able to draw a bead on it. There was Old Reelfoot – so named because it left a twisted track with one hind foot; it'd been shot through at point-blank range in an apple orchard, a surely fatal wound, and had fled into the forest to die but kept coming back to eat more apples in the same place for years afterward, even though dead.

There was the one he and Father hunted. *The* Bear, Absalom called it. None had ever been so big or smart or fierce or so uncommon in its ways. Cassandra had known Father to hunt bear all her life; normally he took them as he found them. For him they held no mystery. But this one seemed to have cast its spell on him too. He thought of little else. And that was long before the winter when its rampages grew so frightful.

The cold weather came on. They rode the country and she watched the great heads of the mountains slowly darken as the woods went bare from peak to foot. Soon the farthest ranges bulked cinder-colored in the distance and the nearer hills got as gray as so much slate or lead or iron and when you looked close you saw that the dullness of them bristled too with millions of tiny black spines that were the now-naked trees. And when that had fully happened, you saw revealed all the features of the hills that the leafy woods had covered up before. You saw the contours of the ridges, you saw every cove and hollow, seams and pleats of sooty black with the clustered green of the roughs and laurel hells at their heads. You saw outcrops of rock and sometimes whole big ledges of rock layered like grainy cakes. And in seeing these things you began to see also the source of the dark magic the country folk perceived in the snake and the bear and in all about them. The hills bred it. It lived in them.

He took her to a place he called The Herrycanes. It was on a branch-head up high on the side of a mountain and the whole shoulder of the mountain was nothing but a tangled clutter of uprooted and shattered trees. They had lain there thirty years, he claimed. About the time the war ended a mighty storm of wind had come. It had torn trees out by the roots or twisted the tops out of them and then tumbled the wreckage together in great heaps and mounds up and down that whole mountainside. Now most of the bark had rotted off the fallen trunks and branches and the bare wood was smooth and bleached like old bone. Thousands and thousands of bones. It resembled an immense catacomb but roofless and not underground as in Rome, nothing but the vast glare of the winter sky arching over it – a catacomb whose masses of brittle old skeletons it seemed some unaccountable force had come violently and without warning to stir and churn and intermix.

He took her high up to a place called Nigger Head where two ranges met – the Tusquittees and the Valley Rivers, he said. Here a narrow sharp-topped ridge ran north and west, its steep flanks choked with vines and laurel and the spiky black wedges of spruce trees. Far off bulked a tawny round summit – Weatherman Bald, according to Absalom. She gazed long at the prospect. What secrets might be harbored on those heights and in all those deep-cut ravines and thickets? What wraiths and ha'nts, boogers and varmints? What spirits? What magic? It all spoke to her and she heard it just as she'd heard Absalom's power that first time and she answered to it now just as she had answered to him then.

Here, he told her, a creek took its headwaters and flowed down the south face of the Tusquittees and passed by his father's farm. Tuni Creek, it was called. The family sawmill was down there now, in the bottom. You couldn't see it from this point of the ridge on account of the way the fold of the mountain lay. But it was down there. It was where he grew up. He was born in a different place, his father's first place. That place was higher up, poorer. "Land so steep you had to do your planting with a shotgun," he laughed. Later his father squatted on a piece of bottomland another man had vacated. Absalom shook his head chuckling. "He's squatting there still. But nobody seems to care, especially now we've got some means."

◄

As the season passed he grew more and more comfortable in her presence. He seemed to feel himself a friend now, though he never presumed anything approaching intimacy. He related his tales, each more amazing than the last, never repeating a one. He took her to ever more lovely and intriguing places, sometimes on the train as well as by horseback – the Nantahala Gorge, Red Marble, Big Snowbird, Hanging Dog, Pot Rock Bald, Rainbow Springs. In the fastnesses he always carried a rifle and kept a sharp lookout for The Bear and on occasion he and Father went out to hunt The Bear, always returning empty-handed. Those were lonesome times for her – times when she realized how fond she had become of him and how much she wanted to know how he felt about her – if he felt anything. For long weeks he gave no sign of what might be in his heart; he was unfailingly courteous, kind, thoughtful, eventually even relaxed and amiable. But still, always, inscrutable.

Then, all of a sudden, miraculously, he started to come clear. It happened like sediment settling in a pool of water. She did not know how it had happened, only that it had. One day he was an enigma and the next she simply began to see inside of him. He had seldom asked about her life and she had wondered why. Then one day she knew the answer. Just knew it. It wasn't because he had no interest in her life; it was because her life was so strange to him that he didn't know *how* to ask; and even if he did know, he wasn't entitled – wasn't worthy – to ask such a thing of a person of her ilk.

So, grasping this at last, she resolved to tell him without his asking. But no sooner had she started to speak than she sensed how meager her story was, how spare and vacant compared to what he'd told her of himself and his world. Almost at once she grew weary of the drone of her own voice in her throat, the knocking of her tongue against the roof of her mouth. It struck her then that her own life had become boring to her. She cut off her account and sat pondering the new realization with a kind of slow astonishment – till now she'd thought her life had been crowded with incident and accomplishment. Now it seemed empty as a drained eggshell. Then, as the silence built, she saw with her new clear sight that in stopping she'd hurt and disappointed Absalom, that he suspected she'd shut off her talk thinking him too slow and backward to grasp its meaning – when the truth was that she was ashamed of it. Ashamed of her own triviality. His life, she felt, was more real than hers, larger, more dense, more worthy of respect.

After this revelation she concluded she'd been wrong to think his tales were no more than a device to hold her distant or to fill up hours that would otherwise have been awkward and void. She realized they were his way of telling her who and what he was, and what his world was, and how he saw it. He was telling her these things because he wanted her to know him even if he thought he wasn't worthy to know her. It touched her to see that. And for the first time she became a little afraid of him and of what he might offer and demand. And underneath the fear the old arousal rolled like a sea, the deep tide in her answering to the pull of his moon.

◄

"My mama loved to read," he told her one afternoon as they rode back from an expedition up to Mr. Alex Monday's at Aquone. "Mama went to Mr. John O. Hicks's academy down in Hayesville when she was little. Not long, though. She got married to my daddy when she was thirteen. And my daddy, well, he didn't truck to books. If he saw one, he'd burn it. He thought if a boy wanted to read, he was a sissy. He's a severe man, my daddy. Somebody gave him a banana one time, first time he'd ever seen one. He ate it and didn't say a thing, so the fellow that gave it to him asked him, said, 'Mr. Middleton, what did you think of that banana?' And my daddy said, 'Just one more thing to crave.' That was him all over. Life was hard toil to him and any pleasure was a temptation to weakness.

"But I had Mama's love of books anyway. Don't know how – it must've just come to me through the blood. She taught me on the sly to read. Then I'd read anything. Labels on tomato cans. Signs on store fronts. Of course we had to have a Bible – we were Christians, after all – and I'd read that. Mama had eleven more younguns altogether, prac- tically one a year; and the two that came after me were boys and then there were some sisters and then two more boys. So my daddy had a good deal of help around the place, boys and girls together, once they all grew some. So then, somehow or other, Mama argued him around into sending me to Mr. Hicks's school too. I was big then, twelve, thirteen, I don't know how old exactly. I'd be the only one, you see. All the others would stay home and work.

"Lots of times in these hills you'll see the mother claim the youngest boy that way – keep him back from the hard life. And the fathers'll put up with it, if they've got enough older ones to work the place. But Mama, she turned it around and favored me, even if I was the oldest. I'm not sure to this day how she did it. But I've always suspected she struck some sort of a bargain with him – someway gave him my brothers and sisters, in trade for me. Them and her too. Maybe gave him their right to be other than what he wanted. Maybe gave him that forevermore.

"So off I went to school, big and gangly as I was. And one day at Mr. Hicks's an Episcopal missionary came by looking for boys to go to a boarding school he was starting up. The school was over across the mountain in Macon County on Cullasaja. He picked me and one other to go to this school. Picked us on account of our grades and on account of our being poor. It never cost my daddy a nickel, so again, he put up with it.

"That time when the missionary picked me, that was the second time in my life that I knew I was poor. The first time wasn't long before that. We've got a neighbor, Captain Moore – Irish Bill, they call him. When he and my daddy started out, they were both poor; but then the Captain, he got rich. One day after he was rich he was out plowing and he thought about us and how poor we were. I've heard him tell this story – he tells it to his advantage, you see. So being struck with the notion of our poverty, he left his plowmule standing there in the field and went to his sheepfold and took out a sheep and killed it and carried it over to our place on his horse and gave it to Mama for us to eat.

"So after those two things happened I knew I was poor. Before that, I'd thought the life we had was just . . . well, just the way it was. Knowing I was poor made me ashamed. So after Mr. Hicks and those Episcopalians got done with me, well then, I figured I was equipped so I didn't have to be poor any more or feel that shame. And I've not been poor or ashamed since. Nor will I ever be again. Especially now that your father – "

She interrupted before he could finish; she didn't want to hear how grateful he was to Father. She didn't want to think about Father and his schemes. "It sounds to me," she said more sharply than she'd intended, "as if you should thank yourself. Yourself and your mother." She paused and drew a breath. She had been too harsh and she saw his brows knit with perplexity. She took a moment to compose herself, then added less brusquely, more in a tone of gentle warning, "You shouldn't be too grateful to Father."

He watched her for awhile. His eyes had changed but she couldn't have said how, save that they seemed a touch cooler. Maybe wiser. She wondered whether what she saw was comprehension, whether he understood far more than she knew. A waitful stillness divided them, then presently the frown left him and she felt his mood turn and he sighed and that topic was done. He said, "I'll take you to see Mama one of these days. I want you to meet her."

Then his temper changed again. He brightened and told her of the books he loved. "Shakespeare – now he's a feast. I enjoy to read all of him. *Hamlet*'s good, only I can't figure out when he's crazy and when he's not. And the Bible, of course. I like the stories of the patriarchs and prophets and kings and soldiers in the Old Testament. But there's nothing as fine as the Jesus stories and the Acts of the Apostles. Now *Pilgrim's Progress,* I liked that. *Paradise Lost. Gulliver's Travels.* But my favorite book's *Moby Dick.*" Wistfully he smiled. "One day I'd like to sail the ocean and hunt whales." Here a twinkle of mischief lit his blue eye. "Only with a better outcome, I hope."

Listening, she noticed how selective his education had been. Yes, it was remarkable that he'd had any learning at all. But orthodoxy had bridled him. The dead hand of religion had censored him. She wondered at his thirst for knowledge and mourned for what she imagined had been denied him. But the next time he saw her he brought along his old Lippincott's Fourth Reader from his days at Mr. Hick's academy. He held it out to her with an air of reverence.

It had a cover of heavy cardboard that may have once been white, decorated with fancy scrollwork, now rubbed and faded from much handling. The spine was brown leather embossed with floral designs, lettered in gold leaf. The pages were of slick heavy paper that were soft-edged with wear but still turned stiffly under her fingers. Paging through, back to front as was her wont, she glanced at the delicate little engravings of waterfalls, partridges, a family crossing a stone bridge over a brook, some boys seated around a table, a sprig of sea-island cotton. She read the chapter headings: "After the Reading of Bertie's Letter"; "A Huckleberry Party"; "Where There's a Will There's a Way"; "How Mr. Raymond Taught Grammar". Then she came to the flyleaf where an inscription in red ink slanted across the page as if overeager to complete itself. She held the little book up to the light and read:

"Oh had I the wings of a dove then would I ascend to the heavenly mansion above where all is love and peace and hear the little angel voices singing in paradice above and see them hovering a round our Fathers Throne where sorrows will be ended ever more and where happyness will never sease and where we will hear our savior calling his little sheep home and oh could see them greeting their dear ones on the golden streets and gathering in to the light a bove where all is love and peace. wrote by A.T. Middleton, May the 7 1887."

Her last ounce of fear of him dissolved as she read. Her judgments about the narrowness of his education faded. When she'd finished she handed the book back and turned away blind with tears. It occurred to her then that Father had been right, but only in part. Yes, Absalom was pure. But the purity wasn't of the blood. It was of the spirit. That was what Father had not understood. To him the goodness in Absalom was a pleasant attribute of a lower order of being or, perhaps more charitably, of a child – admirable perhaps, even worthy of some imitation, possibly edifying to a pampered daughter, but ultimately too simple for the hard and demanding world. It must be fashioned into something better and more practical. Something equal to the task of saving the race. But Father was wrong. Absalom needed no bettering. He was pure already. Father was not his better, bending down by *noblesse oblige* to raise him up. Absalom was better than Father. He was better than the man who would perfect him.

◆

He was as good as his word too. The next time they rode out, he took her over the gap and down Big Tuni Creek to visit his mother. It was a cold and gusty day. The wind spat pellets of ice in their faces and there were patches of old smutty snow in the lee of every boulder and deadfall and all about them the hills loomed dark and forbidding under a sky the color and texture of old beaten tin. Once it would have been a day for curling up by a warm fire to read a racy novel. But Absalom had changed all that and the country he had showed her had changed it too and now she reveled in the bite of the cold and the dimness of the light and the roughness of the trail. Her heart pounded lustily, her lungs swelled to take the crisp air. She felt more alive than she ever had.

On the way down they passed the ruins of a newly-burnt house, its charred timbers outlined with pitted snow, starkly black against the soiled white. She remarked on the pity of a family dispossessed in wintertime by the cruel happenstance of fire. "Wasn't no happenstance to it," Absalom told her. "Fellow owned that house, he got in a dispute with a neighbor over the line of a fence and took him to court. Sued him. Won his case, too. So the neighbor, he came over one night and burnt the fellow out to pay him back."

She gaped at him. "Burned him out?"

"That's right," he nodded. "It's a remedy folks use hereabouts, from time to time." She marveled at how casual he was, relating such an atrocity. She could detect no judgment in him, no least flicker of condemnation. Nothing about his face had changed in the slightest. He seemed content with this terrible knowledge. For an instant her whole conception of him reeled. Like any Northerner she had heard sensational accounts of the bloody feuds that supposedly racked the Southern mountains; but till now she'd seen no evidence to support them and had been inclined to disbelieve. Now she held a wary eye on him. She remembered his gentleness, his inscription in the Lippincott's Reader, what had seemed his innocence. Did he countenance such acts? Had he, God forbid, committed them? She wanted to ask. But she couldn't. She was afraid to. She would rather not know.

They passed on down out of the forest onto the lower slopes that the Middletons had logged out. Suddenly the sky was stunningly emptier and more vast, the side of the mountain more shrunken, scarred now by deep gullies, its miles and miles of denuded ground spotted with thousands of stumps that looked like the pustules of a wasting disease. She was shocked by the scale of it, the completeness of the ruination. Absalom viewed it impassively but with a proprietary air. After all, it was his doing. This had been the means of his ascent.

The Middleton farm was a squalid place, a log hut of two wings open through the middle with a chimney made of sticks and clay, the ragged roof shakes held down with rocks and poles, two lonely poplars in front, the only trees in all the stripped expanse surrounding it. It had but a single unmullioned window covered with a scrap of greasy cloth. It sat amid a family of eroded hills of raw red dirt that were dotted with the same contagion of stumps she'd seen above. Beyond it on the edge of a scummy pond choked with logs stood the portable sawmill spouting rooster tails of white smoke, its screams and howls filling the valley. Even in the bitter cold the dirt yard swarmed with half-naked children and pigs and dogs and dozens of scrawny chickens. Cassandra felt a mild swoon of misgiving but for Absalom's sake quelled it and mustered her pluck as she would when riding at a challenging jump.

Inside, the house was dim and stank of filth. Absalom's mother – the woman who had passed to him her love of books and used her wiles to set him on the path toward all the good that she could never have – was a bony, listless hag with dead eyes, ruined by work and childbearing. She smelled of snuff and fried hog fat. The look she turned on Absalom was as desolate as anything Cassandra had ever seen; but Absalom drew her to him, tenderly, as if she were made of bird bones or dry twigs. He folded her slightness in his strong arms, kissed her. His love for her filled the room. But she hung there limp, arms dangling at her sides. She did not seem to know him. She accepted Cassandra's kiss with the same apathy, though as Cassandra stepped back from the embrace she thought she saw a flash of dread in the dim eyes, as if when they touched her the mother had felt or seen some sign of woe to come.

The father who had abused him for a reader when he was a boy fawned on him now as the author of their prosperity, though no sign of prosperity was to be seen in that stinking hovel. Mr. Middleton would have been as tall as Absalom were he not stooped and bent from labor. He was painfully thin but had huge big-fingered hands and thick wrists and altogether gave an impression of wiry strength and endless endurance. He showed the countryman's face that came of long years of outdoor toil, sunburned below the line of his hatbrim and pale as ivory above it. He had narrow eyes set on an Indian slant and hard cheekbones and a cruel mouth that stayed cruel even when he tried to smile.

Everything about him spoke of unrewarded labor and hard luck and anger nursed long and deep, but his new joy overlaid it like a pale halo; he was happy now, radiant. He was proud of Absalom. Proud now of the boy he'd once called a sissy, whose books he'd burned. He greeted Cassandra with a cringing deference that he seemed to think he owed her as the daughter of the great man who had so favored his son. She could tell that Absalom hated him.

And seeing all this, she thought how brave Absalom had been to bring her here, to show her this. What a risk he'd taken! She might have recoiled in disgust. She might never have spoken to him again for so offending her. Yet he'd done it. And in doing it he'd said, *This is not me any more. But it is where I came from and you ought to know it.* He'd said it proudly. She thought it was the bravest thing she'd ever seen.

The event was as awkward as it had to be, given the strangeness of Cassandra's presence. The father could hardly bring himself to speak lest he give offense to the lofty personage his son had so inexplicably fetched home. The mother kept guarded watch but still never lost her wasted and listless air – it was as if not even the danger she sensed in Cassandra could rouse her from her torpor.

Mercifully soon the visit was done. Outside among squalling children and barking dogs they found a visitor, the wealthy neighbor Absalom had mentioned, Captain Moore, politely waiting. He was passing the time in talk with two of Absalom's brothers, one lean and dark-eyed and ugly, the other younger, blond, slack-jawed with wonder as he stared at her. Moore had brought over a man he thought Mr. Middleton might want to hire. This man, a mulatto the color of a peach, sat his mule watching them with surly eyes that held the eerie blue-green fire of an opal. Moore said he was called McFee. She didn't like him. She was primed to dislike the Captain too, on Absalom's behalf – she'd thought that business with the sheep a bit too conspicuous for true charity. But to her surprise she took to the old fellow at once.

He was a tiny leprechaun of a man, smiling impishly in a white beard, sitting an enormous black mare that he controlled with a cavalryman's perfection – that was where his rank came from, she learned, the Confederate cavalry. His eyes had a saucy snap and he spoke with a lilt and there were still faint hints of red in his hair and she could see why they called him Irish Bill. He told her she was the most beautiful woman he'd ever seen – save his own wife of course, the exquisite Miss Hattie, who was the loveliest female ever made. Or Nannie his youngest. Or his other daughter Jennie. Or Addie. Or . . . They burst into laughter. Then he got down off his huge horse and kissed her hand and she forgave him for the sheep.

◀

On their way back to the gap they passed the same burnt house. They walked their mounts up the track past it and then Absalom drew rein and turned Pequod and sat gazing thoughtfully at the black timbers coated with old snow, and then looked to her and said, "You know who burnt that fellow out?" He smiled and for just an instant it was the same smile she'd seen on Mr. Middleton, cruel even when it didn't want to be. "I'll tell you who did." He nodded and gave a short, harsh laugh. "It was my daddy."

It was snowing at the top of the gap. The flakes were fat and soft and fell with a feathery slowness like goosedown. The way would be slippery going down and Absalom wanted to steady her saddle before they started, so they dismounted under a broken spruce and Cassandra stood aside and watched him through the falling snow as he worked. He raised a fender and hooked the stirrup over the horn to keep it out of his way and then drove a knee hard into Omar's belly to make him blow his air out and when the horse had obliged him he yanked hard at the cinch strap and fastened it.

Watching him with a new acuteness, she wondered, *Who is he?* So many times she'd thought she knew. She'd thought his spirit was pure; that he was still the schoolboy who'd written his dreams of heaven in his Lippincott's Reader. But then he might be a man who could set fire to another's home or at least condone it. Or he was shy and gentle and without guile. Or he was ambitious and proud. He adored books and longed to sail the seas and hunt whales. He ravaged the forests for gain. He revered his mother. He hated his father. He was as much of a mystery as the mountains that had borne him. In the face of that mystery some of her old fear of him came back.

But this time the fear was heady and stinging like too much champagne and something broke loose inside her and before she knew it she had crossed to him through the blowing snow and put a hand on his arm. He turned to her in surprise – there had been no touch between them till now, save for the lift of his cupped palm under her elbow as she rose to the saddle or stepped into a train carriage.

"What?" he asked; and she heard a quaver of warning, hope and denial in his voice. Under the padding of his coat sleeve she felt hard muscle and bone. Her heart roared in terror but she had to act – he never would, it was up to her – and she stood on tiptoe and took his face between her mittens and saw his eyes widen with the same terror that was in her, and she drew his head down and gave her mouth to his and his lips were soft and moist and had a strong flavor like the taste of wild game and she was lost, lost for good but found too, found and never to be lost in the old way again.

◆

Then on that frozen February day on Tusquittee Bald The Bear broke Father's arm and crippled his man Poindexter. Some weeks later it attacked and killed a workman at Mr. Middleton's logging camp quite near the spot where Absalom had shown her the sharp-topped ridge of Nigger Head and the source of Tuni Creek and where they had kissed and where the want in her had changed to love. After that Absalom was often gone in the wilderness, scouting for Father and the hunters. Underlings ran the mill while he and Father thrashed about in the bush in search of a brute of nature.

Now it was summer and still they hunted. Father had changed. The Bear had changed him. He was no longer the poised and confident man of high achievement she had always admired as equally as she had disparaged what he stood for. He was harder now, shriveled like an old nut, bitter as gall. His humor was gone, his balance. Like Ahab in Absalom's favorite book – he was even maimed now like Ahab – he was on a blasphemous quest to wreak vengeance on a creature of God that had done no more than act according to its nature. And he had recruited Absalom in his unholy mission just as Ahab had drawn Starbuck and Queequeg and the others to their watery doom.

The Bear had transformed Father into a person she no longer recognized and now it had taken Absalom away as well. A part of her hated them both for giving themselves over to a thing so unnatural. And in time another part of her began to hate The Bear too for having brought this about; and then she herself partook of their blasphemy. Like them, she defied Providence. She saw the wrong of it but could not, would not, forswear it; its root went too deep, as deep as the place Absalom had touched. Still, she sensed that so much wrong could not go unpunished forever. She began to dread that when Father and Absalom finally cornered The Bear it would deal them the awful fate of Ahab and his crew. God would use the Bear to repay their sin. She would be widowed and orphaned at a stroke. And that would be her penance.

Chapter Fourteen

When Yan-e'gwa was just a cub, he was in the forest feeding on tasty worms and roaches at a fallen log when an eagle suddenly swooped out of the sky and grasped him by the head in its strong talons. The eagle was very large and would have borne him off to its nest to eat had Yan-e'gwa not proved too heavy for it to lift. But even though it could not carry Yan-e'gwa, the eagle still clutched his head in its talons and kept trying to rise with heavy beats of its wings. It did not give up trying till Yan-e'gwa's mother heard his bleats of fear and came and chased it away.

The pain of that eagle's claws in his head had been very sharp and fierce and he had bled freely but the worst of the pain had lasted only for the short time the eagle kept him in its grip. As soon as the eagle flew away, the pain had begun to ease and before long it had stopped altogether. That was the worst pain Yan-e'gwa had felt in all his life till the Ancestor pointed his stick at him on the bald of Where the Water-Dogs Laughed and the stick made its hard shaped noise of thunder and the new pain came to his head which was sharp and fierce like the pain of that eagle's talons except that it did not fade afterward. It was much more pain than he could stand but it did not wane even by a little so he had to stand it although it was past standing.

At first it felt as if it were a thing made of ragged edges and deep roots. But after a time that changed and it grew round and

176 Charles F. Price

hard like a stone embedded in his skull. But the changes did not assuage it and there was never a time when it could be borne. It stole his sleep all that winter. Day or night he could not rest. He could not find a way to sit or lie or be that would lessen it. It possessed him. He forgot to eat. He became gaunt from hunger and his pelt turned coarse and staring and some of it fell out in big tussocks leaving patches of bare hide.

He was desperate to dislodge the stone of pain. Repeatedly he ran his head into boulders and the trunks of trees but this only drove the stone deeper and made it worse. He lay on his back in the shallows of the river hoping to soak it out or soothe it but this did no good either. If he had known where his mother was, he would have gone to her and bade her lick away his hurt but it had been a long time since he had seen her in the woods and he suspected she was dead and anyway he began to understand that nothing – not even the healing tongue of his mother – could release him from the pain.

He plunged through the woods squalling his rage at what he could not abide but also could in no wise escape. In his frenzy he pushed down small trees and tore the bark off bigger ones with his claws. He uprooted laurel brakes. He dashed to pieces the blown-down logs that he would ordinarily probe with delicate care for insects on which to dine. He caught rabbits and ground squirrels and crushed them in his jaws but spat them out and did not consume them.

Near the top of Where the Water-Dogs Laughed he took the life of an Ancestor who was in a gang of Ancestors that were killing the world but it was because he did not like the smell of the Ancestor and not because of the war he had once been fighting. He broke into the camps of the Ancestors and destroyed many of their things and killed more of their beasts but this was not because of his war either. Not any more. He had forgotten his war. Instead, because of the pain he could neither endure nor lose, he had begun to make war against everything.

The weather grew warm and the hardwoods of the forest put forth their clothing of leaves and the flowers bloomed and the deadfalls swarmed with ants and larvae and under patches of *fern the fat salamanders drowsed and there were woodchucks scuffling in their burrows and the blueberries waxed plump in their thickets but Yan-e'gwa did not notice. All he knew was the stone of pain which grew old and more round and harder but never quieted. Sometimes he seemed to remember that he had some mission, but the memory was dim and fleeting and did not tell him what the mission was; and soon even the faint memory quit coming at all and that was the end of his plan to keep the Ancestors from killing the world and to restore the forgotten covenant between his kind and theirs.*

Finally the pain took away every one of his old memories and all of the thoughts he used to think. It even took away whatever was his power to think at all. He did not know who he was or remember that he and the Ancestors were kin. He did not recall that winter day on the peak of Where the Water-Dogs Laughed when the Split-Noses turned him and he fought them in the snow. Nor did he recall the Ancestor who had hurt him with the loud stick; nor the other Ancestor either, the one whose fear he had smelled and pitied that other day in the gap and then again on the bald in the snow. He no longer knew the songs his mother had taught him while rocking him in her arms in their cave den by the river. He did not know that he had ever had a mother.

Nothing was in him now but endless pain and the rage born of that pain. He dashed through the forest breaking down everything before him. All the small beasts fled from him in terror. From far away the creatures in other places heard his roars echoing across the steeps of Where the Water-Dogs Laughed and trembled at the sound of him.

Though Captain Moore had inspired in him a mighty zeal to rush to Dad right directly and demand permission to pledge his troth to Lillie Carter, Will was wise enough to know he must tread carefully and await the most propitious time. Not that he believed for a minute that Dad would ever be inclined to favor his suit; no, Dad would be opposed no matter when or how the notion came up.

But like anybody, Dad had a temperament that was changeable; he wasn't always mulish. Moods would sometimes come on him that softened his nature. They came rarely but they did come. Then he was as open to reason as he ever got. It wasn't much of an opening – more like the slit of a trout's gill, and mighty hard to aim at – but it was there if you knew how to recognize it, as Will had learned to do.

So whenever the next such mood struck, that would be Will's one chance and he steeled himself to make the best use of it he could. Everything would depend on how well he made his case. Or cases. For there were two. First he had to get Dad to agree he was even fit to wed Lillie at all, bad blood or no. Then he had to convince him they needn't wait till Will was of age but could marry any time they wanted, sooner rather than later.

Either possibility looked as unlikely as the moon turning to a ball of lard. Will quailed before the challenge. He'd never yet felt entitled to stand up to Dad over anything important – was still ashamed of having sent Grandad to speak for him last fall. He wasn't certain he had it in him to do it now. One thing was sure; there'd be no second chance.

So he thought and thought about what he'd say. He went to Dad's unabridged dictionary and looked up the best words he could find. Night after night in his garret under the gable he composed the speech in his head, changing and shaping and refining it as he found newer and better words. In the meantime he damped down the eagerness Captain Moore had kindled and summoned up his patience to wait for one of those milder moods to arrive, all the while clinging fast to the new resolve the Captain's fine words had put in him. Especially he cleaved to the notion that had come to him on his way home from the Captain's talk – that a man's blood wasn't good nor bad by descent but was whatever he wanted to make of it.

He had a long wait. The work of plowing and planting had aggravated Dad's rheumatism and laid him up crippled and since he was far from a graceful sufferer – for all his preachments about fortitude and moral fiber and the virtues of self-denial he was actually one who loved and savored every bodily comfort – the aching of his joints seemed to him an affliction nearly insupportable. Constantly he bewailed it, forgetting how he had denounced others for their want of the sturdy faith of Job.

It would have surprised his admirers in the congregation at Chestnut Grove to hear how he whimpered and whined and made the sobbing noises usually associated with a fretful child while Maw bade him chew ginseng root and celery stalks and dosed him with teas boiled from goldenseal and barbell and witch hazel. They'd be shocked worse were they to hear how he snapped at Maw and vilified her by way of thanks for the tender nursing she gave him. She suffered her own ailments, some maybe worse than his, but if the corns on her feet hurt till she limped or the hay fever troubled her so bad she could hardly breathe or if her own bones were inflamed or she had the sore throat from her bad tonsils, she never uttered the least complaint; nor did Dad take any notice of her ills but only kept book on what he insisted were her failings of duty to him.

Will had learned to love Dad just as he remembered his mama had taught him he must. It had taken him a long time and it had been a lot of toil but he'd done it. Still, when Dad took sick, that was when it was hardest to keep the love up. For weeks Dad lay on his daybed plucking at the edges of the afghan that covered him, sobbing and complaining, snapping at Maw and Will as irritably as a cur with a briar in its paw – save of course on Sundays when miraculously he would rally and rise from his bed of anguish and drive the buggy out to Chestnut Grove and do his churchly offices hobbling on his cane and wearing a strained smile of forbearance so that everyone could see how bravely he bore his burden.

All that while Will impatiently held his peace. Often he meditated on what the Captain had told him about the valor of the wild old clans and sometimes he got downcast thinking he was a frail and puny sprig of that warrior strain, piddling about as he was, biding his time, waiting for Dad to mend. But he saw no remedy for it. If he owed it to himself and to Lillie to come at Dad straight-on as he'd never come before, it was also true that he ought to come at Dad with respect. For respect was Dad's rightful due. He was worthy of it.

From time to time Will would go to the marble-topped table in the parlor where the big leatherbound Bible lay just as it had lain that first Christmastime long years ago when he was six and his real daddy brought him here to this same room and left him in the care of the strangers he now called Dad and Maw, strangers who had been willing to take him in when his own no longer wanted him. He would open the Bible and draw out the folded paper that always rested there between the pages, the paper that proved how much respect Dad was owed:

NORTH CAROLINA
CLAY COUNTY

To all whom these presents shall come – Greeting.
James M. Cartman having applied by petition to the undersigned Clerk
of the Superior Court of Clay County for the adoption of William

Hannibal Price an orphan child for minority and the said James M. Cartman having satisfied the undersigned that he is a suitable person to have charge of said orphan and an order of the court having been made granting the petition of the same James M. Cartman These are therefore to authorize and empower the said James M. Cartman to take charge of the said William Hannibal Price an orphan and to enter upon his duties as parent of said orphan, during his minority, to the end that the relationship of parent and child may be fully established between said James M. Cartman and said William Hannibal Price agreeable to an order made by the Court.

> *Given under my hand and*
> *Seal of said Court at office*
> *(Seal)   in Hayesville the 23rd day of*
> *December 1889*
> *G.W. Sanderson, Clerk*

Orphan. Parent. He lingered over the words. Even after ten long years and even in the face of all that Dad was and was not, they still struck their pangs deep, the one a bolt of despair, the other a soar of pure grateful joy that was like he imagined his welcome of the Resurrection would be, when at last it came. Orphanhood had been a black abyss into which he had been about to plunge headlong; he could see it gaping before him like the pit of an abandoned well, and just as in a well he knew that when he pitched downward he would be completely and horribly swallowed up and so utterly lost in its deep maw that it would be as if he'd never been born.

But then without warning, in the nick of time, a parent, a real parent – Dad – had saved him from that fate. Saved him from being swallowed by the black pit. How could he ever be thankful enough? Dad had saved his body as surely as Jesus had the power to save his soul, bad blood or no. Praise was due the Savior. Praise, not blame.

You worshiped the power that saved you, you didn't carp and grumble and find fault. You blessed the Savior's name. Oliver Price swore that Dad had adopted Will only because he and Maw were childless and Dad needed a hand to work the place. That Uncle Andy had done the same with Minnie and for the same reason. That love had no part in it. Others said it too. Maybe it was even true.

But if it was, what did that matter? Love wasn't everything. Shelter, food, clothing, a family to be part of – all these weighed on the scales, even if love was absent and no name came with it. Anyway, Maw loved him, he knew that. And Dad, Dad's reasons . . . well, they didn't count. Will's obligation did. You owed thanksgiving when you were saved, without reckoning the whys of the saving. Will had given thanks all his life since. He'd been dutiful, compliant, uncomplaining. He'd blessed Dad's name. Whenever unworthy thoughts had come – and he was human, they did come on those occasions when Dad, as now, fell into foul behavior and tried his patience – he'd banished them; he'd prayed to the Lord to forgive his ingratitude.

Mulling these matters over, Will would slip the paper back into its place and close the Bible. The Bible was so big and heavy it was the work of both hands just to close half of it. He reflected that what he owed Dad felt heavy that way. It felt too heavy to move. Yet he must move it. If he truly wanted to make Lillie Carter his betrothed and in his own time, he had to move it. But he couldn't help wondering if he was wrong – sinful – to try to shift that weight. Thanksgiving, gratitude, obedience were his foremost habits. To go against Dad felt so much like betrayal that his stomach rolled over in nausea whenever the notion came.

But there was that other word the paper used. *Minority*. All these years he'd tried not to hold it too much in mind and if others spoke it he'd made shift to shut it out. But sometimes it wouldn't be stilled. Sometimes it tolled in his head like a big bell. *Minority*. Yes, like the Clerk of Court's paper said, he was Dad's son and Dad was his father and Maw was his mother and this was his home. But not for always. Only till he came of age. As soon as he turned twenty-one Dad would be quits with him. He'd be free – that was one way to see it. Free to marry or not marry, free to take a job on the railroad as he'd always dreamed, free to get out of Clay County at last, free to wander the great world on his own. Free as he'd never yet been. He longed to taste that freedom.

But something lay deeper than the longing. It lay far down in darkness like a serpent whose fangs were fastened in him sapping away the rapture he might otherwise have taken in the freedom that awaited. It wasn't that he coveted an inheritance, though everyone he knew said he'd earned a fine one. For himself he was indifferent to the goods of this world, though he did wish he could offer something of substance to Lillie and to the children when they came, something to build a future on.

It wasn't even that he wanted the proof of Dad's trust and affection that a legacy might imply – he'd already made his peace with the idea that maybe Dad didn't love the way some did, or easily confer trust. No, the snake that was coiled in the sump of Will's soul was the worst thing he could know – that in five years' time Dad was going to do to him exactly what Ves Price had done. Yet right up to the moment he abandoned him, Dad was going to hold the power to bar Will from all his fondest wishes. And that was the power Will had to break.

◄:

Dad always put in his corn checkerboard fashion, plowing and planting a field both ways – at right angles – so as to save on hoeing. He contended this was the most efficient manner of doing and maybe it was, but Will believed it was also because Dad just admired the pattern of a field planted that way, the rows lined up straight and orderly like soldiers on parade no matter which way you looked to see the crop. And Dad being Dad, he insisted on precision. The rows had to be exactly two and a half feet apart – he'd measure it with a yardstick when Will was plowing – and he'd watch close behind you to make sure you dropped three kernels in each and every hole, no more, no less, and after the seed corn sprouted he'd follow along again to satisfy himself that if three had sprouted, one got pulled up.

His fussy ways galled Will and confounded him and Will was often at his prayers begging God's pardon, but even with the blessings of Heaven over him, Will was always glad when they got done planting. Normally that was when Dad eased off. This year, of course, he'd got the miseries and it was well into summer before he was up and around – and before his temper mellowed and the time got right to approach him.

The way Will knew the time was right was this. One afternoon he and Dad were mending the fence along the lower pasture by the river and as was his custom Dad was using old rails rather than hew out fresh ones. He never disposed of anything outright; he'd use it till it fell apart rather than spend a penny or an hour of extra toil he didn't need to. Naturally some of those old rails were pretty rotten and didn't want to hold a nail, but while Will held a rail in place Dad would pound the nails into the mushy wood anyway. And at every lick he'd give his head a rueful shake. "Ah," he'd say in a mock-sorrowful tone, "it's like driving into a cow pie." And he'd grin and toss Will a sideways glance of mischief. And Will knew.

Will sucked in the biggest breath he could get and feeling his heart thumping in his chest he took his leap – that's exactly what it felt like, like diving off the high limb of the old sycamore that leaned out over the swimming hole downriver by the Sanders Carter place. The same giddy exhilaration with a slippery swooping feel of fear in it. "Dad," he commenced, trying to hold his voice level, "I want to talk to you."

"Hold up another rail," muttered Dad, twisting the words around his mouthful of nails. Will did. Dad hammered. Then he nodded. "What about, son?"

Will lifted another rail, stood a moment holding it crosswise before him. His heartbeat was so loud he was sure Dad could hear it. "About bespeaking Lillie Carter."

Even holding the cluster of tenpennies, Dad's lips twisted in sarcasm. The skin around the edges of his eyes crinkled up. "Aren't you forgetting something? Hadn't you better go and fetch your grandpa?"

The sting of Dad's scorn made Will blush dark red. But he held his peace and stepped to the fence and hefted the rail and put it in place and Dad hammered. Then when Dad had finished hammering Will stood back and took another large breath and told him, "No, Dad, I aim to witness for myself."

Dad spat the nails into the palm of one hand and dumped them into a pocket of his overalls and swiveled himself around mighty lively for a man recently bedridden with the rheumatism and sat down with his rump in the grass that grew thick under the line of the fence. Idly he juggled the hammer back and forth between his big blacksmith's hands. His denim-hued eyes peered narrowly up at Will twinkling as if he were greatly amused. "That'll be a change, won't it?" he drawled in that same mocking way. "Well, go ahead on. I'm interested to hear what you think you can say that'll change my mind."

Will gulped down some more wind and waited till he was sure of his voice. He hadn't expected Dad to tease and tweak at him in this sly fashion. But whatever Dad essayed, Will had resolved to hold himself steady, though he realized he'd forgotten all the fancy words he'd looked up in the dictionary and couldn't recall a single sentence of the speech he'd so painstakingly composed.

Instead he bent an earnest look on Dad and confessed, "I don't figure I *can* change your mind. Not by arguing at you." Then he motioned toward the pile of rails and Dad tipped his head in permission and Will moved some of the rails around till they were set firm enough to hold him and took a seat; and he and Dad sat facing one another in the weedy corner of the fence.

"Well, at least you've learnt that much," Dad remarked, mopping his bald dome with a handkerchief. The day was hot and they had no shade but he looked to be enjoying himself in spite of that. "I declare, I don't know what's got into people's heads of late. You know who came to me the other day exhorting me to provide for you? My own brother, that's who. Yes, your Uncle Andy, he came to speak to me on your behalf."

That puzzled Will. He couldn't imagine Uncle Andy doing that –
Uncle Andy who'd promised Sister a miserly dowry of a hundred dollars if and when she ever found a husband. He surmised Minnie might
have gone to Aunt Samantha and won her over – Sister liked to torment
him about Lillie being plain but he knew she favored the union – and if
she'd done that, then he reckoned Aunt Samantha might have gone to
Uncle Andy in her turn and inspired him to take up the cause. Next time
he saw Sister he'd ask. But just now all his mind was on Dad.

"Everybody likes you," Dad was saying, stuffing the handkerchief inside his shirt. He resumed tossing the hammer back and forth
between his hands. His air of biting humor was fading now and in its
place Will thought he sensed something harder and darker coming
in, something that felt near to an envious dislike. Never before had
he apprehended such a thing and it shocked him to feel it now. "Everybody takes an interest in you," Dad went on with a cutting edge
in his voice. "Folks praise your singing; 'I love to hear Will sing
that Christian Harmony', they say. Or they say, 'I love how Will
tells those funny tales.' Or they say, 'That Will, he's a mighty good
son to you, Uncle Jimmy.' Or your grandpa comes to me in the office of a marriage broker. Brother Andy wants me to settle my estate
on you. Even Cousin Lillie . . . "

Will was startled to hear that name. "Lillie?"

Dad bobbed his head and the edges of his face hardened. In her
case it was clear that he felt himself betrayed. "Yes, even Cousin Lillie,
she's come urging me to do right by you." He gave a scoffing laugh.
"Whatever that means. I wonder what it means?" He leveled a cold eye
on Will. "Do *you* know what it means?"

Will met the look mildly but without a waver. "I reckon you've
done right by me already."

Fiercely Dad nodded. He slanted his look aside and sat staring off
across the pasture, the hammer dangling loose in one hand. There was a
silence and in it they heard the shrilling of the jarflies and the distant
cawing of crows. Then Dad stirred and dropped his gaze to the hammer
and examined it as if he saw it for the first time and wondered how it had
come there. "Well, I reckon I have," he agreed, and for a second or two
he seemed flushed with what seemed vindication; he colored and grew
stern but then his manner changed again and he seemed no longer triumphant nor envious nor angry either but only wistful, even sad. "I'm glad
to see you know it," he finished in a murmur.

"Anyway," Will continued, "I don't care about any legacy. What's yours is yours to do with as you like. That's not what I want to talk about."

Wearily Dad sighed. "I know what you want to talk about." A flash of resentment came over him. "The same thing you sent your poor old grandpa to beg when you didn't have the gumption to beg me yourself." Then as quickly as it had surged, the annoyance passed and he seemed jaded and sorrowing again. "And you've got my answer. It's the same answer it's always been. You're Ves Price's boy. I don't care how much folks love you and extol you and carry on about what a sweet-natured soul you are, I don't care how fair you sing your shaped-note music or what entertaining tales you tell, you're still Ves Price's boy and my feeling is, if you marry into quality, you'll ruin it."

Will went utterly still inside, save for the throbbing of his heart. He was an empty vessel in which Dad's three conditional words *my feeling is* hung suspended like heavy iron balls somehow defying the laws of Creation, implausibly afloat in space. He couldn't fetch a breath though he badly needed to. Disbelieving yet half believing, he leaned at Dad, straining to hear confirmed what he dared not hope would come next.

"The blood's in you," Dad went on, but now as if to resume his old harangue about the blot on the name of Price; and Will's hopes started to dim even before they were fairly born. Maybe he'd heard wrong; he must have misunderstood; there'd been no condition after all. Dejected, he hung his head. The will of God often seemed harsh but was always for the best. "It's not your fault, it may even be a shame, but it's the truth," Dad went on. "The blood's in you and it'll tell. One day it'll tell and you'll go wrong, unlikely as it may seem now, as we all look upon your shining innocent face." He scowled and cast the hammer aside into the weeds. "And my question's this: What's the rush anyway? When you're twenty-one you can do as you want whether I approve or not. Pity though it be. Calamity though it be. Then you can wreck the fine old family of Judge Madison Curtis and I can't do a blessed thing about it."

Will could see how he'd hurt Dad and he was sorry for it. But he couldn't relent, not even now when he knew his case was hopeless. He'd promised Lillie; he'd promised himself. He tried to recall the brave words of Captain Moore. He gave Dad a lingering, searching look. "We don't want to wait, Dad. We want to get engaged now. And we want to marry as soon as we think it's right."

"Well," Dad grumbled, "I'm sufficiently acquainted with the ways of this world to know what a lively boy and a willing girl with the fires of youth in 'em are apt to do. And nothing I or anybody else can say or do'll change it either." He sighed. "Nor do I want to be the author of –

what-you-may-say – of a mortal sin on account of my obdurance."
Now Will's spirits bounded up anew – he was growing giddy from
riding the highs and lows of his hopes as Dad talked on, first seeming to
encourage, then to chide – but this time he counseled himself to be
wary, to be patient, to wait and listen. He watched Dad, expectant,
trying to guard against being cast down one final time.

"I'll repeat," said Dad, "my feeling is that you ought not marry
Cousin Lillie, soon or late or ever. I'm convinced you bear the seed of
decline in you. But I've been pondering on it. Been pondering and
tusseling. Wrestled with it as Jacob wrestled with the Angel. I've talked
to Lar about it. I've been on my knees to the Most High and I've prayed
so hard I've sweat drops of blood just like the Lord Jesus did in the
Garden of Gethsemane. And what's come of it is this – I'm going to bow
to the opinions of those who insist you're not as I believe you are." Will
moved not a muscle. Each new word Dad uttered fixed another ball of
iron in the void within, to join the others that still hung there eerily and
impossibly afloat.

"Now I want you to listen and hear what I say," said Dad. "I've
not changed my opinion about you. I think you'll fail at whatever you
do. Not because you want to; no, you'll *try* to do right. You'll try hard,
I give you that. I know how hard you try; it pains me to see it. But you'll
fail. You'll quit because – what-you-may-say – because it's in you to
quit. If you marry Cousin Lillie, or if you get this farm, or even if you
leave here and go off and join the railroad like you've longed to do –
whatever you attempt, you'll quit it in the end. Because that's what's in
you. Quit is what's in you.

"Others say different – Brother Andy, your grandpa, Cousin Lillie,
even Lar, folk at church, all my friends and neighbors. They love and
trust you. Bless his betrothal, they say. Make him your heir, they say.
All right, all right, maybe I'm wrong. I don't believe it, but maybe I am.
Maybe it's possible. But that's not why I'm doing this. No, sir. I'm
doing it because I can't *not* do it. Not any more.

"I have to live in this community. People look up to me. I'm a
beacon of the spirit. Should the folk think me unfair to you, or cruel, or
selfish, or any such – to you that they cherish so – why, they'll start to
doubt the goodness of my heart. They'll lose faith in me. I can't have
that. Rather than that, I'll let you wreak your damage. Then, when you've
done that – failed, quit, run off, whatever scoundrelly thing you do –
they'll know I was right all along. Then – " His chin jutted fiercely.
"Then they can reckon up the cost of their misjudgment.

"But for now, I concede to them. And to you. So I'm going to make you a – what-you-may-say – a proposition. I do this with woe and regret, for if I'm right about you – about what's *in* you – then it's a proposition to my detriment and I'll rue it all the balance of my life. But if by some unlikely chance I'm wrong about you, if in fact you're the fine Godly boy everybody says you are and you'll grow to be a fine Godly man, then this proposition will benefit us both. For it'll provide me and Lar a great service – I'll explain it in a minute – and . . . well, it'll give you what you want – the right to bespeak Cousin Lillie and wed her. Bespeak and marry her whenever you say."

He paused. Cows lowed in the distance and somewhere a dog was monotonously barking. On his pile of rails Will did not stir as much as a hair. For all the ugly things Dad had been saying, still by a miracle it seemed Will was on the cusp of gaining his goal and his senses reeled to imagine it. But a certain shrewd look had crept over Dad as he spoke and Will had seen the look and dreaded it and so he tried hard to hold himself back from the joy he wanted to feel.

"We'll each make a pledge, you and I," Dad said. "I'll pledge to give you an inheritance – after Lar, everything I have'll be yours. And I'll give my blessing to your union with Cousin Lillie. Give it here and now, without any condition or compromise."

Will was afraid to ask but must. He drew a last long breath. "And my pledge to you?"

"As I am, I've naught to succor me when old age comes. I'll falter and fail in my dotage, for it's God's plan that all shall weaken and die. Your pledge to me'll be that as long as the two of us live, Lar and me, you'll stay by us. And care for us, even before your own. And the gamble I take is that you're not the son of your father after all – that you're man enough to make that pledge and honor it, swearing before the Almighty."

Will didn't hesitate. "I make the pledge," he said. "And I swear before God to honor it." And that was how his prayers were answered.

Uncle Jimmy lived another fifty years. Will married Lillie Carter in 1902 – when he was nineteen, not twenty-one – and they had eight children and Will proved himself a good husband and father and a fine provider. He rented a piece of farmland and every evening after finishing his own chores he drove his wagon the three miles over to Uncle Jimmy's and worked that place too. In 1928 Uncle Jimmy sold him a plot of land near the home place and Will was able to build his own house. He and Lillie cared for Uncle Jimmy and Aunt Laura in their declining years. His whole life long Will revered Uncle Jimmy. He never allowed any of his children to speak ill of him. Uncle Jimmy died in 1948. The inscription on his tombstone reads, *"He died as he lived – a Christian"*. Will lived only three years more. He died just before Christmas in 1951.

A month earlier, Ves Price had passed away in Los Angeles, California. He was ninety-two.

Chapter Fifteen

Corntassel's place looked the same but different too. The difference wasn't anything obvious, it was the sum of a few small things. The whitewash still shone, the frames of the windows and door were just as blue, the same Indian doohickeys hung from the jambs and lintel. The sun gleamed as brightly on the tin roof.

But at the edge of the dooryard where Hamby had drawn rein, the grass – normally so neatly mowed – came to the fetlocks of Captain Moore's loaned mule. The oilskin curtains were drawn to. Behind the cabin the corn stood high but choked with leafy weeds. The doorstone had not been swept. There were only four or five old half-rotted chunks of poplar in the woodpile.

Frowning, Hamby stepped down, gave the reins a couple of turns around the lower limb of a young buckeye tree and crossed to the doorstone and knocked.

From within came the choking bark of Cattywampus Dog, then after a few moments Corntassel's voice, unnaturally weak and quailing, "Come". He pushed in the door and entered.

A fetor of shit and old vomit smote him, so foul he had to cup a hand over nose and mouth. Because of the drawn curtains the room was dim and at first he couldn't distinguish a thing; then Cattywampus Dog came scuttling to him out of the gloom and he sank to one knee and the poor deformed beast crowded against his leg and commenced to shake and whimper and lick his palm and from the dark Corntassel said in that same whispery way, "That you, McFee? You'd best not come near. Reckon I got the typhoid."

Hamby nodded. He knew the odor. "You stink like it," he answered. His only thought was, *This what come next*. It struck him how fast things could change. One minute he was running an ordinary errand and the next he was plunged deep in the smell of dying. He remembered something he'd heard a preacher say a long time ago: *In the midst of life we are in death*. He had no use for preachers and couldn't recall why he'd even been listening to one – maybe it was a chaplain during the war and he hadn't had a choice – but anyway those words had stayed with him because he'd thought they sounded true. They were true enough now.

The old man gave a cackle that sounded like a sick pullet clucking. "Never did smell none too good."

"Well, whatever you smelt like before, you done topped it now." Hamby rose from petting the dog and started to the bed. The dog came sidling after.

"Stay away," Corntassel quavered. "You'll catch it."

Hamby grunted and came on. "Hell, what *ain't* I caught?" At the bedside he looked down on the small figure shivering under a grimy quilt and even in the bad light he could see the yellowish eyes unnaturally bright, the wizened face greasy with fever sweat framed by a mass of lank white hair. The stench welled up over him. "How long you be like this?"

The old man coughed and it sounded like somebody rattling pebbles in a gourd. "Eight days, ten. Can't say for sure." He made a vague gesture with one claw of a hand. "I'm all swimmy- headed."

"Shit," said Hamby. Cattywampus Dog was still leaning against him and he had to step over the critter to go to the windows. He drew back the curtains and propped the windows open, flooding the room with light and letting in some welcome draughts of air. The dog trailed behind creeping sideways. It was sounding a high whine like a whistle. Hamby was mad. He turned back from the windows, demanded, "Where that Sanders Carter supposed to look after you?"

"He's down with it too," the old man wheezed. "And Miz Martha. And all their get."

So it was a contagion. Somebody's bad water had bred it in the summer heat. Corntassel, the Carters, the Cartmans, next the whole goddamn valley; he thought at once of Carter's Cove – Tom Carter's place – and of Miss Becky's gal, of Lillie Dell. A cold rod of fear probed at the pit of his gut. *Damn*, he thought. *Goddamn*.

Corntassel hawked up a gob of matter and rolled his head over the side of the bed and spat it on the floor – a sin against his neatness that was a measure of his pitiful state. Hamby noticed the dog didn't go for the Indian's spittle the way it was always going after his. Corntassel rolled his head back and looked at Hamby with his too-shiny eyes. "What you doing here?"

Hamby came to the bed again and Cattywampus Dog followed along still making that whistling sound. "Tell you later," said Hamby. "Right now, I be fixing you."

He threw aside the quilt and opened his mouth so as not to take into his nose the stench that surged up so vile it almost had the force of a physical blow. He unbuttoned the old man's vomit-encrusted shirt and exposed the bony form. He'd been sick more than any eight or ten days. He was scalding hot to the touch. He was drenched in sweat and shivered and jerked with spasms. The skin hung on him like a drapery of flimsy cloth. His tongue was as dry and brown as a strip of burnt bacon. He was naked below the shirt and in its sparse nest of white hairs his peter had shriveled to the size of an acorn but his balls were still as big as walnuts though they did lie slack and forgotten. The manful parts were another thing that could be mighty precious one minute and useless as a turd the next. Corntassel's old shit that was caked on the bedding around him was pea green but the newer stuff had blood and tissue in it and on the coppery hue of his chest and belly the rose spots had already come and gone leaving their telltale rust-colored blemish.

"I've got bad gripes in my belly," Corntassel confessed, like he was ashamed of it. Hamby felt. Sure enough, there was a big squashy swelling down there on the right side. Hamby hunkered and took thought. The fact the old man had puked and there were bits of gut in his stool meant his bowels had started to go to pieces and the blood poisoning had got in him. There wasn't a thing in the world to do but try to make him easy.

Hamby felt sorry for himself, thinking what he was in for. He sighed. *This what I get for opening my big mouth to them Middletons.* He dragged a footstool to the bed and sat on it. The dog sat too, hindforemost beside him. It kept on with its whistling whine. Over its shoulder its pretty eyes watched up at him with a pleading look.

Corntassel grinned out of a face that already resembled a skeleton's. "I'm a goner, ain't I?"

"Naw," Hamby scoffed, "ain't nothing wrong with you. You just be slacking."

Again the old man made his weak cluck of a laugh. "That's right. Got tired of tending that corn. Pulling them suckers off that 'baccy."

"When fall come, you be hunting bear. You and this ugly goddamn dog." What had at least been barely possible when Hamby rode up – the very reason he'd come – was now as remote from this world as the farthest star in the heavens. The Middleton boy that worked for Weatherby had come to camp asking if anybody knew the Indian on Downings Creek that claimed to have the wisdom of bears and Hamby'd said he knew him and it was true the old man boasted he'd killed many a bear with his charms. Go and fetch him, Middleton had said, tell him there's a hundred dollars of Weatherby's money in it if he guides Weatherby to this bear that killed Boatwright. Hamby had surmised the old man would never do it – he knew Corntassel's heart had changed toward the bears and he hadn't forgotten the tales the old man had told him or what he'd said about what bears were. But going down to ask him was a chance to get away from camp and Middleton had paid him a dollar and a half to do it and he'd gone. Now look at the fix he was in. He shook his head, disgusted.

Corntassel regarded him shrewdly. "Come fall," he croaked, "I'll be feed for the worms. You know that."

"What you got," Hamby remarked, "I be a worm, I wouldn't want no bite of you." They both laughed then, the old man making a dry noise like sandpaper rubbed against itself. Hamby blew out a resolute breath. "All right," he concluded, "I gots to clean you up. And feed you some eats." To himself he secretly spoke every cuss word and blasphemy he could think of.

He lifted Corntassel from the soiled bed and the old man felt so slight in the cradling of his arms that he might have been a bolster stuffed with feathers. He was raving now, sometimes in a strange tongue that Hamby took for Cherokee. Or maybe it was only the wordless babble of a fevered brain. Hamby bore him to the hearth and laid him on the bearskin there and covered him with the cleanest blanket he could find. He took a coon pelt from the wall and rolled it up and put it under Corntassel's head for a pillow. Then he fetched a bucket and went outside to the well and pumped it full and brought it in and held a dipper of water up to the old man's mouth and he lapped at it daintily like a cat.

There was no food in the house save some old canned goods, so Hamby pried open a tin of beans with his buckhorn knife and struck a fire in the fireplace and heated the pot of beans over it, then mashed up the beans so they'd be easier to chew and fed them to Corntassel in pinches held between his fingers. The old man ate but little. The dog sat with its back to them watching them over its shoulder. It had stopped its whistly whine but occasionally it would shudder so hard it nearly toppled over. Presently Corntassel fell into a delirous stupor and

Hamby gave the dog the rest of the beans and poured it a dish of water and it fed and drank with a desperate greed and after a time it quit its shaking.

After that, Hamby stripped the bed and tossed the bedding into the dooryard. Next he undressed the old man, lolling him from side to side so limp he might have been dead already save that he kept on with his mumbling and muttering. Hamby threw the soppy shirt outside onto the pile of bedding. He heated a pot of water on the fire and took a rag and wiped the old man clean. All of Corntassel's bones stuck out sharp under his loose and waxy skin. No sooner would Hamby dry him off than the fever-sweats would spring out on him and run again like streamlets. Convulsions made the old man jerk and twist under his hands like some animal trying to get loose. After a time, though, Corntassel slept. He slept so sudden and so deep that Hamby thought he might've died, but he leaned an ear close and heard him give a faint breath. He got up then and went about pulling the other furs off the walls and dressed the bed with them and covered them with a quilt and then carried the old man back and laid him in the mounded softness of them and spread the blanket over him. Cattywampus Dog scuttled crabwise to and fro, following his every move.

It was evening then. He went outside and unsaddled the Captain's mule and turned it into the pasture where it could graze – he'd rub it down directly. He checked the chicken coop and the hens all looked moulted and bedraggled from neglect and two were dead and the rooster was down and gasping, ready to die. He turned the hens out and found the feed and fed them. He twisted off the rooster's head and hung him by the feet from the lintel – they'd have him to eat tomorrow – and he threw the dead ones on the heap of stuff in the dooryard and set a match to the whole of it.

He settled on the doorstone and lit his pipe and smoked and watched the fire. *Gots to cut some wood*, he reminded himself. A siege of coughs shook him, he spat blood. The dog came and licked it up and then leaned against him and laid its head sideways on his lap. Dark came on.

Hamby had dragged the bed across the room and set it catercorner to the fireplace where Corntassel, who was freezing and burning up by turns from the raging of the fever, could at least get a spell of comfort when the chills took him. Hamby sat by him in the same old barrel chair he'd used when he came back from the war and old Daniel welcomed him like the prodigal returning home and fed him cold squirrel meat and pone and called him son. That time he'd slouched in the chair sulled up the whole time, thinking himself a grander man than Daniel for keeping his resentment hot while Daniel was letting his cool. It made him a touch sad to think of that. He'd thought the chair hellish hard on his bottom then. Now it felt good to sit in. When he was at Corntassel's before, he hadn't been able to see a thing he remembered in the old place save the fire-dogs. Now there was this chair that Daniel had made with his own hands.

He smoked and reflected. Cattywampus Dog was at his feet in a tortuous tangle, softly snoring. The old man lay partly on his side gazing into the flames. Just now the pangs of the sickness had lulled. He roused and spoke. "You never did say why you come."

Hamby grunted. "That Weatherby, he hear tell you a heathen witch-doctor, hunt bear by some goddamn Injun voodoo. Want to hire you." He cackled a scornful laugh. "Pay you a hundred dollar if you take him out to fetch that bear with you magic root or whatever shit you use. Gone make you red ass rich. That oldest Middleton boy sent me to ask you."

The old man coughed into a curled hand. "Which bear is that?"

"You know which," Hamby said, shooting him a look. "Only one they is, any more. That killer bear."

Corntassel's head moved in a small nod. "I done told you somewhat of that-'un."

"I know you did. I remember. Visitation, you say." Hamby took his pipe from his teeth and leaned and spat blood into the fire and chuckled. "Jesus and the Devil all roll up together."

A tremor passed through the old man and he gathered the blanket closer around him. His eyes were bleared and his voice but a wisp of itself yet his features had sharpened with interest. "You believe me? What I said of him? Of him and of all the bears?"

Hamby puffed volumes of smoke. He shrugged. "Can't say as I'm believing all *that* shit. I remember it, is all."

"What *do* you believe?"

"Me? Hell, I don't believe nothing. This child ain't the believing kind. But I *do* wonder."

A bolt of pain struck Corntassel's middle and his features twisted into a knot of wrinkles and he doubled up with his knees almost to his chin, drawing the blanket askew. But he clamped his mouth tight and kept himself from crying out and only uttered a low husky groan. The sweat was rolling off him in drops the size of gold dollars. There was a certain kind of river clay Hamby'd seen that was the same whitish-gray that the old man's face now had. But in a moment Corntassel lay back and took a series of ragged breaths and quieted. Tidily he rearranged the blanket that his contortion had disturbed. Then he asked, "What d'you wonder then?"

Hamby scowled, remembering. "Sorry piece of white trash working hisself up to kill my ass, up there in that Middleton camp. Even tried it one time. Done his best to put my light *out*. Crazy-mean son of a bitch. Want to kill me, kill that bear too. Stand in the woods and holler for that bear to come. Brag how he gone kill it. Kill it and fuck it after it dead. Toted a pistol to shoot it with.

"One day that bear come just like he bid it do. Bust out of the woods, straight at him. Tore his ass flat *up*. Ate his face. Single him out, didn't mess with nobody else. And all them others walloping, trying to drag it off. So I wonder. Be hard to say what I wonder. But I do." He hesitated, unable to frame words that were right enough to say what he felt. "Seem like . . . like we come together someway," he stammered on, "this bear and me. Like . . . hell, I don't know." His own confusion balked him.

The old man eyed him slyly. "He taunted Yan-e'gwa."

"What you mean? Who did? What that name?"

"Yan-e'gwa," Corntassel answered. "The Great Bear – that's the way the white man'd say it. It's his Cherokee name. He's all the bears in one. That feller taunted him. Yan-e'gwa reckons to be hunted, even to be feared and hated; but he's due some honor for what he be. For he's all the bears, you see. That's why he come – to *be* them. To insist on what's owed 'em. But he can't forget he's us too. He's them *and* he's us. We're his kin."

The old man spoke till his wind ran out and his voice dwindled to no more than a faint rustle. He fell silent and lay panting and Hamby could tell he meant to go on when he was able and so said nothing, just sat smoking and watching the fire, waiting him out. He thought maybe Corntassel was going out of his head again.

The fire popped and crackled and made its searing sounds and somewhere outside they heard the hoot of an owl. The dog lay coiled on the hearth in fretful slumber and sometimes it let out a low squeak. Then the old man stirred and resumed, his talk as hushed and reedy as river cane stirring in a breeze. "You recollect how I told you before in my tale that the bears come of us?"

Hamby nodded.

"But we've forgot," Corntassel went on, "and he aims to teach us to remember – if we'll learn. In his heart he means us no mortal harm. He didn't kill ary soul, not till this-'un that taunted. He only ruint goods and kilt dogs and stock. And when Weatherby and them turned him that time on the bald, why, he hurt 'em, yes; but he never kilt, did he? And Lord knows he could've."

The old man stopped again to gulp for air. He was atremble with chills now. He hugged the blanket close. His mouth worked like the mouth of a fish will do when you pluck it from the water. Some of what he was telling sounded like the raving of the fever. But some didn't. Hamby knit his brows together, looked down at him, remarked, "By what you say, ain't a thing 'tween me and this bear then, 'spite my wondering."

Corntassel wagged his head on the coonskin pillow – a mighty spry move for his condition – and his voice got edgy with impatience. "Didn't say that. No, sir. They's plenty betwixt you."

"Howso?"

The old man held still again for a long space. More convulsions ran through him and he suffered several more seizures of the gut that drew him up into a ball and made him rock from side to side giving out small croons and bleats that were almost prim, he tried so hard to quell them. After that he worked on getting his wind back. His sides whipped like the flanks of a greyhound after a long run on a hot day. He sweat torrents. His color got paler and paler, went from that clay tint to the hue of dingy chalk. Hamby waited, blinking at the sting of the smoke backing up into the room from the bad flue.

Finally the old man was ready. His words came so soft they might have been so many pinfeathers drifting out. "When I talked of Yan-e'gwa before, I said he didn't act according to the nature of a bear. I didn't have the right sight then, though. Now I've got it. Your regular bear's timid, seldom lashes out. Yan-e'gwa lashed out. I took that for wrong behavior as bears go. Thought him a visitation on account of the wrongness. But now I see different. The visitation is, he's us and them both. He's the bear and the man together. Not one come from the other, but both joined in the same body and spirit."

He raving now for sure, Hamby thought. *Hell, let him. Why not? Hocus-pocus, mumbo-jumbo, maybe it soothe him when his mind run like that.*

Once more Corntassel had to wait to muster more of his waning strength. The rasp of his breathing was harsh now, dryer than it was, more coarse, like the grating of a file on a scythe blade. When he was ready, though, he pushed on, the talk coming with more and more effort. "Long time ago all the bears met in council and considered going to war against the men that kilt them without doing them the right honor. But in the end they decided not to, that they was bears and if they took up the ways of men they'd be bears no more. But Yan-e'gwa, he taken up the ways of men. He's a-waging war as men do, not keeping the peace the bears decided on. That's his visitation and his meaning. And it's his dream."

Hamby wagged his head and raised his eyes to the ceiling. *Dreams,* he scoffed. *Visions. We be beating the tom-toms in a minute.*

Still Corntassel went ahead. Something new had come into his speech though. A kind of rhythm, as if he meant to sing or chant or maybe say a poem. It was the same singsong Hamby remembered from before, when the old man had told him the tale of the bears and the tale of himself. "But Yan-e'gwa's sore hurt now," Corntassel intoned. "They say he carries a wound that festers and mortifies. A wound of the head sunk deep. Deep enough to eat away his sense. Yep." He raised up a little at this, he bobbed his head sharply. "I reckon it might've took his wits. It may be his dream's gone or dimmed or fouled somehow and he don't know any more what he's a-doing or why. That he's run plumb mad and the fine purpose he had, to teach us by the war he wages, be lost in the addling. That he's just on a ruction and a rampage no better'n a hydrophoby dog."

He dropped back then, weak and shaky. The lyric pace of his talk faltered, he was fighting now for every breath. But he wasn't going to stop. "Think how he done you the favor of taking off this taunter," he said, "that taunted you too and aimed to kill you just as he aimed to kill Yan-e'gwa. Even if he done it without knowing or intending, still it's a favor. Or if he done it part knowing and part rabid and not knowing. So him and you've crossed." The yellow eyes glazed, widened. "I see a figger of things in that, I do. A mighty figger. For you owe back to Yan-e'gwa a favor the size of the one he done you."

Hamby had turned to him as his talk got more and more strange. "Do what?" he blurted, getting testier now. "What favor?"

Pleated lids closed over Corntassel's eyes and Hamby wondered again if he'd gone to sleep or even died, but then he saw the twitching of the eyeballs under the lids and the quivery voice resumed and the old man lay there talking with his eyes shut, the talk spinning out now no longer like pinfeathers but like a thinner and thinner thread. "He give you the favor of your life, that the taunter was fixing to take, didn't he? I expect you owe him back the favor of what he's lost."

Hamby stood and knocked the ashes out of his corncob against the stones of the fireplace and slipped the still-warm pipe into the pocket of his shirt and turned to bend and glare down on the old man who seemed to talk while asleep or dead. He was mad as hell at the words he'd heard but he didn't know why they irked him so. "What you mean?" he stormed at him, loud enough to startle Cattywampus Dog awake. It clambered to its feet and looked warily up at Hamby with its cranked head, its nub of a tail trying to wag but afraid to. "What I be giving back?" Hamby hollered into the gnarled face with the hooded eyes.

"Why, his dream," answered Corntassel.

Hamby swore. He straightened and stomped away to the door and then came stomping back. He stood over the old man wanting to snort like a bull. But he wasn't as riled now as he pretended to be. Something was sneaking into him, some question winding like a snake. "You the one lost his goddamn sense, not no bear," he blustered to hide it. "How in hell I do that?"

Corntassel held silent for so long Hamby feared a third time that he'd drowsed or passed on, till he saw the old man's bony chest rise and saw the throb of a twisty blue vein in his temple and knew he was only gaining strength for what else he had to say. The same owl hooted in the outer woods and Captain Moore's mule in the pasture answered it with a bray and the fire on the hearth snapped and Cattywampus Dog stood between them looking anxiously from one to the other trying to decide whether or not to wag its stub of tail.

Then Corntassel gave a toss of his shaggy head and opened his eyes and fixed a gaze on Hamby and Hamby felt it against his face like the slap of a bird's wing – a mockingbird guarding its nest had swooped on him once and come too close and had clipped him and that had stung just like this did. The amber eyes shone bright as gems and the voice wasn't trembly and leached-out, it was still frail but this time it was limber and had the narrow crackle of a whip in it. "Listen to me, McFee. You got to listen now. I told you two tales, didn't I? One was about the bear. 'T'other was of you. How you nursed your spite and couldn't get shet of it. Couldn't rid yourself of it even by setting the good of others before your own, like you done with that Ves Price. Your stepdaddy – him that lived in this same house – he done it. Had rancor in him but got to where he could lose it and laid hisself down a sacrifice for them as once owned him a slave. I reckon now you're a-trying hard to see how he done that. For you want to do it too. Life's long – mighty long to parch it all the time with malice and grudgement. Presently now I'm a-going on from this place; and I'm ready to go. Ready for the ease of it. Nor will you be far behind me. You know that, don't you? Knowing it's why you want to learn how he done what you couldn't. You don't want to pass on parched like that cinder."

Hamby couldn't move or form a thought or turn his tongue to

speech. All he could do was listen to the beat of the song or chant or poem that the old man's voice had once more become and know that what he heard was a truth that he'd been wanting to find without ever knowing it was lost.

"I told you I've got the right sight," Corntassel sang at him with a crooked hint of a smile. "Well, I do. And it's give me to see what you want to know. What I see is, you know already. You know but you've let yourself forget. *He* told it to you. Same night he died, he told it. What'd he say?" Corntassel started up partway off the bed. "What'd he say? 'They're family', he said. 'They'd save us; we got to save them.' He saved them Curtises not 'cause they deserved it but 'cause they was folk in peril of their lives and saving them was what was decent to do." He fell back shivering but still sang on. "Now you saved that scamp, sure enough. But you scorned him as you done it. The saving of him was a taste of ashes in your mouth. That same night your stepdaddy died, you run in front of a bullet meant for a white man, one of them Curtises."

Hamby gaped, disbelieving. *How he know?*

"Yep," Corntassel assured him, seeing his shock, "My sight showed that too. You offered yourself a sacrifice. But you held contempt for that Curtis you saved, same as for that scamp. And all your life that's been so, ain't it? You done some good in this world – more'n you'll admit to, I expect – but you despised the doing of it. For by your lights none deserved what you was giving. None save *her*. That youngest gal of old Squire Curtis. You give her all – all but the love of the body. And she give the same back. Lord knows how or why. Hearts set to loving and it's a mystery. It's a sign none can read save them that loves. But here's another truth my sight gives me – that she loved *past* you. Past you to others. To all others in the world. But your favor stopped with her. Loving only her. Keeping yourself apart – "

Hamby wouldn't abide that. Every slur and hurt ever done him on account of who and what he was came over him and he lurched at the old man on his bed and balled both fists and shook them at him in deadly menace. "My goddamn yellow skin keep me apart, you damn old scut!"

At his roar Cattywampus Dog scrambled away in terror to hide in the dark and emit a piteous howl.

"It niggered me," Hamby snarled, "just like your red hide Injuned you."

But Corntassel met the outburst with calm. "Maybe that's so. Maybe it's the blood in us that acts and not us. Maybe we got no say. Maybe it's only the blood and how it's mixed and all that counts is that folk see the mix and mark it. It's hard, I know that. Hard as hell. But I reckon I'm a whole lot more'n any goddamn cracker imagine I be. And I'm satisfied with that. You – well, you can reckon it out any way you want. Anyhow, you got to listen now. You got to give back that favor you got. Give Yan-e'gwa back his dream. I'd do it if I could, but I couldn't even if I was well and not like to perish of this sickness. For I don't owe the debt like you do. The one that's owing has to do it."

Hamby stood back away and opened his hands and looked at them and saw that they were shaking. He felt light of head. Weakly he protested, "You talking nonsense. Damn you nonsense talk. What you driving at?" He sat again and stared emptily at the old man in the bed who seemed to be shrinking more and more the longer he talked, as if the talk were substance and every word of it reduced him more. "What you think you make me do?"

Corntassel gave him a gentle look. "Once I told you every man's got the power to end the world. You remember that? You loathe the world, don't you? Condemn the folk in it? You can't mend a hate that black. Maybe you'd like to, but you can't. Maybe you dread to die like a cinder all parched with hate but you'll do it anyhow, for there ain't no other way. You can't purge the poison out. You can't be what your stepdaddy was. For he saw it's not our place to set in judgment but to put judgment aside and take for kin what folk we can, and leave the rest to the mercy of Whatever Made Us. You can't come to that. Not in the time that's left to you."

He sighed. He was grieving but he was hoping too. Sad and hoping, he smiled. "You hate all the race of men. But my sight tells me you do hold a care for the beasts – the stock that labors in the field and men abuse; and the critters of the wild too, the ones like Yan-e'gwa, that won't bow the neck or grant us rule over 'em. So I'm a-going to tell you how to end this world that you hate and how to end the people in it that you hate too. You can end it by giving to a beast the grace you can't give a man. By giving Yan-e'gwa back his dream. And I'm going to teach you how."

❦

Two days later Hamby rode the loaned mule over to Sanders Carter's. Cattywampus Dog wouldn't come. It wanted to lie on the grave. Hamby found the Carter turnaround full of rigs. One was a Studebaker that he remembered belonged to Oliver Price. It used to be red but it was faded now to the color of a tomato that hasn't got enough sun. There were three more buggies he didn't recognize and then Tom Carter's beat-up old phaeton. Seeing the phaeton made him think of the time he'd come when he'd spied Miss Becky's Lillie Dell on the gallery and turned back to go lie up in the woods and drink blockade rather than stand meeting with her. Now he reckoned she was there in the house nursing her Aunt Martha. Maybe he'd see her, maybe he wouldn't. If he did, he thought he could stand it this time.

He came down the gravel drive between the lines of fence. Some of the horses were still in the traces of the rigs biting at themselves and lashing their tails at the flies and some had been turned out to graze in the meadow before the house where Hamby recalled topping tobacco a long time ago when it was cropland. Some younguns played around the boxwoods and one was up in the big magnolia shade tree hollering down to the others. There was a flat stump where the second magnolia used to be. A pot of flowers was sitting on the stump. A number of dogs bounded about. Some men were squatting on the front steps watching him come. *Let 'em watch*, he thought, *I a sight to see*. Dead man riding a mule, that was him.

He fetched up at the bottom of the tunaround and got off the mule and tethered it to the fence and then climbed up on the top rail of the fence and perched there facing the house. He got out his corncob and tamped it full and fired it and commenced to smoke. This made him cough and he hacked awhile and then spat blood and went back to puffing. The men on the gallery steps watched him and he watched them. The younguns quit their didoes to gawk at him but when he didn't do anything more than just roost and smoke they dismissed him and went back to their playing. One of the dogs ran up and sniffed at the toe of his boot. It was a setter and its silky coat was the same coppery red-gold that Corntassel had been before he sickened and its yellow-amber eyes were almost like his. It sat and looked up at him grinning with its tongue hanging out. It had a swollen tick under one eye. When he didn't stir it lost interest and trotted off. Captain Moore's mule nibbled at the middle rail of the fence. Hamby smoked.

Right in front of him, five or six steps away in the turnaround, was the spot where he'd got shot. More than thirty years ago now. *Like to died that time*. Maybe he should've. Maybe he'd have been better off. Old Daniel, he did die. *He* was better off. Folk thought of him transfigured, a hero or a saint. Giving his life for others not even of his kind. A mighty figger, the old man would say. Hamby thought if he'd have died then, he'd be a mighty figger now too. Instead of what he was – a dead man sitting on a fence with an empty life behind him. He smoked some more. The mule nibbled. The men watched him and he watched back.

After a time one of the men got up and went inside and in another

minute Tom Carter came out. Hamby cursed. He hadn't wanted it to be
him. Tom had got paunchy and his thick beard was shot with gray. He
had the careworn and threadbare look of one who'd been bad-luck poor
all his days. He descended the steps and walked between the boxwoods
nervously rubbing his hands on the sides of his trousers like he was
drying them. Hamby slid down off the fence to meet him.

Tom gave him a short nod but wouldn't fix a look on his face.
Between them stood the ghost of Miss Becky that Tom had wed and
killed with his ill fortune and with the long years of toil he'd forced on
her and Tom saw the ghost too just as Hamby did and at least he had the
good sense to feel ashamed. "Heard you were back," he said in a mutter.
He put his hands in his back pockets and dropped his pale eyes to the
gravel under his feet. "I'd like to've seen you before this," he lied. Bound
to be lying.

Even with her ghost between them, the fool could say that. Even
full of shame as he was and ought to be. Hamby's temper flared. He
wanted to box Tom in the face for saying it. Here was another goddamn
white pretending Hamby mattered, hailing him like a friend. Hell, Hamby
was no friend to Tom Carter or to any of them, nor they to him. He
didn't matter to them save as something to slight and abuse, and in
Tom's case to steal from and spoil all that Hamby had ever held dear.
And they sure as hell didn't matter to him. Let the typhoid take them.
Tomfool Carter most of all. He couldn't figure why they all went to
such a deal of trouble keeping up a sham.

With all this boiling in him he eyed Tom straight-on and talked at
him dry and short, "I come tell your brother his Injun died. I tend him,
bury him when he die." He flicked a thumb toward the Moore mule
where he'd used plowline to fasten the old man's Winchester to one side
of the saddle and the trapdoor Springfield on the other. "Injun give me
that truck. Give me his dog too." He hated to ask what he must, but did:
"Want to know. Can I keep that dog and saddle, them guns?"

Tom brought his look up off the gravel and settled it on Hamby
and Hamby could see the grief in it as well as the shame and knew that
while some of Tom's sorrow was for his brother and his family, much of
it was for the ghost that stood between them and Hamby had to admit
now what he'd understood all along but always wanted to deny, that
Tom Carter had held Miss Becky as dear as he had, and in losing her
had lost what Hamby had lost and maybe even more beyond that. And in
spite of everything some of his own bad grace started to drain down.

"I'll go tell him," Tom said. "But I don't know if he can say. It's
a bad time just now. Fever's here too." He stopped and gazed past Hamby

into the pasture where the horses browsed in high grass. "Sanders's wife passed this morning. And his girl. And two of the boys are fixing to go."

Hamby couldn't help asking, "Which two?"

"Zeb and Virge."

"Which gal?"

"Daisy."

They were all mostly grown now and Hamby didn't know how they'd turned out; but he remembered them as younguns running around like these younguns here in the yard. He sloped his head to one side and considered. Hell, saying a word wouldn't hurt nothing. "I sorry," he said.

Tom nodded, turned then and crossed the turnaround and Hamby was downcast but not surprised when the ghost went with him. Went with the husband. Tom climbed the steps and went in. Hamby got back up on the fence and smoked. While he smoked he reached inside his shirt and rolled between his fingers the smooth oval of blackened wood hanging by its cord there that had once been the carved angel he'd given her and she'd given back on her deathbed. To fly him up to heaven, she'd said. As if he was going to any goddamn heaven.

The men on the steps had quit watching, so he quit too. Instead he watched the Moore mule while it munched on the fence rail. "You, mule," he said. That was a rickety old mule but it had a good gait. The younguns in the yard dashed around squalling. Two of the dogs were humping. Miz Martha, he thought. He remembered the last time he'd come by, looking for work. Miz Martha had wanted to feed him. "Can I give you a bite to eat?" she'd said. She'd looked like a worn-out old lady. *Them Carters, they bad on they womenfolk.* She didn't seem like she was pretending when she wanted to feed him. But she must've been.

◣

Pretty soon Tom came out again and some old gent was with him, silver-haired, gaunt-faced, grinning behind a walrus mustache, hobbling along on a cane made of knobby hickory. There was something familiar about the stranger but at first Hamby couldn't place him. Then he saw how the grin made the old gent's eyes squinch up into two little narrow half-moons and he recognized Oliver Price – Oliver had always grinned that way in the old days, save at the end when he'd left off grinning on account of his second wife dying on him and his boy Ves turning out so ill. Now the old fellow was more tottery and crippled-up than ever; but somehow he'd got his grin back.

Here he came, hurrying ahead of Tom as quick as his bad leg would let him, his eyes squinched up with laughter, one hand stuck out to shake.

"Hidy," he was crowing, "hidy thar, Hamby!" Hamby had little choice but to slide down off the fence and oblige him. The fine-boned shoemaker's hand he took in his paw was big-knuckled with arthritis. "I've been a-missing you!" cried Oliver. "You ort to've come to see me!"

Hamby couldn't think what to say to that, so he just stood there nodding while Oliver pumped his hand and turned to Tom and declared, "Remember when I used to come over to the Curtises' every summer with Miz Henslee and my boys and us and Hamby'd pull the horn-worms off the tobacco?" He'd always called his wife by her widow's name, Hamby didn't know why. Eagerly Oliver glanced back to him. "Wouldn't we, Hamby?" And Hamby kept on nodding. He didn't mind Oliver. As a matter of fact, if somebody was to put him to torture to make him confess the name of a white man he could halfway abide, most likely Oliver would be the one he'd pick.

Oliver burbled on. "Last time I seen Hamby was when – " He stopped then, bridled himself before he went too far; he could glimpse the ghost too, Hamby surmised. " – was the last day I seen my boy Ves," he finished up, completing a pretty neat change of course, Hamby thought. Hamby knew why too. Ves had been there when Miss Becky passed. Yes, Ves Price – sorry goods as he was – had loved Miss Becky. Loved all her life a woman too good even to spit on him. And when she lay on her deathbed he'd come to say her a goodbye. And once he'd done that, he'd vanished. Vanished for good. Had blown away like a dust devil on the wind.

"What ever come of Ves?" Hamby asked. Not that it mattered. He was just making talk for Oliver's sake. If there was a hell he hoped Ves was roasting in it.

"Last we heard he was away out West," Oliver replied with a wistful look. "Colorado. Place called Littleton." Then he brightened. "His boy's here, though. Name of Will."

Hamby was surprised and intrigued; he hadn't known Ves to be married. And with a youngun. Tits on a bull, that was. And running off to Colorado. *Probably be out there robbing banks or stealing cows. Be wearing a kerchief over his face.* What kind of sprout would the damn fool sire? "Ves had a boy?"

"Girl too. Her name's Minnie. Jimmy Cartman adopted Will and Andy adopted Minnie." Damn, Ves had run West leaving his kids in the hands of the likes of the goddamn Cartmans – that was clear without Oliver bothering to say it out loud. Nonetheless Oliver beamed. "Will's bespoke to Tom's daughter," he said. He paused and crossed his hands on the head of his cane; he looked right through the ghost that stood between them and added, "Rebecca's gal, Lillie."

Hamby blinked, wrinkled his brow. Lillie Dell – Miss Becky's Lillie – promised to a son of Ves Price's? Why was old Oliver so happy about that? He was Ves's daddy, he knew what Ves was, had despaired of him, surely he must dread what any offspring of Ves's was apt to be. Better he should be as vexed as Hamby felt himself becoming. Once Ves had crassly coveted Miss Becky; a union of Lillie with his boy sounded just as vile. Hamby flicked an eye to Tom to see how he fared. But Tom was only studying the gravel under his feet again. "Is that so?" Hamby said, rounding back.

"It's so," Oliver proudly attested. "The Prices and the Curtises is marrying up."

Hamby marveled anew. "What this boy of Ves's be like?"

Oliver gave him a smirk. "I know what you're a-thinking. Don't blame you, neither. But if you was to take Ves and turn him inside out, why, you'd have Will. He's all that Ves ain't. As fine a boy as you'd hope to see."

Some of Hamby's ire eased. It might be so; likely old Oliver wouldn't be so pleased if it wasn't. He guessed if this Will was fixing to marry Lillie, it meant Lillie saw some merit in him. And if she was as fine as her mama, she'd have Miss Becky's good judgment. Pretty soon Hamby was going to have to see Lillie Dell; he'd see this boy of Ves's too. And make up his own mind about him. "Jimmy Cartman," he said bitterly. "He still a saint of the Lord?"

"Yep," Oliver laughed. "Still got hold of a Bible in one hand and the first penny he ever made in the other."

At this point Tom raised his head. He wouldn't put a look on them – gazed past them into the pasture as he'd done before – but he wore a dogged expression and Hamby thought maybe the spate of gab about Miss Becky and Lillie and Will and Ves had shaped the ghost all too real before him and had hurt him and prodded him to speak so as to shift the talk to safer ground. "Sanders says you can have the old Indian's place and anything in it you want," he told Hamby. "Corntassel always claimed he never had no family. Anyway, Sanders says the place was yours before it was the Indian's – and your stepdaddy's before that."

Hamby dipped his head. "I be obliged," he mumbled. Tom couldn't make himself stay any longer. He had to go, Hamby could see it. But before he went he shocked Hamby by putting out his hand. For an instant Hamby just stood regarding the hand. Its palm was covered with yellow calluses and the nails were horny and rimmed with black. It was a hard-luck hand for sure. Hamby gave a small nod and touched it and let it go and Tom turned away then and crossed the turnaround and mounted the steps and went into the house and once again the ghost went with him and Hamby was both sad and reconciled to see it go. Of Oliver he inquired, "Miss Lillie. She inside tending her cousins?"

Oliver assented and Hamby sighed. "She not sick?"

"No," Oliver assured him. "She's not sick."

"Good," said Hamby. He unwrapped the reins of the Moore mule from the fence and fitted one foot into the stirrup and swung up and sat his saddle a moment looking down at Oliver, who gazed up at him with a cocked head. The grin was gone now but Oliver still had an air of pleasure and contentment, as if seeing Hamby had really buoyed him up on this day otherwise steeped in sadness. "We had us some grand times back then," he recalled.

Hamby shrugged. "Some grand, some not."

Oliver nibbled at the bottom of his mustache, then gave a little sideways smile that seemed gently to mock how he once was. "I don't study the bad no more," he said. "I did for a long time. But now I find no profit in it."

Hamby gathered his reins and saluted him with a tug of his hatbrim. "I come see you, 'fore I go."

"Where you going?" Oliver wanted to know.

But Hamby didn't answer. He only turned the Captain's mule and kicked it lightly in the ribs and started away up the drive.

Chapter Sixteen

As a husbandman inclined to the old ways Captain Moore might nourish certain misgivings about the benefits of the railroad, but as a provider he knew how to draw a line between his ideals and the hard practicalities of life; like most every other farmer in Clay County who owned a stand of timber he regularly cut crossties and sold them to the agents of the Southern or the Atlanta, Knoxville & Northern.

On the big hill behind the house above the Jack Holler was a fine grove of hardwoods and every wintertime his boys Jim and Charlie would cut trees up there and then during the warm-weather months trim out the ties and stack them; then sometimes they would take a load by wagon over to Murphy and at other times the railroad would send contractors to come and fetch a consignment.

Irish Bill suffered no twinge of conscience to be treating thus with the powers that he thought were ruining the customs of the country. The railroad was a fact – a lamentable one, but a fact all the same. The old ways were going and that was a fact too. A man had to face facts. It did no good to wail and maunder and wring the hands – though he was honest enough to admit he'd done more than his share of that; he reckoned it was the Irish romantic in him and excusable. But the carping didn't change the facts, and another fact was that the railroad paid good money for ties and when a man had a house full of mouths to feed, money weighed heavier on the scales of this world's value than any amount of principled misgiving.

On this particular sultry day in July an agent of the Southern had just paid the Captain seventy-five dollars for his latest two shipments of oak crossties and it was necessary for Moore to ride into Hayesville and deposit the funds in the bank. As a progressive man he was a great believer in the banking system of the country; often he disparaged those timid souls who hid their money in mattresses and kitchen jars lest panics such as that of four years ago wipe out their savings. But it was also true that in secret he harbored a motive far lower and less civic minded: A trip to town to do the banking afforded him an unequaled opportunity for showing off.

So on this humid morning he dressed in his best broadcloth suit and donned his favorite throwing hat – its broad brim made for good sailing – and he took his old Confederate bugle from its peg by the front door and slung it over his shoulder by its braided cord; then he sat on a bench in the shade of the pear tree behind the house and shined his riding boots till they gleamed and after that he polished his old brass cavalry spurs with fireplace ash and buckled them on the boots and strutted around the yard admiring how they twinkled and chimed. He polished up the bugle too, and drew on a pair of yellow deerskin gauntlets that reached to his elbows.

When he thought himself suitably magnificent he returned inside to take his bear rifle from its rack. That killer beast was still raising Cain in the vicinity and if he met it Irish Bill meant to be the one to wind it up. On the back porch he paused with the Winchester in the crook of his arm to refresh himself with a dipper of the spring water that ran live through a wooden trough keeping cold several crocks of butter and jars of milk and cream. The water tasted of the tin of the dipper and of the clean rock and moss and fern that grew around the place yonder on the hillside where it rose. A line of locust poles he'd augured hollow fed it downslope to the trough and the Captain never drank from the trough without feeling a warm burst of pride at the excellence and utility of the arrangement.

His thirst assuaged, he left the porch and crossed to the barn to saddle Dixie and commence his trip. And there at the threshold of the barn he found Nannie crouching on a milking stool wiping away copious tears with a corner of her apron.

Irish Bill was startled. "I thought you were in the orchard helping your mother."

"I was," Nannie miserably replied. She turned up to him a face that was wet and swollen with weeping. "Then I remembered I was supposed to feed Dixie this morning and I came down to do that." A great sob burst out of her and she hid her face in her apron. "But I got afraid again," she wailed.

With a frown Moore set the butt of the rifle on the ground and crossed his hands on the muzzle; his countenance clouded over. "How many times do I have to tell you?" he lectured her. "There's nothing to be scared of. Dixie'll not hurt you. She's not like Crockett. Crockett was a stallion and high-spirited and I admit could maybe hurt you if you surprised him. But Dixie's gentle. Big but gentle."

"A whole lot bigger'n me," Nannie tearfully concurred. "She could step on me by mistake. Or lean against me and squash me like a bug."

The Captain blew out a raspy sigh of impatience. "She wouldn't do that. Did you ever get her fed?"

"I tried," wept Nannie. "I *think* I fed her. Sort of. I think I got some of the corn in the manger."

"What'd you do, child? Stand outside the stall and throw it in?"

"Well . . . I think I got some in."

He glared sternly. "You're fortunate, young lady. It's just as well Dixie's not grain-fed today, since I'm taking her out and she can graze on the way. But next time, you must be a braver girl than you've been this morning. You must go straight in and give Dixie her feed and not be puling and whining about it. I'll not tolerate cowardice in a daughter of mine."

As soon as he said it he was sorry, even before he saw her go pale under the rebuke and give way to a fresh spate of crying. Curse his rash tongue! How unfair to accuse of cowardice a little girl who'd just shown the very essence of courage – attempting to do a thing she dreaded above all else. But he dared not relent now even in the face of his blunder. After all, firmness in a parent was the worthiest virtue; it was the foundation of all discipline. He straightened, cleared his throat. "Now stop blubbering, child," he ordered her, but in a tone somewhat less gruff than before. "Clean yourself up and go on to your mother. Tell her I've gone to town and will be back before dark."

She huddled on her stool hiding her face once more in her apron, sobbing, "I'm sorry, Daddy."

The sight racked him with guilty woe. He knew he was her hero and he had wounded her beyond calculation. What he wanted most in the world just then was to sweep her up in his arms and smother her with kisses and beg forgiveness for his intemperate words. But he could not. Adults must never show weakness before the young lest their faith in the steadiness of grownups be shaken.

"I know you're sorry, child," he assured her. "But you must stop carrying on now. Show me you're sorry not by crying, but by feeding Dixie properly next time. Now do as I say. Go to your mother."

"Yes, Daddy," she sniffled, rising. She rubbed her face clean of tears with the bottom of her apron, gave him a last winsome look that tore his heart out by the roots, and left him. He turned to the business of saddling and bridling Dixie and then shoved the thirty-thirty into its leather boot under the stirrup fender. He led Dixie out and mounted her and walked her around the house and past the mulberry tree in the front yard and into the road and turned her toward town. He was surely in his splendor, so finely dressed and accoutered. But he could not see the road before him for the smarting of his own tears.

❧

By the time he came cantering into the Hayesville square, though, Captain Moore's spirits had rebounded. The agent for the Southern had written him a check which was in the poke he carried looped around the horn of his saddle. In the poke along with the check were a hundred dollars in eagles, double eagles and silver dollars which he'd saved over the month for deposit. All together the coins gave the poke considerable heft – enough so he was confident of performing one of his very best feats. Briskly he glanced about. Fewer persons were abroad than he'd have liked, but he reasoned it was an adequate audience for a weekday.

Guiding Dixie to the open door of the bank he reined her back and hollered in, "Count this; I'll be back around in a minute," then tossed the poke in through the door, spun Dixie on her hind legs, screamed out a hair-raising Rebel yell and set off at a mad gallop around the square. Halfway around, he set the bugle to his lips and blew a piercing cavalry charge, snatched off his hat and sailed it ahead of him so it came to rest crown-high in the dirt just before the bank. Dashing at the hat on the dead run, he swung himself sideways from the saddle and down, reached out and caught it up with a flourish and pulled Dixie to a plunging halt in a storm of dust exactly opposite the bank's hitch rail.

He'd never done it more expertly and was full to bursting of contented pride as he dismounted, replaced his hat and glanced expectantly about, ready to bask in the accustomed cheers and huzzahs of the townsfolk. But the few present only stood and stared and the looks they gave him were not of the admiration he thought he'd earned but of scolding disapproval. Never before had he inspired such a reaction. Puzzled and embarrassed, he fidgeted with Dixie's reins and patted her heaving barrel trying to imagine why his nimblest trick had met with such a sour reception. Then he spied Oliver Price limping from his shop with an agitated gait. Oliver crossed to him scowling. "Moore," he hotly declared, "sometimes I think you're just a frivolous sort of a man."

The Captain was aghast. "Why, what d'you mean?"

"Don't you know there's typhoid here? And all through Downings Creek? Folk are suffering and dying and here you are riding around yelling and blowing your horn and doing your confounded carnival pranks. You ort to be ashamed of yourself. You ort to show some respect for the trials of others."

Fiercely Irish Bill blushed. "Typhoid? When? How?"

"Days now. Some loggers working in the Tusquittees took it and come down to try and get tended. Laid up at the Craigses and the Mostillers on Downings Creek. It spread from there. Ain't you seen it up your way?"

Speak of fear, Moore knew fear then. He went cold with it. Typhoid was brewed in water tainted by the seepage of human excreta; and where was such foulness worse than in the latrines of the Tusquittee logging camps, often so carelessly sited near springs and streams? He thought of his own lovingly wrought piping system, drawing from its fine bold spring, feeding into the back-porch trough where the clear water sparkled and ran – was it poisoned too, from faeculent matters higher up?

Here was another kind of fact to conjure with, about how the coming of change could break in on the safe world of old and transform it overnight to one of mortal danger, erase his foolishly imagined line between the ideal and the practical. Timber companies and railroads were not just dire things in themselves, they dragged behind them dragons' tails of consequences even more dire. They imperiled the innocent – Miss Hattie, Jim, Charlie, Nannie – Nannie whom he'd crudely wronged and hurt.

Nannie. Regret flooded him. Reproachfully the image of his sobbing daughter came. In self-righteousness he'd unjustly chided her and in stubbornness he'd not asked her pardon after he saw the error of what he'd done and in vanity he'd ridden off preening himself in his finery leaving her to shed tears of unearned remorse, undeserved shame. How could he have done that to his lastborn, to sweet Nannie the child of his old age who meant more to him than his own life?

"No," he answered in a hush, his mind reeling, "not a lick of it up Tusquittee that I know about." He paused, gape-jawed. He'd been cutting hay all week, he'd seen no one, heard no news. "Downings Creek, you say?" He struggled to think, then remembered. Remembered the Cartmans and young Will Price and all the Carters at the old Curtis place. "What of Uncle Jimmy and Uncle Andy, and Sanders Carter?"

"So far the Cartmans and their people are all right. Sanders is yet living. But his wife and Daisy and two of his boys are dead of it. Dead and in the ground at Chestnut Grove." Irish Bill didn't hear the last of what Oliver told him. He forgot his banking. Already he was in the saddle, sawing at the reins, whirling Dixie into the square. He struck his spurs deep and Dixie's powerful hindquarters bunched and sprang and he was off in a spew of clods and pebbles, hammering across the grass of the courthouse yard, dodging between the maple trees, heading for the bridge at Sanderson Ford, heading for the Tusquittee road.

◆

In his anxiety Irish Bill wanted to cover the whole distance home at a gallop but he knew Dixie would never last at such a pace and so he was forced to rest her with spells of walking that maddened him with impatience. He kept thinking that in little more than a month – on the twenty-fourth of August – Nannie would be eleven years old; and on that same day Charlie would turn twenty-five. The date shimmered in his mind like a candle flame about to gutter out. The new danger had transformed everything. Suddenly what had seemed firm and fixed had become conditional. He saw now what he'd once known all too well but the long years of peace and comfort had lulled him into forgetting; what the war had taught him – that all is impermanent; that nothing could be counted on.

Around him the peaceful countryside unfolded, bathed in the gauzy light of a late-summer day. Behind the haze of heat the mountains were the same whitish-blue as always, on either hand the corn stood robust in the fields. Dogs barked in the distance, birds sang, buzzards wheeled high overhead. Nature cared not that man had bred a plague from his desecration of it. Moore remembered that in wartime he'd often marveled how God's world could go serenely about its business untroubled by the bloody battles humans waged. When his company stood in reserve behind Vance's regiment during the fight at New Berne he'd lain on his belly watching a beetle calmly eating a leaf in the wet grass before him while shells from the Yankee gunboats on the Neuse exploded on every side. He remembered how at Chickamauga he could hear the whirring of the locusts in between the bursts of musketry; and how once in East Tennessee, pinned down behind a deadfall by tory sharpshooters, he'd seen a garter snake slowly shed its skin. Now today, as then, all Creation still abided, indifferent to what mischief mortals wrought.

He did cover the last mile at a gallop. Dixie seemed to sense his urgency; he could feel her great heart thudding under his knee. Her breath came in ever more ragged grunts. A creamy lather started out around the edges of her saddle; clots of foam broke from her muzzle and streamed back, some striking his face; he tasted her salt in his teeth; his beard was wet with it. She swerved through the gate and into the dooryard and slid to a stop and stood with legs atremble and sides pumping as Irish Bill leaped down, bounding for the house, then abruptly stopped when he spied the empty mouth of the barn. His bowels gave a sickening squirm. The buggy was gone.

Just then Charlie came around the back corner of the house carrying a sickle – freshly sharpened, judging from the shine on its blade edge. Charlie stared stupefied, his mouth a small oval framed by his curling black mustache and goatee. "What's wrong, Papa?"

"Where's the buggy?"

"Why, Mama and Nannie took it."

Again the Captain's guts writhed. "Took it where?"

"To the Middletons'."

"The Middletons'?" Farther up Tusquittee. Farther up toward the logging camps and the polluted water and the typhoid. He went to Charlie and laid a hand on the boy's shoulder to give himself a prop, for he truly felt as if he might swoon from dread. "What for?"

Charlie dropped the sickle and grasped him by an elbow; he'd seen the Captain lose all color. "One of their scawny younguns showed up right after you left," he explained, white with forboding now himself. "Said Miz Middleton had took sick."

Oh God, thought Irish Bill. *Oh God, no.*

"Asked if Mama'd come and nurse her," Charlie went on. "So Mama got some of her things together – boneset, some feverweed and horsemint, rabbit tobacco and whatnot. Me and Jim hitched up the rig and she took Nannie to help her with the nursing and off they went." He crooked his knees so he could lower himself and look straight in the Captain's eyes – he was as big and strapping as Moore was tiny. "What is it, Papa?"

Moore told him. And told Jim too when Jim came to see about the uproar. Then he ceased and took a long breath and his head cleared and he was no longer faint. He reached deep within and found the old air of command that he hadn't had to call on since he put by the Confederate gray. Then he was crisp.

"Saddle me another horse," he ordered. "Get me Rebel, he's the fastest. I'm going after them. You boys stay here. Take care of Dixie, she's about rode down." They wanted to go too but he told them no and reinforced it with a rare oath. It was enough that Miss Hattie and Nannie were at risk. He wasn't going to set the boys in harm's way too.

It mortified him but he had to visit the privy before he could go.

That was how badly the news had stirred his bowels. How he despised being old! He reckoned hazard was mostly a young man's game. But in ten minutes' time he was astride the little dun gelding and trotting up the road toward Big Tuni. He was cool now. His bottom might be shamefully raw and dirty from his hasty job in the privy and he might be old when he wanted to be young, but in spite of it all he'd begun to feel again what he used to feel when the bugles blew and the sabres came out and the guidons snapped in the wind – that however flawed he was, there wasn't any choice – he had to be the equal of what was coming.

❧

It was late in the evening when he checked Rebel where the road opened out to show him the broad flat bowl of the Big Tuni bottom silvered with misty light from the three-quarter moon that hung on the rim of the mountains. Around him the denuded hills raised their big round tops and he thought they resembled the severed heads of giants set about for warning by some tribe fatally at odds with Goliath and his kin. In the moonglow their slopes covered with stumps looked like big pitted faces and the gullies that scarred them looked like wrinkles in the pale flesh of the faces. Somewhere high on the range a painter squalled and from the darkness ahead several dogs answered with a frenzied barking. Down where the dogs rioted shone an orange light – Middleton's. He rode to it.

As he approached, the point of light divided and became two and when he turned in through the broken gate he saw that one was a bonfire for the burning of soiled bedclothes and the other a fire to heat a kettle of water suspended over it. Between him and the fires stood his buggy, unhitched, shafts-down in the yard. The buggy horse was tethered with a long line of rope to an armrest of the seat and was browsing in the scant grass at the edge of the yard. In the glimmer of the firelight he saw something lying on the seat – a bundle – and riding nearer discovered to his relief that it was little Nannie, curled up asleep in a swaddling of blanket as cozy as a kitten. He sat his saddle with bowed head and mouthed a prayer of thanksgiving.

Despite the lateness of the hour the yard was crowded. There were the dogs, a homely assortment of fyces and curs that quieted after a minute or two and soon crawled back under the house to resume the slumbers the painter and Moore had interrupted. Rufe Middleton sat on a stump by the bonfire with his forearms lank in his lap and his big hands dangling from his knees in an attitude of utter defeat that was somehow irksome to see – it bespoke a state meaner and more narrow than grief.

Young Seth squatted on his hams nearby staring into the flames now and then using a sleeve to scrape snot from his nose – he was silently weeping. Two small Middletons hunkered beside him shooting marbles in the dirt. Three men Moore didn't know lounged at the edge of the light – some of the Middleton logging crew, he supposed. There were no neighbors come to console; over the years Rufe had managed to turn them all against him by means of one affront or another.

The oldest boy, Absalom, was pacing up and down before the open door of the house. Lamplight streamed from the door to make a long yellow rectangle on the beaten earth of the dooryard and every time Absalom passed through it he cast a crooked shadow that exaggerated the slump of his shoulders and made him look weighed down with sorrow – though as Irish Bill rode closer he could see the boy wasn't so much sad as enraged; when Absalom glanced up to speak there was a flat feral glint in his eye.

Moore stood down, tied Rebel off to the spokes of a buggy wheel, shook with the menfolk and made his manners. Rufe was too listless to speak but Absalom thanked him for Miss Hattie coming. Seth could only manage a miserable dip of his head.

Irish Bill was turning toward the house when Miss Hattie emerged, sweaty, disheveled, her hair awry, wiping her forehead with the backs of her wrists, her sleeves pushed up above her elbows – and for all that, still looking as lovely as he'd seen her, an angel of mercy if one had ever descended. He hurried to her and caught her by the hands and kissed her greasy brow. Then he fixed a reproving look on her. "You've got to get out of here. You and Nannie. It's . . . It's . . . "

Miss Hattie shook him off frowning. "Heavens above, I know what it is. I knew the minute I looked at the poor woman. Four of the children are down with it too. And you know better than to tell me to leave. Who's going to take care of them?" She glared dismissively at the helpless males in the yard. "Seth? Absalom? Rufus? The oldest girls are the sickest; they can't help. Anyway, I've already sent Luther to town to fetch Dr. Sullivan or Dr. Killian. When a doctor comes, I'll leave. But not before."

Oh, that mulish streak; every one of the Gashes had it. He felt his nostrils tighten with exasperation. "There's typhoid on Downings Creek," he told her, meaning to be harsh in hopes of stirring her caution. "Craigses, Mostillers, Sanders Carter – poor Martha and three of Sanders's children are already dead." At that news he saw her start with hurt, saw the tears spring into her eyes to glimmer in the firelight. "It's in Hayesville too," he hastened on. "What doctors we've got'll likely be – "

"Then I'll have to make do till one can get here," she cut him off, scrubbing away the tears with the heel of a hand. Instantly he regretted the roughness of his speech. Her chin hardened and went up and he despaired – when the Gash chin rose, all argument had to end. "Main thing is," she said, "we've got to get Nannie out of this." She sighed and bit her bottom lip, aggravated at herself. "I shouldn't've brought her. I never thought . . . never dreamed it was typhoid; it just sounded like a common ague; I thought she could help me with the nursing. Soon as I saw what it was, I sent her out of the house. Told her to stay in the buggy or by the fire but not touch anything we're burning. God forgive me if I've exposed her . . ." Her voice trailed off and her eyes went blank and she gazed beyond him, suddenly distant.

Again he took her by the hands, essayed to fetch her back from wherever she'd strayed. "You couldn't've known. Don't fret yourself about it. What's done's done." She came back a little then; he saw her eyes clear. But there was still a remove, she still felt the sting of her remorse. He squeezed the small and delicate hands with his rough ones. He inclined his head toward the house. "How do things stand here?"

She sighed. "Bursheba's done for, I'm afraid." That was Rufe's wife. "The oldest girls'll pull through, I think. There's no telling about the two littlest ones." She was exhausted; he could see the dark circles under her eyes like bruises, the slackness of her mouth. But then fresh worry flooded over her, sharpened her look. She grasped his arm. "Take Nannie home, Bill."

He knew he should, knew he must. But how could he? It was like having to choose between them. Both were too precious; he couldn't choose. But he also knew it wasn't really a choice. Not yet anyway. He peeked past her into the lamplit house, saw the rude log wall, a dirty shirt hanging from a peg, a row of cheap tin flatware stuck behind a strip of wood, a hen pecking on the floor. All the feathers were gone from the chicken's neck and the pale naked flesh of the neck was repellent to see. He put his eyes back on hers. "I don't want to leave you."

"I know. But take her back. Take her now." Confidently Miss Hattie nodded. "I'll be home – soon as a doctor comes."

He drew her to him and hugged her tight. She smelt of sweat and the sickroom and woodsmoke and her own warm and strong and capable self. "Lord help us," he whispered into a cluster of her damp curls.

He felt her hands softly patting his back. "He will. You know He will."

He didn't know any such thing. What he did know – what he'd remembered in spite of his prayer – was that the Lord would permit worse calamities than any man could imagine. But he bobbed his head obligingly and released her and stepped away. "I'll take Nannie," he said. "But I'm coming back for you."

She gave him a wan smile. "There's carbolic spray in the cellar. Bring it." She turned quickly then and mounted the doorstone and was gone and Irish Bill stood grinning to himself. Those Gashes and Sauers. Authority was in their blood. He'd seen major generals trained at West Point who didn't have the habit of command that Miss Hattie could call on at will. He stepped back, spoke to the Middletons and started away to hitch up the rig; but as he passed the bonfire Rufe reached out one of his gnarled hands and snatched at his sleeve and stopped him.

"What am I going to do, Moore?" It wasn't an appeal. It was too hard for that. He held onto the sleeve with a downward pull that was sharper and more insistent than it should've been unless he meant it to be some sort of rebuke. Moore met Rufe's eyes. For an instant the envy in them was like a polar light. But that faded and something else that was coarser and less pure came, something that insinuated and accused; and then Rufe twisted his head away as if the sight of Moore had all at once revolted him. Bitterly he regarded the house. "That woman dies, who's going to take care of all these younguns?" He gave a snort. "Everything happens to me. Just when we get to prospering, that woman takes sick and half the younguns takes sick and I'm cast back on hard times." He snorted again and the snort changed to a small dry mocking laugh that sounded like a crumpling of a handful of twigs. "Hit ain't fair," he mused. He nodded with a conclusive emphasis as if he'd just seen the proof of some long-held theory. "Hit ain't fair."

Seth rose and spoke an oath and walked from the fires toward the privy cussing under his breath. Irish Bill stood frowning. By ordinary Rufe was a reticent sort, holding all his complaints and grudges sourly close, the better to nurse and cherish them; spite brewed in him but its poison usually leaked out meagerly at a dozen different places and times; never before had so much of it spouted all at once. The Captain could think of no rejoinder suited to a display so ill-suited. He was ready to concede Rufe some right to deplore his lot; but what Rufe had said was beyond the pale. Yet he couldn't think how to upbraid him without seeming rude himself.

He was still trying to mull that out when Absalom tore off his hat and threw it on the ground and tromped it flat with his big calked logging boots. "God damn you!" he bawled, then came at Rufe in a rush head-down like a mad billy goat, crossing between the two fires to lean down and bellow into Rufe's face, "God damn you, it's your fault Mama's dying!" Moore was stunned to see it. Always before, Absalom had seemed a quiet and biddable fellow, composed, refined, soft of speech, a dutiful son; folks marveled how he could be so mild, sprung from such roots. But Moore also recalled how, when he arrived, Absalom's eye had showed that baleful spark; he reckoned the outburst had been a long time coming. God only knew why.

"You talk about prospering," Absalom roared, spewing beads of spit over Rufe's face. The two boys ceased their marble game and crouched in the dirt staring wide-eyed; what entertainment was finer than a quarrel of adults? "Did *she* ever see any of it?" Absalom demanded. "Did you ever buy her a new dress or hire some help around here to spell her? Hell, no. You wore her out worse'n you'd wear out a mule. Bad times and good, it didn't matter, you wore her out. Got younguns on her one after another till she was all busted up and empty inside and dry as a chip. . ."

He had to stop for breath. He stood hunched over Rufe, red-faced, raggedly panting, both hands shaped into claws as if he wanted to use them to rip Rufe's vitals out of him. Miss Hattie had come to the door of the house, the boys watched transfixed with delight, the men from the logging camp slunk quietly into the dark. One of the dogs emerged from under the house and lay down by the doorstone and pointed its nose to the sky and commenced to howl, till Absalom turned and kicked it hard in the ribs and it yelped and withdrew whimpering whence it came.

"Well," Rufe remarked in that same hard tone, "when this plague's done I won't have half the younguns I had. Then who's going to do the work around here?"

"You son of a bitch!" raged Absalom. From the dog he swung back to Rufus. "Selfish! Miser! Abuser! House burner! I swear before God, if you weren't my own flesh and blood I'd kill you with my bare hands. That poor husk of a woman in there, why, what little's left of her is so much better'n you, so much higher, so much finer, you're not good enough to kiss the heel of her foot."

Rufe didn't even cringe. He just sat on his stump shaking his head before the enormity of his misfortune. His unrepentant self-pity stoked Absalom's rage even hotter. "I tell you, old man," he yelled, "when she dies, when my mama dies, I'm done with you. Done! You'll get no more help out of me. No more of my work. No more of my money – the money I earn with my notions and plans, money that you can hoard and fondle and play with in secret, while your wife and your younguns toil and scrimp and go hungry. Damn you! Damn you to hell!"

He'd worked himself into a frenzy. Moore stood by appalled as Absalom's clawed hands finally went where they'd wanted to go all along, went to Rufe, clutched him by the shoulders and commenced to shake him all limp and limber like he was of no more substance than an apple-head doll.

"Hell's where you belong!" Absalom was hollering. "By God, I want to put you there myself!" He shook Rufe so hard that Moore heard Rufe's teeth rattling in his mouth. Then he hit him – hit him with a fist, a short chop of a blow that knocked Rufe sideways off his stump. From the doorway Miss Hattie spoke Absalom's name in a way that straightened him where he stood and made him raise both hands in disclaimer and step back wearing a look in which vindication and shame were mingled. "All right," he murmured. "All right."

Rufe lay on the ground. He seemed serene. "Everything happens to me," he repeated. "What am I going to do?" He rolled over on his back and raised a bony finger and pointed it at Irish Bill. "Tell me, Moore. You tell me. How come you to prosper and me to fail? How come? Hit ain't fair. I worked hard – hard as you. Harder even."

The Captain blushed. He wanted to be anywhere but where he stood. He hadn't wanted to see what he'd seen. He wanted no share in whatever had parted this father from this son. He wanted no knowledge of Rufe's life of misery and want, ironically transformed now into a bounty made of briars and thorns. But he *was* part of it. He wondered if he might even be the cause of it, or some of the cause anyway. For he'd enjoyed good fortune and his neighbor hadn't. In some way he felt he was to blame for some measure of Rufe's failures. And even if he wasn't – even if he was innocent of any guilt at all – he was still a part of Rufe, and Rufe was still a part of him.

These many years they'd led their lives but a few miles apart and if their lives had been separate they'd also been bound, bound by time and place and acquaintance and by the seasons and the weather and by war and peace and by all that had transpired for both of them, work and marriage, children and growing old and then older yet, and then somehow – not because he'd been more virtuous or diligent or ambitious or in any way more deserving – his life had turned out mostly good and Rufe's had gone mostly bad; Rufe's had been like the shadow side of his.

So each had a stake in the other, just as every man has a stake in every other man; and when Moore recognized this he finally regained some of his pity for Rufe and forgave him for what he'd so crudely said. And then he could surmount his embarrassment and nod and answer, "Yes, Rufe, I know you worked hard. Harder'n me indeed, sometimes. But I reckon we've still got to bear what comes. Whether we deserve it or not. For I think we've all got some bad times heading our way now."

Rufe lay on his back gazing up at the white chunk of moon which had moved off the rim of the mountain and was floating free in the heavens, surrounded by a foggy corona of light. There was a smear of blood on his mouth where he'd been hit. Absalom stood by the house swearing and weeping. But Rufe still kept that odd calm. He gave a small twisty smile. "I've done that already," he said. "I've done borne more'n any man ort to stand."

◆

Moore drove Nannie home in the buggy with Rebel trotting behind on a lead. She drowsed off and on, but as they neared home she wakened and sat up. They chatted awhile – all was forgiven between them now; graver events had supervened – then she fell to thinking. After a time she assumed a serious mien. "Daddy," she asked, "will those girls die?"

"I don't know, sweetheart. Mama thinks two of them might. But they might recover too. We can't tell. It's in God's hands."

"God must have big hands."

"What d'you mean, Nannie?"

"Whenever bad things happen, everybody says, 'It's in God's hands'. I was thinking His hands must be real big to hold it all."

"Well, yes, sweetheart. I reckon they are."

"But I guess even as big as they are, they can't hold everything. Because bad things keep on happening, in spite of Him holding them. Like if those girls were to die? Do you think if they die, it would be because they fell out, because God's hands were too full?"

Wistfully the Captain smiled. *Out of the mouths of babes*, he thought. Aloud, he said, "Maybe you're right, Nannie. Maybe the ones that die do fall out by accident. For I don't believe God wants them to. And I believe He's sorry for it when it happens."

They traveled awhile in silence. Nannie reflected. Then after a time she remarked, "It must be hard being God."

Moore nodded. "Yes, sweetheart, I think it is."

Ten days later Nannie came down with typhoid. The following morning Charlie took it and by sundown Jim was sick too. That night Irish Bill began to suffer the first symptoms of headache and lassitude, thirst and fever. In a week's time all three of them were deathly ill. Miss Hattie alone escaped the sickness.

Chapter Seventeen

Absalom Middleton had suffered a tragedy; and Weatherby understood that Cassandra wanted to sustain him in his time of grief as was proper in a friend and patroness. But owing to the pestilence raging everywhere roundabout, he felt he must forbid her to leave the grounds of Wildwood till such time as the epidemic showed signs of abating. To be sure, the quarantine was a troublesome inconvenience – after all, it kept Weatherby himself annoyingly confined when he chafed to be out tramping the woods on the track of The Bear or even down at the mill on the Nantahala tending to such business as The Bear would let him think about. But Cassandra resisted the internment with a special vehemence that he thought striking and somewhat out of character.

True, Absalom was a worthy retainer and had lost his mother and two sisters to the disease and under ordinary circumstances it would have been best for Weatherby and Cassandra to show their sympathy by being present for the funeral at the rude little Baptist chapel beyond the ridge on Tusquittee Creek where the Middletons worshipped. But the circumstances were not ordinary and to Weatherby's way of thinking Absalom for all his excellence hardly merited the running of a personal risk. To go abroad now was to court infection, was therefore irresponsible, indefensibly so.

But Cassandra bridled at the restraint. "What sort of unfeeling tyrant are you?" she harangued him. "No one has been truer to you than Absalom. Why, he's your protegé. You praise the purity of his racial stock and manipulate it to demonstrate your theories of breeding; have you no care for him as your fellow man? Despot! Oppressor! How can you be so . . . so medieval?"

Her outburst amused him. He reminded her that at the outset she herself had thought it an insult to be cast into Absalom's unrefined company. She quieted at that, but continued to sulk. Of course her criticism was unjust. No one thought more highly of Absalom than Weatherby. Who else of Weatherby's station would've done as much for one of Absalom's? Weatherby believed himself an enlightened and forward-thinking man, a man of the modern time. He trusted reason and science. However much he might ridicule Cassandra's collectivist notions he conceived himself a true democrat. He eschewed the false distinctions of class. Unlike Margaret, he never forgot that his own father had been a common working man. He believed the only legitimate aristocracy was that of brains and talent.

These Absalom possessed in abundance, and in addition bore within him the precious elixir of the pure blood. He was the coming man. The man of the future. But it should not be denied that he was also different. Not less. Not lower. Just different. He was still in the act of becoming. In time, with Weatherby's help, perhaps he could become nearly what Weatherby now was. In time. But for now, he was all potential. And today his potential was insufficient to strike a balance with the achieved value of Cassandra and of Weatherby. He was not yet worth their imperilment. To say so was but to express the simplest and cleanest logic.

He could not expect her to understand. But still the heat and persistence of her feelings surprised him and after a time his amusement at what seemed her fallacious zeal faded and he began to remember Margaret's warnings so oft expressed; then when he saw where that line of thought might lead him, he had an inkling of something he dared not imagine and thrust it aside and let his mind go white rather than open the door he had glimpsed.

As a diversion he suggested they visit the target range; he'd purchased some new shoulder arms that he hoped might serve for The Bear and wanted to try them out; and it had been some little time since Cassandra had sharpened her shooting eye. Grudgingly she agreed. The range lay in a grassy swale behind the stable; target frames of wood stood against a bank overgrown with honeysuckle and morning glory. It was the duty of one of Weatherby's groundskeepers to set up and replace the targets.

Handling a long gun was harder for Weatherby now because of his injured arm. But he'd learned how to compensate and could shoot now nearly as well as before. He sighted in the bolt-action .45-79 Remington-Keene magazine rifle and fired off enough rounds to see that it shot a bit high and to the right. The recoil was smooth but he found the newfangled bolt awkward to manage. Next he took up the .40-60 Marlin sporting gun and its factory sight proved dead-on and the whole piece had a good tight feel and the lever action was easy and he put ten rounds in the black with it and set it aside to use the next time he went out for The Bear.

Finally he tried the large-framed Colt slide action. It was chambered for .40-60-260 and had a half-magazine and a peep sight. It had good power, more than enough to knock down The Bear, but the act of racheting the reloading pump to and fro was hard on his bad arm and he concluded it wouldn't do in the field. So he repaired to the Marlin.

Meantime Cassandra was idly popping away with her pump .22, which was a miniature of the big Colt. Absorbed in choosing the best gun for The Bear, he hadn't been paying much heed to her shooting; but now as he stood reloading the Marlin he did, and he saw the careless way she handled the gun, saw that she was missing the black almost every time. "What in the world is wrong with your aim?" he cried, aghast – ordinarily she was as sure a shot as Annie Oakley, yet here she was, spraying bullets about like some hapless schoolgirl.

She turned to him a face crumpled with anguish and streaming with tears but the green eyes held a fierce glint of defiance too; and suddenly he felt a large and terrible force bearing down on him, a force coming from her to him that threatened to bowl him over as if he were no more than a tenpin. "Father," she told him firmly, the rifle hanging forgotten in her hands, "I'm going."

He knew what she meant but pretended not to. He stood frowning as though puzzled and bent his attention to the work of reloading the Marlin. "Going?" he asked, feigning innocence, unwilling to meet that gaze or the force it portended, thumbing cartridge after cartridge into the receiver of the gun in blind ritual. "Going where?"

She leaned the .22 against a bench and faced him with a toss of her head that shook out her coppery tresses in a way he recalled with a pang from her childhood. "To the funeral. I'm going to the funeral tomorrow."

With a show of fatherly patience he sighed a denial; but still he could not look at her. "No, dear," he said, trying to hold his tone kindly but unyielding, firmly paternal. "You can't. I'll not put your health in danger so you can make some silly gesture to demonstrate your fellowship with the downtrodden." He realized it wasn't a gesture just as he realized what it really was. But his mind was still white. He musn't concede what he feared even to imagine.

He felt her steadiness, her resolve, that force bearing down. He was almost proud of it. She had his fire; her weeping face was bright with it. "It isn't politics, Father," she answered. "And I'm going. I'm just going, that's all."

The Marlin was full now and he had no choice but to put it down. He leaned it against the bench alongside the little .22. Then he had to look at her; and when he did, he was sorry, for he sensed that he was accountable for the torment he saw in her. But that could never be; he could never have made such a blunder; he was too wise in the ways of the world. No. No, he hadn't done that. He *wasn't* accountable. He couldn't be. He was himself; he was sound, he was capable; he was the equal of every challenge. "My dear child," he implored her, hoping for a reply that he knew he would not get, "what's wrong?"

"I'll tell you what's wrong. I love him."

Still that whiteness of the mind. But the force that had been coming struck him now, jarred him like a blow. He stammered, "Him? Him? Who?"

"Absalom," she declared, as he'd known, dreaded she would. "I love him and he loves me. We're going to be married. And I'm going to the funeral, I don't care what you say."

Always he had been a supremely rational man. Contradiction vexed him, he could not abide an inconsistency, he pounced on every instance of deluded argument, oxymorons were irksome, he was peeved by incongruence, logic was his lodestar. How then could he travel the road of evidence now so plainly marked out before him? It was there; he saw it; but he dast not recognize it. For if he allowed himself to recognize it, the rationality to which he was wedded would impel him to follow it; and if he followed it, then he must travel according to the rules of the logic that governed him. And logic – remorseless, pitiless logic – would lead him where he could not go without bringing into question every conviction he'd ever held about himself. It would bring him to contradiction, to the very thing he most despised. Once before he'd been to that woeful place; The Bear had forced him to it, that first time on the bald. He would not willingly go there again.

From the welter of his confusion he dredged up but a single word and huskily spoke it, "No." It was not enough, but at that instant it was as much as he could find in himself.

"No what?" she pressed him, demanding precision as always. Had he meant to deny her the funeral? The marriage? Both? Her eyes flamed; he was smitten afresh by her beauty, all roughened and inflamed by high temper. Dear Cassandra, so insistent, so literal, so determined to clarify whatever seemed muddled. How he loved her! Yet the old rift was opening again, yawning hugely and irreparably; and across its widening gulf he saw her start to dwindle, to recede. This time, he knew, he would not get her back.

"Just no," he repeated. He was beyond reply. He was simply unable. He could never allow her what she wanted, all she wanted. That much was clear and not subject to debate. But the rest – the why of it – remained but a dim shadow hovering beyond the rim of his volition. He guessed it, vaguely apprehended it, it tickled the nose of his sense like a feather. But it had no shape he wished to witness. He would not declare it. He must never divulge it, not even to himself. For if he did, it would make a fool of him. And he refused to play the fool, even for Cassandra's sake.

So he simply turned and left her. Amazed, caught in a kind of stupor, mystified by his own actions, he strode unsteadily across the lawn toward the house. From behind she called to him and called again and then called a third time with a screech of outrage in her voice, but he was deaf to it all. He mounted the back stairs of the house clinging to the balustrade lest the weakness of his legs betray him and he tumble headlong. He was trembling. His cheeks were seared with shame. He wept.

◄

If not for The Bear he would have forestalled it. The Bear had claimed too much of his mind. The very day of Cassandra's arrival from Swarthmore, what had he been about? He'd been crashing through the wilderness in a vain effort to start The Bear that had confronted him on the bald and made him see more of himself than he'd wished to. He'd been intent on wiping out what he'd seen by wiping out the thing that had made him see it. So Cassandra had been an afterthought that day; and because of The Bear she'd been an afterthought ever since.

Absent The Bear, Weatherby would have seen the dangers, anticipated them, hedged them about with safeguards. Would not have left the matter in the bungling hands of Margaret, poor mule, whose imagination was as empty as her womb. What good her hectoring admonitions? Her tearful reproaches? Action had been required. Decision. He'd have acted, had he realized. Margaret had only wrung her hands, entreated him, expostulated, laid blame, foretold doom. And owing to his preccupation with The Bear he'd dismissed her. He recalled a line of Abbot Kinney's: *A woman without children is a mere sewer to pass off the unfruitful and degraded passions and lust of one man.* Think how even more inutile was such a creature as Margaret – a void chamber, unworthy even of receiving the milt of rut, much less of breeding young. Yes, had it not been for The Bear, he would not have leaned upon so weak a reed.

That evening he skipped dinner and sat in his study nursing a bourbon instead. At his feet, propped against the stones of the fireplace, stood the Winchester he'd been carrying that foggy day on the bald when he first saw The Bear. The big gun's bent iron and claw-torn wood spoke of the mighty power that had smitten it from his hands. Weeks later, in the snowstorm, the same power had smashed his arm, crippled him. It had reduced him, cut down the size of his life, narrowed his choices, squeezed all excess out of him, hardened him, honed him till there was scant room left anywhere in his realm for Cassandra, once so beloved. The Bear had moved her to the margins. To the farthest edge. Though he'd still doted on her in an episodic and absent-minded way, in actual fact he'd hardly noticed any more what she did. What he'd dwelt on was The Bear – its largeness, its cinnamon hue, its rank and woodsy scent, its knowing eye, all the several ways it had broken in on every facet of his life. That sharpened focus had cost him dear already. He'd suffered countless wounds and outrages. The Bear owed him for those. And now it owed him for Cassandra too.

◀

Father did not join them for dinner. Cassandra and Aunt Margaret dined in an awkward silence made even more wearing by Duncan's inflexible rule of butlering, which was that every room should seem emptier when he was in it than when he wasn't. He floated behind them ghostlike; his tread made no sound; plates of food appeared and vanished and wine glasses were replenished as if by magic. The silence of his ministrations cast into even sharper relief the terrible unease they felt.

After her interview with Father, Cassandra had confessed all to Aunt Margaret and the poor thing had lapsed into bitter despair, taking on herself the guilt for the calamitous turn of events; now she sat picking listlessly at her food, from time to time wagging her head in rue, her eyes puffy and red-rimmed from crying. At intervals she miserably gave voice. "It's all my fault," she'd moan. "George gave you into my care. I should've been more persistent in my representations. I knew disaster was coming. But even when I did speak of it, he wouldn't listen. No. Not to me. He disregards me. He loathes me. He always has. And now he'll hate me even more. It may be that he'll spurn me. Cast me out. I, with no prospect in the world . . ."

The bewailments droned unheard in Cassandra's ears. The roar of her own racing blood shut them out. She knew that all the world had changed; but she could not yet guess how much it had changed or what the change might mean for her. Perhaps nothing would ever be the same again. But what would that be like? She couldn't imagine a life in which she and Father were parted in enmity. So how could she possibly decide what to think or feel or do or be, now that all was different from the way it had ever been?

She longed to be with Absalom, grieving on the far side of the mountain. He needed her. It was true that he had lost but the shell of his mother. But she knew how he had revered that husk; how gratitude kept fresh for him what in the eyes of others had long since shriveled and gone hollow. Her place was by him.

But she had never yet defied Father. She might think and preach rebellion and rail against the evils of the system he lived by and her convictions might be true ones, but nonetheless they were of the head and Father was of the heart. She was a daughter and like any daughter she loved her Poppy – her girlhood name for him – and she wished to please him, the more so because he had been both mother and father to her for as long as she could remember. Now her belief in him and the duty she owed to Absalom were at odds. And in spite of herself she couldn't resist a daughterly suspicion that she might have failed her Poppy – been somehow unworthy or untrue – rather than contrariwise. Yet in the next moment she thought how cruelly he'd served her and she bristled with a righteous wrath.

Obsessively her thoughts circled, like a dog chasing its tail. Aunt Margaret whimpered on. Duncan wafted about like a wraith. The food was so much clay in her mouth. The room oppressed her – its dense red draperies, the dark paneling of the walls closing in on every side, even the glow of the candelabras on the table seemed forbidding, funereal. Unlit by sun, the stained glass of the windows looked as dense and impenetrable as lead. All in the room that had finally grown intimate and familiar to her now glowered, became suffocating and portentous.

After dinner they retired to the music room where they pretended to read: *Munsey's Magazine* for Aunt Margaret, for Cassandra a small red volume (Number XXV) in the International Science Series entitled *Education as a Science* by Alexander Bain, LL.D., plucked at random from the shelves of Father's library. For half an hour she had been staring without sight at a single sentence on Page 88 – "The opposition of the Concrete and the Abstract, while but another way of expressing the opposition of the Particular and the General, brings into greater prominence the highly *composite* or combined character of Individuality." – when she suddenly became aware that Father was standing under the Moorish arch of the entryway balefully watching her.

He was ashen; he seemed to have dwindled, become slenderer, frailer, weaker than she'd ever seen him – so much so that for a moment she feared he'd taken ill, that in a quirk of ironic fate the typhoid had claimed him to spite his every precaution; yet for all his apparent fragility there was something hard and ramrod stiff in his stance, something that might have once bent but never would again. The gaze he fixed on her was desolate; and seeing him so stricken yet contriving to be so strong, she melted with her old love for him, was half inclined to beg Poppy's pardon, forswear Absalom, throw herself on his mercy. But then he spoke.

"Cassandra." His voice was as empty as his look. "Tomorrow I'm sending you and Margaret back to Swarthmore. We'll take the Climax and leave for the flag stop at Beechertown in the morning. You'll go out on the noon train."

She heard Aunt Margaret gasp and begin to sob but mostly she heard – in disbelief – the unalterable decision in his voice. As each word came, more and more of what she'd started to feel for him ossified and crumbled away like the dust of old bones. There was to be no discourse, no stating of cases, no persuasion, none of the old jocular back-and-forth. Not even a quarrel. He would not give her even that. The confident figure who till now had always relished a jousting of ideas, who'd loved to argue every contentious point – that strong sarcastic scornful and humorous man – had utterly gone; and in his place was this glum unbending ruin, this shade cored with a bolt of iron that spoke horrors in a reedy hush.

Appalled, she opened her mouth to dispute him. But before she could speak, he turned and was gone and she was alone in the dimness with Duncan and her weeping aunt and with the piano and the organ and the harp that nobody in the house would ever learn how to play.

◆

The horse she took was Mazie, her birthday filly, the little blaze-faced chestnut Father had given her last month when she turned seventeen – it seemed an age ago now. Necessity forced the choice. Her own Omar Khayyam was lame, had thrown a shoe and bruised a hoof; and she dared not spirit away any of Father's stock. But Mazie was hardly a choice to be preferred. Only partly broken to the saddle, she had a nervous and flighty disposition. Nor did she know the road over the mountain as Omar did; and the track was a steep and rocky one that Cassandra herself had never traveled without Absalom to lead the way.

Yet she was resigned. *Beggars can't be choosers*, she reflected, tightening the cinch in the dark of the stable. *By the time this is over, that's probably just what I'll be. Aunt Margaret and me, beggars to-*

gether. Anxious as she was, the improbable vision evoked a giggle which she had to quell behind a hand. *I'm hysterical*, she thought, *I've got to calm down.* The humor passed then, but a black terror replaced it. Instantly she was soaked with a clammy sweat. Leading Mazie out, she found she was shaking head to foot. Her heart leapt in her chest like a trapped creature frantic to escape; it beat so hideously she was certain it could be heard at the house.

But the house stood silent. It would never have occurred to Father that she would disobey him – a thing she'd not done once in all her life. So he had taken no steps. Locked no doors. Posted no spies. He'd gone to bed confident that his will would prevail as always. It had been an easy matter to creep from bed and don her riding gear and slip downstairs and out a rear door and across the dark lawn to the stable. Now by the rear of the stable she stood to the saddle. Mazie humped her back and took a couple of jumps but Cassandra was ready for her and kept her seat and then curbed the filly with a sharp word and a jerk of the reins and Mazie quieted and stood snorting and blowing, the muscles of her legs aquiver.

Holding Mazie's head firmly down Cassandra gave the monstrous pile of Wildwood what she hoped and believed and feared would be a last look. Tears blurred the view. She tried not to think of all the things she wanted to think of. Or of all the things that terrified her – the typhoid, wild animals, the night, the treacherous trail. She had never felt so alone and yet in an odd way she had never felt freer or more exhilarated. Everything was new. New and awful and sublime. An adventure.

A silly laugh burbled out of her. *Perhaps I'm going mad*, she thought. She drew a shuddery breath and softly expelled it, *Goodbye, Poppy.* Then she whirled the filly and cantered down the back lane under the spruce trees to the road, scrubbing the tears away with a back of her gloved hand. At the road she turned east and south, down Wolf Creek. Ahead in the night – how many miles away she reckoned not – was the place where she knew she would meet the path that led up the mountain. Up to Tuni Gap; and over the gap. To Absalom.

❧

Where was she going? To whom? She loved him – was sure of it – but who was he? The dreaming boy who wrote poems in his Lippincott's reader, the mild soul who adored his mother and loved Shakespeare and Milton and Swift and *Moby Dick*, who wove galax wreaths, told beguiling tales, played the gourd banjo, showed her the glories of the highlands? Or the man whose strangeness she'd sensed that time on Tuni Gap, who casually spoke of house burning and feud, whose force she had felt in the searching of his hands on her breasts and in the hot moist bloom of his mouth and the hardness of his body against her own?

She'd been afraid of that force; yet somehow it was her very fear that had toppled her over into loving him; and she understood now that part of what she'd loved was the force that she'd known was coiled inside him like a beast in its lair. Maybe she mistook him, maybe the force that drew her was cruelty and not just a manly strength. It was possible – she'd thought she knew Father too. But she didn't think she was wrong about Absalom. Surely she couldn't afford to be – not now. And after all, love was faith, wasn't it? Every romantic novel said so. She would have faith in him; and her faith would make him what she needed him to be. What she believed he already was.

The night was humid and cloying and tar-black under lowering clouds. Lightning played continually along the cloud bottoms and each flare of it showed her the narrow stony road and the jagged masses of pine crowding close on either side and the bushy heads of mountains higher up. Every time the lightning came Mazie would flinch and begin to plunge and Cassandra would have to shorten the reins and calm her with caresses and soothing words that belied the increasing impatience she felt with a horse so useless it was ready to panic at the least noise. How she longed for her bold Arabian!

They had traveled this way – in fits and starts – for an hour or more when thunder rumbled in the distance and presently rumbled again and the second time it sounded closer, though Cassandra tried to convince herself it had not. Soon a wind came up and began tossing the peaks of the pines making them softly roar and Cassandra could smell rain on the wind and then she knew with a sink of despair that she was in for a storm. *I hadn't counted on that*, she thought bitterly. Hadn't counted on any obstacle at all. Hadn't brought a waterproof or a blanket or food or her rifle or anything but her reckless self and her mother's wedding ring of white gold which she intended Absalom to slip on her finger when they were wed. *What'll I do?* she wondered in sudden alarm. Then she recalled a phrase of Absalom's that made her smile: "You'll just have to bow up your neck and take it." *Bow*, he'd said, to rhyme with low. The notion warmed her. Yes, she'd bow her neck and take it.

The wind lashed harder and the thunder drew nearer and at every bolt of lightning Mazie dodged from one side of the road to the other as if trying to pick a direction in which to flee. Cassandra fought her, jerking grimly on the reins, wishing the bit of the bridle had a higher port – she'd chosen it in the dark of the stable, fearful of striking a light. She wasn't sure how much farther she must go to reach the place where the path to Tuni Gap turned up the mountain. Ordinarily an hour's ride at a walking pace might cover as much as three miles of good ground – perhaps four at a jog or a trot. But given the roughness of the road and all the stops she'd had to make to quiet Mazie, she had no idea how far she'd come; maybe no more than a mile or two.

Worry pinched at her insides. She remembered there was a big boulder wedged into the mountainside just before the Tuni Gap cut-off; it had some ancient Indian carvings on it. Would she find it in the dark? In the rain when the storm hit? Hundreds of big rocks littered the slope; how would she recognize it? How would she see the carvings? Maybe the lightning would reveal them. Maybe the storm would pass around; they often did in the mountains, Absalom had said so.

Then, as if to spite her hopes, the rain struck, first a stinging spray blown in the wind-gusts, then a downpour slanting in cold sheets. Instantly Cassandra was drenched, chilled to the bone where moments before she'd been sweating in damp heat. Lightning seared the night, gave her one blinding glimpse – the rain a slashing curtain of silver, the road a dancing foam – then thunder pealed overhead, ran off crackling and booming over the summits of the mountains; and Mazie squealed, jumped, swapped ends, bucked Cassandra off and bolted.

Oh, she thought. *Oh, dear.* She lay on her back in the rain. The wind had been knocked out of her and she tried to get her breath but gagged on rainwater and tried to cough but couldn't and for an instant feared she might strangle or suffocate or both. Then the breath came; but it came with an excruciating suck that was like the stab of a knife in her chest. Fighting to breathe, she choked on the water in her windpipe; a fit of coughing convulsed her. She rolled over in the mud, retched, retched again in violent spasms. When that had passed, she sat up, sodden, muddy, her chin ropy with her own drool.

She glanced about. Mazie was gone. "Oh," she howled, undone, "oh, you horrid, horrid horse!"

She must find the stupid beast. Must go on. Giddy from the fall, she made as if to stand; but pain lanced her left ankle and that leg doubled under her and she fell sideways into the rocks of the road. Shaken, she lay bemused. Drops of rain as big and hard as pebbles hammered at her. *Why can't I stand up?* It made no sense that she couldn't gain her feet. Chagrined, she made another try. And tumbled as before. *Strange, it doesn't hurt except when I put my weight on it.*

Then it struck her – the ankle was sprained. Or worse. Maybe it was even broken. It must've happened when Mazie threw her. She must've landed wrong. How unlikely, to break an ankle and not an arm or a head. Or a bottom. She'd broken that often enough, taking the jumps. Absurdly the thought triggered another siege of giggles.

Soon though, fear claimed her. Weakened by shock and exposure, she might take pneumonia; wolves or bears – maybe, by some quirk of ill fortune, even the very *The Bear* that had become the bane of all their lives – might come to feed on her; she might perish of hunger. Worse and worse fates traveled through her imagination, a train of horrors.

Curled in the road, pelted by the rain, she began to cry. But after a time she grew weary and ashamed and she stopped. She was acting like a girl. She wasn't a girl, she was a woman. A woman who was in love. A woman making her way to the man she meant to marry. She sat up, wiped her nose with a cuff of her sleeve. *Stop your sniveling*, she commanded herself. *Think*.

Mazie would run home. To the stable at Wildwood. One of the stableboys would find her there. He would tell Father. Father would set out, he would backtrack Mazie in the soft ground. He would find her. By dawn or shortly after, he'd find her. And he'd take her back by force. He'd bundle her off to Pennsylvania – to Philadelphia or Laurel Hills or Monongahela where in time she must wed some brainless plutocrat and breed young of proper American stock and eke out the rest of her life in meaningless ease among her own effete kind. She would have the idle existence of a hothouse flower. Life as an ornament. As a vessel for the propagation of the race.

No. No. She'd sooner die. Sooner take pneumonia, sooner give her flesh to the animals, sooner starve in the wilderness. No. She'd be like the heroines of all the novels she'd ever read. Her love would triumph over adversity. Heedless of her hurts, she'd go on to Absalom, crawl to him if need be. Drag herself on hands and knees up the flinty mountain path, over the high gap, down the other side, mile after tortuous mile. Collapse at his door bloody, briar-torn, mud-smeared, half-dead of selfless love.

As she relished this vision of high sacrifice the rain slackened, became a drizzle and then a mist. The wind died and all about her the dark woods slowly went silent save for the patter of rainwater shed from millions of leaves. The thunder receded to a faraway growl, the lightning to but a wan flicker that occasionally limned the uneven horizon behind her, above Wildwood. Fog thickened in the air; the world smelled deliciously of wet. It was as if the very elements had fallen still, tamed by the power of her unconquerable love. Yes, she would go to Absalom. Go to him no matter the hardships.

But she would need her strength to do that and suddenly she was very tired. She was as logy and flop-limbed as a newborn pup, her eyes were sore and grainy, her bones ached from the fall, the ankle had begun to hurt. She would rest, she would sleep and gather her faculties for the ordeal ahead. A catnap, no more – she couldn't rest long; Father would be coming soon; might be on his way this very moment; she'd lost track of the time.

She hobbled to the roadside, knelt, blindly groped about on the soggy ground for a fit place to lie. Under a pine she found a smooth slippery bed of needles, soft if spongy with wet. Here amid the heady fragrance of pine she curled herself into a ball for warmth and waited for slumber.

On the cusp between wakefulness and sleep she saw herself lying spent and broken on Absalom's threshold, saw him gather her in his powerful arms, saw him bear her to his bed and lay her down and undo the buttons of her clothing one by one and strip away her bloody rags and wash her bruised and battered body with an infinite care and when she was fresh and clean and bright and ready he would kiss her and begin to touch her as he'd not yet touched her, touch the flesh and not just the shape, her breasts and the nipples of her breasts and her arms and her legs and her flanks and the mound of her belly and its little bush of maidenhair; and he would reveal himself to her at last and she would give herself to him and he would give himself to her and they would merge into one in the mystical way she did not yet understand but ached to know and they would be safe together, safe, safe and never to be parted, never for all time.

She awoke in bright daylight. Father was sitting his horse in the road. He had Mazie on a lead. "Come, Cassandra," he said.

❧

Weatherby had granted Absalom a week's absence from his duties at the mill – more than ample time, he'd thought, for the burying of a family and the settlement of the necessary affairs. Actually it had been a far more generous allowance than could be justified on purely business grounds. It couldn't have come at a worse time – the epidemic had played hob with the work force, production was down, orders were backing up; and Weatherby could hardly be expected to venture down to the mill and manage operations in person at the risk of his own contamination. But he was fond of the boy – had been at the time, that is – and because of his fondness had fallen into a leniency that he now regretted.

Of course everything was different now. Weatherby regretted that too. He'd reposed great hopes in Absalom and had even begun to see some of them borne out – he'd managed the mill not just diligently and well but shrewdly and with imagination, finding new ways to improve working conditions and efficiency and to boost output; and of course with his woodcraft he'd proved indispensable in the hunt for The Bear – his loss there could never be supplied. Worst of all, Weatherby's scheme to use Absalom's gifts to show how the mountain white could be perfected must now go glimmering. Every last hope of him had been dashed.

So when he returned – punctually, one week to the day after going home to arrange the obsequies – he found the gates of Wildwood locked against him. The gatekeeper sent word up to the main house by a stableboy. Weatherby came down to the gate on foot, found him sitting his mule before the iron grillwork wearing a look of amiable perplexity. He shrugged and gave a sheepish grin as if he thought the gatekeeper had barred him in error. "Sorry you had to step in," he murmured with a bashful duck of his head, "but this fellow won't let me through."

Weatherby folded his arms and studied him through the black bars. The figure of his treachery shaped itself before him and his rage flared to think how Cassandra in her innncocence must've been beguiled by his low cunning; and when he answered, his voice cracked like the report of a rifle. "That's by my order."

Absalom's jovial frown of confusion deepened. "How come?" Then an idea came to him and he waved a deprecating hand. "If you're worried about the fever, you can't get it from me. You have to drink the bad water or . . ."

Weatherby bridled. Was he accusing him of cowardice, of being too afraid of disease to step outside his compound? How dare he presume so? "It's not the typhoid," he snapped back. "I'm discharging you."

The frown vanished as if wiped away by an invisible cloth. But he didn't seem in the least surprised. He slouched a bit in the saddle – casually, as if settling in for a long and friendly conversation. He put his head inquiringly to the side and watched Weatherby with a flat vigilance. "You're what?"

Weatherby hadn't expected this coolness; it intrigued him. Some deep part of him admired it even as a part closer to the surface took it for impudence and resented it. "Discharging you," he repeated. Then he took thought of the circumstances and made a vague motion with one hand and added, "I'm sorry, it's a bad time, I know; I regret the tragedy you've sustained. But I feel I've no choice but to dispense with your services. Much as I have valued them."

Absalom nodded as if this were not the end but still only the beginning of that long and congenial chat. Slowly he shook one foot free of its stirrup and lifted that leg and hooked it over the horn of this saddle and leaned foward resting an elbow on the knee. His air was languid, he looked like a man who had very many fine choices to make and much time to make them in. "I see. And how come you're doing that?"

"For deceiving me," said Weatherby. "For taking advantage. For abusing my trust."

His smile came back, thinner this time, more insinuating, almost indulgent, as if he'd known the answer from the first and had only been waiting for Weatherby to offer it up. "She's told you then." He nodded again. Idly he began playing with the reins, drawing them through his hand, releasing them, drawing them through again. He dropped his gaze from Weatherby to watch himself do it, as if it were an important task. "She wanted to tell you from the first, soon as we knew. You need to understand that. It was me held out against it."

There was something intrusive about him now, something overly confidential; it pushed against Weatherby, prodded at him as when someone stands too near and violates the space a man needs to keep clear around him; Weatherby actually stepped back a pace to try to free himself of it. "And why was that, may I ask?"

The smile widened but hardened too, became sly. But he didn't look at Weatherby; he kept his attention on the business of drawing the reins through his hand over and over. "I figured your notions were a gooddeal bigger'n you could hold," he said. The comment smote Weatherby like a slap in the face; a hot flush seared him; the door in his mind that he could not afford to go through flew open and he glimpsed the road beyond it and glimpsed where the road led and forced the door shut.

But the effort left him speechless and when he didn't respond Absalom went on. "She believed in you, though. Believed you'd take a man for his natural worth. Believed you'd let a poor man marry her. Oh, she was scared of telling you, I'll not deny it – feared you'd oppose it; but thought you'd oppose it for *her* sake, lest she be shunned and scorned by her own kind and her life spoilt. She thought you favored her that much."

Weatherby heard the condemnation in the last remark and resolved to hear no more; he forced himself past his swelling temper, found and used a remnant of his voice. "Your pay's at the mill office," he croaked. "Collect it and clean out your room and go. I want you off the premises by nightfall."

But Absalom wouldn't stir. He kept his easy seat in the saddle, leaning negligently on the knee he'd thrown over the pommel. Incredibly, he seemed to believe that he, not Weatherby, had charge of matters. "I'd like to see Miss Cassie," he said.

It was revolting to hear the endearment on that tongue. "*Cassandra* isn't here," Weatherby told him, speaking the full name to override what he'd called her.

"Where's she gone?"

"Pennsylvania." He gave this word too a special flavor, knowing how it would hurt. "She won't be back. You'll not see her again."

Annoyingly, there was no reaction that Weatherby could see. Absalom slouched in the saddle sorting his reins, watching himself do it. The mule stamped impatiently in the gravel of the driveway and he said a word to it and it steadied and he sat awhile longer, downlooking, pensive. Then he raised his head, set a look on Weatherby; it was not an unkind look; it seemed almost pitying and the possibility that he might be pitied rattled Weatherby, alarmed him, then made him indignant – who was this yokel to sit in judgment on him?

He wanted to say this but couldn't think how to express resentment for a thing he'd only inferred, that hadn't been actually spoken. Absalom broke the silence. "You bore with a mighty big augur, don't you, Weatherby?" he drawled. "Snap your fingers, folk just disappear. Hopes die, dreams blow away like so much dust. Love, a man's job, his chance in life, all of it's gone. On your say-so. Never costs you a minute's sleep either, does it? Your head rests easy on your pillow of a night, I'll bet. Well, I reckon you can do what you want. You've got the power." He paused then, his gaze hardened, his tone went level. "But I'll tell you something. Nothing's done ill in this world without it's answered back in time."

Weatherby blinked. "What d'you mean by that?" Something seemed to be happening that he couldn't understand. His mind floundered, tried to grasp it. Then it came clear. He stood aghast. "Are you threatening me?"

Absalom gave another careless shrug. "I'm telling you a thing I believe to be true – a thing I've observed in life. Something that might profit you to ponder. Ponder and maybe get ready for."

"How dare you?" Weatherby burst out.

But Absalom cut him off and the flatness of his voice had an edge now, an edge like a honed knife. "I'll tell you how I dare. I was born as good as you. And I was as good as you the day you hired me. I took your wage and did your bidding, but there was never a time when I wasn't as good as you. It's the way God made us. You were born rich and I was born poor but in His eyes we two were good the same."

He stopped and smiled and the pity was back now but there was scorn too. And something like vindication. "But today I'm *better 'n* you. For I'd never do what you've done – part a daughter of mine from the man she loves, give that man a chance to rise and then whisk it away once he starts. Pretend to believe one way but do another. I guess you think because you're rich it gives you the right to mess with people the way you've done. I guess you think being rich is the same as being worthwhile. Well, it's not. You're higher'n I am, that's all. Not better, higher. *I'm* better."

He straightened then, unhooked his leg from around the horn of his saddle, slipped the toe of his boot into the stirrup and gathered his reins. His face was stony now, the eyes as hard as pellets of lead shot. "I damn you to hell for what you've done," he said, not loudly or in bombast, not wrathfully; but in a voice deadly small, "and I tell you, you'll answer for it. And the answering'll go hard with you."

Weatherby gaped; he wanted to reply – say something taunting and cruel and clever and strong – but he couldn't think what to say; he was empty of words and feeling both; and while he stood trying to think, wanting to act, needing to, Absalom was turning the mule from the gate. After its long stand the mule was anxious to go. It made as if to break into a trot; but Absalom reined it down, held it to a walk. He rode between the rows of dying Lombardy poplars, rode without hurry, rode away taking Weatherby's hopes with him, Weatherby's hopes and maybe more, maybe much more, and the hooves of his mule crunched in the dry litter of dead leaves.

Chapter Eighteen

Hamby squatted at the edge of the yard watching the cabin burn. It was an old cabin – Old Man Curtis had built it years before the war, which meant it was older than Hamby himself; its chestnut logs were dry and split and warped with age. It burned fast and well except for the new tin roof. The fire scorched the strips of tin till they were black and crinkly and their nails popped out and they curled up at the ends; and then the roof beams burned through and the curled pieces of tin fell inside with a roar and a burst of sparks and the cabin became a delicate hollow tissue of charred timbers filled with a mass of fire. The heat of it seared Hamby's face. Greedy gouts of fire spouted from the windows and gushed up from the broken roof; smoke rose in billows to form a huge brownish-black column that stood motionless in the still air and covered the sun and dimmed it to a disk of corroded copper. Folk would be seeing it for miles.

"What's that burning?" they'd ask. "Why, it's over by Sanders Carter's; d'you think the poor man's set his house afire from grief?" They'd never figure it was nothing but the Indian's place – McFee's place, old Daniel's. For such a sorry little shack it sure as hell made a fancy blaze. It tickled Hamby to think how everybody would be fooled.

The tissue of timbers got more and more frail as the fire ate away at it. Presently it swayed and commenced to totter and then collapsed in a shower of burning brands and ash and clouds of soot. There was a last big burst of yellow flame and a soar of sparks. Soon what had once been a home of sorts to old Daniel and to Mordecai Corntassel and to Hamby himself was nothing but a bed of smoldering embers with the curled ends of the strips of roof tin sticking up out of it. It hissed and sizzled and popped and whined. It stank. It stank of old stuff burnt up. Old lives. Old times. Old memories. Shit that the years had leached of any meaning.

Good riddance, he thought. Cattywampus Dog sat next to him in the uncut grass peering with his head awry as the last of the fire burned down; the Moore mule waited by the road tethered to a fence-post. Lashed to the mule's saddle were the Winchester and the Springfield and two of the best of Corntassel's bear pelts and a poke with some ammunition and canned goods and a part of a deer ham and some corn dodgers in it; the Cherokee doohickeys that used to decorate the jambs and lintel of Corntassel's door now dangled from the pommel horn. Everything was ready.

Now, he thought, *we do what come next*. There were five more things. He owed Oliver Price that visit. He had to stop by McCrae's Fort Hembree store to trade the Springfield and the pelts for supplies and some extra forty-four shells for the Winchester. He had to go to Miss Becky's grave. He had to return the borrowed mule to Captain Moore. Then he had to do what he'd promised Corntassel.

He rose and stood rubbing the flats of his hands on his rump meaning to turn his back on what he'd just burnt up and never take thought of it again and go on and do his five things. But instead he waited a spell longer and kept watch on the lapsing fire. He told himself it was to make sure the coals didn't catch the grass alight and spread the blaze. But the truth was, he'd commenced to remember some things and in spite of himself he didn't want to stop.

He was remembering how he'd come home from the war to find old Daniel living in that cabin – owning it, owning the cabin and the forty acres around it and as proud of owning it as if he was Old Man Curtis himself and the little patch of poor cornland and its miserable tumble-down shack was a fine farmstead and not the pittance it was and that he and Old Man Curtis were equal before the law just like Abraham Lincoln said. And Hamby believing no nigger ought to settle for any pittance a white man was willing to give him, believing instead that the nigger deserved to get it all – to take to himself every goddamn thing the white man had hoarded all those years he held the nigger in bondage. Hamby hadn't wanted to get equal, he'd wanted to get even.

He'd sure enough got even in the war. When he was fourteen years old he'd gone through Georgia like a case of the cholera. Gone through it with the bummers' army of Uncle Billy Sherman. He was a gangly boy wearing a battered blue hat with the acorn insignia of General

Davis's Fourteenth Army Corps on it – a boy as hard as a bayonet, as hard as the hardest man and nursing a worse hate than any – a hate that glowed in his belly like a white-hot ingot that never cooled, a hate for that white man from Asheville who'd lain with his mama and a hate for his mama for giving herself to that man and for remembering that man with fondness; and a hate for himself for being neither white nor black because of what his mama and that man had done; and a hate too for the whole goddamn world, the world of whites and the world of niggers both, the world that insisted on naming him neither one thing nor the other then condemned him for what he wasn't. Yes, he'd got even with Georgia. Then he'd come back to Clay County to get even with it too.

A spate of coughing took him – the smoke had aggravated his lungs. He hacked and hacked and when he was spent he stooped and spat a bloody clot in the grass and wiped his mouth with the back of a hand - this time the dog didn't come to taste what he'd spat; it kept on morosely watching the last of the fire. Get even, that had been his whole notion in those days. Torment the Rebels – and through them get back at all else that riled him too. But old Daniel wanted no more than to be taken for as much of a man as any white. He'd fight for that; but for nothing beyond it. He'd kept no accounts. "The Rebels are whipped," he'd say. "Let 'em stay whipped. We got our own business to do now."

Hamby had scorned him, taunted him for still thinking like a lowly slave. Hell, in the end he'd even died like one, died for the goddamn whites. Died like slaves had been doing for a hundred years but did it after he was free. Made up his mind to do it. Sacrificed himself. Why? It was the mystery Hamby had wanted to solve and now he reckoned it *was* solved. But he hadn't solved it, Corntassel had. The old man had said it right. Daniel, he reasoned, hadn't so much loved the Curtises as he'd just done what was decent to do. Made the free choice of a free man. *Chose* to do right. And no part of having been a slave was in it.

Hamby couldn't reach that, Corntassel had said so. Sometimes he'd tried. With Ves Price. Or on the night Daniel died, when he'd got shot trying to help. But whatever he'd reached for, it always lay just beyond his grasp. Once in his travels he'd gone up to Hot Springs in Madison County and stood on the bank of the French Broad River where his mama told him his white daddy had drowned himself after she was sold away from him; and standing there he'd tried to feel something about his daddy other than the hate. Abbott, his daddy's name was. Mama said Abbot loved her and wanted to marry her and Abbott's daddy parted them by selling Mama to Judge Curtis and Abbott killed himself in despair for his loss. Mama said Abbott's hair smelt like new-mown hay in the sun. She said he was a good man. A soft and tender man.

But standing on that riverbank all Hamby felt was the hate. He couldn't get hold of anything else. Too much of having been a slave and a mixed-blood had stayed in him. It was funny – he used to scoff at Daniel for keeping a slave's mind when the truth was, he was keeping a slave's mind himself. His daddy was part of him – had to be; some of the good, some of those tender ways – but the slave living in him wouldn't let him get to it. To that or to anything else that wasn't hateful.

He took the Cartmans' carriage road to town. Cattywampus Dog trotted sideways behind the mule and as usual somehow managed to keep up pretty well despite his disadvantage. Till now Hamby had been calling the dog an it. Today he decided to call it a him because the critter had a stubborn way about him that Hamby liked. Nothing was going to stop him, not even being twisty as a corkscrew and having to look up his own ass to take a shit. Hamby would see if he was as good a bear-dog as Corntassel used to boast.

Nobody was abroad for fear of the typhoid. The fields stood silent and untended, cows lowed unmilked in the pastures, the road was empty of travelers. Nearly every farm had its kettle of water boiling in the yard and a fire going so as to burn up infected clothes and bedding. The smoke of these fires, wispier than his from the cabin, stood up in thin straight lines and then leveled out high in the air to a long flat whitish-gray plume that was his smoke and theirs too; all the distances were blurred with a faint film of it. He'd thought folk would take note of his big smoke and question it – now he understood that one smoke was the same as another and they all meant the same thing. He passed a place where they were burying somebody and several more places where he saw the red-dirt mounds of fresh graves on high ground in back of farmhouses and at another place he heard folk wailing and somebody singing a dirge. The weather hung heavy and hot and dampish as if it had taken sickly too.

He crossed the Sanderson Ford bridge and rode into town. As he went uphill to the square Cattywampus Dog had no option but to fall behind owing to his afflictions. On the streets nobody much was astir. A wierd quiet held the place. Crossing the empty square Hamby fetched up before Oliver Price's shoe shop, dismounted, tied off the mule and stepped to the boardwalk. By then the dog, delayed but never daunted, had caught up again; and when Hamby took his seat on the bench to wait to be discovered, the dog sank panting at his feet, head hindward, tongue hanging slack.

Nearly an hour passed before old Oliver poked his head out the front door and found Hamby biding there. "Hidy," he said, without the least surprise.

Hamby gave him a nod and Oliver stripped off his leather apron and came out and joined him on the bench and they sat together for another hour. Hamby loaded his pipe and smoked it. Oliver fished out his case knife and whittled on a stick. The dog slept. The town lay before them nearly silent and lifeless. The air smelt of smoke. Idly they watched hens pecking in the street dirt. The mule broke wind. They paid heed to one farm wagon that passed, a gaggle of geese that waddled by, a pair of men loading a coffin into a hearse in front of the undertaker's. Miz McClure swept the front steps of the hotel. The bell of the First Baptist Church tolled – another death probably. Hamby emptied his pipe and refilled it and fell again to smoking.

Neither spoke. Neither had to. They'd never yet relied on talk; they wouldn't now. Time was what mattered – time that you improved by meditating on its passage and savoring it and taking it into you without remark in the same way that you might linger over sweet water from a fine spring. Two men could hardly be more different; yet they were the same in this one thing of time. A little sameness couldn't help but come with so many years of knowing. They'd been parted for awhile but that hadn't counted for much; they'd known each other so long over the course of their lives that the edges of their difference had worn smooth and they could fit together like two pebbles nestled in a creek bed. That it was a leavetaking made the fit even closer, the flavor of the time they were tasting that much sweeter.

Finally though, the time had to run out. Hamby knocked the ashes from the bowl of his pipe and got to his feet and slipped the pipe into the pocket of his coat and gave his head a dip and said, "I be going now."

With a grunt old Oliver pushed himself up from the bench, stood hiked over to the side favoring his bad leg. He put out his smooth little hand and Hamby took it and quickly let go of it and turned and spoke gruffly to the dog and the dog bounded up wagging its ugly stub of tail, ready to go wherever the road might lead. Hamby left the boardwalk and unhitched the Moore mule and swung aboard. One last time he nodded; Oliver nodded back. Not once in the whole hour had their eyes met, nor did they now. Hamby jerked the mule's head, started to wheel and leave; then paused, swung back, sat his saddle looking down and to the side. He coughed, spat blood. "I be obliged," he said.

◄

Lillie Carter was worn out and depressed, and whenever she got in that state it was her custom to go to the old Methodist cemetery and sit by her mama's grave and tell her mama her troubles. Today the need was more urgent than ever, for Lillie had been called on these last two weeks to help her stepmother nurse a host of kinfolk and neighbors stricken with the fever. She'd even been present in the sickroom when her beloved Aunt Martha passed; and later when her cousins Zeb and Virgil and Daisy died, she'd been not twenty feet away in the front yard of Uncle Sanders's place boiling bedclothes.

Not till then had Lillie been in the presence of death – save the passing of her mama which she hardly recalled – and it had alarmed and fascinated her and made her think of her own death to come and of Will's. It seemed queer to her that folk had to go to the trouble of getting born and living and putting up with all the commotion of life only to die, sometimes a lot sooner than was convenient, as with her cousins and with her own mama.

Of course she knew the Bible said it was all just a way of getting ready for eternity and for reposing in the bosom of Jesus. And it was true that in the case of Aunt Martha death had come as a needful rest after long years of hardship and toil. Still, by and large it appeared to Lillie that dying made living look like a whole lot of useless bother. She had wanted to relate this to her mama and see if her mama had something helpful to say about it from her place on the other side. Will had come by Carter's Cove in Jimmy Cartman's wagon, making a detour on his way back from delivering a load of crossties to Murphy. He'd agreed to take her – they were promised now, so it was all right for them to go.

So that hot August afternoon Lillie was sitting by the grave in the shade of the maples with her feet tucked under her talking to her mama about death and Will was hunkered nearby helping to comfort her by singing a hymn he was going to lead next Sunday morning at Chestnut Grove.

The fever had so far spared the Cartman households and while Will sympathized with Lillie's losses and joined her in mourning them, he'd lost no dear ones himself. Also, he was used to Jimmy's ways – business had to go on, epidemic or no; and he'd done his business by going to Murphy and earned some free time and meant to put it to good use. So he could be in a temper to sing. His high tenor rang out over the gravestones:

> *"Oh, when shall I see Jesus*
> *And reign with Him above?*
> *And from the flowing fountain*
> *Drink everlasting love?*
> *When will I be delivered*
> *From this vain world of sin*
> *And with my blessed Jesus*
> *Drink endless pleasures in?"*

After he stopped Lillie communed awhile longer with her mama, then turned to Will no longer glum. It was true she'd got no improving counsel; but it had been a relief just to unburden herself to her mama who she knew always patiently listened even if she seldom talked. Lillie's heart felt lighter; it put her in a sprighty mood. "You're mighty vain about that voice of yours," she tweaked him. "I believe vanity's your besetting sin."

"It's not vain to recognize the truth," he replied with confidence, "and the truth is, I've got a fine tenor voice that I sing regular and distinct and without pain or a weeping sound, and with a sufficiency of breath, just like William Walker says in his book. And I sing the pure Christian Harmony. Anyway, it's not my doing, it's the Lord's. My voice is a gift from Him and I use it to praise Him."

"I still think you're vain and you're using the Lord to hide it," she teased. Still, he did have a glorious tone. She knew how he practiced his *fa sol las* in the parlor at Jimmy Cartman's every evening after supper and how sometimes of a night in his gable garret he'd study the shaped-note songs in William Walker's big book by candlelight till he fell asleep.

He'd attended any number of the ten-day Christian Harmony singing schools – Jimmy was willing to part with the fifty cents each school cost because whenever Will sang so good in church it made Jimmy look more and more holy. Will's last singing teacher had lent him the Walker book – *Hymn and Psalm Tunes, Odes and Anthems* – and Will couldn't have prized it more if it were Holy Writ itself, for the old books were mighty hard to come by these days. Whenever the singing teacher passed through Clay County again and asked for it back, Will was going to have to give it up; so he was learning everything in it by heart.

Ignoring her criticism he now sang for her the tenor part of the grand old hymn "French Broad", which spoke of the very highlands they lived in:

High o'er the hills the mountains rise
Their summits tower toward the skies;
But far above them I must dwell,
Or sink beneath the flames of hell.

Oh, God forbid that I should fall
And lose my everlasting all;
But may I rise on wings of love,
And soar to the blest world above."

Even if it was only the tenor it was pretty. After he sounded the last note they sat quiet for a time, though now and then Will would hum another tune. From the hill they had a good view of Chunky Gal and back of her, the Nantahalas. In the smoky air the nearer mountain was a royal purple and the range behind it a blue so soft it looked like it belonged in a dream. A bird was hopping about nearby and it had a white head and Will pointed it out and wondered what it was. Lillie said it looked like a robin but robins couldn't have white heads. Will surmised it was a misplaced seagull, though he'd never seen a seagull to know.

They drank buttermilk from a stoneware crock and nibbled on some crackers. Across the way a small bunch of folk were burying somebody and Preacher Chalmers Moore was praying over the grave, which meant the deceased was a Presbyterian. It was a mystery why a Presbyterian was being buried with the Methodists. Even so, Lillie and Will watched and listened with due reverence and when Preacher Moore got finished Will said *amen* and Lillie said *amen* too.

Then Lillie fell pensive again. The sight of the funeral had reminded her of all her recent trials and sorrows. But she couldn't let herself get but so low in spirit, not now that she and Will were to sure be wed in time. It was funny, all the worries that used to plague her were gone now – whether Will would ever ask her, whether she ought to tell him yes or no, whether he'd stand up to Jimmy and demand his own; but all the same, other worries hurried to take their place and she guessed there'd always be some; sickness and death were some.

Another came now. She picked a grass stem and put it in her mouth and asked him, "Are you sorry that if you marry me you can't be a railroad man?"

He frowned. "Grandad said that too; I don't see why I can't marry you and be a railroad man both."

She gave a sigh of impatience; she thought the answer to that was painfully obvious. "Because if you were a railroad man, you'd be gone all the time. And what would I do then? Besides, railroad men experience temptations and often fall into sin. And if I was to find out you'd fallen into sin, why, I'd split your jenny."

Mischievously he grinned, showing his white even teeth. "Well, I'll bet the *wives* of railroad men sometimes fall into sin too – if their husbands are gone so much. What about that?"

"If the husband's gone so much," she sniffed, "maybe it'd serve him right."

Will shrugged, plucked up a handful of early-fallen leaves, scattered them. "Oh, I've given up that notion anyhow." He didn't seem sad and she was relieved to notice that. "I mean to farm," he said.

She sent him a sharp look of her bright eye. "Farm for who? You and me? Or Jimmy?"

He reddened and his mouth went flat the way it did when he felt pressed. She knew he was proud of himself for having stood up to Jimmy; she was proud of him too; but she thought it likely Jimmy'd got the better of him in spite of everything and she wanted to warn him to watch out. He'd be awful sad when he learnt how hard was the bargain Jimmy'd driven. He was so trusting. So hopeful. He couldn't see how bad it was going to be, trying to take care of his own and the Cartmans too.

"I've explained that," Will insisted. "Us first, then him and Maw."

Lillie vented a little snort. "So you say." Sarcasm tinged her voice. "He's going to make everything over to you, is he?"

"That's what he's promised."

"Promising's not doing," she pointed out. Her chin went up in a show of resolve. "Well, he's my cousin – I'll make him treat you right. Or know the reason why." She would. She'd go to him once a week for the rest of his miserable life and remind him what he'd pledged to do. Even if he never did it, she'd make him wish he had. Jimmy Cartman! She shuddered. "Oh, thinking about that man gives me the mullygrubs."

Will brightened, anxious to change the subject. "I'll tell you a story then, to cheer you up."

She squinted doubtfully. "Well, all right. But it better be a good-'un."

"It will be." He took thought for a minute, composing the tale. Then he commenced. "There was this family that had a flock of guineas. One

Sunday the family went to church. While they were gone, the guineas got into some fermented fruit and got drunk on it and passed out. So when the family got home from church they found all their guineas lying around in the yard and thought they were dead, that some sickness had killed them.

"Seeing as how the guineas had all been wiped out, the mother of the house decided she wanted feathers for ticking for a featherbed. So she plucked them. When she finished, she had her husband take the dead guineas across the field and throw them in the ditch. And next morning the family woke up and looked out of the house and all these stark-naked guineas were running around the yard. They'd all come to, you see, after being drunk. Well, it was wintertime and the mother got worried about the welfare of those naked guineas, so she crocheted little jackets to keep them warm."

Lillie made a sour face. "That's not much of a story. And you know she never crocheted any little jackets."

Will looked sheepish. "Well, I added that."

"I wouldn't tell that story any more," she advised. "With jackets or without them either one." Her look went past him toward the road and sharpened on what she saw. She shaded her eyes with a hand. "Who's that coming yonder on that mule?"

He turned to see what she was seeing – a raggedy-looking nigra; no – not a pure nigra; his skin had the pinkish-orange hue of peach pulp. He was a high yellow. He got down and busied himself tying the mule to a crape myrtle bush. There was some kind of ugly malformed dog with him. When he finished with the tethering he started into the cemetery, moving with a sort of long shuffling walk. The dog didn't follow; it made a queer quick motion rearward and sat by the mule with its bottom toward the cemetery but its head twisted back over its shoulder to watch after the yellow man, who'd come to a stop now that he'd seen them there by the grave. He stood undecided as though surmising he might not be entitled to come any nearer.

But Lillie knew at once that he was. "I'll bet you're Hamby McFee," she burst out. "Aren't you?" She sprang up from the ground and jumped eagerly from one foot to the other, hugging herself. "I've been wanting to see you all my life," she exclaimed. "Come over here and talk to me. D'you know who I am?"

The yellow man peered narrowly as if her enthusiasm had unnerved him and he was reconsidering his visit. He had pale gray-blue eyes and his face and the backs of his hands were covered with ginger freckles. After taking his squinty look at her, he dropped his attention to the grass under his feet and muttered, "You be Lillie Dell Carter."

As happy as she was to see him at last – besides her daddy, the nearest living link to her mama – she couldn't help noting with disapproval that he made no move to doff his hat. Faintly scowling she asked, "How d'you know that?"

His heavy shoulders rounded then dipped. "I knows."

Lillie reached out and gave Will's arm a touch. "Hamby, this is my intended, Will Price. Will, this is Hamby, who saved your real daddy."

The pale eyes brushed Will before slanting down to resume his scrutiny of the ground. "Ves Prices's boy," he allowed.

Will confirmed it with a tilt of his head and Lillie could see that he wasn't any too pleased to have the man who'd kept his real daddy from getting killed show up and call back to mind how Ves Price had shunted him off and run away.

An awkward moment passed, then Hamby remarked, "Heard he had him a boy." A flicker of his light eyes went from Will to Lillie and then down again. "Heard you two was bespoke."

"You came to bless my mama's memory, didn't you? I know you did." But the business of the hat was nagging at her and she couldn't help making mention of his failure to show a proper respect. "If you did, though, how come you don't take off your hat by her graveside?"

"I took it off for her one time," Hamby replied – a bit doggedly, Lillie thought. "Day she die, I took it off. Know what she say? She say put it back on, my head too ugly to show. I keeps it on all the time now." He hesitated, darted her a sidewise glance, added, "You got a sassy tongue in you head, jus' like her."

Lillie wasn't sure if this was a compliment – there'd been a hint of a complaint in it, she thought. Nor could she tell if his answer about the hat had been altogether satisfactory; but it had been unusual enough that she decided not to pursue the question any more – especially when she recalled what her daddy had told her. "My daddy," she remarked, "says she loved you like a brother. All my life I've been wanting to know why. Come on over here and tell me why."

Hamby waited; he seemed to be considering whether it was wise or even safe to oblige her. He was stubborn – she could see that; he wanted whatever he did to be his own notion. He frowned; his attention darted here and there over the ground before him as if in search of a weapon he might use to defend himself.

Then he blew a little derisive puff of air out of his nose. "Tom Carter say that? He just a fool."

In spite of being glad to find him after all these years, Lillie was disappointed and displeased to hear him deliver such a rude remark. "I've been wanting to see you for the longest time," she said, using her most severe tone, "but I won't stand for you to say anything against my daddy. He's a good father and a good man and a good Methodist. He's just had a lot of bad luck, is all." When she saw how her rebuke made Hamby blanch she decided that was enough scolding and relented. "Now will you come over here and tell me why my mama felt so strong for you? Daddy says she did. So does everybody else. I'm her daughter, seems to me I ought to know why. So you tell me."

Still looking down and sideways, he edged grudgingly toward them. Coming under the shade of the maples out of the sun, he seemed to darken, he lost that peach hue and took on more of a tint of bronze; the eyes that had appeared to be pale blue in the light now seemed as green as the underside of a laurel leaf. He shifted a look Will's way and – as if to postpone the subject Lillie wanted so badly to pursue – remarked to him, "Ves Price's boy. You remember that scamp?"

Grudgingly Will shook his head; he had no wish to speak of that. "Not hardly atall," he answered in a clipped way.

"Give you to Jimmy Cartman, didn't he?"

"He did."

Lillie's impatience overcame her; she stamped her foot in the grass and blurted, "Hamby McFee, are you going to tell me or not?"

He shot a short glance to her, past her. She saw him gather a breath, knew he resented her probing at him. *Well*, she thought, *he just said my mama was sassy; he liked her sass, he can like mine too.* She folded her arms to wait him out.

"I remember you," he finally said. "You had on a little yellow pinafore. Old Moore, he rode up on that Crockett. You went to that old brown stud to pet him."

"The day my mama died," she nodded. "I've got a stepsister now who wears that same yellow pinafore, though it's near wore out. I can't bring you to mind, though – what you were like that time. You didn't smell bad, I remember that. Most other times you smelt like you do now." The way he smelled and the dingy condition of his clothes and his rebellious temper were making her wonder more and more what her mama ever saw to admire in him. But it was certain her mama did; and the certainty was enough to keep Lillie after him.

"I was setting on the fence," he said.

"I remember that. But not what you looked like." Lillie sighed. "Now you tell me. Why were you and my mama so close?"

Hamby lifted his head, gazed off toward the mountains; his irritation faded; something of him seemed to drift loose and go away over the air and come to rest as far off as those mountains were. "One time she made tea with a little tea-set," he mused. "Served me tea."

"Was that how you knew she favored you?"

Whatever had left him came quickly back. He made a little deprecating click with his tongue against the roof of his mouth. "Naw. That was just serving tea. Play-like. She was just a little bitty thing. But I always think of that." He stopped then; his mouth clamped shut like a trap. It was as if he'd said all he could afford to say without making something happen that he was determined to prevent. He skated off the topic as before and turned to Will and asked, "Jimmy Cartman, he good to you or not?"

"He's right good." Will was getting put out.

"I bet he preaches at you."

"He does."

A deal of time passed. Nobody spoke. Hamby observed the ground. Then he commented, "That Ves, he a scamp."

"I've heard that."

Hamby seemed to have brought the matter up on purpose. He could tell Will was vexed – anybody could've; Will'd darkened like a turnip – but there was an obstinance about Hamby now; it was like he'd made up his mind to go on and say a thing to Will whether Will wanted to hear it or not. "Tell you what, though," he went on. "He done all he could with what was in him to do. Didn't put up no lie. He be what he be. He a son of a bitch and make no never-mind about it. Always got him a plan. Gone be rich, rise high, be a swell. Need to be big, I 'spect 'cause he know he so damn small.

"Dumb." He wagged his head and let out a small dry chuckle. "By God, he dumb." But then a sudden earnestness came over him and for the first time he fixed a steady look straight on Will's face. "But he be trying," he said, laying a special stress on every word. "All the goddamn time, he be trying. Take all he got just to get through the day. He pay his debts, I say that for him. Pay every last red cent. He sure enough paid me."

He'd uttered several vulgarities and taken the Lord's name in vain and used the worst cussword there was and Lillie was hurt and offended to hear such crude speech from the mouth of this strange yellow man her mama had cared for and whom Lillie herself desperately wanted to know and come to like and understand but found mighty aggravating. It brought back the irksome matter of the hat too. She opened her mouth to call him to account for his misbehavior but then happened to notice the look of

wonder that had crept over Will's face as Hamby talked. All his bad
feeling had started to melt away. He leaned at Hamby now, stammered
out, "Dad – Uncle Jimmy – he says . . . he says I'm bad seed on account
of coming from Ves Price."

In a further revolting show of bad taste Hamby bent aside and
spat, though Lillie noticed he did it in the direction away from her mama's
grave. He turned back laughing bitterly. "Jimmy'd say such a silly damn
thing, wouldn't he? And him a bigger son of a bitch than anybody."

The same bad language whisked by again; this time Lillie was too
eager to hear what might come next to complain of his crudity – besides,
she agreed with his assessment.

"Tell you what," Hamby continued. "Tell you what I think. Ves
know he dumb and small and never be a swell. 'Spite of all his schem-
ing, he know it. He know he never be a good daddy to you. He know he
never amount to shit. And he so dumb, he think Jimmy Cartman a good
man. He believe all that Bible-thumping Jimmy do. He figure, I give my
boy to Jimmy, Jimmy raise him right, make him a Christian; I keep him,
we both go to hell together. That how dumb Ves be."

Will stood gaping. "You really think that's how it was?"

"Yep."

It was good Hamby was giving Will sentiments of solace that
he'd never got before; it was good that Will was taking them to heart;
Lillie was overjoyed to see the sudden brightness of his face and feel his
soul lifted up. But she'd been denied *her* wants and she'd asked first.
She'd wanted to hear the truth too. And she'd made up her mind that no
matter how much her mama might have loved him, Hamby McFee was
mulish and hardly housebroken and needed to learn some simple manners. She wasn't going to be put off any longer.

"Well, if it rained honey, my plate would be upside down!" she
exclaimed. "I've been standing here all this time waiting for you to talk
to me and all you can do is go on about Ves Price! I've been waiting all
my life to hear the truth. Why'd my mama treat you like a brother?"

While talking to Will, Hamby had actually faced him; but now,
with Lillie, his look dropped back away and down. "White folk see me
for colored," he mumbled.

"What's that mean? I know you're colored."

"Well, white folk just see me colored, that's all."

Will spoke up. "He's afraid somebody'll think wrong about it,"
he offered. "Because your mama was white."

Lillie faced Hamby impatiently. "Is there any reason to think wrong
about it?"

The green eyes flared and there was danger in the glow they took on. "That ain't it," Hamby shot back. "Wouldn't give a shit if they did. Any goddamn white got something to say to me, he can try and do it. See if he can do it and live. No, that ain't it. Most whites see me be colored. Your mama . . ."

She didn't even hear the profanity any more. "My mama what?"

He hesitated, groping for words. Then he started to speak but before he could shape a phrase a cough choked him and he turned away and bent over and a long spell of violent coughing racked him. They stood appalled till it ran its course. When it was done he spat again and what he spat was dark red and the sight of it made Lillie's stomach roll over and her gorge rise. He straightened, wiped his bloody mouth on the cuff of his threadbare coat. It took him a minute or two to catch his breath; they waited till he did it.

Finally he was ready. "She not see that," he said, hoarse from coughing. "Just . . . not see it." Then without warning a great rush of talk broke out of him like a torrent of water dammed up for a long time and suddenly finding an outlet. "She see I be *me*, not a colored man. Just me. What I *be*. What I want, what I hope, what I be hating, what hurt me, what please me. Nobody else see that. Nobody in the whole world. Not even me, *I* couldn't see it. She could. Did. Made me her brother. Made herself my sister. That a gift. Fine gift. Finest I ever got."

He stopped – had to, for he'd run out of wind. He stood gasping, looking down. Now his air turned sad. "I couldn't give it back, though," he confessed. His head moved from side to side in a motion eloquent with regret. "Couldn't see . . . free, the way she done. Couldn't give her what she give me."

Again he fell still, panting with a husky noise. Then very deliberately he raised one big hand to his throat and with it lifted something out of his shirt and over his head – it was a kind of necklace, a greasy cord with a lump of something black suspended from it. He held it up. "So when she first get sick," he continued, "I carve this. Give it to her. *My* gift. 'This a angel,' I say. 'Fly you up to Heaven when it be time.' Day she die, she give it back. 'Fly you up too,' she say. I be keeping it ever since. Not 'cause I fixing to fly." He chortled emptily. "I ain't going to no goddamn Heaven on no angel's wing; I gone roast in hell next to Ves Price and that damn Jimmy Cartman. No, kept it to remind me 'bout that gift."

With an upward gesture he proffered the necklace to Lillie; closer to, she could see little rudimentary stubs on the lump of black – angel's wings. "You take it," he was saying. "It be dirty from handling. But it got her and me in it, the both of us. Mostly her, though. Keep that. It be yours now."

She took it. It smelt of him but she folded it to her bosom anyway. She'd begun to cry. The sight of her tears made Hamby turn aside; he cast nervously about till he spied the bird that Will had pointed out before, perched now on the top of her mama's gravestone watching them with alert twists of its head. "See that robin?" he said. "Got hisself a white head. I never see that before. Not no white-headed robin. Not till last time I come. He was here then. Hopping around your mama's headstone. Not afraid nor hanging back. Bold, sassy. Like she was." A corner of his mouth rose a fraction of an inch; maybe it was a part of a smile. "Like you be."

Lillie wiped her eyes, smiled, nodded. "He's always been here when I've come too. Maybe . . ." But she didn't finish. Didn't need to. She could see that he understood.

There was another long stretch of silence. Then he took one step back, and as he did Lillie thought he looked strangely different – lighter of weight, smoother of outline. Like he'd divested himself of something rough and bulky. The step carried him back into the sunlight and he was peach-colored again and his freckles showed up brighter. It was a signal of goodbye. He didn't remove his hat but he did lift a hand and tug the brim of it downward in a solemn gesture that looked like it could be part of some ceremony. "I be going now," he said.

Gratitude flooded her. "I'd been waiting all my life," she told him. "I'm glad you finally came. Can we talk some more sometime?"

But he wouldn't answer that, only took another pace backward; then Will stirred and crossed to him and pushed out his hand. Hamby grasped it; Hamby's palm was horny as emery paper and his grip like a vise – not to be showing off, Will could tell, but because Hamby didn't know his own strength.

"I'm obliged," said Will, "for what you told me."

Hamby shrugged. "He was a scamp. It don't mean you got to be."

Will tried to talk but had to stop and clear his throat. Hamby turned and strolled off between the headstones toward where the mule and the misshapen dog waited. Lillie called after him, "Where're you going now? Are you coming back?"

He didn't answer that either. The crippled dog got up as he approached and wagged a little nubbin of a tail. It licked the toe of his brogan as he untied the mule from the crape myrtle. When he swung to the saddle it watched him fervently, as if he were a god; and when he rode off, it followed along behind him trotting sideways, doing its best to keep up. With a flutter of wings the white-headed robin rose from the headstone of Lillie's mama's grave and flew away among the maples.

◀

After finishing at the Fort Hembree store, Hamby rode on up Tusquittee to give back Captain Moore's mule. On his way he passed more farms each with its black pot boiling in the yard and its bonfire sending up a line of smoke and the buggies and saddle horses of visiting kinfolk clustered in front. Opposite the mouth of Peckerwood Branch he met a carryall coming down the road drawn by a sorrel horse; and as it came nearer he saw it was the rig of Sullivan, one of the two doctors in the county, with Sullivan himself slumped over in the seat dead asleep from exhaustion and the reins trailing on the ground underneath it where he'd dropped them. That horse was headed for its barn no matter where old Sullivan had meant to go.

Hamby turned the Moore mule to bar the road and the horse stopped and Sullivan awoke and sat up scrubbing at his face first with one hand and then the other, and commenced searching about for the reins, not even seeing Hamby right there in front of him. His face was as gray as putty, the eyes raw-rimmed and sunk deep in their sockets; his jaw hung slack, there was a line of drool on his chin and a glistening streak of it on his coat lapel. His clothes looked like he'd had them on for a month.

When he finally did catch sight of Hamby he stared in disbelief as if he suspected him of having dropped from the clouds. He tried to move his mouth but it only flopped and gaped in a rubbery way and nothing came out and Hamby got down from the mule and fetched the reins and handed them up and Sullivan took them with fumbly hands. His deep-sunk eyes touched Hamby but didn't focus on him, just seemed to have wandered there by accident. Hamby stood to the saddle and guided the mule out of the road. Sullivan gazed dumbly ahead, the reins loose in his hands. The sorrel horse started for home again.

◀

Captain Moore's big white four-gabled house was no different from the others – the same kettle on a boil, the same bonfire, the same clutch of turnouts and wagons and saddle mounts in the yard. Hamby was sorry to see that. He swung down and tethered the mule to the gate, unsaddled it and and set to grooming it with the currycomb he'd found in the saddlebag. When he'd got the mule neatened to his satisfaction, he took Corntassel's saddle and laid it astraddle of the Moore fence; he wouldn't be needing it now and maybe it would serve for interest on the loan of the mule, if the Captain was yet alive to reckon up such accounts. After that, he turned to making up his budget of goods.

He took a coil of whang he'd bought at the store and made a sling for the Winchester. On the shoulder of the road he spread out one of Corntassel's wolf pelts and laid on it his poke of eats and the ammunition boxes for the Winchester and the charms he'd taken off Corntassel's door; and he wrapped these up in the pelt and tied the pelt into a bundle with some more of the whang. Finally he used the last of the whang to make a sling for the bundle. Then he was done. Since nobody had yet noticed him and come out, he climbed up on the road fence across from the house and filled his pipe and perched there smoking.

In another twenty minutes or so somebody must have spied him, for Miz Hattie emerged. Others – a man, two women, a girl Hamby didn't know – stood in the doorway curiously peeking; kinfolk, he reckoned. He slipped off the fence as Miz Hattie passed through the gate pushing it open with an impatient flourish. She looked older than he remembered her, older and grimmer. Smaller. Mad, too. Her eyes were mad at what was happening.

She came at Hamby as if she had it in mind to bless him out for intruding or maybe for being somehow responsible for it all; he dragged off his hat – the first time in nine years he'd done that, the first time it had seemed right to do since the day he'd stood by Miss Becky's death-bed; hurriedly he spoke up, explaining, "Cap'n Moore, he lent me this mule." She couldn't have glared at him any more smartly if she suspected him of telling a lie. He looked down, commenced turning his hat before him in his hands, muttered, "I be bringing it back."

"Put it in the barn," she told him; her voice stung like a leafy branch lashing into your eye on a mountain track. "We've got bigger things to tend to just now." But standing there with his eyes down, he could see how she twisted her hands in her damp apron and how badly her hands shook.

Embarrassed, he gave an awkward nod. "You got the sickness here."

"We do."

He wanted to know more but feared it might not be meet to ask. Who was down? Who was dead? Was it old Moore himself? He stood mute, head dropped, watching his hands rotate the hat. Then he thought, *What the hell, she just a old woman beset.* He straightened, took a breath, forced himself to speak. "Anybody . . . anybody pass?"

Whatever was making her bristle went out of her then like air squeezed out of a bladder; she sighed, raised one hand, put the back of a wrist to her brow. All of a sudden she was a just a vessel so fragile she might break at a touch – a vessel full of more woe than she could hold. "Yes," she told him. "Two."

"The Cap'n?"

"He'll live, I think. And Nannie, my baby girl." For an instant her face collapsed, the vessel burst, tears sprung into her eyes and spilled over; one sob caught in her throat but she gulped hard and swallowed it and forced herself past it and it was done; and save for the tears which still silently flowed, she was as she'd been before, just grim and mad. "But I've lost my boys," she said in a steely hush. "I've lost my Jimmy. I've lost my Charlie." She teetered then, as if she might swoon.

Hamby was terrified that she might; what would he do then? But the kinfolk waiting in the doorway saw her reel and came bolting to her aid. The women took her in their arms with cooing noises; the man gave Hamby a scowl as if he'd done her some bad turn; the girl clung to Miz Hattie's skirts crying. In a bunch they all bore her off to the house. Hamby stood in the road turning his hat. Then he went and sat on the road fence again to wait for Cattywampus Dog to catch up.

◀

He walked to the Middletons'. When he got there he found the typhoid had beat him there too. Half the logging crew was down with it; Miz Middleton and two of the girls were already dead and buried; the old man was gone off somewhere – drunk, Seth said. Seth and Luther were trying to make up a load of tanbark and wanted Hamby to help; but he told them he'd quit. He asked after Absalom. "Weatherby fired his ass," Seth crowed. "Sent that fancy gal of his back North too. Reckon he's come to earth with a wallop."

Hamby found him back of the house filling a demijohn with coal oil. "I hear you and Weatherby be finish," he said. Tersely Absalom confirmed it. Hamby squatted. "'Bout that bear. I found that old Injun that knows the medicine; but he dead of fever now. He give me the secrets, though. I was aiming to go and get me that bear. But now – "

Absalom cut him off. "Go on ahead. It don't mean a damn thing to me, not any more." Then he paused and seemed to ponder. A pleasing notion must've come over him then, for he smiled – though the smile was a narrow one. He nodded encouragingly. "Yes, you go on and get that bear. Put its head in a bucket, take it to Weatherby. He'll pay you two hundred dollars for it." He looked mighty smug for a fellow who'd lost his gal and been put out of a job both; Hamby studied him, trying to think why. But Absalom just kept smiling, kept filling that crock with coal oil.

Chapter Nineteen

If Nannie Moore was going to have to die, she hoped it wouldn't be for another fourteen days – not till the twenty-fourth of the month when she and her big brother Charlie were supposed to celebrate the birthday they shared. She was going to be eleven and Charlie was going to be twenty-five and she thought it would be a shame to have to die and still be only ten. She didn't know how Charlie felt about it – hadn't seen him since he took sick too and they put him in the downstairs bedroom. But it seemed sensible that as a grown-up man Charlie would rather have a sister that was eleven than one that was but ten and still a child – even if she was destined only for the grave.

It was pretty certain she was going to have to die. All the signs pointed to it. She'd been abed more than three weeks with her fever going higher every day save the times of a morning when it would ease off a whit and then come raging back more fierce than ever as if to tease her cruelly with small respites. It had raged so hot she'd shrunk to half what she'd weighed before taking sick.

She was so weak she could hardly lift her head and there were still some rose spots on her middle and her belly was swollen and hurt worse than it ever had and sometimes instead of night soil she voided blood. It was true her head had come clear – after several whole days when Mama said she'd been raving. But Nannie knew that wasn't the hopeful sign it seemed, was in fact the opposite; she'd heard a clearing head was an unfailing prelude to death.

Also, they'd laid her in the forbidden upstairs front bedroom – a place Mama had never before let her spend the night lest she sleepwalk and wander out on the second-floor balcony and topple over the railing and fall. Instead of the Old Testament tales she loved best, Mama was telling her the Easter stories of Jesus and the promise of the Resurrection and the Life Everlasting. And when Daddy came in to visit he kept shedding big fat tears though he tried not to. Mama explained this was because he had the fever too and was feeling light of head and not himself. But Nannie knew it was because she was bound to die.

She wasn't especially afraid of dying. Quite a few of her friends had died of one sickness or another – whooping cough, diptheria, scarlet fever, milk sick. Lots of infants got born dead. Till now she'd thought it was a normal thing for the ones to die to be the young – adults hadn't seemed to die all that much before the pestilence came.

Anyway, dying was supposed to be sort of a privilege. Everybody said it meant ascending up to Heaven and joining with the Saviour and seeing God Himself and becoming an angel and being in bliss forever and ever. All that sounded nice but not as interesting as candy pullings or going to singing school or riding horseback up to Pot Rock Bald to camp out under the clear skies and eat roast mutton in the cool of a summertime evening with Mama and Papa and Charlie and Jim and all her married brothers and sisters and her aunts and uncles and cousins.

But if she'd get to meet Jesus, she guessed that would be fun. So she didn't mind the idea of dying too much. But she did mind *having* to die right in the next few days. It wasn't fair to be forced that way. She'd never liked having to do anything according to somebody else's notion of time – always preferred to have a choice.

Not that she ever had. Girls got precious little choice – it was another reason she'd wanted to be eleven and not ten; she'd be that much closer to being a woman and having a say. At least that's what she'd always imagined. On the other hand, Mama was always telling her it didn't matter what age you were; if you were a female, the menfolk did your choosing for you. But Nannie had been watching Mama pretty close all her life and it had seemed to her that one way or another Mama could get Daddy to do just about anything she wanted, and when she wanted it too. And that was what Nannie would've preferred, if she hadn't had to die.

She wasn't sure that seeing Jesus would be better than some of the things she'd have enjoyed by living on. Getting married and having children of her own, for instance. By dying she wouldn't get to be anybody's wife – not even Clarence Smith's. Clarence was somebody she'd noticed and had thought she might marry when it was time. She didn't know if it was an advantage or not to never get married to Clarence.

Maybe there would've been somebody else besides Clarence that she might've married. But then when she died she wouldn't even get to see Clarence ride by the house on his mule at the start of every summer, driving stock up to the grazing range on the bald with his brothers; or hear him tell how he meant to go to Colorado someday to work on his uncle's ranch; or notice how silky his hair was or how chocolate-brown his eyes.

Nor would she ever again taste the corn muffins and teacakes Mama baked for her Sunday School class or for visitors or for the mail carrier. Or bite into the plump red-gold pears that ripened on the tree behind the house so the juice filled her mouth and ran over to drip off her chin. Or crack open the walnuts that fell from the huge tree in the side yard and pick out the tasty wrinkled meats to chew. Or walk her friends home after play till Mama yelled after her not to go any further than Rattlesnake Branch. Or try to feed Dixie and be afraid and have Papa frown and grumble, "Shucks, she'll not hurt you." Or watch with wonder as Daddy threw his hat before him in the road and spurred at it on Dixie and bent down to snatch from the dirt. Or listen while Daddy tapped out rhythms on his drum or blew notes on his cavalry bugle. Or listen to the stories the government surveyors told when they spent the night – stories about big cities and paved turnpikes and cement dams and telephones and electric lights, ferries, ocean-going steamers, buildings that stood higher than Goldmine Ridge, trains that ran underground, people who flew high in the air hitched to balloons, music that came out of machines, machines that printed words on paper when you played them like a piano, machines that could see through the human body, machines that could capture sound, machines that showed pictures that moved.

That was a lot to give up just to be with Jesus – and it would be even worse if she had to die before she and Charlie got to eat their birthday cake. So the next time Mama came in to nurse her, Nannie asked, "Mama, do you think I'll live long enough to have a birthday cake with Charlie?"

Mama took a good deal of time answering, had to gulp and swallow and hold her mouth tight, and when she found her voice it didn't sound like normal, was husky and almost like a whisper; but she managed a narrow smile and declared Nannie wouldn't die before her birthday came – Dr. Sullivan had sworn it. She even told a white lie and said Nannie wasn't going to die at all. Nannie felt some better after that – not because she believed she was going to live, but because Dr. Sullivan had pledged she wasn't going to die before the twenty-fourth.

It never occurred to her that anybody in the family other than she might be taken. Yes, Daddy was sick; so were Charlie and Jim – Jim was in the same bed with Charlie downstairs. But they were grownups; and while it was true that some grownups had died already in the epidemic, Nannie knew hers wouldn't – couldn't; they were far too strong to pass. She was the one who had to go.

That was why she couldn't credit what she overheard Mama tell that nigra Hamby McFee. The bedroom window opened out onto the road and the sash was up to let in what little air was stirring on this sultry day, and the speech exchanged down there by the gate came to her as clear as if uttered by her own bedside. The nigra asked if there were any deaths in the house and Mama said there were two and Nannie thought maybe the delirium had come back and she was raving again and imagining things that could never be. In the dream – if it was a dream – Mama said more but said it in such a hush that Nannie couldn't hear if she'd told who was dead. She pondered. It was she who was to die; and she was living yet. If two were dead, who could they be? Not Daddy, not Jim or Charlie. Surely not Mama, who stood there talking. No one else was in the house. It was a vision conjured by the fever. Had to be.

But she wanted to make sure. That was hard, though; when you were deathly sick, the truth got mighty scarce; everybody told lies and because you were sick you had no power to compel the truth out of them. All Nannie could do was try to find out if she'd dreamt or not. And if by some awful chance she wasn't dreaming, she had to learn who'd perished – she'd seen Daddy that morning and he'd looked all right, so she figured it was between Jim dying and Charlie, if anybody was dead at all. And because of the birthday she picked Charlie to ask about the next time Mama came upstairs. "Mama," she said, "will there be a cake for me and Charlie on our birthday?"

"There'll be a cake, sweetheart," Mama replied.

"But will Charlie be there to help me eat it?"

Mama didn't say anything, so Nannie had to insist. "I thought I heard you tell that nigra down in the road that two of us had died in here. Well, I'm not dead yet and Daddy isn't and you aren't. Did I dream it? Or did Jim or Charlie die?"

Mama gave a long windy sigh and took her by the hands and held them. "I'm afraid to tell you, sweetheart," she confessed. Tears came to stand in her eyes. "But Charlie died just this morning. And Jim, he passed two days ago. We didn't tell you because you were so low yourself we thought you'd go next, from the shock of hearing it. They're gone. Your brothers are gone. We took them out the back window downstairs so you wouldn't see them."

"Are they in the ground?" Nannie wanted to know.

Sadly Mama nodded. "They're in the Presbyterian graveyard. Your father was too poorly to go and I couldn't leave you. So their brothers and sisters and the other kinfolk buried them. Preacher Moore said the service."

Nannie was surprised. "I didn't think *they'd* die."

"I hoped they wouldn't," said Mama. "But they did."

"Will Daddy die?"

"Dr. Sullivan says not. Nor will you."

Nannie scowled and turned her head and looked out the window where the sun shone bright and hot. "You're just saying that."

"No," Mama assured her, "I'm not. Your fever's broken, you're on the mend. You're going to be fine."

"Will I be eleven?"

"Yes, you will. And you'll have that cake. Charlie just can't have it with you."

"Well, all right," Nannie conceded. But she didn't believe she was going to live to be eleven or to grow up and marry and have children and enjoy all the other treasures of life she'd been thinking of earlier. Of course she was going to die. And she didn't mind it at all now. She'd be in the ground next to Jim and Charlie and after the Resurrection she'd be in Heaven and Jim and Charlie would be in Heaven too and they would all be with Jesus together. And she'd bet that if Heaven was any kind of a place at all they'd have some cake there to eat and if it was heavenly cake it was sure to be pretty good.

❧

Every day now Irish Bill went riding. It was harvest time and the stock ought to be brought down off the highland pasturage and much of the work of the farm had lain untended during the sickness and needed doing now, but the Captain had no heart for such toilsome trifles. Nor had he spirit for matters far more pressing – not even for paying comfort to Miss Hattie who was sunk deep in grief and needed his succor nor for little Nannie whom he'd nearly lost, who was riven with a pain he might've helped soothe. No, he hired men to bring in the crops and fetch the stock and catch up the chores – tasks Jim and Charlie would've helped him do. And he turned away from his own who were bereft. Every morning he rose and went out to the stable and saddled Dixie and turned her through the gate and rode. He took no drum, no bugle, no throwing hat – all his hijinks were as dead as his boys. He rode and rode.

Sometimes he had a purpose. He went to town to pay off Dr. Sullivan, visited Sanders Carter to condole with him, wept over the two fresh graves in the Presbyterian cemetery. But most often he just wandered restlessly, without aim. The contagion had run its course, gradually the rhythms of normal life were resuming; but people were chastened, subdued; a kind of oppressive hush still lay over everything, as if all the world yet held its breath, bewildered by the horrors it had witnessed.

The same suspension lived in him. He remembered having told himself at the start that the sickness, like war, was bound to change everything, that he must be strong enough to meet what came. How hollow that sounded now! What old man – hell, he was almost seventy – what father his age could've guessed he'd be called on to bury his youngest boys? What father could abide it?

It was beyond abiding. So he rode the silent country. Miss Hattie needed him, Nannie needed him; but it wasn't in him to give what they needed. He was in sore need himself – he needed his boys back, his old life, his faith, his soul, everything that had gone down into that cold ground with Jim and Charlie. Miss Hattie was hiding her agony behind a shield of temper, had turned snappish and irritable. He didn't blame her – after all, years ago he'd dragged her from a fine home and a life of ease up in Macon County to this hard place where she'd had to toil all her life like a slave till a pestilence rose up to carry off the sons of her body. His health had returned but he owned no power to beat past her rightful rage. Nor had he the wisdom to explain to Nannie what he himself couldn't understand. So he rode.

Once he rode as far as Big Tuni. He sat Dixie on the creekbank gazing across the denuded hills that once were the Middleton woods. Unimproved despite Rufe's new prosperity, the house looked smaller and shabbier than ever squatting at the base of those bare slopes. Above it row on row of raw red-earth summits mounted higher and higher, all the way up to Tuni Gap, all the way over the ridgetop, and not a tree or a shrub on them, nothing but black stumps and piles of slashing and countless crooked erosion ravines eating them away. Mounds of sawdust where the donkey mill used to be had caught alight and dully smoldered, sending up a thick rank smoke that caught in the creek bottom and in the mouths of the hollers like a dismal fog. Big Tuni moved slow and blood-red with the silt washing out of the stripped hills; downstream, Moore knew, even the upper Tusquittee ran cloudy from it.

Rufe had cut everything he owned, even the shade trees before his own house. Moore wondered if he was content now, with five hundred acres of scalped hills leaching away around him and a wife and two younguns dead of the fever and a son who hated him; but with money under his mattress at last, more money than he'd ever dreamt of having. His family was wrecked, the timber gone, the land played out – wouldn't come back for a generation. But Rufe was somebody now. He'd cured all that bad luck. He'd finally got ahead of Irish Bill. Maybe the envy didn't gripe at his vitals now like it had. Maybe he hadn't minded losing what he'd lost to gain what he'd got. And maybe if all that was so, Irish Bill needn't feel any longer that somehow his own success had cost Rufe his.

He thought then about Miz Middleton and those two poor dead girls and about Absalom and what Absalom had said that night when death came to take his mama and his sisters, about the hate he'd seen twist Absalom's face into a mask, how the boy had smitten his own father down. He reckoned that cost. Maybe Rufe didn't reckon it but Moore did. And God would. God would reckon it to Rufe's woe, in the Hereafter if not in this life. And Moore reckoned up his own losses, his precious boys who'd never marry nor make children nor live long nor grow old. But he counted his blessings too – Miss Hattie, Nannie, his seven children yet living and their spouses and host of offpsring, a good farm enriched by husbandry, a respected name. For all his losses, he owned yet what Rufe Middleton had paid out. And what Rufe had bought was low and mean by contrast.

In the buying he'd put this ugly sore on the land that would be a long time healing. And his was but one of many. Others like him, like Weatherby, had left their cankers, had hewed roads into the mountainsides and leveled the forests and washed out the coves with splash dams and marred the ridges with log slides and fouled the rivers with sediment. The railroads had left their wounds too, and transformed the lives of everyone in the district. And the tanners, the sawmillers, the miners for corundum and iron and clay and copper and mica and gems, all had dealt out hurt and change.

Even Irish Bill had inflicted weals of his own, cutting for crossties and tanbark even as he deplored how the country was ravaged and its customs turned in new directions. And in time all the sores together had festered – had mortified till they hatched a disease that swept over the land like the plagues God sent on Egypt in the olden time.

Moore fell to reflecting. His uncle had been the first white man up Tusquittee. Old John Covington Moore came in through the Nantahalas and over Chunky Gal and down Perry Creek and built a log cabin in the midst of what was then a boundary that belonged to the Cherokee. It was said of Uncle John that after he got settled he decided he needed a wagon and since none was available in that wilderness he had to go out to Tennessee to buy one and fetch it back; that he'd made harness from cornshucks to put on the horses to draw the wagon; that he'd come back trimming out a road with an axe; that when he got to the shut-in at Leatherwood Bluff he found the trail up the Hiwassee so narrow he had to take the wagon apart and haul it up piece by piece and reassemble it on Tusquittee. The country was that hard then.

Uncle John's brother Joab Lawrence – Irish Bill's daddy – came in later. Came from Rutherford County. He picked himself a place up Tusquittee and cleared the land and made a farm too; and that was the farm Irish Bill held today. But the country hadn't been pure even then – not even when Uncle John found it, much less when Daddy came. Already the Indians had hunted out the game, already they'd cleared some of the timber – torched some of it – for crops and settlements and ball grounds. Porcelain clays had been dug out of it to make Wedgwood china away off in England. Spanish explorers had mined it for gold and diamonds. When Uncle John made his farm and Daddy had made his and Irish Bill improved and enlarged what his daddy had made, the country had already been changing for two hundred years or more; and not for all that time had any man – red or white – seen it as the Almighty fashioned it.

His whole life Irish Bill had watched it change, had even done his own part changing it. Had cut trees and girdled them, had burnt some, had chopped the forests back so as to make room for cropland and pasture, had burned some patch of woods nearly every year to free up ground for tillage, had grazed livestock free so the hogs and sheep and goats consumed the undergrowth. Had built dams and weirs and sash mills. Had sunk wells. Had made roads. Had been a ruiner and a pillager no better than Rufe Middleton or G.G.M. Weatherby.

How then could he rightly complain? Change was what happened. The land bore it. Had to. And could. It would be scarred, sure. Scarred and deformed, depleted. But it would come back. Not the same. Not pure as from the hand of the Creator. But something of it would come back. It always had. He was nothing but an old man hating to see the world he knew give place to one he didn't. That was it. The villain of the piece wasn't Middleton or Weatherby or even Irish Bill Moore. It was age. It was growing old. It was the cruelty of being mortal. You lived long enough to see what you knew and loved fade away around you, to be replaced by something new and strange – when your fondest wish was to die before it was lost, before you forgot how it used to be when you were young.

◄⁙

He rode back downstream and at a place near the mouth of Chairmaker Branch he tethered Dixie to a fence rail and strolled to the creekside and sat on a boulder around whose nose the water curled, running clear now, the last of the Middletons' runoff settled out of it. Sycamore and thickets of sumac lined the creek and there was still some late goldenrod growing and on the far bank a laurel hell. It was shady under the trees and he felt the cool of the water breathing up to him and he listened to the rush of the stream and to the slow stir of the leaves overhead. He pitched a pebble into the creek and a trout rose thinking some insect had fallen in; it broke the surface and saw its mistake and dove, leaving a round ripple. Moore threw in another pebble. The trout rose again, poked its head out, gave him a blaming look and sank.

Moore laughed, then realized it was the first time he'd laughed since the sickness came; guiltily he choked it off. What right had he to laugh? How could he feel levity with his two boys dead? Better he should keep somber from now on, better he should wear black all his remaining days. What finer memorial to Jim and Charlie than to devote himself to perpetual mourning? Gloom would be his companion always. A pall would shroud him. Never would he smile, never tell a joke, never spin another yarn or do a riding trick or make a spectacle of himself. He'd make that vow. But while he was vowing the trout popped up again, looked him in the eye and dove; and Moore laughed. And laughed and laughed. He laughed till his sides hurt. Then he cried.

◄⁙

The rattle of a rig and the noise of hooves on the road roused him and he stood and climbed partway up the bank craning between the sumac boughs with their reddening fronds to see who was passing by. He recognized Jimmy Cartman's buggy and Jimmy's white mare in the traces, then young Will Price handling the reins and Lillie Carter next to him on the seat, one arm linked through his. By ordinary Moore would've bounded over the lip of the bank and hailed them, but today in his pensive frame of mind he held back, content to watch and muse. He'd heard Will had proposed, had gained Lillie's hand; he wondered whether his own fulsome advice that day in front of Oliver Price's shop had stiffened the boy's resolve, wondered if the union to come might be due in part to his eloquence. He hoped so. It made him proud to think so.

They saw Dixie tied to the fence and knew her. Will drew rein; they looked about for Moore. But he'd withdrawn behind the sumac. Not finding him, Will made as if to go; but Lillie chose the moment to lean at him and turn her sweet face up; he bent his to her; they kissed. A swift chaste kiss, no more. Then they parted and Moore heard the tinkle of her laugh. Will slapped the reins, they rolled on.

Moore watched them go. He reflected how their love had flourished with death raging everywhere around. They'd trusted they could grasp a future as man and wife even when contagion seemed ready to sweep the future away wholesale. Jim and Charlie had trusted in the future too. But they'd lost it – lost the gamble that life was.

Yes, life was a gamble. In peace as in war. It was hardly safer here in the peaceful fields and farms of the Hiwassee Valley than it had been in the army when the balls were flying – on outpost duty in the swamps around New Berne when he was in the Cherokee Rangers, or later with Folk's Battalion, chasing tory bushwhackers in East Tennessee or fighting regulars in the Georgia woods. A sip of bad water could kill you as quick as a shot from a carbine. A fly could walk across your mashed potatoes and put you in your grave just as easy as a round of spherical case on the battlefield. Jim and Charlie were casualties of life just as so many boys had been of the war.

He'd let himself forget it, that was all. Peacetime and prosperity had lulled him. But he remembered now, remembered what the war had taught him that he'd let slip his mind. You couldn't dwell on your losses. You numbered them, yes. You even grieved for them if you had the time. But you had to go on. Their dying wasn't your fault, it was the fault of war. War didn't give you the luxury of an abundance of time; you had to make the next move or you'd soon be dead yourself; what you did was call the roll and see what troops you had left, then figure what you could do with the boys you had on hand.

Life was a little different; it gave you more time than war did. But because it *was* life – was ordinary and commonplace – you failed to make the best use of the time, thinking there'd always be more of it. But it always ran out – slower than it did in war, but always sooner than you'd expected. And as in war, you couldn't linger to mourn or beat your breast; you had to go on; there was always more to do, more of your own life to live.

There was something else he'd come to see; Lillie and Will had showed it to him. There was almost always some love. It grew amid the offal of war and of peace, like a flower on a grave. Where you saw death, you found even more life; and where life was, love was too. It came back like the land came back from ruin. He thought again of Miss Hattie, Nannie on her sickbed, all the others – the blessings he'd counted before, his love for them and theirs for him; and that was when he knew he could go home.

＊

That night Wildwood burned. First there were only small tongues of flame licking at the base of each of the many corners of the house, triangles of yellow light that appeared improbably one by one as if the element of fire had somehow gained the power to reason and made up its mind to start in unnatural orderly sequence. The weather had been dry and the ornamental plantings at the corners quickly caught and burst alight the same as so many torches, and each shrub soon touched off its neighbor till a chain of fire ran to girdle the whole house; and for a time the turreted mass of Wildwood seemed to sit like a great doomed ship berthed in a bed of low flame.

Then the circlet rose – the ship sank lower in its fiery slip. Blazes lapped at the eaves of the porch. In no time the porch itself began to burn – its row of balustrades, its finials, its gingerbreading – and then the lesser of the towers. The enclosing woods glared and gleamed in reflection; above, the cloud-bottoms commenced ruddily to glow; sparks and brands and ash surged upward in a rush; an incandescent smoke mounted high. In their peaked gables all the windows of the first floor like tremulous jewels shone with flickery light. Then the heat blackened them and they broke making sharp popping noises and fire gushed from the holes they left and roared upward to embrace the foot of the highest tower.

All that seasoned chestnut and redwood, heart pine, oak, poplar, primavera, Philippine mahogany, burled walnut, all of it went up now with a flash and a thunder that shook the woods. Weatherby had gotten out, Duncan too. They stood before the conflagration helpless in their nightshirts. Duncan clutched a ewer and a silver tea service, Weatherby had saved no more than his own bare shanks. The gatekeeper, the gardener, the stableboys – all watched dumb with awe as flames sprang greedily to the tower's tapered crown and lifted its shingles off by the hundreds, blowing them away like fireflies.

The chimneys reeled and fell. The porch sagged, its pillars toppling domino-like; the mansard sloped, collapsed; with a mighty groan the whole colossal pile of Wildwood settled, all its seams opened, fire belched from every crack, the heat of its burning seared everything for a hundred yards around, driving the watchers back to the edge of the woods with singed hair and eyebrows. The grass of the yard shriveled to a carpet of smoking soot. Even the dead Lombardy poplars lining the drive flared and lapsed like struck matches. A moment longer the house hung together in the heart of the blaze; in half an hour it had dwindled from a grand edifice of weight and substance to this delicate quaking skeleton of char. Then whatever held it up failed and it slumped, it sank upon itself. With a rumble and a crash it fell, not heavily – most of it had been devoured; only its remnants remained to tumble weakly together. From the ruin a giant mushroom of sparks and embers rose twinkling in the night. Then at once its glow began to fade.

At the back line of the Wildwood property Absalom Middleton threw the empty demijohns over the spiked iron palings of the fence and heard them thump hollowly into the soft cushion of moss on the other side. He grasped the grillwork with his powerful hands and pulled himself up and crossed over and dropped. The suddenness of the move startled Pequod and the white-faced mule shied back but Absalom spoke his name and Pequod quieted with a snort and stood.

Absalom went to his knees, felt about in the dark for the demijohns, found them, fetched them up, fitted them into the wicker panniers lashed to either side of Pequod's saddle. They still smelt strong of coal oil. When they were secure, he took up the reins and mounted and turned the mule away from the fence and rode. Behind him, beyond the screen of the forest, the glare of the fire was already waning. He didn't even look to see. He knew. Most of what he was, he'd got from his mama. But this hadn't been from her. This had been from old Rufe. And he reckoned if it turned out that the nigger could get The Bear – could get it before Ahab did, could steal Ahab's vengeance from him – then that, together with this, would almost be enough to cost Ahab what he damn well owed.

Part Three

The Hunt

Chapter Twenty

Yan-e'gwa ranged far. In his madness he did not know why; he was compelled to wander without reason. He had forgotten many things but he had not forgotten how the world was made, how it was a great island afloat on a lake, kept from sinking only by the four cords tethered to its corners; the cords hung down from the vault of rock which was the sky. He had been roaming for a long time, and he thought by now he must have crossed nearly the whole island of the earth; and pretty soon he was sure to reach the place where one of the cords was attached.

When he came to the cord he was going to look to see if it was old and frayed, for if it was, that meant it was almost ready to break and the world was soon to fall and be swallowed up by the waters. Then all the creatures would drown. That was supposed to happen when the world got worn out; and since the world felt badly worn out to Yan-e'gwa, he was confident the end was near and that when he found the cord it would show this. Of course one of the things he had forgotten was that if the world was ending it was not because it was worn out but because the Ancestors were killing it.

Without meaning to, he went as far as Yanu-unatawasti'yi, Where the Bears Wash, the pool of purple water at the head of a creek in a gap of the mountains a long way from his home on the bald. Yan-e'gwa had never been to this place before but recog-

nized it immediately anyway because many of his kind loved to come to the pool and wallow in the cold deep water the color of the evening sky and often spoke of it. And he found that what the others had said was true, for when he came down out of a thicket of rhododendron and mountain laurel on the verge of the pool he saw several of his kind luxuriating in the water and resting on the stony banks.

Because of the wasting sickness occasioned by his wound Yan-e'gwa had become thin and bony, and one of the young males approached him by the pool and asked, "Are you not Kalas'-gunahi'ta, the Long Hams, the one so lean that the Ancestors will not hunt him, whose legs are long and his feet small, of whom we have heard?"

And Yan-e'gwa told his true name. But the young male would not believe him and asked why he concealed his actual identity; and this impudence angered Yan-e'gwa. He no longer suffered from the stone of pain embedded in his skull that used to make him ravage all in his path. The stone of pain had worn down to a small hard pebble not of pain but of bad temper and what the young male had said made the pebble burn white-hot and caused Yan-e'gwa to bow his back and raise his hackles and begin to pop his teeth and walk about in the heavy prowling low-headed way that showed he was ready to fight.

While it was true that he was worn and weak from his ordeal, Yan-e'gwa was still more than twice the size of the young male and the madness that came from the pebble in his head made him very fierce, so that when they fought he attacked with great savagery and quickly overmatched the other. He caught the young male's muzzle in his jaws and tore it terribly and then ripped a gaping wound in his throat with his teeth and opened his belly with his claws and the young male fled whimpering into the forest where it was certain that he must die. Yan-e'gwa was not even scratched. All the others left the wallow then and some peered at him in fear from cover, for it was almost unknown for one male to treat another with deadly violence. He entered the pond of purple water and bathed there till his temper cooled.

After he had bathed, he was standing on the rocky bank

shaking himself dry when he sensed a footfall on the other end of the suspended island of the world. The weight of a gnat would have been heavier and it was many, many miles distant, but he felt it anyway. Something smaller than the smallest being alive had stepped onto the pad of floating earth that rode on the waters of the lake of Creation and Yan-e'gwa felt its tread and its purpose too; knew at once that it had come to meet him, that if the cords that held the world did not break and cause the world to sink, he and this being must come together and discover some great prize that could not now be named.

This knowledge did not come to him by way of reason, for his reason was mostly gone. It came by way of his madness. And it drew him away from Yanu-unatawast'yi, into the balsam woods and along the ridgetops and crags and knobs, toward the place where the sun went down into the lake on which the earth floated, toward the bald of Where the Water-Dogs Laughed.

With his wolf-pelt knapsack on his back and Corntassel's Winchester strapped over one shoulder, Hamby left the Middleton place and started up the drainage of Big Tuni. The road to the gap had been hollowed so bad by ox teams dragging logs down and then washed out by a year's worth of rains till it was nothing but a mess of ruts, some of them nearly waist-deep and every one choked with rocks and exposed tree-roots. Going up was hard and tedious work – one misstep and you'd snap an ankle – but here at last Cattywampus Dog discovered he had an advantage; he could leap effortlessly from stone to stone and master the root-tangles as if they were rungs on a ladder; Hamby guessed his four feet were better than two when it came to going over rough ground, even if he was bent double as a damn hairpin.

More often than he wanted, Hamby had to stop and catch his breath. He'd clamber out of the sunken road and drop the knapsack and rifle and sit himself down on an old half-rotted fender log and wipe away his sweat and cough and spit blood and wheeze and blow till he felt ready to go on. Cattywampus Dog would stretch out across the top of a rut farther up the track to wait him out. He suspected he wasn't fit enough for the job he'd taken on. It annoyed him to think so, but it looked like the truth. He was sore and sick and old and had weak lungs. What made him think he could get this big troublesome bear when no hunter in the whole blessed country could do it? And why in hell had he decided to go up Big Tuni anyway? He ought to've backtracked down Tusquittee from Middleton's and come up by way of Matlock Creek and Julie Ridge and Pot Rock Bald. It was a longer way but bound to be easier on a fellow that was windbroke worse than any rode-down racehorse.

It took him most of the day to get halfway up, stopping as often as he had to. Late in the afternoon he took what he swore would be his last rest – he wanted to be on the top of the Tusquittees before night. He sat chewing a ball of middlin meat watching the sun dip toward Dead Line Ridge. The ridgeback wore an inky cloak of spruce but lower down the Middleton logging crew had shorn off all the hardwoods giving Dead Line a soup-bowl haircut. Back of Dead Line, Hamby knew, Tusquittee Bald and Signal Bald looked the same; but above the soup-bowl line their woods were as thick and wild as ever, and got thicker and wilder the higher you went, till they thinned out again on the scanty tops; and somewhere up yonder lurked the varmint Old Corntassel had called Yan-eg'wa, the Great Bear. A bear that was man and bear together. That had nursed a grand notion of how men and bears ought to be, a notion now fouled and fuddled, maybe lost. A critter that gave Hamby his life by killing that fool Boatwright who'd tried to murder him; that Hamby owed back now, owed the favor of the lost dream. Hamby lit his pipe and sat smoking. What was it Corntassel told him? *Give to a beast the grace you can't give to a man.*

What a load of bullshit. It was crazy, it was medicine-man mumbo-jumbo. But the old duffer had made him pledge his word and grudgingly he'd done it, afraid to balk a dying man's wish lest he court bad luck – no less a superstition than Corntassel's own, he saw now. But he'd promised. And his word was good even when he knew he'd been wrong and dumb-assed to give it. That was something he'd held to all his life. He'd held to it not because of what it might mean to others but because of what it did mean to him, to his sense of who he was. Besides, there was two hundred in specie at the end of it.

He finished his smoke and trudged up another hundred yards or so till he came to where one of the logging paths split off to the left and went switchbacking up more westerly than the gap road. It was washed out too but not as bad as the main track and was sure as shit not as steep. What the hell, it was easier; he wasn't proud; he made up his mind to take it. He and Cattywampus Dog turned off and followed it across a waste of stumps and slashing and wood-litter and sawdust

mounds with a few spindly young trees leaning this way and that looking amazed to find themselves so alone in such an expanse. Overhead
the autumn sky was a vast space the color of a kingfisher's back that
shaded to a lighter blue nearer the rumpled rimwork of the mountains
roundabout; wispy white mare's tails marked it. The weather was warm
for October – thank God for that; he felt the cold worse every year – but
it was a sweaty business hiking along in the glare and heat even if the
sun was sinking lower all the time.

Presently though it slipped behind Dead Line and the whole Big
Tuni watershed fell into shadow and at once the temperature plummeted
and Hamby's sweat-soaked clothes turned clammy and pretty quick
he was chilled to the bone and shivering. He stopped and glanced
about to get his bearings and saw from the way the hills lay that he
was right near the spine of the range, probably somewhere close to
Bearpen Gap, the next one west from Tuni. Likely the summit was
just above. He nodded; he'd make that and camp for the night. Up
and up he plodded, sucking hard for breath, blowing plumes of vapor in
the deepening cold, now and then twisting his head aside to split a dollop of red. Cattywampus Dog always stopped to sample the red and
then came scrambling after.

At the top he stripped off the knapsack and laid the Winchester
against a downed log and stood in the fading light and took in the prospect, using the time to do it even though he felt nearly frozen and needed
that fire and had to hug himself to try and keep warm. It was worth it.
On his right hand was the north-facing wall of the range with the old
Middleton log slide curling down it where he'd nearly tumbled to his
death last winter when Boatwright pushed him in. The soft red of the
evening sun lingered on the crest but the slope dropped away sharp out
of the twilight and into the dark of the valley; and a long ways off down
there where it was already night he could just make out the pale ribbon
of the Nantahala winding dimly along.

The other way, westward along the broad saddle that had been
sheared all over now like a sheep, Signal Bald loomed up with the big
dome of Tusquittee Bald standing next to it and the high purple line of
the Valley River Mountains frowning beyond the two like the ramparts
of a fortress. Maybe Yan-e'gwa was over there on that big dome, he
thought. Yan-e'gwa the Great Bear. Bear-man. The bear-man with his
lost dream that men and bears should keep the old bargain. Somewhere up here, maybe on the very spot where Hamby now stood, Yan-
e'gwa had come into the logging camp to take Boatwright in his arms

and gut him like a goddamn fish and so save Hamby's life. Did Hamby really owe him for that? Did such things happen for cause? Or did they just transpire by blind chance? Shivering, he fired his pipe and smoked. The bald was a mass of black, inscrutable, keeping its secrets. He studied it. He puffed. Cattywampus Dog huddled at his feet. He watched brooding as night came down around him and the first of the stars winked to life.

After he got his fire going and pitched his camp in the lee of the fallen log, he ate some more middlin meat and a corn dodger and washed this down with a swallow or two of the white whiskey he kept in his tin flask. Cattywampus Dog nestled close beside him and put his front paws over his ankles and watched him with his pretty eyes in the worshipful way that dogs do when they've decided to give themselves up heart and soul. Hamby sat smoking. "You better not do that," he told the dog. "Better not get me to liking you. We find that bear, you be jumping down his goddamn throat. Do your job, that bear gone eat you alive. That, or rip you to scraps. How'd that be?"

The dog licked his chops and kept up his reverent study. "You better not look at me like that," Hamby counseled, "I the one gone put you on that bear." But the dog never stirred. Soon they slept.

He awoke in the middle of the night badly needing to make water – a vexing custom that had come on him of late. Groggily he shook himself loose from the wolfskin, gathered it around him for a robe and stood. A quarter moon rode high overhead, its crescent seeming to trail a brilliant fretwork of stars. In the piercing cold every bone of his body ached; he gave a moan of misery, shuddered, stumbled away from camp clutching the pelt with one hand and unbuttoning himself with the other. Cattywampus Dog looked up, watched him closely to see if he meant to stray far. He came to the place where the edge of the gap shelved over and started its long drop to the Nantahala. Here he jiggled himself out and commenced.

There was a tiny crumb of light far down in the abyss of the valley; he saw it kindle, flicker, grow brighter. Soon it was shining like a hot coal aglow on a shovel-blade, save that it wavered and waxed and waned where the gleam of a fire-coal would hold steady. It ate a dazzling hole in the black of the night and as it grew a sort of halo formed around it which he could tell was the glare of it lighting up the encircling woods. Something big was burning. He peered at the shape of the peaks above it, hoping to reckon out the place that burned by how the hills set. But he couldn't. He grunted, finished his business, buttoned his britches one-handed while he held the wolfskin close. Somebody's house going up, he surmised. *Somebody's bad luck. Be a heap of bad luck in this damn world.* He hawked up a wad of phlegm and spat, turned, crossed back to the camp, stirred the fire and added some wood. He lay down again; with a whimper of comfort Cattywampus Dog snuggled warmly into the small of his back.

He had to make water twice more in the night but this didn't keep him from having to unleash another bountiful piss in the morning. He stood over a pile of punk timber ruefully observing the seemingly end-less yellow stream that gushed out of him smoking in the cold. *Hell,* he thought, *I ain't drunk a damn thing but one little old sip of whisky. Where all this come from?* Along with the cough and the pain in his bones and his lack of wind, it was one of the mysteries of what he'd come to be these last years. As if equally perplexed, Cattywampus Dog closely watched him at his dreary task, backturned head atilt.

They breakfasted on two greasy hunks of fat meat and then Hamby rolled up his plunder in the wolfskin, tied it with whang and slung it on his back. "Time to get off you ass," he told the dog, looping the Win-chester over one shoulder by its strap. The dog got up a little gingerly. Hamby grunted, "You sore too, huh?" He shrugged. "Well, we both too goddamn old and beat-up for this. But here we be."

Remembering the fire he'd seen in the night he crossed to the edge of the drop-off and scanned the valley to find what had burned; but the valley lay hidden beneath a flat blanket of fog – or was it smoke? But in the light of day it was easier to tell how the blaze had lain in relation to the shapes of the hills above it; and he thought maybe the burning had been somewhere between Wolf Creek and Big Choga. What was there? he wondered. He hadn't been in that country since coming back from the mica mines. Maybe it was a woods fire. He dismissed it, turned away, lit his pipe, hitched the knapsack higher on his back and started out. Cattywampus Dog gave one whine of com-plaint and followed him.

Yan-e'gwa traveled only by night and at the end of the third night he knew he was close because the wind was from the west and bore to him the distinctive smell of Where the Water-Dogs Laughed, its mixed odors of damp hemlock and fern and nutty mast and pure flowing waters. It also carried the bracing fra-grance of the beginning of the changing of the season, the grow-

ing-old of the hardwood leaves, the night-frost, the crisp air that spoke of the harder cold to come.

It was good to smell these things of the forest up ahead because he had been wearied and dismayed having to cross so much ground where the forest no longer was, where all he could smell were dead tree-stumps and stale sap and shattered bark and where the land was so littered with dry heaps of old wood scraps that he could not walk on it without making an unseemly noise, where it was almost impossible to find enough cover to travel safely.

The wind brought him other scents too; one was of a Split-Nose and the other was of an Ancestor, and the Ancestor was leaving a spoor more rank and wild than most, smokier, woodsier, smarting in the nostrils, a smell more akin to Yan-e'gwa's own than to the smells of other Ancestors; and Yan-e'gwa's madness told him then that this Ancestor must be the very same being whose tread he'd felt at the edge of the world's island. And he thought it was right that the Ancestor smelt more nearly like a bear than like its own kind – it had something to do with why in his derangement Yan-e'gwa had known at once that he and this Being must meet and that their meeting would be to some important purpose.

Yan-e'gwa slept that day in a thicket that clung to the side of the mountain. When night fell he resumed his journey. Presently he came to a place where the Being and its Split-Nose had eaten and slept and which the Being had marked as its own by repeatedly making water. This insolence offended Yan-e'gwa because the place the Being had marked was well within his own range. So Yan-e'gwa made water over the places the Being had marked and reclaimed them.

After that he moved swiftly toward Where the Water-Dogs Laughed, whose sweet scent grew stronger and stronger in his nose all the time now. He was eager to be home and eager to confront the Being who had come to find him and eager to learn why he had come and what the purpose of their meeting might be. His thinking had been growing clearer; he could remember his home. But his temper was still pretty bad. The hard little pebble *of rage remained lodged in his head. He was as dangerous as he'd been at the Place Where the Bears Wash when he'd wounded the young male so sorely that he had to die. If the Being had come only to trespass and to challenge him, he would kill the Being just as he'd killed the young male. But somehow inside his rage and his willingness to kill there was also a certain expectancy, as if he were on his way to meet one of his own kind with whom he'd once been close but whom he had not seen in many a long year, maybe a brother or a sister, or maybe his mother who used to rock him in her arms in their cave-den and sing songs and tell him the stories he could sometimes still recall when his mind came clear. But as with any of his kind, it was as likely that they would fight when they met as that they would not; and either way he would be ready.*

On the fifth night of his journey he reached the lower slope of Where the Water-Dogs Laughed and soon left the cut-down wastelands below and entered the untouched forest. The big woods were the same as ever; he recognized them with a deep satisfaction – the trees towering so high that he could not see their tops nor distinguish how the tops met and grew together to form one thick sheltering canopy. Just as before, he could smell all that he could not see and so knew everything about the woods and all that was in them.

In the night he had followed the two scents of the Being and his Split-Nose and when they camped he had smelled their fire and the queer food they ate; and finally, some time before the sun was due to rise, he drew near the place where they slept and got downwind of it and crept quietly through the bracken as close as he dared without rousing the Split-Nose and lay silent on his belly working his nostrils to take in and sample every vestige of how they smelled.

With his poor sight all he could see was the hazy blur of their fire, not even the shapes of their sleeping bodies; but his nose told him many things about them and he lay a long time savoring each one. He was going to go on, get ahead of them, let them strike his trail and follow him; then he would lead them to the place he had remembered, where he meant to turn. But first

*he was going to learn as much as his nose would tell him. He lay
in the dark delicately sniffing.*

Hamby preferred to hunt alone. Admittedly it was a preference that been been forced on him – few were the hunters in those parts who relished his company – though some would say it was his prickly nature more than his color that caused folk to avoid him. However it had come about, he scorned to hunt bear the way others in the uplands did – with gangs of men and a mob of dogs thrashing about in the woods raising an unholy ruckus more likely to chase a bear into the next county than to corner one. Half the time the men were drunk and the dogs lost and the whole enterprise was more of a shivaree than a hunt. For his part Hamby thought a bear was a solemn thing and shouldn't be hunted with anything less than solemn intent.

He'd always used but a single dog. Not a fancy one either. Not one bred for a cold nose or to run by sight or to strike or to tree and or to be a fighter, not any pure-blood Plott, Airedale, black-and-tan, pit bull or whatnot – he liked a plain old cur dog, half-hound, half-cur, able to track like a hound but severe enough to tree a bear and fight him. He'd hunted with black-and-tans and liked them better than any of the breeds. But the crossbloods were best, the mangier the better.

Whether Cattywampus Dog would fit the bill or not, he couldn't yet say. God alone knew what strains the poor twisted-up critter had in him. He was companionable enough, but was he any good? Corntassel had sworn he could follow a cold track and worry a bear like hell too. So far there'd been no occasion to try his talents out. That was going to change today, for they were in the deep woods and could cut sign any minute; and if he was any kind of a hunter it was going to show up pretty damn quick.

Till now he hadn't acted as if he even knew he was *on* a hunt. Hamby hadn't seen him smelling around for a scent or even paying particular attention to anything. Mainly he just followed Hamby everywhere giving him admiring looks. "You on the job or not?" Hamby asked him. "Making mooney eyes at me ain't getting us no bear. Is you a bust?"

Cattywampus Dog offered no reply. They tramped on.

It was the third day out. Hamby was tired of the hunt already – frost had come in the night and worsened his cough and his joints hurt like hell from the cold and from sleeping on the hard ground – but nonetheless it was good to be in the woods after traipsing all those miles of clear cut with nothing about you but empty sky and hundreds of red-dirt hills covered with a stubble of stumps making them look like so many faces that needed a shave.

Here on the heights the woods stood tall and thick and imperially still, already brilliant with autumn, the Spanish oak as crimson as a new Rebel flag, the white oak a pinker red like that same flag faded out, the maple like a cluster of gold dollars, the buckeye a butternut brown, the beech and birch a ruddy yellow. In the coves were stands of hemlock whose soft boughs of dark green were delicately fringed with a shade of yellow brighter than that of the beech and birch – their millions of tiny needles soon to be shed. Under all the big trees were brakes of laurel and ivy and chokeberry and beds of fern giving the forest a denser look than lower down, where the farmers had burnt off all the undergrowth making every glade look barbered like a park – though all that was gone now, he remembered. He'd never thought much about that till today, how so much of it had vanished. Cut it down, it would grow back; that had been his notion. Still, it was good to see what was left. To see it and be in it and smell it and feel its peace around you. He reckoned maybe the woods were as solemn a thing as the bears that lived in them.

They flushed a flock of wild turkeys and started a doe and a yearling buck from a copse of spruce and even came across a little hundred-pound he-bear that had been eating grubs out of some rotten logs in a blowdown; it trotted off with a bawl of aggravation, stopping a time or two to turn back and give them accusing looks. Later they found the sign of a sow bear and two big cubs by the side of a branch where they'd been drinking. All this activity Cattywampus Dog serenely ignored; either he was such a wonder of a bear dog that he had no interest in any game but Yan-eg'gwa – and how could he know Yan-e'gwa was the one they were after? – or he had the hunting instinct of a toad.

They kept on. The oaks had dropped such a fine crop of mast that the acorns crunched under your feet like popcorn. With such a feast on the ground Yan-e'gwa was sure to feed on it if he was near. They poked about awhile in the oak groves and late in the day when Cattywampus Dog had bestirred himself enough to go sniffing in the mast, he found a spot where a bear had fed and then stooled to show he was finished with the place. Hamby settled on his hams over the pile of glistening black turds. "Well, leastways you know bear shit when you smell it," he told the dog. The stool was fresh, not even a day old. Nearby in the soft loam of the forest floor were some tracks – flat rectangular tracks with the long marks out front of the claws that never retracted. Cattywampus

Dog nosed these eagerly.

"He a *big* son of a bitch," Hamby remarked. In fact it was the biggest sign he'd ever seen. He turned to the dog, who watched him alertly with his cranked head; there was a new look in the pretty eyes. A narrowing, a sharpness, a glint. Maybe he was remembering how he'd got hurt and changed into a freak; maybe he was tasting again the flavor of his hate for what had made him as he was. He twitched his nub of tail. "All right," Hamby said, "you the boss now. Find me this big old boy, we gone split that two hundred."

But before he could finish, Cattywampus Dog had bounded off into the woods, running sidelong, his squarish head awkwardly back and down, nose to the ground. He didn't bark or bay or bell like your common bear hound; he ran silent as a trout in water. He looked like he might know his trade after all.

Hamby sighed. The two hundred didn't have a damn thing to do with it. Not now that he was close. This was Yan-e'gwa. He knew it now that he'd seen the sign. And if any bear was a solemn matter, this one was the most solemn of all. You didn't go after him for any goddamn two hundred. You went after him because he needed somebody to come. You went because he was what he was. Because he'd dreamt what he'd dreamt and lost it. Because you and he were part of the same thing far more than you'd ever been part of the hateful world of men. And because in going after him you could take to yourself the power to do what Corntassel said – get shet of all you hated. So you were going after Yan-e'gwa not for money but in solemn and rightful ceremony. *You was right, old man*, Hamby thought; *you was right about it all*. He offered his salute. He stood then, unslung the Winchester and followed the hurrying dog.

Y an-e'gwa lay on an outcrop of rock and watched them as they came up through a stand of pitch pine and scrubby white oak below him. It seemed that they were hunting him. He had been hunted many times but never in this way, by one Ancestor only and by a single Split-Nose whose shape was bent like a wind-blasted cedar and which moved in a fashion no creature had ever moved – sideways, like a snake backing up to coil and strike except that it was going forward; nor did it make any noise whatever as it tracked such as other Split-Noses did when they hunted.

*It was as strange as the Being it served. Just as the Being smelled
more like a bear than an Ancestor, so the Split-Nose smelled both
like a Split-Nose and like something else.*

*What that something was, Yan-e'gwa could not tell. He knew
only that it was not the odor of a body or even exactly any odor at
all but something that partook of a scent but was more than a
scent also; perhaps if a thought could have a smell, it would feel
like this in the nose; and if the thought was bad, it would sting as
this did. Two nights ago when Yan-e'gwa had lain secretly in the
woods by their camp, the Split-Nose had not caused this sting in
the nose. The sting had come only after the Split-Nose had struck his
trail. Now the more it stung the more Yan-e'gwa disliked it, for it told
him that the Split-Nose was hunting him individually and that this
one was worse and more dangerous than all the other Split-Noses
that had ever hunted him, that its spirit was full of bad intent
where the others had only done what nature told them.*

*Yan-e'gwa studied the Being too. The Being carried one of
the sticks that could make the hard shaped noise which had hurt
Yan-e'gwa so badly last winter. This implied a hunt also. Yet the
thoughts of the Being did not sting. So its intent did not fit with
the intent of the Split-Nose; but the stick was a menacing sign
and to make matters worse the Being kept relieving itself indis-
criminately as if to mock Yan-e'gwa on his own ground.*

*Yan-e'gwa had hoped that he and the Being might be nearly
the same – the Being was an Ancestor, after all – and that the
purpose of their meeting was to be good. While in his confusion
Yan-e'gwa no longer remembered his war to keep the Ancestors
from killing the world, he did remember fragments of the old
tales his mother had told him about how his kind and the Ancestors had long ago been one. But now he began to mistrust the
Being almost as much as he mistrusted the Split-Nose. He began
to think the Being had come to kill him as so many other Ancestors had tried to do. And as his mistrust deepened his temper
began to worsen and he started to think he must kill the Being
and the strange Split-Nose to save himself.*

*Only one thing gave him pause – that the thoughts of the
Being did not sting. If its thoughts were indeed a part of how it*

smelled, they were hard and firm and deeply settled and, yes, dangerous too; but they lacked the tang of evil intent that was in the mood of the Split-Nose. This was a mystery that intrigued Yan-e'gwa. So even as he began to lose his temper he decided to wait awhile longer before he acted.

He watched them as they climbed. Then when they were close enough he rose to a low crouch and backed slowly away from the lip of the rock ledge and into the forest of red spruce above it. Then he turned and climbed higher through the trees. He would lead them to the place he had chosen. There he would decide.

Between the bear that was making a beeline up the mountain and Cattywampus Dog that was trailing him closer than stink on shit, it was all Hamby could do to keep up. It was true that if he fell too far behind the dog would stop and linger impatiently till he came scrabbling back in sight; but no sooner would he round a laurel woolly or a grove of trees or a pile of boulders and spy the dog waiting up ahead than the damn critter would whirl and light out again lickety-split and disappear in the woods quicker than you could say Jack Robinson.

Hamby would cuss and swear and have a fit of coughing and then go stumbling on after him. Getting a snootful of that heap of bear shit had worked some kind of black magic on Cattywampus Dog. It didn't matter any more that his head was on wrong and he was as bent around as a barb on wire, he had that goddamn bear in his nose and meant to run him down and corner him if it killed Hamby and him both. It was hard to remember now how he'd lollygagged and hung back before. Panting and gagging, stopping now and then to cough up blood, Hamby followed as best he could, up and up through the forest of red spruce.

The bear wasn't trying to be sly. He was taking game trails and open ground where his tracks would show or his passing would leave sign plain as day. He wasn't even hurrying all that much, just keeping up a steady and stately pace – the prints of his big paws were flat in the soft earth, not torn out in back as they would be if he were in a rush. He wasn't running. He wasn't trying to lose them, wasn't trying to escape. He was going somewhere. He was leading them, taking them to a place he wanted to go. A place he wanted them to be. Where he and they could meet.

The notion was so queer and so big that it made Hamby break out in a sudden rush of hot sweat; his peter shrank to thimble size – not so much in fear, though he was sure as hell scared; but in . . . what? He didn't know. But some of what he felt was good. More of it was good than was fear. Sure, he'd go. He'd meet the bear. That was Corntassel's prophesy, wasn't it? *It what this be for*, he thought. But it amazed him to think that the bear knew it too, that he and the bear could have in mind a thing they both understood. It seemed a privilege to know that. It gladdened him to know it almost as much as it scared him.

He plunged higher and higher up the steeps, sometimes having to pull himself along grasping roots and shrubs and tree-branches or loops of creeper or hanks of grass. The weight of the knapsack dragged at his shoulders and its strap of whang cut into his chest; the buttstock of the Winchester that was slung over the knapsack kept banging him annoyingly in the ass. His shoes were loose; on the tilt of the hill his feet kept slipping and turning inside them, wearing big blisters on his heels and the sides of his feet; every twisting step he took hurt worse. *Shit*, he kept saying like a chant, *Shit shit shit*.

The time came when he had to stop and regain his wind. He was ashamed of himself but he couldn't help it; he was used up. He dropped the rifle, dumped off the knapsack and hunkered panting on a carpet of spruce needles. *Fine bear hunter I be*, he wheezed. His lungs felt like bundles of pins all thrusting at his insides every time he tried to fetch a breath; he coughed and spat up a big clot of something warm and grainy that he didn't want to look at. The slimy feel of it coming up made him want to puke. Bathed in a sweat of nausea he leaned forward, put his hands flat on the ground, went to all fours, saw the pattern of fine brown spruce needles under his face start to spot with bright red. "Shit," he said aloud.

Something was by him then. He looked; it was Cattywampus Dog, come back to see how he fared. The dog's moist nose touched his, its rancid breath blew on him, the hot wet tongue licked at his face and bloody mouth.

"You laying down on the job again, ain't you?" Hamby managed to gasp. But he was glad to see him. He let himself all the way down on his belly with his chin in the soft bloody spruce needles. Then he rolled over and lay on his back in the shade of the trees, examining the intricate tapering shapes of their boughs and the way their peaks pointed to the sky like church steeples, thinking how cool it was in their shadow, smelling their spicy fragrance and the bitter-dry odor of their needles under him. A bundle of the needles clung to his chin, stuck there with blood; he scraped them away. The patch of sky above him was a pure periwinkle blue; up there a buzzard wheeled by. He heard a ground squirrel chirp, the chatter of birds. He was shaking and there were cramps in the backs of his calves and the muscles in the tops of his thighs were jerking like they wanted to get out from under the skin; but he felt peaceful and his wind was coming back, slowly coming back. He lay waiting for it to come all the way back while Cattywampus Dog sat beside him with his backturned head closely watching.

◀️

After a time he thought he was strong enough to stand. He was still weak and a little giddy of head and inclined to tremble but he thought he could go on now, though the sides and heels of his feet were sore as hell from those loose brograns. *I get that two hundred,* he thought, *I buy me a goddamn pair of good shoes.* He stooped and picked up the Winchester and the wolf-pelt knapsack and slung them and recovered his hat and put it on. Cattywampus Dog studied him with an air of doubt. "I be all right," Hamby assured him, "You look out for you own ass."

As if he'd understood, the dog obligingly turned and started up the slope and Hamby came limping after. It was evening now, the sun was resting on the top of the range. When you glimpsed it full-on between the trees it dazzled you, it might have been a blob of molten metal spilt from a ladle up there to cool. When the trees blocked it the light came through the woods broken into soft slanting shafts that cast long shadows down the hill behind you.

Hamby plodded on, sweating torrents, head-down, fighting for breath, stopping betimes to cough and spit blood. Cattywampus Dog no longer pushed on; now he'd smell out sign for a few rods, then pause and turn and wait anxiously for Hamby to come halting up. He looked worried. Hamby thought about reproaching him, telling him to mind his own business and track that bear. But what the hell, this bear wasn't going to let them lose him. This bear would wait. Let the damn dog play mother hen if he wanted to.

A blustery wind began to blow, making the big spruces toss and sway and roar like muted thunder. It clouted the banks of laurel so the pale bottoms of their leaves all turned up and waved like a crowd of little hands. It was a cold wind; the light began to fail; looking up, Hamby saw a curdled bank of gray cloud coming over the top of the mountain from the west, blotting out the ingot of the sun. The air smelt like rain.

That all we need, he thought. He climbed higher on his sore feet, the dog hanging back just ahead and sometimes trotting down to him to sniff anxiously at his legs, which felt more and more like they were made of lead. The wind blew colder and harder, whipping at his clothes, making them flap and flutter like washing on a line; once it tore his hat off and blew it into a tangle of ivy and he had to go and retrieve it; he couldn't lose that hat. When he got it back, he jammed it low over his ears – making himself look like a goddamn idiot, he reckoned. Well, he *was* a goddamn idiot.

When it got too dark to see, he stopped and shook off the knapsack and leaned the Winchester against the nearest tree trunk and slumped down and fell asleep right where he lay without taking any account of where he was or of the cold or the buffeting of the wind. His sleep came at once and was as heavy and impenetrable as a rock; a boulder of sleep mashed him into the ground, pinned him flat, crushed him. He was vaguely aware that the wind and cold were at him as he lay; but they were lashing at the heavy rock of his sleep that pressed him down and couldn't penetrate that rock to trouble him. He did sense Cattywampus Dog quaking against the small of his back. That was all. He didn't even dream, save once when just for a moment he felt certain his stepdaddy Old Daniel McFee was close by; he smelt the pomade Old Daniel liked to put in his air, smelt it as strong and real as could be, that tart mineral odor.

He awoke with that odor still in his nose thinking to speak to Old Daniel but instead found himself lying on his back in a cold rain, drenched to the skin and scalding with fever. The rain felt like a million slivers of ice stabbing him and he was burning up so bad with the fever he wondered why the rain didn't sizzle when it hit him, as it would if it fell on a hot stovelid. Shudders passed through him in spasms; his bone ends felt like tenpenny nails had been driven in them. His back teeth were making a dry clicking noise that sounded like some damn nigger playing the bones.

All he could see was a dense white pall and at first he feared he'd lost his sight too; but then the pall divided and part of it drifted aside to show him the brown trunks of the spruce woods and he realized that a shroud of mist had come with the rain in the night to cover the top of the mountain. Relieved, he made as if to take a breath. But it snagged in his throat and he heard his lungs wheeze like a bad set of bellows; he began to cough and the fit shook him hard and long till it passed. He brought up a gooddeal of blood, more than ever before; it spilled out of the corners of his mouth and around his neck and some of it spread over his chest in a red pool till the rain thinned it out and trickled it off his sides in pink runnels. He lay weakly panting. *Jesus Christ*, he thought, *I done it now.*

He discovered he was lying in a goddamn puddle. He forced himself to rise to an elbow and roll out of the water and came face to face with Cattywampus Dog, who'd crept to him from the nearby laurel slick where he'd had the sense to crouch while Hamby laid out in the weather like a fool. The dog flicked his tongue lightly over Hamby's face, giving little whines of sympathy; the tongue felt good on his scorching skin; the brown eyes gazed anxiously at him.

Hamby grunted, gathered what was left of his strength, began to drag himself toward the shelter of the laurel slick. The dog took a sleeve in his teeth and tried to help pull him along with his sidewise head; that looked pretty funny and Hamby couldn't help breaking out in silly giggles – he guessed the fever had addled him. Then he saw the dog freeze and turn loose of the sleeve and heard him growl; and as soon as he saw and heard this, he knew; and he slewed around in the mud to confirm what he'd already divined, looked upslope to where Cattywampus Dog was looking; and the mist thinned and yonder between two big spruces not ten rods away he saw the bear standing on his hind legs higher than any man, his front paws curled over his chest, his back hunched, his reddish-brown coat soppy with rain, his squarish head pushed forward as if straining to see; big, yes, he was goddamn big, bigger even than his tracks had promised; but so slim and rangy was he, so wasted down to pelt and bones, so tattered was his fur, that for all his size he looked oddly fragile; you wouldn't have been surprised to see him sway and fall. Hamby felt a pang to see him. He cocked that big boxy head as if he meant to ask a question; but just then Cattywampus Dog made a gutteral noise that was half a snarl and half a hacking bark and bared his yellow fangs and ran like a shot directly at him, broadside, head-cranked, the only goddamn way he could run.

The Being and the Split-Nose seemed to have stopped tracking and Yan-e'gwa had grown curious and had come down to see why they no longer followed him. The spot on the bald where he wanted to confront them was very near and he had thought that if he went to them and showed himself, they might rouse from whatever sloth had delayed them and take his trail again. Then he would lead them up out of the spruce forest and over the place of the broken trees and the field of boulders to the rock that jutted out over nothing, where he would turn. Then he would see if they had come to kill him as he suspected; or if, as he hoped, the

Being wished to meet him as kindred so they could compose between them some matter of importance.

Because of the weather the smells of the morning were muddled. There was rain and fog and wet moss and stone and damp spruce and mud and standing water and then the scent of the Being and the sting in the nose that was the strange Split-Nose, all blended together. It was hard to tell what was near and what was far. So by mistake Yan-e'gwa ventured closer than was wise; almost before he knew it a rent opened in the fog and he saw the Being and the strange Split-Nose huddled together by some rhododendron in a little swale – close, too close; and in his surprise he reared to his full height and the pebble of bad temper in his head flared hot and he bristled and assumed a posture of menace even as his nose told him something was wrong with the Being, it had lost the power it had smelt of before, the settled hardness, the flavor of the woods and the wild, the danger, the musky odor reminiscent of bear; now it smelled sour and flat, a smell of a stale spirit. Yan-e'gwa tilted his head to look more sharply at it. He regretted that the power of the Being had waned because that implied it was just a commonplace Ancestor after all and that like all the other Ancestors it had come only to hunt and kill.

As he looked, the strange Split-Nose charged. It came fast, coming with that queer motion Yan-e'gwa had noticed when he watched from the rock ledge, its body wanting to run to the side even as its head wanted to run straight, the backcoiling of a snake reversed. The stinging of its bad spirit came with it like a bunch of briars flying in the air and it pricked Yan-e'gwa's nose and he smelled the malice in it and even though the day had already dawned he wondered if this Split-Nose were not actually a witch like Atsil'-dihye'gi, the Fire-Carrier who haunted the darkness; perhaps the witch had taken the form of a Split-Nose so as to haunt the day as well as the night.

Before he could do anything the strange Split-Nose was on him, had bounded from the ground to his belly, came scrabbling upward digging his hard toenails in the soft flesh that hung slack from the hunger that had come with the wasting, it thrust vio-

lently with its back legs, mounting higher, plunging up and up over his chest, a force of pure evil, implacable, worthy of a witch; and it fastened its jaws on his throat and sank its teeth deep and then shook its head viciously from side to side tearing the flesh, then opened its jaws to get fresh purchase and snatched another mouthful, more this time, a great ball of flesh, and bit even deeper and shook that till it tore, and Yan-e'gwa's blood gushed over it in a fountain – all this in a twinkling; then Yan-e'gwa recovered from his amazement and his world went red with rage and he closed his front paws over the Split-Nose and pushed it down and away and it ripped loose from his throat fetching in its mouth another bloody chunk of flesh and hair; it dropped at his feet floundering and flopping, trying to get its legs under it to spring at him again – its witch's malice was that great; and Yan-e'gwa stooped and swung his paw and struck it a single blow and heard all its bones break at once; the blow tumbled it over and over; and as it tumbled the litter of the forest floor stuck to its bloody coat making it look not like a Split-Nose or a witch any more but only like a limp ball of spruce needles.

In its weakness the Being had not moved but the wounds in Yan-e'gwa's throat were very bad and very painful and the attack of the witch had made the pebble in his head sear like fire and he was filled with an awful wrath; he knew now that the Being had sent the witch, that it had come not as kin to do good but as a murderer like all the other Ancestors and that he must kill it to purge away all the bad it had brought when it stepped onto the floating island of the world; and he lunged at the Being and caught it up in an embrace and was a little surprised that it did not struggle but hung almost passive in his grasp giving only a slight wriggle; he closed his jaws on its head and tasted its blood and heard some of its ribs pop and only then did it resist, it squirmed, it made a twisting motion; then Yan-e'gwa felt a stab of pain through his middle and knew that the Being had hurt him some- how, had hurt him badly, had maybe even given him his death; and he released the Being and backed away from it feeling rage and fear and woe, feeling the blood pulsing out of him, and now that he was so badly wounded he thought maybe he need not kill the Being after all, that maybe the bad that the Being had brought did not matter any more because the world was so worn out that the cords that held it up were going to break and it would fall into the waters of the lake and sink and all life would drown anyway; so it would be best to quit, to go home, to climb up to his chosen place to rest and wait for the world to end; and he backed further away and left the Being huddled where it had fallen next to the dead witch; he slowly turned and started up the slope toward the bald, already sensing the draining away of his strength and with it now the worst of his rage and fear so that what remained was mostly sorrow and a wish for rest.

Hamby tried to sit up. He heard a crunch inside him and knew it was his ribs and then the pain came and he lay back down. *Can't stand a whole lot of that,* he thought. He was having trouble seeing and that was worrisome till he managed to lift one hand and feel gingerly around his face and find that a piece of scalp had got peeled partway off the top of his head and was hanging down over his eyes. That was better than some things. *Leastways I ain't blind.* He slid the piece back, tried to fit it where it belonged. But the pain wouldn't let him do much and pretty soon he quit.

He lay in the drizzle trying to fix his mind to go on past the pain and get him up. Everything had gone wrong and it was his job to put it right and he had to get up to do it. His body was telling him he couldn't get up; but then it had told him he couldn't grab hold of his knife when the bear had him too, and he'd done that. Grabbed it out of his pocket and opened up one of its four blades and shoved it hilt-deep. If he could do that, he could get up no matter how it hurt.

His sight dimmed again and he realized the torn scalp was bleeding into his eyes. He wiped the blood away and tilted his face up to the rain so it would help wash his eyes clear. But more blood surged and ran and blinded him and he guessed he had some other cuts too that bled differently from the big one on his head. Some of the blood ran into his mouth and rather than spit it out or agitate his bad ribs with a cough he let it fill his mouth and run over and out the corners. All this on top of the fever that had him quivering like a doused pup. *I one big mess.*

Cattywampus Dog was worse off, though. But Hamby noticed that he looked like a regular dog laying there dead – all his kinks were straightened out and his head was on him the way it was supposed to be. The bear must've done that when it swatted him, must've mashed him back to normal. It was peculiar and a little sad to see he was finally in the right shape but wasn't alive to enjoy it. But hell, he'd got what he needed to get, had got himself a big helping of revenge; and no bear dog had ever gone out meaner or better; Corntassel would've been proud. The old man would've frowned on the rest of it, though – it was likely none of them save the dog did what they'd meant to do. That was part of what had to be put right.

He wasn't going to get it done laying up on his ass in the rain. So he forced himself beyond the pain and eased to a sitting position and then pushed himself even more and tipped forward onto his hands and knees and then willed the pain to be bearable and stood. Blood poured over his face, his ribs crackled, a white light burst over him and the world slipped up and up past his head and then turned over with a sickening roll and he fainted and Old Daniel was close by him again smelling of that pomade in his hair although Hamby couldn't see him. And Old Daniel was saying something and Hamby had to strain to hear him because Old Daniel always had a soft voice, soft but firm; and Old Daniel said, *I've got some cold squirrel meat and pone; sit yourself down and eat. After that we'll talk.*

Hamby wanted to talk with Old Daniel. He hadn't ever really done that, he'd been too proud. Now he was looking forward to it. He'd never wanted anything as bad as he wanted to talk to Old Daniel now. But no, instead of a meal and a talk he felt himself commence to swim slowly up out of the swoon; he tried to keep it from happening but couldn't. The pain and the fever came back; the cold rain soaked him; his sense cleared and he saw where he was and remembered what he had to do and said, "Shit."

The fever was like a heavy liquid, dark and thick and as clingy as syrup or molasses that had got stiff in cold weather; you'd fallen into a vat of the damn stuff and were trying to get out, but doing anything at all was harder than hell – the shit dragged at you, held you back, slowed you down, wanted to suck you to the bottom.

You had the shakes too, and the chills and hot spells kept coming, and worst of all your head wasn't right, it was slow and numb-feeling and the notions it got didn't always match up. You thought of Strickland's mule that turned the windlass at the Axum mine and some of the roosters you used to fight and a jenny you once had and how a certain run of moonshine tasted so velvety smooth and the tart smell of rosin on the blade of a crosscut saw and Miss Becky in her kerchief pulling horn-worms off the tobacco and the orange of a harvest moon and none of it meant a goddamn thing. But that wouldn't have been so bad if he hadn't been so weak and if his knees didn't keep giving way under him so he wobbled around like a drunk man.

He used the Winchester for a crutch to stop him falling all the way down, for if that was to happen he didn't want to think what it would do to the pain in his side. That gun was a lot to tote when you were this bad off. But you had to keep it. You could leave everything else – he'd even left that piece of scalp that was always falling over his eyes; had cut it off with the knife to stop it pestering him. Left the knife too. And the knapsack with the eats and the whiskey flask. He wouldn't be wanting much after this. But the Winchester, he'd have need of it.

Worse than trying to walk and not fall down was the coughing. Every fit of coughing brought new bursts of the pain and the white light and he'd have to hold still hoping to bear it without squalling like a babe and hoping too that he wouldn't pass out and fall and have an even harder time. If there was a God he'd have prayed to Him not to have those fits. But he had them anyway. Whatever he coughed up, he got rid of it quick without looking. Then it was a case of waiting for the next one.

He was following the blood. It was easy. There was a lot of blood spattered all along, through the spruce woods and out of them and up onto the open bald where there was no big growth any more, just a mess of laurel and ivy and scattered mats of cotton grass and heath shrub and hazelnut and beyond that a bunch of scraggly trees. The knife must've gone in the vitals, maybe cut an artery; the bear was bleeding bad, pos-sibly was even done for – queer how one little buckhorn-handled clasp knife could do such bad hurt to a varmint so big. But then look what little old Cattywampus Dog had done to him. On the other hand, a crit-ter seven foot high and weighing at least six hundred pound had just ripped hell out of Hamby McFee and he was still shuffling along. Shit-fire, you couldn't figure any of it.

At least the rain had stopped. He was glad of that. He was damn tired of being rained on. The mist was beginning to drift off too. It opened up the distances and he could see across most of the bald now, low masses of limby dwarf woods yonderways – stunted oak and wil-low and ash with swatches of dull color still on them even this high, some yellow birch covered with a moss that looked like old men's whis-kers. And the big sky, washed clean as a whistle by the storm. *Small favors*, he thought. To see the sky. To see what was ahead, even if it sometimes got twisty and shimmery from the fever like looking at the rocks in the bed of a river through a running current. But if he started to take too big a breath the pain would come again and show him the white light. Blood kept running into his mouth from wherever else he was slashed on his face or head; he'd take little sips of it till he had enough to spit, then he'd spit as easy as he could; but no matter how easy he spat he'd feel it in those damn ribs.

He went on following the blood. He came to a peat bog and past it found a seep and saw where the bear had stopped to slake his thirst; there was plenty of blood all around on the wet lichen-spotted rocks. He bent down as careful as he could and drank too, cupping up water in one hand trying not to aggravate the ribs; the water tasted like minerals, made him think of Old Daniel's pomade. Damn, he'd have liked to talk to Old Daniel. But he reckoned he'd had his last talk – unless this bear could talk. To hear Corntassel go on, the damn bear was smart enough to argue politics or religion. Maybe they'd have a conversation.

He kept at it. Was hobbling over rocks. A scatter of flattish gray-white rocks. More blood on them. His and the bear's both. It continually oozed up from within to fill his mouth, from without it ran down his face in ropy streams. He spat, scrubbed it away with a shirt cuff. Was in a patch of fallen trees. Dozens of trees. A windstorm had knocked down a whole stand. Long ago. So long ago the bark had fallen off and they were all bleached white and smooth as picked bones and so rotten you could put your hand through a trunk half a foot across and their brickly branches snapped and broke under you as you tried to walk on them. When they broke he'd drop down a ways and get jolted and jarred and that would start him coughing and the pain and the white light would come and it would be as bad as it had ever been till it passed. Then he'd go fumbling on, probing ahead with the Winchester to search out the easiest way through. He was burning up with fever. The fever made the big deadfall look like a whole field full of deer antlers. He couldn't help but grin. *Somebody be planting antlers, grow theyselfs some deer.*

Ahead through a blur of fever he made out a rubble of boulders, one gnarly old dead tree leaning to the side, beyond it a great gulf of sky and distance – hell, it was the rim of the bald. A piece of nearly level rock stuck out over the void and the bear was lying on that spread eagled on his belly. He lay with his chin rested on the edge of the shelf gazing off into blue space. The place where he lay was pooled and smeared with blood and Hamby could see the rapid heave of his flanks as he panted. He hated to see that. But if the bear was alive, what had got set wrong down in the woods could still be put right; and that was good, that was what he'd come for.

He was nearly out of the deadfall and the bear hadn't seen him so he shoved past the pain one more time and made himself kneel behind the last of the downed trees. He hunkered there trying to open a hole of clarity through the muddle in his head. The Winchester was fouled. He had to remedy that. He waited till he was ready for the pain again and then working very slowly he reversed the piece and used a forefinger to scour the mud out of the muzzle. It wasn't easy; his hands were numb and the mud was packed deep from the gun being used as a crutch and the pain was so bad the white light started to glimmer around the sides of his vision. He had to find a stick straight enough to poke down the barrel to get the worst of the plug out. Blood was running into his eyes and he had to sop that up with a sleeve and then more pain would come and he'd stop to stand it and then go back to work waiting for the next onset of pain getting ready to stand that too. Spells of dizziness swept over him, he couldn't get a decent breath. *Don't you cough*, he told himself, *Don't you dare go to coughing.*

When the gun was as clean as he could make it, he turned it rightway around again and held his wind and gently and quietly worked the lever to chamber a round. Even so, the action made its steely clank. Then there was the little snick when he lowered the hammer. But the noises failed to rouse the bear, he was too deep in his own hurt, he laid panting on the rock as before. Hamby crouched awhile longer pushing through the fever and pain and weakness. He was trying to call to mind from very far away all that Corntassel had taught him. It wouldn't work if it wasn't done right. He'd promised to make it work. If he did it right and it worked, then he'd be done. And by God he was ready to be done.

It hurt to sing but hell, everything hurt now. The Cherokee words felt queer in his mouth and he'd never had a voice for song; but then it wasn't a song so much as a chant; and anyway this was what he had to do and he did it, sending his cracked voice to the bear, asking what had to be asked, giving what was due:

> He-e! Hayuya'haniwah'
> Tsistu'yi nehandu' yanu' – Yoho-o!
> He-e! Hayuya'haniwah'
> Kuwa'hi' nehandu'yanu' – Yoho-o!
> He-e! Hayuya'haniwah'
> Uya'hye nehandu' yanu' – Yoho-o!
> He-e! Hayuya'haniwah'
> Gate'gwa nehandu'yanu' – Yoho-o!
> Ule'-nu' asehi' tadeya'statakuhi' gun'age astu' tsiki

This is what Yan-e'gwa heard:

> He! Hayuya'haniwa'
> In Tsitu'yi you were conceived – Yoho!
> He! Hayuya'haniwa'
> In Kuwa'hi you were conceived – Yoho!
> He! Hayuya'haniwa'
> In Uya'hye you were conceived – Yoho!
> He! Hyuya'haniwa'
> In Gate'gwa you were conceived – Yoho!
> And now surely we and the good black things,
> the best of all, shall see each other.

He had been waiting for the world to end. He had been looking out over the blue space thinking that when the cords attached to the four corners of the earth frayed and broke and the world fell into the lake of Creation, from this height he would be able to see the waters of the lake start to rise. That would be something to see. He was hoping he would not die before it happened. He was badly hurt and thought death was near; so he lay completely still except for the motion of his breathing, hoping to conserve his energy and stave off dying till he could watch the spectacle of the lake rising to overwhelm all life.

He was weak but no longer in pain save for the ache of hunger and the parch of thirst. While he lay waiting with his chin resting flat on the cool stone he was thinking of all the things he liked best to eat, crunchy ants, sweet berries, mice, meaty roots, every kind of nut and acorn, plump grubs, bees, honey in the comb, tree seeds, the delicate dogtooth violet. These were his favorites and he thought of feeding on them and then finding a stream and lapping up the cold clean water afterward to wash them down. He hardly thought at all of the meat he had sometimes eaten when he must, the fish and deer and the pigs and lambs he used to take from the Ancestors when there was little else to be had.

He was thinking he was so hungry and thirsty now that he would eat carrion and drink stagnant pond water if he could only find some; but then he heard the chant coming to him on the air, heard the singsong of it and its words sung badly but not so badly that he could not understand them, the incantation four times repeated, then the song twice, then the prayer itself, the prayer he had never heard except in the stories of his mother and had waited all his life to hear – the prayer of kinship, of the invocation of sacrifice, of the begging of pardon, of the honoring of the old covenant, of respect, of gratitude, of love, And now surely we and the good black things, the best of all, shall see each other.

The world was not ending. What was ending was the war he had fought to save the world. He had forgotten his war. The prayer had called it back. Now he remembered it. He remembered how he had made himself an outcast from his own kind by fighting the war against the Ancestors which all the other bears had forsworn. He remembered the hard fight he had waged. And now he knew from hearing the prayer that he had won. He had stopped the Ancestors from killing the world. Because of him they had remembered the covenant they had made with the Ani'Tsa'guhi so long ago. From now on they would honor the sacrifice of the bears that gave them the food of life. They had come to tell him. Their singing was bad because they had not sung the prayer for many generations, but there was reverence even in their bad singing. They had come in a sacred manner. They had come with honor as he had always wanted them to. He could love them now without being sad that his love was misspent. As he listened a great peace stole over him. Rest was coming. He wanted to raise his head and look to see them coming to him and singing, but he was too weak now to stir. But it did not matter any more. It was enough to lie gazing out over blue space listening to the singing of the prayer and knowing that the world would be saved after all.

Hamby finished the chant. If he'd owed a favor like Corntassle argued, it was paid back now. And if he hadn't owed a favor, well, he'd just pulled the most mortifying damn-fool stunt ever and it was a good thing nobody but a beast of the woods had seen it. The effort of it had brought the pain again and the white light and had turned his vision all spotty and piecemeal like looking into a mirror whose backing had flaked off; and he thought time was probably getting short and he needed to do the next thing.

He cocked the hammer of the Winchester and laid the barrel across the trunk of the dead tree to steady his aim and drew a bead on the bear's head. He laid his finger on the trigger and got ready to shoot. He had him dead-on; when he shot, it would take him in the brains – a sure kill even on a critter his size, even with just a forty-four. He closed his finger on the stiff trigger; in his sights the bear lay panting on the rock. There was a small brown knot on the crown of his head that resembled a walnut; it must be what was left of the wound that maddened him. It didn't look like much now. His coat was bloody, matted into hundreds of wet little red triangles, though the sun still found some of the cinnamon and russet of his pelt and made it dully shine. His flanks whipped faster and faster. It looked like his eyes were half-shut. Hell, he was bled out, done for. What was the point of shooting now?

It was part of the ceremony, the old man had said – you asked pardon, then you shot. Still, he waited. Hell, he'd asked the pardon. And it had been given; he'd felt it, had felt Yane'gwa give it, had felt it come as he sang. It had come like a soothing puff of wind, it had blown soft through the pain and the white light to tell him he'd not only put things right here on the mountain but had done pretty damn good all around with the cards that had been dealt him. He was pardoned now, and not just for this either. He was pardoned for all that had held him back from what he'd wanted of life and never dared wish for.

He'd asked; Yan-e'gwa had granted. What did it matter how death came now? Death was death. He leaned against the fallen tree squinting down the barrel of the Winchester. In the notch of the sight the figure of Yan-e'gwa got more and more shimmery. The white light grew. Still he waited. And waited some more. He waited till he saw he didn't need to shoot at all. Then he let the rifle slide. He eased himself down and lay back on a dry crackly bed of rotten tree limbs and stared up at the vast bowl of the sky.

He'd never seen such a sky. It went up and up, a dome of indigo going higher and higher. If the sky and the mountains and the woods and the bear and all the creatures of the wild were what the world was – were all it was – he wouldn't want to fetch it to a close, wouldn't want to use the power that all men have. They were the only pure things. They had shown him all he'd ever known of purity – all there was of it in the world, most likely. There should've been more. But he could think of folk that had given him a little grace, one or two who'd offered love. That was something. And it was more than he'd given back. He was far from pure himself. But he'd been pardoned for what he'd done and for what he'd not done, and he reckoned he could give pardon as well as get it. So in his heart he gave a pardon. What there'd been would have to be enough.

He lay gazing at the sky as it got wider and higher and more and more blue. Hell, he thought, it had been all right.

Acknowledgements

I am grateful beyond measure to my uncles, James Price of Hayesville and Fred Price of Asheville, for sharing with me their memories of their parents Will and Lillie Price and their foster grandparents whom I have called Jimmy and Laura Cartman. I hope James and Fred will be able to embrace the uses I have made of what they told me.

Although I would not have thought it possible, C. Edwin Smith of Decatur, GA, grandson of Irish Bill Moore, actually improved on the very generous cooperation he afforded me during the writing of *The Cock's Spur*, this time providing priceless information about his mother – Irish Bill's youngest daughter Nannie – her brothers, the typhoid epidemic of 1898, and Irish Bill himself. He also read and commented on the manuscript and is responsible for Miss Hattie's corn muffins and teacakes in Chapter 19, more authentic fare for the time than the blueberry muffins and oatmeal cookies I had mistakenly put in her oven.

In August 2001 Edwin kindly invited me to a Moore family reunion in Hayesville, where I was generously received by members of that fine clan and gleaned many wonderful stories, including the ones I have put into the mouth of Absalom Middleton about snake dogs; about a solemn man eating a banana; and about Irish Bill stopping in the middle of plowing to kill a sheep to feed a poor family. Edwin also entrusted me with some wonderful old photos of the Captain and Miss Hattie, which I shall always treasure.

It is a source of deep sadness to me that Edwin passed away on the very same day this work was accepted for publication. By the time I e-mailed him the news, he was gone. I can only hope he knows somehow that our book did find a home.

Additional material on Irish Bill Moore came from an article about him in *Foxfire 9*.

For invaluable advice and assistance about land ownership in the Tusquittees and about the nature of old-time forest and the methods used to log it, I am indebted to forestry expert John Alger of Buckdancer Consultants, Swannanoa NC, who read the manuscript, made sure I had the right trees growing at the correct altitudes, and taught me the difference between a log flume and a log slide; my thanks also go to Interpretive Specialist Pat Momich of the U.S. Forest Service in Asheville.

I also owe thanks to Wanda Stalcup, director of the Cherokee County Historical Museum in Murphy for directing me to two useful sources published by the museum, *A Pictorial History of Cherokee County* and *Marble & Log: The History & Architecture of Cherokee County*.

As always, I am grateful to my sister, Wanda P. Galloway, and my nephew, David C. Galloway, for helping launch me on my voyage into the past of the Curtises and the Prices. Others have encouraged me in my writing career when my spirits flagged – Anne Kohut, Rob Neufeld, Peggy Weaver, Ed Sheary, Ron and Caroline Manheimer, Stephen Kirk and Byron Ballard.

I am indebted to Bob and Barbara Ingalls and Judy Geary at High Country Publishers, for believing in this work and especially for falling under the spell of Yan-e'gwa just as I had; and Bob is to be most profusely thanked for his gift to me of the three-foot carved bear which now adorns my living room. Judy proved a willing collaborator as well as a fine editor with a sharp eye for the proper length of a paragraph; working with her was not only a privilege, it was fun.

Among the most useful written sources I consulted on logging were *Tumult on the Mountains: Lumbering in West Virginia, 1770 – 1920* by Roy B. Clarkson; *Miners, Millhands and Mountaineers: Industrialization in the Applachian South* by Ron Eller; the *Americanized Encyclopaedia Britannica* of 1902; and the *Foxfire* series. The scheme for using a portable sawmill which Absalom Middleton relates to Weatherby is based on an explanation given to *Foxfire 4* students by old-time logger Millard Buchanan, while some of Absalom's snake stories are taken from the first volume of that collection. Railroading lore comes from the Cherokee County Museum books and from *A History of Railroading in Western North Carolina* by Cary Franklin Poole. I also consulted John Preston Arthur's *Western North Carolina: A History from 1730 to 1913*; Horace Kephart's *Our Southern Highlanders*; and Margaret Morley's *The Carolina Mountains*.

I owe special thanks to "'What Does America Need So Much as Americans?': Race and Northern Reconciliation with Southern Appalachia, 1870 – 1900", an intriguing essay by Nina Silber in *Appalachians and Race: The Mountain South from Slavery to Segregation*, edited by John C. Inscoe. That piece first awakened my interest in the role played by eugenics in some of the "philanthropic" thinking of wealthy Northerners instrumental in commercial development and missionary work in the Southern mountains in the 1890's.

I also drew on the turn-of-the-20th-century writings of Abbot Kinney about eugenics (*The Conquest of Death*). While abhorrent to enlightened minds of today, his rantings are worthy of note if for no other reason than that they were once broadly shared by some of the most powerful people in America. Nor do they lack relevance in the modern world – we have evidence that notions such as Kinney's actually inspired the Nazi theorists of Ayran supremacy.

Of course the 19th-century highlander was no more "pure Anglo-Saxon" than he was "almost entirely Scotch-Irish", another tenacious old belief. Appalachian scholars are now uncovering more and more evidence showing that the people of the mountain South in the 1800's were a quite varied lot, coming from many cultures, including the Mediterranean, evidently the point of origin of the mysterious Melungeons. Doubtless G.G.M. Weatherby would be dismayed.

The style and decor of Weatherby's "hunting lodge" is borrowed from photographs and information in Time-Life's volume *The Loggers*. For Hamby's experiences with mining I consulted *Mines, Miners and Minerals of Western North Carolina's Mountain Empire* by Lowell Presnell and *Western Mining* by Otis E. Young, Jr.

Anyone familiar with Cherokee lore will know how much I owe to James Mooney's *History, Myths and Ancient Formulas of the Cherokees*. Most of the bear myths and related tales which I quote are drawn from this monumental work. As I present them they are very little changed from the way Mooney wrote them down.

Will's story about Preacher Fanshaw is adapted from a traditional Southern Appalachian tale known as "The Devil and Preacher Dix". I am indebted to Howard and Susan Smith of Burnsville for bringing it to my attention and for providing me with an audio tape of it as performed by the talented Burnsville actor Milton Higgins (Volume 1 of the tape "Roan Mountain Anthology") and for a text of it as told by Dallas Young (*Stories 'Neath the Roan*, Blue Ridge Reading Team).

The story Will tells about the drunken guineas being plucked is apocryphal; variations of it – told as gospel – are heard in various sections of the Southern Appalachians and one comes, surprisingly enough, from as far afield as Colorado; it substitutes geese for guinea hens and includes the improbable detail of the crocheted jackets. I found it, believe it or not, in a "Dear Abby" column. One version, called "The Resurrected Guineas", appears in the privately-printed *History of Jarrett Road Community* in Hayesville; it ascribes the event to the Padgett family of that neighborhood.

Information on shaped-note singing was drawn from articles on Christian Harmony in *Foxfire 7*.

If I have made errors of fact or interpretation in drawing on any of the above sources, the fault is mine alone.

Finally and most signally, I must thank Ruth Perschbacher, the woman who shares not only my life but also the imaginary lives I write about. Her sharp editorial eye and relentlessly truthful criticism have kept me on the right path; and she has often known far better than I where that path led.